Maya

Alastair Campbell

Random House Group Limited supports The Forest Stewardship
Council® (FSC®), the leading international forest certification organisation.
Our books carrying the FSC label are printed on FSC® certified paper. FSC is the only
forest certification scheme supported by the leading environmental organisations,
including Greenpeace. Our paper procurement policy can be found at
www.randomhouse.co.uk/environment

arrow books

Set by Palimpsest Book Production Ltd, Falkirk, Stirlingshire
Printed and bound in Great Britain by CPI Bookmarque Ltd, Croydon, CR0 4TD

Published by Arrow Books 2011

2 4 6 8 10 9 7 5 3 1

First published in Great Britain in 2010 by Hutchinson

Arrow Books
Random House, 20 Vauxhall Bridge Road,
London SW1V 2SA

www.randomhouse.co.uk

Addresses for companies within The Random House Group Limited can be found at:
www.randomhouse.co.uk/offices.htm

The Random House Group Limited Reg. No. 954009

A CIP catalogue record for this book
is available from the British Library

ISBN 9780099534648

The R   hip
Council (FS   . All our
titles that are p   e FSC logo.
Our paper pro   nvironment

Typ
Printed and   CR0 4TD

Preface

How lucky is that . . . I got to see an eagle on my very first day here. It was a wondrous surprise, its sudden emergence around the white pine trees at the far end of the water, a deep, hard-edged croak its only signal of imminent arrival. I watched it hover before it began a mesmerising flight from one end of the lake to the other. Mrs Crowley, the colourfully dressed woman who is renting me this log cabin, had said there was an outside chance I might see one. Like most Americans, she's prone to enthusiasm, so I didn't give it much thought. And then, there it came, just hours after I'd unpacked, vast wings outstretched, swooping then gliding, with a soft whooshing sound as it passed right in front of me, maybe fifty feet above the placid water, king of all it surveyed, and, for these moments, of all who surveyed it from their boats and lake-side bungalows.

Maybe it takes the kind of experience I've had fully to appreciate natural beauty like this, but as the bald eagle finally disappeared from view, to the sound of children across the lake hollering in delight, I put my pen between my lips, and sat back to take in my surroundings. There are worse places to reflect on what has happened, and try to make sense of it. The calmness of the water helps. Everything is so still here.

It's out of season, so there are few tourists. The houses are fairly far apart, some hidden by trees, each one served by its own dirt track to the main road about a mile away. It's rare that the sound of a car engine disturbs the peace. That is left to birdsong, or an occasional speedboat pulling a waterskier, and, less frequently, excited screams as someone makes the sixty-foot leap into the water from a mossy lookout ledge on the orange cliff-side opposite. According to Mrs Crowley it's a coming-of-age dare for all who live round here. She says not to try it. 'The water's way too cold for outsiders at this time of year.'

At least now I'll be able to remember the bald eagle as a thing of beauty, not menace. The last one I saw was on the letterhead of Swift International, the firm of spooks and gumshoes that lies at the heart of this story. I was never cut out to get involved with people like that. As my wife Vanessa once said to me, it was my '24-carat honesty' that attracted her. I've always tried to be honest, with myself and with others. As a child I watched dishonest men cause my mother so much heartache; and the kind of women I like are those who can see through a poser at the first smile – women who aren't taken in by guys trying to impress them, who prefer men to be real, to be themselves. Take my friend Maya. She always said that no matter how high she flew, she wanted her real friends, like me, to 'tell it to me straight'.

Maya. Maya is even more central to the story than the spooks. She's the reason I'm here, in this beautiful place thousands of miles from home, writing these words, trying to remember, trying to figure it all out.

PART ONE

Chapter One

It was typical Vanessa to get up at half six on Monday morning to do the test. We'd discussed doing it at the weekend but she'd been reluctant. She hadn't wanted to get a result in case it wasn't what she wanted to hear and put her in the wrong mood for the party. It was her dad's sixtieth, and there was to be a big family do on Sunday. But by Monday morning she'd caved, and got up in the dark, before the central heating went on, because the instructions said 'first thing'. All the time I've known her, Vanessa has been mega-organised, someone who plans everything meticulously. She's also a morning person, whereas I'm not great at waking up. Somehow I've never rid myself of a childhood addiction to the warmth of a bed well slept in.

'Steve,' she shouted from the bathroom. 'Steve, wake up.'

I clung to the woozy semi-consciousness that comes as the eyelids are pricked open, and the mind has a moment to decide whether to abandon its interrupted dream and face the day, or return to sleep. But there must have been urgency in her voice, an excitement in the way she called my name that got through to me how important this was.

'Steve, it's positive. The test's positive.'

I sat up quickly, all remnants of the dream gone, and she

was standing there, her hair an unruly mess of red curls, no make-up, wearing a bra and knickers and waving the pregnancy test in her hand. She gave me a few seconds to take in what she was saying, then ran towards me and jumped on to the bed. I realised she was moments away from crying. She'd been talking about wanting a baby from the day we were married, and now, after six years of trying, the longed-for moment seemed to have come. I wasn't sure how to react. Could we trust this test? After all, it only came from the chemist, not a doctor. But I didn't want to dampen Vanessa's joy by questioning it. I said something suffocatingly trite about how our lives were going to change for ever, and I'd always be there for her and the baby, but it didn't seem enough. Suddenly what had been an abstract idea was becoming startlingly, achingly real. I might actually be months away from being a father. And I realised I didn't know how to feel about it. I found myself stroking her flat stomach and thinking that beneath the lightly freckled skin lay the beginnings of another human being. It would depend on me for everything, look to me for guidance in how to live; it would have colds, flu, broken bones; it would cry a lot, laugh a lot, might be good at maths and hopeless at history, or great at both; it would have a name, friends not yet born, kids of its own; and I thought 'Why am I thinking all this, why can't I just be like Vanessa and enjoy the moment?'

We spent the next half-hour discussing when to see the doctor for official confirmation, and who to tell if we got it (my mum not yet, her mum and dad probably, her sister Judith definitely since she was a nurse at St Mary's Hospital in Paddington, friends play it by ear but in general only after the third month). By now we were running late. Working for a bank in the City, Vanessa needed at least an hour to get across town by Tube. Although my drive to Globus Logistics was theoretically quicker – I worked for a logistics company based in a twelve-storey, dark-glass office block close to the southern perimeter of Heathrow airport – the traffic at that time of the morning could be dire. We washed and dressed quickly, Vanessa now talking ever more excitedly as she rifled through her cupboard for a clean shirt and tights. I found it hard to keep up.

Vanessa is one of those women whose body is made for a business suit. She's almost as tall as I am, thin-waisted and long-limbed; she suits high heels, and her rich-red hair looks good against dark colours. Today, however, I noticed her collar was awry and she'd smudged her mascara. I tried to straighten her out as we said goodbye in the kitchen.

'Now listen to me,' I said, 'you're going to be fine, and you're going to be a great mum. I know it.' I kissed her on her forehead, then on the lips, and gave her a big hug, but I felt like I was play-acting. I knew I should have been feeling happy, and confident. But I didn't, at least not like I guessed you were *supposed* to when you'd just been given the news I'd been given.

'Thanks, darling,' she said, rushing now before heading off towards the Tube, 'and you're going to be a great dad too.' Trying not to think too much about what she'd just said, I locked up the house, threw my briefcase into the car, scraped the ice off the windscreen, and drove as fast as I could through the streets of Hammersmith, only remembering when I got to the Hogarth roundabout, and my head started to feel the nagging ache of caffeine starvation, that I'd had two cups of coffee rather than my usual three.

If there's one thing that stresses me out even more than being late, it's not having enough coffee before starting work. Three cups in the morning, and I'm human. Anything less, don't come near me. I guess I inherited the addiction from my mum who got through cups of tea the way some of her foul-smelling boyfriends got through cigarettes. Anyway, I was thinking I was going to have to make do with the dross that got served in the Globus canteen when I remembered there was a decent enough Coffee Nation machine at the last garage before the A4 becomes the M4.

I kept thinking about the *supposed* word as I tailed a filthy, dark blue Ford Galaxy, a claret and blue sticker in the back window urging me to 'Follow the Hammers' alongside a larger motif which said that Jesus Loved Me. Presumably Jesus told the driver what he was supposed to feel at various junctures in his life. But what if you didn't believe in Jesus? Who set the *supposed* rules then? Was there some secret Supposed Society that decreed that a man, on hearing the news he was to be a father, must feel happy, exhilarated; must communicate this to his wife, and to all others subsequently in a way that allowed them to follow the Supposed Society's strictures on how to hear the news of another's impending fatherhood, namely happiness and exhilaration but in a lower gear to that felt by the parents-to-be? Annoyingly, there was no separate till for Coffee Nation customers at the garage so I had to stand in line with half a dozen people paying for petrol. The scruffy woman in front of me was clearly even more late for work than I was, and getting agitated at how slowly the queue was moving, held up now by a man who wanted to pay for his fuel with a credit card, but then pay cash for a bottle of water. The woman tutted, but I decided to stay calm. Instead of watching, impatiently, for the tiniest forward shuffle of the feet in front of me, I focussed my mind on the tinny radio tuned to Five Live. A reporter was relaying the details of another soldier's death in Afghanistan and I was tuning out of her analysis of how 'public opinion' would react, when she was suddenly interrupted by the presenter breaking news.

'And we must cut you off there, Charlotte,' said her male colleague, 'because we're getting reports, extraordinary allegations, that actress Maya Lowe is to be interviewed by police over claims that she assaulted a 42-year-old man.'

Maya? I almost dropped my coffee. What were they saying? I strained to hear, suddenly irritated by noises hitherto unnoticed – the pinging of barcodes swiped against tills; coffee machines belching; doors opening and closing.

'Yes, reports coming in to us here at Five Live say the 30-year-old film star has been accused of punching a man on board a flight from the West Indies, where she had been doing a photo shoot for an advertising campaign. It seems the man made a formal complaint to staff on the plane, and has now asked the police to investigate. Our crime correspondent Lewis Carlisle has been finding out more. Lewis, sensational allegations against a woman with the near perfect image.'

I had the exact change, and once I'd handed it over, irritated by the cashier's insistence that she give me a receipt, I hurried to the magazine rack to be closer to the radio speaker. Maya's face was on several of the covers propped up on the overcrowded shelves. 'Maya's magic moments' said one. 'My love for Dan, by Maya' said another. I looked away and concentrated on the source of the noise.

'Martin, yes, that's absolutely right. Maya Lowe, the world-famous actress with the girl-next-door image, star of a succession of box-office smashes, now faces the prospect of being interrogated by police over claims of assault. The details are sketchy but what we do know, Martin, is this – she flew last night on flight BA2262 from Kingston Jamaica to London Gatwick airport. We know there was an altercation of some sort, and we know a complaint was made, and now the police are being asked to investigate. So as you say, Martin, this would seem to be more supermodel Naomi Campbell's territory, not a situation we expect Maya Lowe to be in, a woman who recently displaced David Beckham no less in a survey of celebrities people would most like to have as a guest for the weekend.'

I was suddenly conscious of my heart beating faster than it should. Maya, my oldest friend, was in trouble. I think it was the first time I'd ever heard the radio report something negative about her. Putting my coffee down on the floor, I fished out my mobile and punched in a text: 'Maya! What's going on? Are you OK? Call if you can. Steve X'.

I ran to the car. I should have walked. A dollop of cappuccino froth spurted out of the drinking hole of my coffee cup, and spilled on to my knuckles, causing me to wince. Still I ran. I couldn't bear the idea of missing something. But I needn't have worried. This story was going to dominate the news for most of the day. By the time I'd got the radio tuned to Five Live, and manoeuvred my company Peugeot back into the traffic, the presenter was close to the breathless hyperventilation that accompanies 'breaking news', especially when a 'celebrity' is involved.

'So, for those of you who are just back from taking the kids to school' – I hated the chummy assumptions presenters made about what their listeners were doing, what sort of people they were – 'or getting into the car to head for work, and hearing this sensational breaking news here on Five Live for the first time, here's a recap: Maya Lowe, Britain's hottest film star, is to face a police investigation over claims of assault on a transatlantic flight. I'm joined on the phone by Alan Walsh, freelance film critic. Alan, thanks for joining me on *Five Live Breakfast*, what do you make of what you've heard and, perhaps more significantly, what will this mean for Maya's career?'

Over the years I'd heard a lot of Alan Walsh's critiques of Maya's films. He never gave her a bad review. Today, though, he sounded more guarded.

'Well a lot obviously will depend on what actually happened but if the police have been called in, that sounds kind of serious. If she is formally charged with assault or some kind of violence-type situation, then it's hard to see how this can be helpful to her career and her image.'

'Alan, as we were saying earlier, Maya Lowe's profile has been about as flawless as any image-maker could hope for – successful, happily married, does so much for charity, rarely attracting the wrong sort of headlines – so how will she be coping with this?'

'Yes, Martin, she has been in many ways a classic textbook success story in image terms . . .'

Sheldon, I muttered. Where the hell was Sheldon in all this? What was she fucking paying him for?

As if in answer to my question, the presenter again cut in. 'Alan, just wait there, sorry to interrupt, but I'm being told now we will be hearing, shortly, from Nick Sheldon, Maya Lowe's agent, a big name of course in show-business circles, who has called a briefing at his offices, so hopefully that will clear up a few things for us.'

I was on to the motorway now, and the traffic was flowing

more freely, as drivers released their pent-up frustration and made the most of the four or five miles before their satnav machines beeped out the warning of live cameras roadside. I was hoping to be able to get to the office, where there was a TV in reception, to see Sheldon's performance. Sky were bound to show it live.

I was passing Heston Services when Maya called. Her voice was choked.

'Steve, I'm really glad you texted. I didn't want to bother you so early, but I've been wanting to talk to you. I feel as if the world's going mental around me.'

'What the hell is going on?'

'What have you heard?' She sounded more stressed out than I'd ever known her – even worse than when she was breaking up with Mike.

'Well there's this guy on Five Live saying you hit someone . . .'

'Crazy stuff.'

'What – not true?'

'Well, depends how you're looking at it.'

'Meaning . . . ?'

'Are you driving?' she asked.

'Hands-free, don't worry.' It wasn't true, and I could sense the disapproval of the silver-haired lunatic driving too close behind me in his red BMW, who had been flashing his lights to get me to move into the middle lane, but I was anxious to hear what had happened. 'Come on, give me the story. Who was with you on the plane?'

'Some kid Nick sent from his office . . . Only been there a month. Doesn't know shit . . .'

'So . . . ?'

'So, I'm having dinner, trying to sleep but I never sleep properly on planes, so I watch a movie, get up to go to the loo and as I come out there's this guy, in those stupid BA pyjamas, and he positions himself so I can't just slip by; then, you know, he loves my work, and he's just this minute been watching *Fast Track to Safety* and how weird it was to be watching while the star was three rows in front, and what am I up to, so we do a bit of small talk and I'm thinking, well it'll pass the time, but I don't know, he must have misread the signals because he has his hand on my arm at one point and it's like not accidental, it was a move, no doubt about it, so I say "Anyway, I must go back to my seat," and he says "That's such a shame Maya, I am so enjoying talking to you and getting to know you," and he's standing there, like making it hard for me to walk by and I'm feeling bad vibes, so I start to insist, and he gets really agitated.'

'Where was everyone else? Nick's guy?'

'Asleep, eating, how do I know? We were like through the curtain at the front of the plane, just behind the cockpit. It was fairly dark, dimmed lights and all that. And then as I push past, he sort of puts his hand on my back, pretending to make way for me, but actually trying to touch my body with his. He's got his leg against my thigh, and his upper arm brushing my tits, so I kind of pushed him, and he rocked back a bit but then fell towards me, arm on tits again, so I pushed him again and then he falls against the wall. And that was it. End of story. I go back to my seat. Next thing I know, the chief steward comes and says someone has made a complaint. I mean it is too fucking ridiculous for words.'

I had kept Five Live on in the background, and the presenter was getting more excited, announcing that Nick Sheldon was about to speak. He coated the name 'Nick Sheldon' with a layer of gravity normally reserved for presidents and prime ministers in times of international crisis. 'Your agent is about to make a statement,' I said. 'Do you want to hear?'

'Not really.'

'Where are you?'

'Home. I got back about an hour ago. Vultures gathering outside.'

'How many?'

'A couple of dozen. They're still coming though. It'll be the full works by the evening. Grumpy neighbours time.'

'Where's Dan?'

'Had to go to work early for a meeting.'

I was close to the office, almost at the car park, as Nick began.

'Come on,' I said, 'you should listen to this.' I turned up the volume as Sheldon started to speak.

'Thank you for coming, ladies and gentlemen. I have a short statement and then I will take your questions.' Maya's agent was in his fifties, tanned and jowly, with a deep, reassuring voice, carrying the tiniest hint of a West Country burr.

'My client Maya Lowe flew from Kingston Jamaica to London Gatwick overnight last night, arriving in the early hours of this morning. She had been working on a photo shoot. She was accompanied by a representative of my office, who has sworn an affidavit which along with Maya's own account confirms the accuracy of what I am about to tell you and, through you, the public. Maya was travelling first class, in seat 1A. My colleague was in 1B, seated alongside her. During the flight, she made a visit to the washroom. When she came out of the washroom, a fellow passenger, Mr Vivian Gibbs, of West

Indian origin, was waiting for her. He engaged Maya in conversation, then made some highly inappropriate remarks and finally made a pass at her. Despite Maya making clear her desire to return to her seat, Mr Gibbs persisted in his attempts to force himself upon her. After politely asking him to desist on several occasions, she finally pushed past him and returned to her seat. She was shocked and upset, as she reported to my colleague.'

'Are you hearing this OK?' I asked Maya, as I pulled into my parking space.

'Yeah, yeah, shush,' she said.

'My colleague thought Maya had a case for sexual assault because of the nature of the pass made at her. Maya felt that to make a complaint would simply add to an ordeal she wanted to forget. My colleague did, however, ask one of the cabin crew to keep an eye on Mr Gibbs, who was in seat 4c. It therefore came as a total shock to her subsequently, about forty minutes later, to be told by the cabin crew that Mr Gibbs, in defiance of the facts, had himself made a complaint. My colleague sought to speak to Mr Gibbs, who refused all contact and said simply that he intended to ask the police to investigate on landing. We understand he has now done so and as you know, this has been briefed to the media, presumably by Mr Gibbs' associates, since I am confident the police would not be so unprofessional as to do so.

'Let me be clear – as a British citizen, Maya Lowe will of course happily co-operate with any investigation. But this is a complete waste of police time and money. Let me also say this – I understand that Mr Gibbs has already made contact with a newspaper group with a view to selling his story. And there I think we go to the heart of the matter. Maya Lowe is a very famous, very beautiful, very successful actress, of infinite interest to many media organisations. And when he noticed her seated a few rows in front of him, Mr Gibbs saw his chance. I think it is important that the British media resists the efforts to make money on the back of these false claims. And I hope the police will see this for what it is – an attempt to use them to help extort money from a newspaper. Thank you.'

'Wow,' I said. 'Strong stuff.'

'He's bloody good is Nick,' said Maya. 'He told me he was confident he could turn it against the guy.'

'Everything he said true?'

'Give or take a bit in the margins, yeah.'

Nick Sheldon was now facing a barrage of questions from reporters.

'What do you mean by "inappropriate remarks" Nick?' one shouted.

'I have nothing to add on that. The kind of thing men like him may find funny, but any decent person finds offensive, and women find frightening.'

'Nick, can you give us any more idea of what you call the pass he made at her?'

'No, Maya does not wish for me to go into detail on this.'

'Did she at any time feel in danger of being raped, Mr Sheldon?' asked another voice, female.

'Well, at some point the air stewards would have come by, but it was not a nice experience.'

'Might she sue?'

'Maya has many great qualities. Vindictiveness is not one of them. I think you all know enough about her to know that.'

'Where is she now, Nick?'

'Back in London.'

'Will she be commenting?'

'She is double-parked in a no-comment slot. Sorry.' I could hear some of the reporters laughing. With, not at him.

'Do you think the airlines should have special security for A-list celebrities to stop this kind of thing happening?' one asked.

'We have no complaint against the airline.'

'. . . because they give us lots of free flights and upgrades,' Maya chipped in.

Martin, the presenter, was back on in breathless mode.

'Well, quite sensational stuff there and Maya Lowe's agent proving the old adage that there are always two sides to the story. And it seems her side is that she was effectively sexually harassed. He is saying, if I can paraphrase, that the man on the plane targeted her with a view to provoking her so that he could say she hit him, and then use the police to give the story some kind of legitimacy in order to try and get money from the papers. Well listening to that with me was the showbiz editor of the *Sun,* Matthew Kay. Matthew, thanks for joining us and you heard there Maya Lowe's agent challenging you not to buy this story, what do you say to that?'

'I thought he gave a very strong performance there and frankly if it comes to Maya's word against the word of some random West Indian guy on a plane, I know who our readers would believe. Now I am not aware Gibbs or anyone on his behalf has been in touch, so I don't know which newspaper he was talking about, but I would be very surprised if we were interested in buying his story.'

'Mission accomplished,' said Maya. 'I think you can turn it off.'

'OK. Actually I'd better go. I'm at the office now, and I'm already late. But, listen, are you OK? You seem really down.'

'Well, to tell the truth Steve, things aren't so good at the moment.'

It was strange to hear Maya sounding so subdued. For the past year and a half, certainly since she'd married Dan, it was like she'd been on a perpetual high, always chirpy when she called me, full of enthusiasm for new projects she was involved in.

'Want to talk about it?' I asked. 'We could have one of our lunches. It's been ages since we saw each other properly . . .'

I was expecting some excuse about why she couldn't make it. She'd been doing that a lot recently. There was a time when we had lunch regularly, at least once a month, sometimes more often, but her marriage to Dan had changed all that. To my surprise, though, she was enthusiastic.

'God, Steve, you know that would be great! How are you fixed tomorrow? Short notice but I could really do with getting a few things off my chest.'

'Sure,' I said. 'Usual system?'

She laughed. 'Usual system. I'll see you in the Rectangle.'

It was only when she'd hung up that I remembered I had agreed to go with Vanessa to the doctor's tomorrow, provided she could get an appointment. What if I had to cancel Maya? Vanessa hadn't wanted me to tell her about the baby, so I'd have to make up some white lie. It would seem flakey. Also I always made it a priority to be there for Maya. She lived such a mad, high-speed life, she needed someone like me to rely on. I found myself praying that Dr Blake would be fully booked, and then realised the stupidity, or was it cruelty, of putting lunch with Maya before getting confirmation from a doctor that Vanessa definitely was pregnant.

Suddenly the emotion of the morning caught up with me, and I laid my head on the steering wheel for a moment, closed my eyes. Vanessa expecting. Maya in trouble. It was a lot to cope with on a grey, February Monday morning.

A couple of minutes later my phone rang and I jumped, tweaking a muscle in my neck in the process.

It was Jerry, my colleague, kind of friend.

'I'm standing at the window, Steve, and I can see your Peugeot in the car park, so I'm assuming you're here. Better get to your desk fast. Brandon's in one of his warpath moods.'

I didn't know whether I was pissed off at the interruption, or relieved at the distraction. Maya's world constantly intrigued me, but I was glad I lived in the real one, even if it was inhabited by a slave-driver like Mike Brandon.

Chapter Two

It wasn't the first time Maya had made me late for work. As her life was so much more unpredictable than mine, we had an agreement that I wouldn't call her without texting first to check it was OK, but she could call me any time she had a window. The problem was that her windows rarely fitted with my more or less nine-to-five working day. Though she claimed to understand what an office job was like, she'd never actually done one so really had no idea and would often ring me for a chat at ten in the morning, or suggest having tea together at four. And then there were the ways in which she interfered with my work without even trying. I had a Google Alert on my computer so that I could keep an eye on her press coverage. Sometimes there were more Maya alerts in my inbox than work emails. Luckily I shared an office with Jerry, who was understanding, not least because he was completely besotted with Maya. He'd once queued up for hours with his wife and two young children just to catch a glimpse of her going into a premiere in Leicester Square and I could often bribe him to cover for me with Brandon by offering free tickets to see her latest film, signed photos and posters, or a bit of gossip that hadn't made the papers.

'It's amazing you've stayed friends with her,' Jerry would say.

Maybe he was right, but for me Maya was still the same person she had always been – my best friend from Acton. Often I would forget she was one of the most famous women in the world, perhaps because her fame kind of crept up on us. I first knew her as a fellow pupil, then as a friend, then a friend who was best in school at drama and English, then a friend who went to drama college, then a friend who got a few stage parts, enough to call herself an actress without it being considered boastful, then a friend who appeared on TV, then a friend with a leading role in a small British film, then a friend with Hollywood movie directors fawning over her, and finally a friend I had to get used to seeing being described as a superstar.

You adjust, don't you, to someone you know becoming famous? When Maya was 15, and she would rush out to get the *Ealing and Acton Gazette* to see if she got a mention in the write-up of the school play, it would have been fanciful to imagine that in a few years' time she would regularly be getting front-page treatment in all the major newspapers and magazines. But when it started to happen, the front pages seemed to be the natural home for pictures of her. It's the same with money and houses and all the material stuff that goes with stardom. If Maya the teenager had said she intended to buy a multimillion-dollar New York apartment overlooking Central Park, a majorly posh house in one of the swankiest streets in London, and a beautiful early retirement home for her mum and dad in a lovely country village, it would have sounded ridiculous even to people like me who believed in her talent. Yet when it happened, and she jetted over to New York for a long weekend with her favourite interior designer to choose furniture, fabrics, artefacts and paintings, nothing could have seemed more natural.

As for why Maya stayed friends with me, obviously I often wondered about that. There was nothing terribly special about me. At my interview for Globus, I was asked what I thought set me apart from the crowd. I said I knew the score of every League game Chelsea had played in since the year I was born. It was all I could think of, and actually if I was tested, I couldn't guarantee I would still get all of them right, but it seemed to please Brandon who said he liked people with a good memory. My knowledge of football also came in useful to Maya at times, but I think it was my loyalty that cemented our friendship. I had been steadfast through our teenage years, and I continued to be steadfast. In the crazy world of celebrity socialising she now inhabited, that counted for a lot. I was the person she could lean on. The 'rock'. Her word. She didn't want to appear to have rejected the world she came from, and I was part of that world. She mentioned me, or at least I think it was me, in the first major interview she gave after *Picture Frame* became such a massive hit. She said she still kept up with school friends, particularly one, and that it was important to keep in touch with your roots, no matter how far you went. The interviewer loved it – talked about what extraordinary humility and wisdom she had for a woman her age. The interview was headlined 'The Girl Next Door'.

Maya and I first met when I was 12. Kylie Minogue had a number-one hit with Jason Donovan that year. That tells you how far back we go.

I joined Acton High in the second year because my mum and I had only just moved to the area. Before that we'd been living in Southall but my mum wanted to get away from all the memories of my dad the old house held. She'd also got a new boyfriend and it meant being closer to him.

I've always been a bit shy. I was in torment that first day at school, not knowing anyone, not even knowing my way round. I had geography as my first lesson after the morning break, and it was in a different part of the school, so I asked a passing adult where Room 8D was, and when I realised how far away it was, I started to panic, then run, and when finally I found the right place, and walked into the classroom, breathless, all I could focus on was the one spare desk at the front. I made a dash for it, eyes to the floor, shoulders hunched, and sank down on the plastic chair. It was only when I regained some kind of composure that I summoned the courage to look up, and realised I was sitting next to the loveliest girl I had ever seen.

'Hi,' she said. 'You new?'

'Yeah,' I mumbled.

'Do you have a name?'

'Yeah.'

'Which is . . . ?' She was smiling now, and also raising her left eyebrow. It was my first experience of the quizzical expression that has since become familiar to audiences around the world.

'Steve,' I mumbled.

'I'm Maya,' she said. 'Do you know anything about football?' she added after a pause.

'Lots,' I said.

'Go on then.'

'Go on what?'

'I don't know. Tell me something I don't know.'

I began to list every club, manager and stadium in the old first division. She smiled.

'How do you know all that?'

'My dad was a big football fan,' I mumbled. 'Well, Chelsea.'

It turned out she'd asked because she was looking for a member for the school quiz team who knew something about sport. But although I immediately agreed to join, it wasn't until the school trip to Stratford-upon-Avon, later that term, that I sensed the beginning of a friendship. The teacher made us partners, and we sat together on the coach. I was conscious of being physically closer to her than I had ever been before. Our thighs were almost touching. At one point, as the coach driver braked suddenly when a lorry cut him up on the M40, they did touch. I felt my whole body tensing, with a mix of embarrassment and excitement. I cannot really remember what we talked about. If I had had an aim for the trip, it would have been to get through it without embarrassing myself, no more than that. I know that was the day we learned we were both only children, and maybe that created its own kind of bond. She said her mum always called her 'miracle Maya' because there were a couple of miscarriages before she was born, and another afterwards, which made her parents decide one child, Maya, was all they were destined to have. She was acutely conscious of just how special she was to her parents. I wished I could say the same. I kept quiet about my mum and her numerous boyfriends but I did tell her that my dad had died when I was 3, and I can remember how sad she looked, and how touched I was by that look. I think I even saw a little film of water forming on her eyes, and I was having to say no, it's OK, I can hardly remember it, it means nothing, well, not much. Not as much as her look would have suggested.

Maya was definitely the best person to be paired with on a school trip to Stratford. I remember visiting Hall's Croft, where Shakespeare's daughter Susanna had lived with a doctor.

There was a display of gruesome instruments used by medics at the time, which led to some of the boys going off on one, making life a misery for Miss Wendell, the young English teacher who was meant to be looking after us.

'Miss, I feel sick.'

'Miss, I need some medicine.'

'Miss, I want that big stick.'

Eventually Maya turned on them, told them to give it a break, then launched into a mini speech: did they not realise that today was about learning something about one of the greatest men who ever lived, a genius? Every day nearly everyone in the world, whether they knew it or not, said a word or a phrase that was first used by him and yet all they could do was make crap jokes. I noticed how grateful Miss Wendell looked as slowly the party came to order, but I thought also how useless and inferior it must have made her feel to see that a young girl could command the class in a way that she could not.

For the rest of the day, Maya and I stuck together, so much so that one of the boys in my class shouted at us when we were eating our packed lunches at Mary Arden's farm, 'What are you two lovebirds talking about then, *Romeo and Juliet?*'

'At least we're capable of reading it,' she shouted back. Ours was not exactly the kind of class where the other kids expected you to like reading anything, let alone plays by Shakespeare, but Maya always had self-confidence, never worried about standing apart from the herd, some of whom seemed to rejoice in their own dumbness. And even then, she was clear she was going to be an actress.

That night, I lay in bed and wished I had somebody I could ask how you knew if you were in love.

Everyone at school assumed we were an item of course. I didn't mind that it probably looked that way. We went swimming together, sat in the back row of the cinema, sometimes held hands. A couple of days short of my fourteenth birthday, we devised a secret handshake and vowed never to hide anything from each other, for ever, till death. But, however close we were physically, I always felt that Maya had drawn an invisible line around herself – one that I shouldn't cross. That didn't stop me thinking about crossing it though. I thought about it a lot.

'It's funny, don't you think, that my best friend is a boy?' she said, as we sat on a worn, green-brown bench in Acton Park in the summer holiday after our GCSEs were over. She was wearing a white cotton dress and one of the shoulder straps had slipped down on to her arm. There was a long pause while I considered the question, transfixed by the beauty of her lightly tanned shoulder. Should I lean forward and kiss it, I wondered? Was this the moment? Did I not need to do this, to learn whether she too lay in bed at night wishing she knew someone who could tell her what it meant to fall in love? But then I took a deep breath. I had to get real. There was no way that Maya was ever going to fall for someone like me. If I kissed her, I'd lose her for ever. Far better to be her friend.

It was a significant moment for me. I felt both a sense of loss, knowing that Maya would never be wholly mine, but also elation at the idea that, for the rest of my life, I could be a part of hers, trusted to hear her most intimate thoughts.

'What's strange about having a best friend who's a boy?' I said. 'Do you think a girlfriend could name the ground of every single football League club?'

She chuckled. 'How is that useful to me?'

She had a point. I went home feeling depressed, thinking it had come: the long-predicted end to our friendship. But Maya had such a generous nature: the next time I saw her she'd decided to learn the name of every single League ground as a way of improving her memory skills, so important to learning lines. 'If I can learn lists as boring as that, I can learn anything,' she said, reciting the whole lot to me while standing on a kitchen chair three weeks later. This served her very well when, after three years at drama school and a year working in repertory theatre, she auditioned for the part of a footballer's scheming wife in an episode of *The Bill*. She was laughing when she phoned to tell me about the audition. 'They couldn't believe it when I did my party piece. They asked if I knew anything about football. I went straight to division three, and did every ground, then the Scottish second division. Ayr United, Somerset Park. I think they thought I was a bit crazy. But I got the part.'

After that it was only a few months before she was offered her first film role. The director had seen *The Bill* and fell for what he called her 'tough innocence'. 'You weren't so convincing as an embezzling glamour girl,' he said, 'but I think I've got just the role for you.' *Picture Frame* was an art-house movie about an aged painter who became obsessed with a raven-haired beauty he saw looking at one of his paintings in a gallery. It was the surprise success of 1999. The film helped launch Maya's career as a film actress. It also brought her to the attention of Nick Sheldon, a leading agent with dozens of actors on his books on both sides of the Atlantic. Once she was in his hands, it wasn't long before she became a star. She did another UK film, *Please Miss*, before she was swept up by Hollywood. Then, with *An English Rose Abroad* and *Fallen Angel*, the awards started rolling in. And with more awards came more offers, more films, commercial tie-ups, more wealth, more fame.

In the early days of her success, I was convinced Maya would get bored of seeing me, caught up as she was in her new world of agents, screenings, interviews, celebrity parties. There were certainly periods when I hardly heard from her, particularly when she was living with Mike Simmons, her first serious relationship after leaving school. She'd still invite me to things, but I could tell she needed me less. Mike was an up-and-coming theatre director who had done his own translation-cum-adaptation of a controversial German play and turned it into a satire of Britain's class system. He and Maya seemed made for each other, and I tried to be happy for her. But sometimes it felt quite an effort to stay in with her. I can be very impatient on the phone myself, usually with clients and customers, and once or twice I could feel from Maya that kind of 'I have better things to do than talk to you' vibe coming down the line. But then they split up and Maya was back on the phone to me, particularly when something happened that could have shredded her career if anyone found out.

I never got the whole story, but she said she'd had a one-night stand with some Spanish tourist she met when she went into an art gallery to shelter from the rain. Apparently he didn't know who she was. That was the appeal of it: the anonymity. She was on the rebound from Mike and trying to deal with the whole concept of fame. They had a passionate night in his hotel and then he flew back to his family in Seville. Anyway, she got pregnant. It was a massive secret. The only other person who knew, apart from the medics who did the operation, was Sheldon, who organised for her to go to an abortion clinic that he was sure would be completely discreet. She asked me to go with her. I seemed more nervous and upset than she was and I wondered if she was using the same skills that made her an actress to control, even block out, what she must have been feeling. When I drove her home, she said, 'Right, that's that, never again.'

'Never again what?'

'Sex with a stranger, sex without protection, getting pregnant without planning it. Never again.' Then she squeezed my hand but in a way that made me feel she had been talking to herself, instructing herself to learn from a mistake. It had nothing to do with me.

After that, our friendship seemed to rise to another level. She knew that I had kept her secret and I became even more of a confidant. Also she loved being friends with an industry outsider. She could send up the movie world to her heart's content and know that I wasn't going to blab to the press. It was all part of what she called 'keeping a foot in the real world'. Even after I married Vanessa, she still called at least once a week.

'Doesn't it bother you that I spend so much time chatting to one of the most lusted-after women on the planet?' I asked Vanessa one day, half in jest, after Maya had kept me talking for almost an hour about her conversation with Gérard Depardieu at an awards event in Monaco.

'Should it?' said Vanessa with a challenging grin.

'No, but—'

'Well then it's not a problem. I know this thing with you and Maya goes way back. I know what it is and I know what it isn't. I'd hate to be one of those women who stops their man having female friends. I mean, what kind of relationship would it be if there was no trust?'

That's what Vanessa and I had: trust.

We met when the logistics firm I was working for took over a subsidiary that specialised in event management, and I was seconded to the subsidiary for a few months. Their biggest customer was an American bank which was putting on a series of 'stakeholder outreach events'. Vanessa was on the bank's internal team. Later she would insist we first encountered each other at a conference in Canary Wharf and it was love at first sight. Apparently we had an argument about when the coffee break should be. To my embarrassment, I have absolutely no recollection of this. So far as my memory has it, our first meeting was at a seminar for manufacturers in Birmingham. I was overseeing the set. She was looking after the guests, a pretty dour bunch of Midlands businessmen, and a couple of women, one of whom had a really unpleasant mole on her jaw. I noticed Vanessa's bouncy red hair first, then her impressive ability to diffuse conflict.

The unwinding from a fairly tedious day, allied to a few glasses of wine, had us both opening up more, probably, than we normally would as we shared a train ride back to London. She had lovely turquoise eyes and a twinkly smile. She entertained me by mimicking the businessmen at the seminar. At some point I dropped in that the week before I had been on the set of *Please Miss*. It must have been clear that I was trying to impress her, and get her to ask why I was there, but she happily took the hint and showered me with questions. When she found out I knew Maya, she wanted to know all about our friendship. I was surprised by how little she knew about Maya considering that her every move was detailed in the media. It soon became clear to me, though, that Vanessa wasn't one of those women who buys *Hello!* or *Grazia* to gorge on the gossip, and I loved her for it. She didn't care about celebrity: she was interested in what makes people tick, the famous and the non-famous, and she used to love analysing Maya's various dilemmas and suggesting solutions. She would have made a great agony aunt. We had some of our most fun and intimate conversations after Maya's calls, dissecting her problems, trying to work out whether we thought she should or would date her leading man, or take on a particular role.

Still, I didn't always tell Vanessa quite how often Maya called me, and I sometimes didn't mention I'd met Maya for lunch. I was wary of making her more suspicious than she needed to be. Not that Vanessa was the jealous sort. Take Maya's beauty for example. Vanessa wasn't hung up about it. She was confident about her own looks. If Maya invited us to a gala or a premiere, Vanessa would comment on how good Maya looked without any sign that she felt inadequate in comparison.

I've always found it hard to describe Maya's beauty. Now that she is a household name, there is no need. Everyone knows her. Everyone can see it. The long black hair. A forehead as smooth and soft as the day I met her, not a line or a blemish in sight. Dark eyes with the arching brows that an Australian reviewer of *Please Miss* described as speaking with greater power than most actors' voices. The slender nose. A top lip drawn by Cupid, a bottom lip the shape of a crescent moon lying on its side.

She is lucky in her genealogy. Her grandfather on her mum's side was from northern Spain, and Maya inherited her mother's Catalan olive skin and deep brown eyes. It was bizarre sometimes to see her with her father, Frank Lowe, because he was so English-looking, fair-skinned, blue-eyed, podgy round the middle. Maya was blessed. She took her looks from her mother's family, a lot of her strength of character from her dad.

As a teenager, Maya found her beauty a hindrance. Her mother was endlessly fussing over her, forcing her to wear pretty dresses when she wanted to be in jeans, going on about how special she was, how she should make the most of how pretty she was. Anna Lowe is a wonderful woman but her adoration of her daughter is sometimes pretty suffocating, even now. It made it difficult for Maya to have female friends. A lot of the girls at our school thought she was stuck-up. Of course they were jealous. As for the boys, they were always making suggestive comments in the playground, or trying to touch her up. Maya couldn't stand it. There was this one tree in the corner of the playground, a sad old plane tree with mangy leaves, and Maya made it her place to hide. We'd go round the back of its big, peeling trunk and talk about all the things we'd do when we escaped Acton High. Looking back, I suppose Maya regarded me as her protector. Certainly when men wolf-whistled in the street, she'd grab my hand and walk swiftly on, her body stiff with anger and irritation. And there was I, aching with desire, unable to show it, the feel of her hand in mine churning me up inside. I could spend hours gazing at her face. The summer holidays when she went with her parents to see her mum's family in Spain were torment for me. I needed to see her to feel whole.

Did I resent her ever-growing fame as we got older? The main regret, I suppose, was the steady diluting of what she could give me, because more and more people began to think they were entitled to a little piece of her. Being alone with her was the most enormous treat, which was why our lunches were so special to me. I was particularly looking forward to the one after the aeroplane debacle. I hadn't seen her properly for months. There had been her thirtieth birthday party in January, but that hadn't counted. Sheldon had hired a private function room at the Lanesborough, and she'd been so surrounded by famous friends Vanessa and I hardly got to say a word to her. Before that, the last time we'd had lunch had been in the summer, after she finished filming *Fast Track to Safety*. Her marriage to Dan had made a big difference to our friendship in ways that we were both reluctant to admit.

Chapter Three

Look at page sixty of my London *A to Z* and you'll see that the Westway, Edgware Road, Bayswater Road and Queensway create a near rectangle, with Paddington station more or less in the middle. Most of London's best eateries are south or east of this area, but it became one of those little things between Maya and me: when we met for lunch, we met 'inside the Rectangle'. It was convenient for me: I could take the Heathrow Express and get to Paddington quickly, and it was not too far for her to come from Little Venice, where she and Dan lived in one of the big white houses overlooking the canal. The routine was always the same. I booked the table in my name, Steve Watkins, and I arrived first, then texted Maya to say I was there, so that she could get dropped off by Victor, her driver, come in, see me at the table, and head straight over, without any formality or ostentatious welcome from the maître d', or anyone else. It wasn't a 'star' thing. It was simply more practical that way. It meant there was less chance of her being sidetracked or smothered in fuss, so we had more time together.

To my relief, Vanessa had managed to get an appointment with our GP at 9.15 that Tuesday morning, so there would be no clash with lunch. Dr Blake confirmed that Vanessa was pregnant, asked what hospital we'd like to use for the birth, and booked us an appointment with the midwife the following week. It seemed too easy somehow. 'Is that all?' I wanted to ask. 'Prove it. Prove to me that my wife is pregnant.' Vanessa laughed at my doubts. 'You'll have to wait for the first scan for your "evidence",' she said.

I dropped her at the Tube, then headed to the office. Maya had texted me first thing to suggest a new Italian restaurant we hadn't tried before, so I booked it, then checked with Jerry that Brandon hadn't been asking where I was. We were working all out on a pitch for a huge contract with Qatar Airways, which if we won it would give us the biggest bonuses we had ever had, well into five figures. Brandon would do the main presentation himself, out in Qatar, head to head against all the other firms pitching for it, but Jerry and I were preparing the whole thing for him. We made a pretty good team. We both did sales, but Jerry was better at the hard sell, while my forte was admin, research and analysis, so we tended to carve it up that way. 'You're facts, I'm flair,' he once said which though a bit harsh was near the mark. It also worked. We'd landed four major new deals in the last three months.

Brandon did not share Jerry's interest in, or admiration for, Maya. He didn't think work and play should mix, couldn't care less about who any of our friends were, so I asked Jerry to cover for me again when I slipped out of the office at 12.15 and headed to Paddington and La Forchetta. I smiled to myself when I saw what table the waiter was showing me to. It was by the kitchen. When I asked to move, he just shrugged. I wondered how he'd behave when Maya walked in. I saw her silver Mercedes pull up outside just as he was bringing a menu indifferently to the table, and readied myself to witness her entry. It was always a special moment. As the door swung open and she quickly made for the table (I'd texted to tell her it was the one by the kitchen so 'follow your nose'), I had that familiar sensation of a place appearing to change shape and temperature simply because she had entered it. I had grown experienced at scanning rooms like this. In the corner by the main window, a businessman with yellow braces over his shirt and his jacket draped over the back of his chair spotted her the moment she stepped out from the car, and I could lip-read him telling his colleague 'There's Maya Lowe,' then the colleague turned to look in the street but by now she was moving into the doorway and his companion motioned his head in her direction so that now both of them could see her and nod approvingly, doubtless feeling they must have chosen well for lunch if someone like Maya uses the same place. A young couple briefly unentangled their hands and sat up a little to follow her intently as she came to the table, studying us both for a few seconds before returning to their own intimate discussions. Two ladies-who-lunch had the same conversation as the businessmen, but spoke with their blazing eyes only, waiting for Maya to sit before using their tongues to dissect how she walked, how she looked, what she was wearing. And as for the staff, they were clearly experiencing a mixture of excitement and sheer terror at the prospect of having to serve such a famous customer.

Maya had barely kissed me and sat down when the black-suited manager was at her side, like a dog newly trained and suddenly confident it could serve its master.

'Miss Lowe, it is an honour for us to have you here at La Forchetta,' he said, hands held together in an obsequious knot, head bowing slightly.

'Thank you,' said Maya.

'I wonder if you would like one of the corner tables.'

'No, this is fine, thank you.'

One waiter took our order for drinks, another brought a second menu for Maya. The manager went through the specials. A third waiter brought the bread, and appeared to be pained when Maya said with a little shake of the head that she didn't want any. She picked up on his reaction and took from the oversized basket a thin slice of walnut bread which lay untouched on her side plate for the rest of the meal. The manager took our order for food – I had spaghetti vongole, Maya a tomato and mozzarella salad with a side order of salami. She has always had a thing about salami. A fourth waiter laid our napkins on our laps. A fifth accompanied the manager when he brought our food. The service got so attentive, so over the top, that I had to ask them to treat us like any other customers. Otherwise, it risked being a repeat of the time we had tried a newly opened Spanish restaurant near Lancaster Gate where the owner had responded to Maya's arrival by phoning his friends and favoured clients and inviting them to a 'meet Maya Lowe' lunch. It was when I realised he was organising a very English queue of people to get their picture taken with her that I complained. We ended up leaving and going to Pizza Express instead.

The Forchetta manager took my complaint on board but it still took another ten minutes for latecomers to finish their 'there's Maya Lowe' conversations, the staff to quell their excitement and the atmosphere to settle. Usually Maya would be brilliant at cutting out everything that was going on around her and, by the time the starter arrived, be well into some anecdote about the crazy demands some of her more precious co-stars made when they were on set. Today, though, she was quiet, fiddling with her napkin or nervously turning her wedding ring on her finger.

'Sheldon did a good job yesterday,' I said, trying to kick-start a conversation. In the morning papers Gibbs had been subjected to the kind of media vitriol normally reserved for gaffe-prone politicians and convicted paedophiles. It showed two things: Nick Sheldon's skill in a media scrap, when the first hours of battle were the key to winning the war, and the enduring strength of Maya's appeal. The media had invested too much in her being a good story for her to become a bad story. Yet.

'Nick calls it "the Harold Shipman treatment",' Maya said wryly and carried on pushing the food around her plate.

I was surprised to see her looking so low. I'd always admired Maya's ability to ignore the snide little things said about her, and focus instead on her work and the people who were important to her. And after all, this particular story had a happy ending. She'd come out on top.

'Are you going to tell me what's wrong?' I asked, touching her arm.

She looked up at me with sad eyes.

'You know, Steve, I'm beginning to think I'm not cut out for this game.'

'Game?'

'Acting . . .'

She could see I was taken aback. In all the years I'd known her, she'd never had any doubts about what she wanted to do. It was like hearing Tiger Woods say he wasn't made to play golf.

'I can't believe you mean that Maya,' I said. 'I mean, it's your whole life.'

'Well, perhaps it's not exactly the acting I mean, but all the shit that goes with it. The stuff in the papers and the magazines and on the websites and these wretched show-business programmes, every day, every single fucking day. Monday, Tuesday, Wednesday, Thursday—'

'Friday?' I interrupted with a grin, trying to lift her mood.

She frowned, and shook her head. 'OK, I know I'm not being much fun today but you have no idea what it's like. The photographers outside the house. The noise they make. The litter they leave. The botheration for the neighbours. So I try and escape somewhere, but it's impossible to escape people like those two rancid old trouts over there. Look at them, smiling at me like I'm their friend and if I don't smile back, for months they'll be telling everyone they know "Oh that Maya Lowe, she's so bloody unfriendly, so stuck-up, such a bitch."'

She forced a smile as she looked over, but through her teeth was whispering 'Yes, rancid old trouts, it is Maya Lowe and I am smiling at you so you can tell all your friends about it, and you will say how lovely I am and never know that I told my friend Steve I would like to see you taken to the kitchens and drowned in a vat of burning oil.'

I laughed, because I thought that was what she wanted and sometimes the only consolation you can give to people in distress is what you think they want. But I was shocked by her aggression. This didn't sound like the Maya I knew. To Vanessa, and to Jerry at work, who needed less convincing, I had always cited Maya's generosity about her fans as one of the qualities that set her above other stars. This sudden attack of rancid troutism was much more the sort of thing her husband Dan would say, especially since he made it big on TV. For him, there were two main categories of people – the talented and the talentless, and he had an unpleasant off-screen habit of making patronising comments about the devotion of the latter to the former, a group in which, obviously, he included himself and the woman he had somehow managed to make his wife.

'It's the lack of any privacy I guess,' Maya went on. 'I just wish I could do my acting and have that in one box, and live my life and have that in another.'

'That's not how it works though, is it?' I said. 'You're a celeb, you're a star. You signed up for the whole package.'

'But Steve, that's because I didn't know what it was!'

It's true, looking back, that she never wanted to be famous for the sake of it. She loved words and she admired the people who wrote them well. But she admired even more the people who could take someone else's words, and someone else's characters, and make them come alive for an audience. I had kept hundreds, no, thousands, of newspaper and magazine cuttings of interviews in which she talked about her work. At first I stored them in old shoeboxes beneath the desk in my study, later in properly ordered and indexed steel filing cabinets. I've always liked the orderly gathering of factual material. In one of the early profiles, a girl from Acton High, Sophie Newton, was tracked down by the press because she was sitting next to Maya in one of our school photos, and was reported as saying 'Maya always said she was going to be a star.' That was wrong. Maya always said she was going to be a good actress. That was it. Star, let alone superstar or megastar, never came into it.

I remember how she used to tell the girls at school that they were stupid to read magazines instead of books, say they were just pandering to trivia and exploitation of this thing called the celebrity culture, which grew up round the same time that she and her beauty did, and was a full-grown monster by the time she was such an important part of it. She thought there was something not proper about the way these papers and magazines intruded into people's lives. She also had strong views about the way the stars themselves cultivated and managed the intrusion. Long before she was part of their staple diet, she always said the celeb mags were full of lies. She thought it even more now she had been on so many front covers. 'Maya's joy' 'Maya's agony' 'Maya's love' 'Maya hits out' 'Maya eats out' 'Maya says this' 'Maya says that' when often she had said no such thing. The editors loved her short name. Short names make better headlines.

'Listen Maya,' I said, comfortably adopting the role of look-on-the-bright-side encourager, 'this is just a reaction to that lech on the plane and the fact that you're between films. As soon as you're working on your next project, you'll see the point of it all again.'

'Maybe,' she said, pushing her half-finished salad to one side. She hadn't even touched the salami. 'But maybe not. It's not just what happened yesterday. I've been feeling this for a long time now. Like when I went to Rome to collect that award for *Fast Track to Safety*. The whole fucking trip was appalling. Even the prime minister tried to chat me up, and when he introduced me to an Italian producer friend of his, who wanted to propose a film idea, he had his arm so far round me that his hand was almost groping my breast.'

'What a creep. So how did you handle it?'

'Just smiled, and felt sick. At least lechy construction workers are honest and straightforward,' she said. 'They see you coming, they like what they see, they have a moment of fantasy, and they let you know, ask you to share in it in a way, just by waving or smiling at them. It's irritating but you know what they're about. The ones I can't stand are these pinstriped arseholes with their fat jowls and their bellies hanging over their belts, and they're on the phone telling their wives they're at the airport, or they're choo-chooing their kids and telling them they'll be home to read them a bedtime story when the only bedtime story they want has me in the bed, with them on top of me, or maybe vice versa. I feel like, instead of being an actress, I've become some kind of porn star.'

I thought about an interview I'd seen a couple of weeks ago in a Sunday colour supplement with one such porn star. I'd only noticed it because Maya had done a feature in the same magazine, one of those Family Values columns where celebrities talk about their relatives. The porn-star article was itself porn dressed up as broadsheet journalism, a five-page spread of 'tasteful' pictures of an American woman named Desiree who said she was never happier than imagining all the men around the world wanking themselves silly as they watched her having sex, thought about her having sex, thought about having sex with her. I hoped, given her current outlook, that Maya had not seen it, not least because Desiree had more space in the magazine than she had, albeit that Maya was on the cover.

'What does Dan say about all this?' I asked.

She shrugged, and I couldn't help feeling pleased that the shrug was a dismissive one.

'He's just living the dream,' she said. 'Loving every minute.'

'What, of being Mr Maya Lowe?'

'He's someone in his own right too, Steve.'

'What? A TV presenter? Oh, there aren't many of them!' I

was conscious of how bitchy that sounded, and tried to retrieve. 'Seriously, Maya, what does he think? Have you told him?'

'Not really.' She looked petulant all of a sudden, like I had taken the conversation down a route she didn't want it to go. She adjusted a button on her sleeve.

'What about Kirsty?' Kirsty was Maya's friend from drama school, a feisty Scottish girl who was making a name for herself as a character actress.

'Oh Kirsty . . . Well, we don't talk so much any more. You know, it seems to me that the more people I know, the fewer real friends I have. In fact, if I think about who I could talk to like this,' and she gave a thin smile, 'there's really only you.'

Not for the first time, she inspired in me waves of conflicting emotion, on the one hand sadness for her that she felt so alone and confused, yet alongside it, perhaps partially drowning it, an unashamed joy that I was the one she could confide in.

Before long, we were gossiping about Malcolm, her bisexual make-up artist on the Jamaica shoot who was as camp as camp could be, and she took him off, boasting about all the stars he'd done in his time – 'and I mean *done*,' she said – and I was relieved to see her laughing. But when the manager brought over the bill, her face fell again.

'Where's all this going to lead, Maya?' I asked. 'I can't see you retiring at 30.'

'I don't know,' she said. 'I'm seeing Nick this afternoon. He wants to go snap on a big American production. But I'm just not sure. I'll have to spend weeks and weeks in the States if I do it, and I don't have the appetite.'

'How much?'

'How much do I not have the appetite?'

'No. How much will it pay?'

'I don't know. Two or three million basic, but they are suggesting I put some of my own money in, so it could be really big bucks if it works. But something's holding me back.'

'The basic's about fifty years' wages for me.'

'That's not the point.'

'Oh,' I said. 'It may not be *the* point, but it is *a* point.'

'This is not about money,' she said.

'Shall we go Dutch for lunch?'

She laughed, and grabbed the bill. She always paid. Another little rule of lunch in the Rectangle.

As if it were a prearranged illustration of what she'd been talking about, when Maya handed the manager a debit card, one of a dozen she had neatly lined up on two sides of a caramel-coloured Prada wallet, he gave her a business card in return. It belonged, he said, to a photographer waiting outside. Jake Nelson, We-know-the-stars.com. The guy had scribbled a little note on the back. 'Hi Maya, sorry for disturbing lunch. Would be great if you stopped and posed. All the best. Jake.'

'Never heard of him,' she said. 'It's that ghastly new website.'

'I don't know how they knew you were here,' said the manager. 'I am very sorry. I hope it was not one of our customers.'

'It happens,' said Maya. 'Don't worry.'

The sad eyes were back. 'This is what I mean,' she said. 'I can't go anywhere without these fucking creeps finding me.'

She called Victor and told him to bring the car right outside the restaurant in three minutes. I didn't like the way she talked to him. It was a bark, not a polite request, and so not like her. As we waited for the car to draw up, I asked her to let me know later what happened at the meeting with Nick Sheldon.

'OK,' she said. I could tell she was dreading it.

'It'll pass,' I said. 'You know that. Remember you're doing what you always wanted to do, and you are what you always wanted to be.'

'You can do what you want to do without being who you want to be,' she said. It either meant nothing, or a lot. Whichever it was, we didn't have time to discuss it.

She stood, kissed me on both cheeks, with the second peck almost touching the corner of my lips. She was wearing a sleeveless orange cashmere top, and tight white trousers. I put my hand on her arm, just below her shoulder, right on the scar left by the multiple vaccine jab she had in school. I loved the feel of her skin. Like silk. I could see the businessman by the window asking his colleague if he knew who I was. I noted that his braces matched the curtains. Perhaps they were journalists, not businessmen. Perhaps they were the ones who tipped off the photographer. I could understand how annoying it must be for her, not knowing who was watching you, or why, and what they would do with what they saw, or thought they saw.

The manager asked her to sign a copy of the menu, which she did, though without much grace. Her smile was brittle and unfriendly, her 'Best wishes' message perfunctory. Not even 'thanks for a nice meal'. Then she handed back his fountain pen, put on her sunglasses and swept out into the street, the photographer snapping away for every one of the few brief moments it took her to walk through the early afternoon sunshine, into the car, and away. The restaurant slowly returned to its pre-Maya shape and temperature, but with an overhang of excited chatter.

I slipped out a few minutes later, ignoring the photographer's questions about whether I had seen Maya, and if I knew who she'd been with. I took the Heathrow Express back to the airport, then jumped in a cab, clearly irritating the overweight driver who had been waiting in a long line of taxis and doubtless hoping for an American or Chinese businessman heading into town. His sighs, headshakes and heavy gear changes were all designed to make me feel bad for wanting a £3.50 ride to the soulless southside office block where Globus did its business. The only effect, however, was to ensure he drove back to the Heathrow queue without a tip.

As I slammed shut the taxi door and walked towards reception, it occurred to me that I hadn't said anything to Maya about Vanessa being pregnant. Despite Vanessa not wanting friends to know for a while, I was surprised to have got through the whole lunch without confiding my anxieties to Maya. In truth, though, I hadn't thought about the baby once.

Chapter Four

'So, how was she after all the hoo-ha on the plane then?'
Vanessa asked as soon as I got through the door that evening.
I'd called her just before setting off to meet Maya, pretending
that it was a last-minute arrangement. There was a delicious
smell of Spanish omelette coming from the kitchen which
refuelled my hunger even though, unlike Maya, I'd had a big
lunch.

'Oh, you know . . .' I said, not wishing to get drawn into
one of our 'Maya conversations' before I'd had a glass of wine.
'Lots of stories about her make-up artist. It's nice to come
home to dinner on the table. But aren't you supposed to be
feeling sick – or craving weird foodstuffs?'

'Maybe the sickness will come later. Right now I seem to
be ravenous all the time. I had to go back and get a second
sandwich at lunchtime. Shall we have a glass of champagne to
celebrate? My final drink before the baby comes . . .'

Our kitchen was a nice place to be. We'd celebrated my
recent bonuses with new units and a small extension on to
the garden, and now seemed to spend more time in there than
in any other part of the house. We had some of our best chats
when Vanessa was cooking and I was sitting in the comfortable old burgundy armchair that used to be in the TV room,

and which I couldn't bear to throw out when, after a previous pay rise, Vanessa had bought a new three-piece suite for the lounge.

Now, over a glass of champagne, we talked about money. Vanessa had checked the maternity pay deal at her bank. It was better than the national minimum. Money-wise, we were well set for a child. We'd even been putting some aside every month. Vanessa called it the baby fund, which was pretty swollen given how long we'd been trying.

I thought for a moment about Maya's film. In the cab from the airport to the office after lunch, I'd picked up a freesheet someone had left on the seat. There was an article that caught my eye on the business page, reporting the latest National Office of Statistics' figures on earnings. I'd been surprised that the average wage in Britain was less than £450 a week. Higher for men, higher in London, lower for women. To get into the top ten per cent, you had to be on £900 a week. I did a quick bit of mental arithmetic, and with bonuses, I made it. Still, it was pointless worrying about other people's earnings. If I compared myself with that average, I was well off. Put myself alongside Maya and her multimillion-pound film deals, or the clutch of Chelsea players on more than ten grand a day, and I was a pauper.

'Were you tempted to tell Maya about the baby?' Vanessa asked.

'We agreed I wouldn't, right? And anyway, she was too busy talking to me about how she wants to give up acting.'

I told Vanessa what Maya had said about the problems of celebrity.

She wasn't convinced. 'Sounds like she's just having a bad day. There's no way she'll give up acting. She is what she does.'

'She seems to have had quite a few bad days recently. I think she's serious.'

'Maybe she's getting broody. After all, she's turned 30, just like you're going to in a few months' time.'

I laughed. 'I'd love to see Desperate Dan pushing a buggy.'

'Seriously though, Steve, maybe that's the problem.'

'But you're 35! She's got plenty of time.'

'Not plenty. I got there by the skin of my teeth, particularly if we want more. Besides, it might not be about age, it might be about what Dan wants. We're lucky. We both want kids, but what if one of us didn't?'

It was an interesting thought. I'd never imagined Maya with children, particularly as she once got rid of one, but I could see that she might be thinking about it. I certainly couldn't see Dan Chivers getting into nappy-changing and pram-pushing, though, when he was at the height of his fame.

'What does he think about her giving it up?' Vanessa asked.

'She says she hasn't talked to him about it.'

'You believe that?'

'I never know what to believe about him.'

Ever since the beginning of Maya's relationship with Dan Chivers, Vanessa had endured a lot of moaning about him on my part. Maya was besotted, but I simply could not understand what she saw in him. In my mind, he was one of those vapid celebrities reducing TV to the same level as the worst of the tabloid press. And the tabloids loved him, of course, not least because the interviews he did with the stars on his show gave them so much copy. His rise from virtual unknown to Britain's favourite daytime TV presenter had been fast, as Maya was always telling me. It sometimes felt like scarcely a week went by without her emailing me some wonderful new

'Dan fact' – like yesterday's show had even more viewers than the one the day before, or they were doing a compilation DVD for Christmas, and did I know that the interview he did with Daniel Craig got picked up in every single national newspaper in the country, apart from two, and several dozen overseas websites, including in the Middle East? It was the kind of thing that, if it involved anyone else, just would not impress her. But for all her amusement at the ridiculousness of other celebrities, when it came to Dan she couldn't see the funny side.

Before he wormed his way into Maya's life, Dan's name meant little to me. He'd been a presenter for one of those safe, comfortable, woolly-pullover regional TV programmes that comes on after the main national news, up in the Midlands somewhere, and he was spotted by one of the top bods at ITV, whose mother lived in a care home near Loughborough. One of the afternoon presenters on ITV1, a popular but ageing veteran called Joe Hughes, needed to take a holiday and the executive with the mother in Loughborough approached Dan to ask him to step in. By the time Joe Hughes got back from his month away, Dan had persuaded the powers-that-be that their afternoon programming needed a major revamp, with him at the heart of it. Within three months, he had given them a blueprint for a new style of talk show, mixing the serious with the trivial, famous people with 'real people' who had great stories to tell, all woven together by his 'personality'. Apparently he tested well with the women who made up the bulk of Joe Hughes' viewers. More importantly, he did well in focus groups made up of people who watched his rivals on the other channels. I don't like to give Dan Chivers credit for much, but he had a plan, and it worked, which is why after six weeks in the job, with the ratings rising, he persuaded the company to fund a big poster campaign to drive the ratings even higher. How he must have loved seeing his bronzed face on gigantic billboards all over Britain. 'The Big Talk. The Big Guests' and a giant picture of him, all white teeth and honeyed skin. But he did get the Big Guests, you had to give him that, which is how Maya ended up on his programme.

She rang to tell me she was appearing and, since I happened to be working from home, I switched on. I found it almost unwatchable. Short sharp jingle at the top. Fast-moving archive pictures of Dan talking to guests, them all smiles and bonhomie, him brimming with exaggerated animation; the jingle going from brassy to electronic, then back to brassy and then the sight of him, perfectly coiffed, beautiful suit, open-collared white shirt, tanned, smiling, a flick of the head then he races down a short but wide flight of red-carpeted stairs through an almost exclusively female audience, all clapping and smiling. Big smile from Dan as he bounds on to the stage, half-hearted appeal to stop the applause, talking over it with a few trailers for the programme, a couple of corny jokes about stories in the news, then on to the first guest.

Dan was disgustingly chummy, cosying up to his guest on his lurid yellow sofa, or walking around among the audience, getting them to ask questions too. By the time Maya came on – they always saved the Big Guest till last – I was feeling thoroughly nauseated.

I have a tape of that interview. After they hitched up together, I watched it over and over again to see if it revealed any signs of what was to follow. There were none. It's not Maya's way to be as open in interviews as she is in 'real life', as people still call it, even though the masterminds of his sort of programme like to think the gap between real life and celebrity life has narrowed, but if anything when talking to Dan she was even more closed up than usual. When they were discussing *Fallen Angel*, a fairly heavy film about a young woman who falls victim to a religious cult, she was fine. But whenever Dan tried to get her to talk about her own life, even stories and events already in the public domain, she put on that gentle but firm demeanour I knew so well, the one that said 'thus far but no more'.

So it was a shock when she said she was seeing him socially, an even bigger shock when I met her for a drink at the Wolseley one evening after work.

'Secret handshake,' she said. 'I think I'm in love.'

'Not Dan Chivers?' I just knew it.

She looked hurt. 'Why not?'

I couldn't stop myself. 'He's a complete jerk.'

'That's a horrible thing to say. You barely know him.'

'Friends are supposed to tell the truth to friends. I know what I see, I know what I think. Sorry.'

She stared at me, not angrily, but with a mix of hurt, and the desire for me to understand.

'There's something about him, Steve. It's hard to explain. It's like there's the TV personality that everyone sees. But then there's this other person beneath all the showbiz glamour, this warm, vulnerable person trying to get out.'

She admitted that when she first met him prior to the recording of the interview, he made a neutral to negative impression. He was behaving like just another TV chat-show host, obsessed with explaining the mechanics of what was going to happen once they got into the studio.

'But there was a drinks do in the green room afterwards, and he came across very differently. He was relaxed because the show was over, it had gone OK, and he was much more natural in a way, and I thought it was interesting that there was this difference between the successful TV face and a real face that to me was more genuine, more human.'

'So you fell for someone because they weren't as plastic and false as you first thought.'

'Steve, why don't you just stop bitching and listen.'

'OK, I'm listening.'

'We met for lunch a couple of times and when he was talking about how hard he was finding his sudden rise to fame, it was like he was describing my life in the run-up to the millennium, when *Picture Frame* went so much bigger than anyone expected and everything went crazy.'

'Jesus, Maya. He is an afternoon chat-show host. You are a serious actress and a major film star. I cannot believe you think there are similarities between your careers.'

'But a lot of what we went through is the same. You go from being virtually unknown, to everyone thinking they know you, and of course they don't know you at all, they just know an image created through and for the media, and I thought at last, finally, I've found someone who knows what it's like.'

'I can't believe I'm hearing this,' I said. I repeated my main point, raising my voice for emphasis. '*He* is a daytime chat-show host. *You* are a fucking movie star. What has got into you?'

'Well, you may see nothing in him, but I do. And so does Nick. He's planning to take over his contract negotiations and some of his extracurriculars.'

'Oh good for Nick.'

I could tell I was beginning to annoy her now. She knew how to hurt back.

'He's actually incredibly intelligent, Steve. He gets the business side of TV better than anyone I know. He is really into French and Italian cinema. And you might not imagine it from the TV show, but his favourite author is Trollope.'

'Oo-er,' I said.

She made the most hurtful point last.

'Plus he's fantastic in bed.'

'So we're shagging are we?'

'I prefer to call it "making love", Steve. You should try it.'

That one did hurt. I decided to sit back in my chair, say nothing, look pained, see if she apologised.

'He makes me so happy, Steve. He's the first man who really knows what I'm feeling.'

That hurt too, even though I knew our friendship existed on a different level to her romantic entanglements. It was something she could take for granted. When she said 'the first man', she didn't have to explain that she wasn't counting me.

I found it hard, though, watching her fall further and further in love with an idiot. After that first conversation I tried to censor myself every time I was tempted to say something negative about Dan because I was worried she'd stop confiding in me. But I think she knew how I felt. I completely blew up when she told me about how he'd promised to stop taking cocaine if that was what she wanted.

'So the man's a cokehead as well as a dickhead,' I couldn't help saying.

'TV is stressful, Steve, and lots of people do it to relieve that pressure,' she replied sharply. 'And anyway, it doesn't matter because he's giving up.'

After that, Dan became almost a taboo subject between us, and she certainly avoided bringing us together. The day she told me she was marrying him was one of the worst of my life, worse even than the day she told me she had 'gone the whole way' with Nathan, the first boy she slept with. In the end Nathan hadn't lasted. I could deal with Julian, a warm, funny guy she went out with at drama school, and with Mike Simmons, because I could see they suited her. I got them. But not Dan. I could not get Dan at all, however hard I tried.

My mobile rang just as Vanessa and I were thinking of going to bed.

'It's Maya,' Vanessa said, passing me my phone from where I'd left it on the kitchen counter. She grimaced, and I could see it was a bit irritating, Maya calling at ten at night, especially since this evening should have been all about us.

'Hiya,' I said. 'Everything OK?'

'Yeah, fine.' Maya sounded very flat still. 'You asked me to call about my meeting with Nick.'

'Oh yeah – how was it?'

'Nothing decided.'

'Oh, and how did he take that?'

'Like any agent would who is banking on ten per cent of a few million plus a percentage of the percentage, I guess. He thinks I'm mad to doubt it for a second.'

'And how are you feeling about it?'

'Same as when I saw you. Just don't have the passion.'

'It'll come back.'

'Maybe. Anyway, I promised to call.'

Later in bed, Vanessa could tell I was troubled. My inability to focus on my book was preventing her from concentrating on hers.

'What's wrong?' she asked.

'Just thinking about Maya, and wondering what criteria she applies to decide she has a bad life.'

'I know,' she said. 'When you look at it from the outside — fame, success, popularity, millions in the bank, beautiful house in London, flat in New York, never wanting for anything material, a husband who adores her, good friends, doting parents — it's hard to see what's wrong. I'm telling you, she wants kids . . .'

She turned out her light, kissed me on the side of my head, then sighed. 'The Queen and her unborn prince are tired. Night night.'

Her face looked even stronger when she was sleeping. I wished I could borrow some of her strength and inner confidence. On so many nights of our marriage, she had fallen asleep with that calm, serene look on her face, leaving me to stem the tide of whatever anxiety was flooding in. Tonight, it was the fear that the 'unborn prince' inside Vanessa would see little to admire in his dad, a man who was only distinguished by his friendship with a woman better known in every country in the world than he was in his own street.

Chapter Five

I had one of my Dad dreams that night. I don't have them
often, but when I do, they are vivid and powerful, occasionally comforting at the time, but inevitably troubling when I
blink myself into the day. We are usually on holiday somewhere, just the two of us, and we're doing something that
feels special, or dangerous. Sometimes both. On this particular night we were rock climbing, attached by a thin yellow
rope. I was scared, and the fear jerked deeper with every
effort to move a hand or foot, and every accidental glance
downwards at the gargantuan sea of granite below, from which
boulders were rolling with a thunderous roar, cracking into
millions of pieces as they hit rocks that had made the journey
ahead of them. My dad appeared to hear nothing of this raging
torrent beneath us. Just do what I do, he said, do what I say,
and you'll be fine. He was looking down towards me, and I
kept thinking he was going to fall from the rock face and the
two of us would go tumbling down with the boulders, but he
was smiling, and seemed confident. It was a warm smile which
left me feeling secure. But then I noticed something. There
was a small baby strapped to his back in a kind of papoose.
It was crying and beating its little fists on my father's head,
and the papoose looked frighteningly precarious. I came out

in a sweat, imagining how difficult it would be for me to hold on to the rope and catch the baby at the same time, should it fall. Then Vanessa nudged me awake, said I'd been groaning, asked if I was OK.

What is really weird about these dreams is that although I know I am with my father – I hear myself calling him 'Dad', he calls me 'Son' – he looks nothing like the photos Mum and I have of him, or rather had. Our house in Southall used to be like a mini shrine to him, for a while at least. There were pictures of him in virtually every room, the bathroom included. The biggest photo, which used to sit in an ornate silver frame on a square table next to the TV, was of Dad holding me above his head, with me looking down on him, laughing but a bit anxious, and Mum watching on with a concerned smile, a cigarette between her first two fingers. I used to look at that photo a lot. He was whirling me around in the air. His hands were tight on my chest and under my armpits, and my legs were flying free. It was obviously something dads did with their kids. I had seen it happening in the park. But I couldn't remember it happening to me. No memories. No Dad.

I wonder sometimes if my life would be different – I don't know if I mean better or worse, just different – if I had a real memory of my dad, something that roots me to him, makes now a part of then. Sometimes I think I remember him, but whenever I try to deepen that memory with a detail – what was he wearing, who else was there? – or the recollection of a feeling or an atmosphere – how did he smell, what was the mood of the room? – I'm always pushed backwards to the realisation, sad every time, that these 'memories' are tricks of photography; a photo I have seen has forced itself on my mind of today to make me think I can recall

moments of yesterday. That instant of realisation is accompanied by deep disappointment, all the deeper because it is
always as though I am feeling the letdown for the first time.
I ought to be used to it by now.

I remember being conscious as a child of how little I knew
about my dad. Mum didn't talk about him much. I knew he
liked cabbage, was hopeless at ice skating, went abroad once,
to Amsterdam for a stag night, smoked, at a rough estimate,
17,000 cigarettes during his life, and was saving to buy a
caravan when he died. But even those details were hard won,
and did not really tell me who he was, or why Mum married
him. All I had were the photos. I would study his appearance.
He had the same browny hair as I have, but his eyebrows were
thicker, and he had a bigger nose. I liked to think anyone who
saw that photo, and then saw me, would immediately see the
father-son resemblance. It's strange where wishful thinking
can take you.

Now I don't even have any photos. I got rid of them when
I married Vanessa. After all, what's the point of having photographs that stir no memories? They might as well be of anyone.
Like when you look at a picture of a great-grandparent dead
long before you were born and you just think, those people
have nothing to do with me. Nothing at all. They are aliens.

Mum got rid of the photographs too. It was a gradual
process. Once she started going out with other men, three
years after Dad died, the silver-framed photo moved to the
sideboard. Then it moved to Mum's bedroom. But once the
men moved in there too, it was put away altogether, along
with all the others.

I am not saying my mum was promiscuous, or criticising
her even if she was. I suppose three years is quite a long time

to go without a man for someone who had imagined she would spend the rest of her life more or less happily married, and probably with more kids than the one she'd had by the time he died. And once she started having boyfriends, she only had one man on the go at any one time, so far as I can recall. The problem was that most of the blokes were pretty hopeless, men whose marriages had bust up or, frankly, losers who could not believe their luck that they had found someone like her. She's not the liveliest firework in the box, but she wasn't bad-looking. I would say she had about six relationships where the bloke actually moved in. That might sound a lot to some people, but they were spread over quite a long period of time, the whole of my schooldays, and a couple of them were there for days rather than months. I didn't really like any of them. They all tried in their different ways to be nice to me, but they weren't my dad and they were never going to be.

I could always sense Mum's nervousness when she brought a man home, and her desire for me to show first politeness, then approval. But I was no good at it. I was selfish enough to expect Mum to devote herself entirely to me once Dad died, but realistic enough to know it was unlikely to happen. That didn't mean I was just going to roll over, though, and give her what she wanted. By Number 3, I had learned to do the politeness bit as a way of giving added emphasis to the non-approval later. I call him Number 3 because I can't remember his name. All I remember about him was that he was the only one who had a beard, a russet thing with speckles of grey, but his top lip was clean-shaven. As far as I was concerned the only point of growing a beard was that it meant you didn't have to shave, but Number 3 both had a beard and shaved every day, just that tiny strip below his nostrils. Tosser.

Vanessa, who always tried to get on with my mum, and managed better than most people do — another blessing of my life with her — found the whole scenario ludicrous. I told her about Number 3's shaving habits one winter afternoon mid falling in love, when we were swapping the tiniest details of our life stories between fucks. 'Normally,' she said, 'it's the young woman taking the new boyfriend home seeking the approval of the father. With you, your poor mum was the young girl and you were the dad.' I could laugh about it with Vanessa, particularly then, one of the happiest times of my life. But back in my childhood, when dark had fallen and I was in bed alone, and Mum was tucked up in hers with Number 1, 2, 3, 4, 5 or 6, it didn't seem so funny.

Of all her blokes, the one I got on with best was a guy called Mitch who said hello and goodbye and left it at that. He had no expectations of me, I had none of him, and I liked it that way. If he was in the house on his own, because Mum was out at work or shopping or whatever, I went to my room, and was fine there. Or I went to Maya's house, where I was even better.

From the moment I met the Lowes, I loved them. Maya's mother, Anna, was so different to my mother — exotic and glamorous, for Acton at least, and a fantastic cook. As for Frank, he was warm, funny and generous. He would take me to football matches, Brentford and Queens Park Rangers mainly, and show me round the railway sheds where he worked. He never said so, but I think he guessed what my home life was like and felt a responsibility to give me a good role model. I remember how brilliantly he handled our first meeting. He was definitely suspicious, clearly trying to work out if his little princess had a boyfriend as in 'boyfriend'.

'You live nearby?' he asked.

'Hundred yards away,' I said. 'Petersfield Road.'

'Lived there long?'

'Only a few months actually. We moved from Southall in the summer.'

'What does your dad do?'

It wasn't often that I was asked a direct question which assumed my father to be alive. When it did happen, I felt embarrassed and awkward, not for myself but because I knew those who asked would feel awkward and embarrassed when I gave the answer.

'He died when I was 3.'

To my surprise, Mr Lowe dealt with the information in a warm and straightforward manner, rather than looking away as so many people did.

'What happened?' he asked.

'He was an electrician in a factory. It's not there any more. It's a Kwik-Fit tyre place now. He was fixing a generator and he got electrocuted. That was it. Happened just like that.' I clicked my fingers.

I was even more surprised when Mr Lowe came over and put an arm round my shoulder.

'I'm really sorry to hear that, son,' he said. 'I'd just like you to know that you're welcome here any time.'

And I was. I could knock on the door whenever I wanted and Mrs Lowe would squeal a delighted welcome and make me chocolate-spread sandwiches, or soup if it was cold outside, or Mr Lowe would take me off to help out on his allotment.

I thought of Mr Lowe as I lay in bed that Wednesday morning trying to shake my mind free from its frightening dream of clinging to a rock face. All through my teens he had been like a surrogate father to me. We didn't talk much, but there was an understanding between us. How would it be if I called Mr Lowe now and told him I was frightened of becoming a father, that I didn't know how a father should behave? It seemed a difficult call to make, too intimate somehow, even though I knew him well.

Vanessa was bustling about, popping in and out of the bathroom, warning me that I needed to get up. What gave her such energy and confidence, I wondered? Was it her close family? I envied Vanessa her good relationships with her relatives. She saw her parents at least once every two weeks, and had a regular session with her sister Judith for Sunday-afternoon tea. Sometimes I would watch her chatting away to Judith and feel almost resentful about it. When I was 7 or 8, I used to pretend I had a big brother, and I would talk to him when I was on my own, up in my room, just chatty stuff mainly, but occasionally I would confide real worries in him, like where Dad went when he died, and whether him dying young meant that we would die young too, and what would happen to us when we did? I called him Joey, after Joey Jones, who was my favourite Chelsea player when I first saw them play. I grew out of Joey when I was about 12, around the same time I met Maya.

So who could I talk to now if not Mr Lowe? Apart from Jerry, I wasn't that friendly with any of the guys at work. They were a dull lot, for the most part – dull people obsessed with cars and gadgets and women, doing dull jobs in a dull building. And even Jerry was a colleague more than a friend. As for other friends, I didn't have many. At my last job but one, the one I was doing when I met Vanessa, I had good colleagues, and some I would have called friends at the time.

But apart from exchanging Christmas cards and seeing one or two of them for a drink now and then, or going to a Chelsea game on the rare occasions we could get tickets, we had not stayed close. Marriage isn't good for friendships. Nor is being best friends with a movie star. The Acton crowd ditched me long ago. I remember Jim, a guy I played football with and who back then I'd have put down as a likely friend for life, taunting me for being a 'star fucker'. And he meant it.

That left my mum. Could I confide in her? It seemed a strange thought. Since I'd met Vanessa, I'd drifted even further away from my mum. She was living with a welder called Doug now, and seemed happy enough. We saw each other at Christmas and Easter, spoke on the phone every few weeks, and that was about it. Vanessa made an heroic effort to get on with my mum, but if ever we had gone beyond that Christmas and Easter deal, I think even she would have said enough's enough.

No, there was nothing for it but to get up and face the day on my own. Maya was the only person I could really imagine talking to about it all and I didn't feel I could burden her when she had so much else to worry about.

As luck would have it, Maya phoned me that day, but at the most inconvenient moment. I was standing outside the boardroom waiting to go into Brandon's weekly strategy meeting.

'Can I call you back in an hour?' I whispered, then quickly turned my phone off.

'Important business I hope, Watkins?' asked Brandon, striding up behind me.

'As always, Mike,' I said as breezily as I could.

Work on the Qatar deal, which was beginning to obsess Brandon, dominated the meeting, but as soon as it ended, I dashed back to my office and called Maya while Jerry was getting a cup of coffee in the canteen.

She sounded jollier than yesterday, as if she had rediscovered a little of her old self, said she was having a dinner party at the weekend, and she'd like us to come.

'A dinner party? What? At your house?'

'Yeah, where else would it be?'

'Dunno. Just, you've never invited us there before. Sorry if I sound ungrateful. It's very kind of you. Who else will be there?'

I suspected that someone had dropped out and we were late replacements.

'Dan, of course, who would love to see you.'

'Of course,' I said, hoping she would note the hint of irony.

'Nick and his wife Becky, who is great, and the woman who edits the *Observer* magazine, I can't remember her name, with her husband, who is some kind of business guy.'

'Oh.'

She detected my surprise, given what she had said yesterday about hating the media intrusion into her life.

'I know what you're thinking, but the *Observer* woman isn't that kind of editor. She's more on the serious side, you know? Besides, Dan thinks it might be a good idea to pitch our profile a bit more upmarket.'

'*Our* profile?'

'Well, mine, his, both I guess.'

I snorted. 'Seems to me *you* – singular – have a very good profile in the upmarket magazines, not least because you don't talk to them unless you have to. I'm not sure they're terribly interested in afternoon chat-show hosts, unless the presenter happens to be married to a film star.'

She bridled at my obvious put-down of Dan.

'I see. Well do you want to come or not? Inviting you is my idea, not Dan's. I was hoping we could talk more about the film project. Maybe you can help me see what's best. You have a pretty good judgement on these things.'

I felt shamed by Maya's sweetness. Here was I being rude about her husband and, instead of getting upset, she was confirming the strength of our friendship.

'I'm sure we would love to come,' I said. 'I'll talk to Vanessa and text you later.'

'Great. Come half an hour early and we'll find a private corner to chat in.'

'OK, see you then.'

When I called Vanessa at lunchtime, she shared my suspicion that we were late invitees, but oddly when she suggested it, I felt a little resentment. I was allowed to doubt Maya. She wasn't.

'I'm sure it is well intentioned,' I said.

'Well, I definitely want to go,' she said. 'I can't wait to see the house. Don't you think it's a bit odd, though, that she's waited until now to invite you there?'

'Why odd? She knows Dan and I always rub each other up the wrong way. Even at the wedding. Remember?'

'How could I forget?'

14 August 2005. Maya looked especially beautiful. She was wearing a simple white silk suit designed by Vera Wang, white shoes, a tiara of pink flowers in her hair. Dan wore a black suit with a matching black shirt and tie. He had wanted to

sell the picture rights to *OK!* or *Hello!* magazine, but Maya had insisted her wedding was not for sale.

'Sometimes you have to trade cash for reputation,' she told me.

'Good for you,' I said. 'Does he understand?'

'Course he does. It could have been Nick pushing him to test it out on me, but I wasn't having it.'

'Sheldon? I thought he was Mr Judgement?'

'He is. But he's also Mr Ten Per Cent, and these mags pay a fortune for weddings.'

At the reception afterwards, at the Orangery in Kensington Gardens, Maya's parents stuck close to me, feeling out of their depth among so many film and TV people and the over-the-topness of the catering. Although Dan had a natural rapport with Maya's mother Anna, he found it harder to chat to Mr Lowe and I could sense his irritation that Frank and I got on so well.

Vanessa loved the whole day. Stars galore at the reception, high-quality food and drink. Very different from our own wedding four years before, which was a low-key event at St Michael's Church, Camden, and had only one celebrity guest: Maya. We did get a few paparazzi though. 'Maya's First Boyfriend Weds': that was the story the tabloids seized on, even though – not for want of longing – I had never been her 'boyfriend' in the way they imagined or suggested. A few of the newspapers had photos of Vanessa and me leaving the church, but mainly the pictures were of Maya, who had taken time off from filming *Fallen Angel* to be there and came in a gorgeous John Galliano dress. Only the *Camden New Journal* had a bigger picture of us than her. We hung it on the wall of the downstairs toilet.

I was joking about this with Mr Lowe at the wedding when Dan walked up. He thought I was taking the piss out of the grandeur of their event.

'What are you doing hanging pictures of my wife in your toilet?' he said. 'Don't you think she deserves better?'

'Oh, I do think she deserves better,' I said, trying to make clear by my tone of voice that I was referring to him.

Vanessa and Mr Lowe were looking at us, their faces showing anxiety that the banter could turn nasty, violent even, like we were about to roll up our sleeves and punch each other.

Dan looked at me with real disdain and walked off to join Jonathan Ross who was holding forth by a giant pot plant about some seemingly hilarious comment Gordon Ramsay had made about green-room sandwiches when he'd had him on the show the week before. I found the rest of the party a torment. It was unbearable having to listen to Mr Lowe's speech about how joyous he felt that his daughter had, at last, found the right man, and Dan's obnoxious speech, which pretended to be about Maya, but which was really all about him. He must have made his feelings about me known to Maya; why else had we never been invited over to their house during the year and a half they'd been married? OK, so when they got back from their month-long honeymoon in Malaysia, they'd been absorbed with doing up the house, but we hadn't even been asked to the housewarming party to which, as I knew from the pages of *Hello!*, they'd had more than a hundred guests.

I pondered the reason for the dinner-party invitation as I drove home from work that night. I had the radio tuned to Heart FM. Easy listening. Until the commercials, that is, which included one for Dan's show tomorrow. It said he had not one, but two Big Guests – Chris Martin, of Coldplay; and his wife, Gwyneth Paltrow. Bloody hell. The man was unstoppable.

Maya knew exactly how I felt about Dan. Even if another couple *had* pulled out, surely she could have found guests more suitable than Vanessa and me to fill the gap. Chris Martin and Gwyneth Paltrow? No, it really seemed as if she genuinely wanted my advice. I felt proud of that. By inviting me to this select gathering, she was making me a part of whatever decision-making circle she was drawing up about her new film project. But if that was the case, I was being put in a position of great responsibility. For Maya to turn down a major film, which her agent was encouraging her to do, would mark an important turning point in her life. It needed careful planning, a lot of thought. I knew I could help, though. Yes, in this situation, the very fact that I wasn't part of her new world made me better able to guide her. I turned up the radio – 'What Becomes of the Broken-hearted?' was playing. I shouted 'Sod you, Dan!' and drove home singing along with Jimmy Ruffin.

Chapter Six

Vanessa walked slowly down the stairs then stood for a moment or two waiting for a compliment. Despite my warning that Maya would wear jeans, albeit very smart jeans, Vanessa had insisted on going shopping for a new dress. 'You know how Maya is always going on about how much time she devotes to dressing down,' I'd warned her. 'She's made "casual" an art form.' 'I'll only be able to get into something chic for another few weeks,' Vanessa had argued. 'Might as well make the most of it.'

It was a simple, black cocktail dress, not too showy, but elegant, and she was wearing it with a pink cashmere shawl. She'd had her hair done too, and it had that fresh, vital shine that only a professional hairdresser ever seems able to give, and which explains why women spend so much on their hair.

'You look great,' I said. 'Now can we go? Maya said to be early and I don't want to be late.'

'No, we mustn't be late being early.' She laughed. I couldn't tell which of us was more nervous. Me, I guess. I was nervous. She was excited.

We took a cab so that I wouldn't have to worry about having a few glasses of wine. I'm the driver in our household. Vanessa has never learnt. As soon as I gave the cabbie the address, he knew who lived there. He reeled off a few other celebs in the area, including a rap singer I had never heard of, and a couple of Arsenal players. He was a Tottenham fan. I told him I supported Chelsea, though less enthusiastically since the Russians took over.

'You friends of hers?' he asked.

I hesitated for a moment, finding the question intrusive, not sure whether I should answer.

'Yeah. She's an old school friend of mine,' I said.

'Wow! You don't really think about people like her having school friends, do you?'

'Well, I do.'

'No, don't get me wrong, but you know what I'm saying; it's just that, for someone like me, she didn't really exist till I knew she existed, like when she became real famous and stuff. That's all I'm saying.'

'I see, yeah. Well, we go back a long way.'

'That's nice. What's she really like?'

'She hasn't changed much really. What you see is what you get.'

'Thing is you know her the person, we just see the different people she plays, and then the stuff in the papers which you can never be sure of.'

'She'd certainly agree with you on that.'

'Getting worse, innit?'

He maintained a reluctant silence up to the next junction and, had the traffic lights stayed green, he might have held it. But the slowing of the engine to meet the demands of the red light created an uneasy quiet which he felt compelled to fill.

'Come on then, in a word, good thing or bad thing?' He was looking at me directly in his rear-view mirror, smiling, and intended to hold my gaze until I answered.

'Good, I promise you.'

'I can vouch for that,' piped up Vanessa.

'That's nice. What about her old man, the TV guy? Top man or bell end?'

'What you see is what you get.'

'Yeah, thought so. My missus' mum loves him, mind you, watches every single day. Watches that highlights thing too. Religiously.'

The house was in Blomfield Road, not far from a bridge over the canal. It must be nice to look out over water, I thought.

'Welcome to poshland,' said the driver. 'Houses cost a bomb round here, I'm telling you.'

Most of the houses in the road had hedges or simple walls, but Maya's had a rather dramatic, high black fence, perpetually swivelling security cameras at either end of it, a video entryphone to get through the garden gate, then another phone at the front door, where two more cameras peered down on us as we arrived. There was no sign of Maya's silver Mercedes. I assumed it was parked behind the large black gates of the driveway. Dan's black Mercedes was on the street.

Vanessa took my hand and squeezed it hard as we climbed the three broad stone steps to the front door. Perhaps she was nervous after all. It was a crisp, clear February evening and little bulbs dotted into the steps illuminated us like spotlights. It was hard not to feel self-conscious. I was glad there hadn't been any photographers in the street. Or at least, I hadn't noticed any. Sometimes they stayed in their cars and just watched and waited from a distance. Perhaps they thought Vanessa and I weren't worth photographing. Or they had decided Maya was in for the night, going nowhere, and they had gone to doorstep other faces whose pictures always sold, or left for the clubs and restaurants used by the more willing celebs.

The door was answered by a tall blonde woman in a dress rather similar to Vanessa's, though slightly longer. Behind her was a young man, also dressed in black, who was holding a tray of drinks in misted, thin-stemmed green glasses. The woman took Vanessa's coat then showed us through to a large sitting room which ran from the canal side of the house to the garden at the back. Vanessa's heels clicked loudly on the polished floorboards in the hallway, silencing only as she reached the thick cream carpet of the sitting room. There were two huge white sofas opposite each other, a low glass table between them, with a thin purple vase on it. The vase held a large orchid. Vanessa touched it to see if it was real. She nodded, and smiled.

One wall gave testimony to the fact that Maya read more than anyone I knew, or rather used to before she got so caught up in the movie world; row upon row of bookshelves, some of the books looking well thumbed, their spines old and worn, others more pristine, probably presents and freebies. The two middle shelves had framed photos sitting on them, mainly of Maya and Dan, sometimes together. Dotted between them were some of the awards Maya had won. I noticed one that was clearly Dan's: 'ITV Newcomer of the Year'.

I sat on one of the sofas while Vanessa walked round examining every chair, every little ornament, every picture. There was a sculpture of a nude by the fireplace, dark stone, with the woman arching her back and reaching upwards, a sphere in her right hand. It was almost beautiful. Above the fireplace was a huge painting, of nothing in particular, dominated by three large swipes of orange paint. I couldn't decide whether it was Maya's taste or not. It had its own lighting attached, like paintings you see in museums.

Dan came through first, all 'hey' and 'great to see you', and Vanessa and I did our best to respond in kind. I had promised Vanessa I would try to suppress my feelings about Dan, but I was hopeless at over-the-top hello stuff. Vanessa kissed him on one cheek and said how beautiful the house was.

'Yeah, we like it,' he said, then came over to slap me on the back and say 'Did they get you a drink?' which, as I was holding one, seemed unnecessary.

Maya talked so often about the 'real man' behind the TV personality, but I could see no sign of him. Establishing where the TV act ended and the real person began clearly required powers of psychological analysis far greater than mine or Vanessa's.

'Been such a long time!' he said.

'I know!' said Vanessa. 'It was so difficult to talk to either of you at Maya's thirtieth.'

'Oh, were you there?' said Dan. He seemed surprised at the idea. 'Wow! Then we sure do have a whole lot of catching up to do.' His language had become very American for the son of a council worker from Derby. Chivers senior was something in environmental health, Maya had once told me. Glorified rat catcher. I told myself not to let it get to me. Maya wanted us here. Vanessa wanted us to have a good time and she was loving it, like she had walked into the pages of a magazine. Go with the flow, I told myself. It was going to be hard though.

He was even dressed like on one of his TV shows, though without the jacket. Crisp, beautifully ironed light-blue shirt, collar opened wide to reveal the top of a tanned, hairless chest. Little red-ball silk cufflinks, close to his embroidered initials. Wedding ring on his left hand, pinkie ring on the right, with a tiny diamond in the bottom corner. Smart, sharply pressed navy trousers; belt with a buckle that was too big. Shoes that cost more than I would pay for a suit. Pointed. I've never trusted a man in pointed shoes.

Maya appeared in the doorway as Dan was giving Vanessa a rundown of who lived in the big houses on the other side of the canal. Businessmen mainly, but the one directly opposite was owned by a fashion designer I had not heard of, but Vanessa clearly had.

'That's amazing,' she cooed. 'I love his stuff.'

'Hi,' said Maya. I stood. Vanessa turned, Dan stopped talking. Even in her own home, a room changed when she walked into it. 'What's amazing?' she asked Vanessa.

I explained that Vanessa's excitement came from learning they had Gianluca, or whatever his name was, as their neighbour.

'I love your dress,' said Maya.

'Oh thanks. Steve said to come casual, but this is an occasion for me.'

Maya was wearing tight-fitting ankle-length Armani jeans, low-heeled black pumps with a polka-dot bow on them, and a silvery wraparound sleeveless top which, Maya told Vanessa, was one of Stella McCartney's. 'The shoes are Marc Jacobs,' she said. 'Really comfy.'

'Hey,' interjected Dan, 'do you guys want to take a tour of the house before the others arrive?'

I glanced at Maya who gave me a barely noticeable shake of the head.

'Oh, I'm fine,' I said, 'but I'm sure Vanessa would love to.'

Dan eyed me, suspiciously I felt, certainly with a quizzical lift of his top lip.

'Come on then,' he said, taking Vanessa's arm. 'Let's leave these two old friends together while we go upstairs and make friends too.'

As they left the room, laughing, I felt the beginnings of a headache fade.

'Have you heard of John Masefield?' Maya asked.

'Vaguely,' I said.

'Poet Laureate, early last century. See the big house over there, beyond the green and red barge? That was his. There's a blue plaque on the wall.'

'One day you'll have a blue plaque here, and the plaques can stare at each other across the water,' I said, walking over to the window.

'Do you think so?'

'Why not?'

She smiled, and her face filled with pleasure. 'Be amazing, wouldn't it? There aren't many people I'd say this to, Steve. But I would love that. I would love it, a blue plaque.'

'Here or Acton?'

I was sure Acton would win it by a clear margin, but the question seemed to stall her.

'Both,' she said after a few seconds.

'If you had to choose?'

'Here, I think.'

'But Acton's where you're from . . .'

'I guess so. Anyway, it'll probably never happen.'

'You never know.'

There was a squeal of delight from upstairs as Vanessa admired something that Dan was showing her.

'Do those people in black live with you?' I asked.

'Of course not.' She laughed. 'They're called outside caterers, dear. Anyway, sit down and have a chat before Nick gets here. You won't get a word in edgeways when he does.'

'Can I ask you something while we're alone?' I asked.

'Sure,' she said.

'Does Dan ever get jealous?'

'Of what?'

'Of me?'

Her face, which had switched into serious mode when I said I wanted to ask her something while we were alone, didn't change. Maybe she looked just a touch more intense, but no big change. At least she didn't laugh.

'Why do you ask that?'

'Because I think I would be, if I was him.'

'Why?'

'Because you're his wife, and you talk fairly intimately to another man.'

'But everyone has different relationships with different sorts of people. He's my husband. You're an old friend.'

'Does he have other women he talks to like we talk?'

'I don't know. It's possible there are women at work I don't know so much about. But it wouldn't bother me I don't think.'

'What would bother you?'

'I don't know . . . If he came to like them better than me! But I don't see any signs.' She raised her eyebrow at me and laughed. 'Anyway, what about Vanessa? She's not jealous is she?'

'No. That's what led me to ask. Because she doesn't seem to be jealous at all. She loves the fact I've stayed friends with you.'

'Let's enjoy it then. Let's be happy that we both have wonderful partners who are strong enough in our love for them not to feel insecure or jealous about the fact that we are still friends. Now, I want to talk to you about this film . . .'

'Yes, of course,' I mumbled, suddenly embarrassed and wishing I hadn't asked her about Dan.

'Where are you on it?'

'Oh, I don't know, Steve, it's so difficult.'

She got up to fetch herself a drink.

'I mean, I like the role and they've got some fantastic actors lined up as possible lead men, and it'll be interesting to have a financial stake which allows me more say in how the thing is made, but I'm just not sure I can face being away from home for so long. And then there will be all the publicity to do. Sometimes I feel as if I'd like to just settle down, you know, and . . .'

'Have kids?' I said.

She laughed. 'God, that sounded so clichéd didn't it? But yes, I do think about having children.'

There was a silence as she sipped her cocktail and stared contemplatively at the orchid. I felt that she was waiting for me to speak, but I didn't know what to say.

'Do you ever think about it, Steve?' she asked. 'Wanting kids?'

I took a swig from my glass, composed myself, and then blurted out my news.

'Actually, Vanessa's pregnant.' Finally, I had told her. Just not in quite the way I had planned. For a moment Maya looked taken aback. Then, good actress that she was, her expression changed to one of joy.

'Pregnant?' she shrieked. 'Oh my God, Steve, that is fantastic.

I cannot tell you how happy I am for both of you.' She must have said fantastic five times, before running through to the kitchen and coming back with a bottle of Veuve Clicquot. 'Some things you have to drink to,' she said. 'And this is one of them.'

It reminded me of the time I told her of my first kiss, the first time I had sex, the first time I thought I fell in love, the time I told her about Vanessa, the time I said we were getting married and would she be a kind of unofficial best man when it came to the speeches? At all the big moments in my life, Maya had always reacted in this warm, compassionate, excited way.

'Do you want a boy or a girl?' she asked, 'And don't give me that bullshit about I don't care so long as it's healthy.'

'This is going to sound crazy. But I know it's a boy. I just know it.'

'Got a name?'

'Not a clue.'

'Vanessa happy?'

'Ecstatic.'

'It is just fabulous,' she said.

'Well, here's to the baby,' I said. 'And here's to you being not far behind.' She came over and kissed me on the cheek, and hugged me hard. Her hair smelled of apples.

Something upstairs was beeping loudly as I pulled away, somewhat reluctantly, from her embrace. 'Dan's exercise machines,' Maya said by way of explanation. I had a picture of Vanessa trying to be enthusiastic about gym equipment and felt guilty for telling Maya her news when she had wanted us to keep quiet at this point.

'Vanessa thinks we shouldn't tell people until three months are up . . .' I said.

Maya put her hand on my sleeve. 'I understand. Mum's the word.' She half laughed at her tired joke, but suddenly seemed flat, like it had been a real effort to share in the happiness she supposed I was feeling.

'What about you then? Are you trying?' I asked.

Maya looked despondent. 'Dan wants to wait. Thinks it's not the best time.'

'Why not?'

'Our careers.'

The 'our' was enough to diminish my good intentions for the evening. I hated the way he saw himself and Maya as a single entity. I couldn't resist putting the knife in.

'*Your* career is set,' I said. 'You're a success. You have a repu-tation that is not going to shrink just because you take time out to have a kid. If he is trying to keep you in the public eye as a film star because it helps his place in the firmament as a TV presenter, then he is being unbelievably selfish if you ask me.'

I turned on hearing a familiar voice behind me.

'Nobody is asking you, actually,' It was the real-person voice, not the TV star. Dan was standing in the doorway. He stared at me, hard and direct, with hatred in his eyes. 'Tell me,' he said. 'What exactly am I being selfish about?'

'It's nothing, Dan. Steve was just worried that you're putting your career over us having children,' said Maya. 'But of course that's not the case is it?' I noticed that she didn't look at him. She gazed at the floor, and sighed.

Dan couldn't bring himself to answer. Instead, he went to pour himself another drink. I watched him take note of the open champagne bottle on the sideboard, and he looked darkly at Maya.

I tried to hide my glass among the ornaments on the mantel-piece, and asked where Vanessa was.

'Taking a pee,' he said gruffly.

The next couple of minutes were agony. There was nothing I could say without making it worse. Dan looked like he was worried that if he engaged any further with me, he would crack. I could feel the anger in him which, coupled with his muscular presence, made him scary to be around – if you were me and you'd just questioned his conduct. Maya filled the vacuum, unconvincingly, by asking Dan whether he thought Sheldon should sit next to Maggie from the *Observer*. He nodded indifferently, and glared at me. I couldn't remember ever being so glad to see Vanessa.

'Steve, you really have to have a look upstairs!' she cried. 'It is out of this world.' And she gushed on, about the different styles in the seven bedrooms, Dan's study, Maya's study, the little cinema with twelve matching comfy armchairs in three rows of four, the jacuzzi, the sauna, the gym. Her enthusiasm was so infectious that even Dan seemed to soften a little. And then the other guests started to arrive, so we were spared having to make further conversation.

As we all milled through the hall to the dining room, Dan brushed alongside me, his face leaning into my ear and muttered: 'Be her friend if you must, but don't push it.' I nodded, avoiding eye contact. I realised it must have made me look shamefaced, but that was preferable to looking at him.

The other guests were an interesting bunch. Nick Sheldon the paunchy, hardbitten agent overdoing the hardbitten bit, name-dropping as ever but usually negative about the names, grouching because he wasn't allowed to smoke; his wife Becky tall and beautiful but looking rather bored like she was out at dinners like this every night; Maggie, the magazine editor, modestly Botoxed and dressed top to bottom in couture, her husband much older than her, maybe late-50s, seriously overweight but confident in himself, taking it in and, I sensed, taking it all apart too.

I felt tension between Maya and Dan, despite the little touches on the arm or shoulder when they passed each other, and I didn't get the feeling it was purely because of my faux pas. I sensed that Dan liked attention to be focussed on him, and it hurt a little when his wife, without trying, attracted more of it.

Once we were all in the dining room, and the lady in black and her young helper had seated us, spread napkins over our laps and brought through the starters, I made a point of watching how the other guests responded to Maya. Even when someone else was speaking, at least one of them would be looking at her, either full on or out of the corner of an eye. Whenever the conversation lulled, they would look to *her* to pick it up and move it along, though there was a successful businessman, a newspaper editor, a TV presenter and a hugely well-connected agent at the table. She did not scream out 'make me the centre of attention', which Nick seemed to suggest was how most stars behaved; the understated smart-casual look of her clothes, the quiet way she moved if she got up from the table to say something to the lady in black, her soft, slow voice. These were not for most people means of attracting attention. Yet she attracted it.

Dan, by evident contrast, was all loud questions and loud opinions, and laughter that was just a few degrees overcooked for the joke or the jibe that Sheldon had delivered. He couldn't keep still. He was repeatedly jumping up and pacing round the room, or fiddling with his mobile. He even went out a couple of times to take phone calls, as if to show that he was endlessly in demand. I was sure that every single one of us at that table was struck by the same insight, the recognition that there were two sorts of celebrity in the room – Maya who didn't act the star and yet indisputably was, Dan who was desperate to be her equal, yet couldn't quite cut it. It was a source of endless mystery to me, and misery, that Maya was alone in not seeing it.

Vanessa was just eating it all up, smiling the whole time. She tried, just after the starter had been served, to open up a conversation about an appeal she had seen on TV the previous weekend, to fund a clean-water programme for kids in West Africa. But somehow she lacked the sophistication of the other guests, and it went nowhere. Dan looked embarrassed. I felt it. Maya smiled, and asked Nick if he liked courgettes.

The food was a bit on the vegetarian side for our tastes, apart from a little fish course, but it was classy and different, and there was an irresistible array of desserts. Sheldon, Maggie's husband and I all overindulged. Vanessa thought Sheldon was funny, and she couldn't help but be impressed at how many of the world's movers and shakers Maggie had met, and how well informed she appeared to be about them.

'So what do you do, Vanessa?' Maggie asked at one point, and I sensed Vanessa feeling suddenly out of her comfort zone. She seemed almost embarrassed to admit what she did, shuffling a little in her seat before replying 'I do event management.' She could have stopped there, possibly leaving them to think that she staged rock concerts or big sporting events, the London Marathon, Wimbledon, Royal Ascot. But after a pause, during which nobody seemed to know what to say, she added 'For a bank.'

'Oh. Right,' said Maggie. 'And is that fun?'

'It's OK. I'm thinking of looking for something less full-time soon, because Steve and I are wanting to start a family. Body clock ticking away and all that.'

I felt Dan's eyes on me, but I didn't meet them. I looked at Maya, who smiled a thin smile.

'You know that bedroom to the left of the stairs closest to Dan's gym, Maya?' said Vanessa. 'That would be the most beautiful bedroom for a baby.' The lilt almost placed a question mark at the end of the sentence. Everyone got the point, for sure. I cringed. I hadn't had a chance to tell Vanessa about the scene that had taken place while she was in the loo.

'One day maybe,' said Maya, in a way that made clear to everyone she wanted that section of the conversation to end. She pressed the silent bell next to her side plate, which would call through the young man to take away the plates.

It was when we went back through to the white sofas for coffee that Maya's pending film project was raised.

'So, Maya,' said Maggie, 'I see on We-know-the-stars you're about to commit to a big new film. True or false?'

'Where do these websites spring up from?' asked Maggie's husband. 'I mean, if we'd been here a year ago, and you mentioned We-know-the-stars.com it'd be like "What the hell are you talking about?" but now you don't go a day without hearing something about it.'

'It's the pace of change,' said Sheldon. He threw his head back, slouched deeper into the cushion, signalling that it didn't really matter who the question was aimed at; he was the man who was best placed to explain the modern world. 'Phenomena are born more quickly. They grow more quickly, if they hit the button. They die more quickly if they don't. Go back a while and what did Google mean? Facebook? YouTube? Amazon? Nothing. And the explosion in TV? Amazing. When I first got into acting for footballers, there might have been two, three matches a week on the box. Now there's a dozen cameras at every pro game in Britain.'

'Very interesting,' said Maggie. 'But what's the answer, Maya?' She put the question in a friendly, small talk, conversation-moving kind of way. Maya took a sip of her coffee, placed the little white cup in its saucer, and looked first at Dan, who was smiling, then at Nick, who had his grouchy look on as he realised his contribution on the world of change was little more than a pair of brackets in a previous, ongoing sentence, whereas he was hoping to begin a new paragraph, a new chapter even, in the evening's discussion.

'Well, it's not entirely clear yet. There is a project we're discussing at the moment, but it is not pinned down,' said Maya.

'Here or in the States?' asked Maggie's husband.

'Mainly in the States.'

'Do you prefer that?' he asked. 'Working away from home, I mean.'

'No!' said Maya with a laugh. 'I'm a real homebody. I want to be able to pad out in my pyjamas to the set.'

'Lead role?' asked Maggie.

'Leading woman, yes. The title role is the guy.'

'They got someone for that?'

'Not definite yet but looks like it could be a big name.'

'I know I don't need to say this, Maggie, but this is all off the record, OK?' said Sheldon.

'Sure, I don't do news.'

'Oh yeah, sure,' said Sheldon, almost growling, but good-humouredly. 'You work for a newspaper but you don't do news. Like butchers don't do meat, and tarts don't do tricks.' He looked around to wait for the laughter which followed. Dan was laughing loudest. I was probably the second. I thought it was funny.

Maggie appeared to be mildly offended. 'I am proud of the fact the magazine is its own entity.'

'So if you heard Maya was starring opposite Leonardo di Caprio in a new *Antony and Cleopatra* by Baz Luhrmann, you wouldn't tell a soul?'

'This is a private dinner,' she said. 'I accept the rules of that.'

'I would love to see the rulebook,' he said. He winked at Maya. It was a wink that said 'Heard it all before, I would not trust any journalist an inch, and she needs to know where the power lies. Oh, and I have laid down a marker.' He had signalled by his demeanour that he felt the conversation had gone far enough and Maya went into 'no more' mode. It was inter-esting how obedient she was to him.

'Anyway,' she said. 'We'll see. It's a good story, a great part, fabulous director, but I'm just not a hundred per cent sure yet.'

Dan, who I noticed was sitting right beside Maggie, their legs almost touching, spoke next.

'You'll do it,' he said. 'This is all just part of the worrying process.'

'You don't know that for certain,' I said.

I should have kept my mouth shut. But sometimes thoughts

pop in, and it's as though they are operating independently of any controlling mind. They're out before I have had time to tell myself they're my thoughts, I am the one who can keep them to myself or share them with the world. I'm not alone in that. I know it happens to everyone, to a greater or lesser degree.

The second the words left my mouth, I realised my mistake. Given our earlier exchanges, Dan was bound to consider my observation 'pushing it'. He had also had more wine than anyone else at dinner, with the possible exception of Maggie's husband, and I could sense something unpleasant was about to fly back over the orchid.

'With respect,' he said, 'what the fuck does it have to do with you?'

I felt Vanessa's hand fall heavily on to my thigh, a combination of her own shock, and a signal to me to keep calm. I decided to say nothing, but could feel myself going a little pale, and my Adam's apple felt taut and bulging inside my throat.

Maya shifted forward a little. 'Dan, I don't think there is any need for that. Steve is entitled to say what he thinks. He is an old friend.'

'Yeah, well some things are out of his orbit, and he should know when to butt in and when to butt out.'

There was a nastiness there that made me want to respond.

The thought of saying 'I've known her a damn sight longer than you' popped into my head, but Vanessa's grip on the top of my thigh was acting as a good brake. I stayed silent, and picked up my coffee cup. I could feel my heart beating beneath my shirt. Dan had not taken his eyes off me since the words had left my lips. Now he stood up, and walked from the room.

Nick sat up from his slouch, let out a jaded little chuckle, and leaned over to Maggie. 'All off the record, yeah?'

'Sure,' she said. 'Don't worry.'

We got home at midnight, having beaten a hasty retreat after Dan's exit. As we stepped out of the taxi Vanessa realised that, in our rush to be gone, she had left her shawl on the sofa. She had been subdued in the cab, perhaps feeling I had reneged on my promise not to provoke Dan. I hadn't pushed her to talk, sensing that the driver was earwigging, even though he had the radio tuned to a Talksport phone-in. Most cabbies knew where the big names lived, and Maya was sure all sorts of stuff got out through them, even without them meaning it to. It was one of the reasons she'd hired Victor to drive her around.

We waited till we were in bed before we did the post-dinner analysis. Vanessa wanted every detail of my earlier flare-up with Dan.

'Oh my God, I had no idea,' she said. 'So I was right, yeah, she's gone all broody and he doesn't want to know?'

'Something like that.'

Vanessa was fascinating about the little tour of the house. She had discovered that as well as owning the house where the cabbie dropped us off, they had bought the one adjacent to it, and knocked through upstairs. But what Vanessa seemed to find most fascinating of all was the way Dan talked about the house. The woman's touch was so clear in the design, the fabrics, the furniture, yet according to Vanessa, it was like everything was about him.

'"I chose this because this. I thought this room needed to be so and so. I've always wanted a sauna . . ."'

'What ambition!' I said.

'In their bedroom, there were one or two photos of both of them, one on holiday, the other at a black-tie dinner, but they were dwarfed by a big photo of him interviewing Jennifer Lopez, I promise you. And in the bathroom, they have these big his-and-her sinks, and I kid you not, there was as much stuff on his side as there was on hers.'

'What stuff?'

'Pills, grooming products, hairbrushes, gels, just loads of it. He saw me looking and made a joke about it, said the girls in the make-up department were always making sure he took all the new freebie products, but it was a bit freaky. Then he showed me their wardrobes – it was basically a whole room of wardrobes, then loads more clothes on rails – and he was talking about all the deals he got on clothes, and how he had different tailors for suits, jackets and trousers, and do you know he has one shirt – a single shirt – that cost £500 but he got it for free.'

'Jesus.'

'And you should see the gym. I mean, it is just incredible. Treadmill. Bikes. Rowing machine. Huge great weight machines. OK, all fine, like normal. But the craziest thing – all over the walls, pictures of *him*, including one, life-size, which he admitted was his head on someone else's body.'

'What?'

'He said it was the dream body he was working to have. Said it inspired him when he was exercising.'

'Did he know who it belonged to?'

'Some model I think. Then there were all these pictures that really were him. Just with a little towel on, and some of him shaving, modelled on the Beckham Gillette ads.'

'Thank Christ I didn't join you on the tour is all I can say. I cannot see what she sees in him.'

'I have to say even the real body is pretty good. He is a good-looking guy, Steve.'

'I think Maya looks for something more than that.'

'He shaves his chest by the way, I could tell.'

'The guy's a jerk.'

'And has her name tattooed across the base of his back.'

'Jerk.'

'Well, he is a very rich, very successful jerk.'

'It's the one thing about Maya I just do not get.'

'Nobody ever understands other people's marriages, Steve,' she said. 'And that sometimes includes the people in the marriage.'

I could tell something was bugging her. She'd seemed like she really enjoyed the evening, despite the flare-up, and I had been hoping we might have sex but she had rolled herself into the duvet in a way that shouted 'Keep Off'.

'You're not cross with me, are you?' I said, edging closer to her across the bed.

'Not cross exactly. More concerned. I just think you need to be careful when it comes to interfering in other people's relationships.'

'Oh, come on, don't go all wise on me,' I replied. 'I prefer my certainties. He's a jerk. She's a genuine talent and a genuine person, with this one terrible blind spot.'

'I'm not saying he is my type at all,' said Vanessa. 'But I can see he has something that might appeal to someone like Maya.'

After that we did make love, but in a tired, distracted sort of way. I felt she'd rather have been sleeping, and soon enough she was.

It was almost 3 a.m. before I could join her, my last thought something Vanessa had said as she was undressing. 'I'm glad we're us and not them.'

Chapter Seven

One of the worst things that had happened to me since Maya married Dan was that I had joined the millions of 'Dan Fans' who watched his highlights programme every Sunday morning. 'Dan Fans'. When it first became known he was going out with Maya, he was nothing more than an appendage to her. 'Maya's new man'. 'Maya's Dan'. It was always about her. He never made headlines in his own right. But then, suddenly all that changed, and one morning there it was in black and white, in the 'Gotta Watch It' column in the TV listings: 'Sunday 10.30, Dan Fans who missed out Monday to Friday can catch up with the TV golden boy's golden moments.' Who were these Dan Fans? What sort of person could waste a part of their Sunday morning watching him and his reruns?

I once confessed to Maya that I watched the Sunday highlights programme. 'Ah,' she said wryly, '*Schadenfreude.*'

I made a crack about how impressed I was that she knew the name of what sounded like a German third division football team, to which she replied, sharply, 'No, no joke. It means waiting to take delight in the fall of my husband.'

I kind of laughed, but in my heart, I knew it was true. This morning, after what had happened at the dinner party, it was all the more so. I longed to see him fall flat on his face, for some 'real' celebrity to look him in the eye and say 'Listen to me, Dan. You're a talentless dickhead and I can't be bothered to talk to you any more.' But of course they didn't. There was a conspiracy between needer and needed; Dan and his TV people needed the big names; the big names needed to be able to crank up the publicity from time to time. One of today's highlights was Bill Nighy, promoting his latest movie. A proper actor. What the fuck was he doing talking to Dan? Then Heather Mills, thanking him for the chance to put 'my side of the story' and talking up a charity she was apparently supporting, then Will Young promising to come back and sing his next single first on Dan's show. Cue wild clapping from the women in the audience.

I could hear Vanessa coming down the stairs, and was getting up to switch off the TV as she appeared at the door.

'I really don't know why you bother to watch that stuff,' she said, good-naturedly. 'If you hate him so much, why torture yourself?'

What could I say to her? That it made me feel closer to Maya, as if I were keeping an eye on her? I was already worrying about what might have happened between her and Dan after the dinner party came to its somewhat undignified close. Had we left them to a major row? Maya had been so calm, but she had a temper on her when she wanted, and she would not have been happy with the way he had behaved. And then there was the threatening way he had looked at me, more than once. There was a lot of anger bubbling under the surface. I wanted to text Maya but I'd noticed last night that she just left her mobile lying around, didn't really keep it close to her, like I did with mine. If they were to have had an argument about my interference, it would only make matters worse for Dan to stumble upon a text from me, however innocent the content.

'Let's go for a long walk,' I said, hoping that a bit of fresh air would help me forget about it all.

We walked for several miles, went for a pub lunch in Richmond and then strolled along the Thames beside Kew Gardens. Every few yards, there seemed to be a harassed parent trying to stop a child from doing something dangerous. Had they always been there when we had done this walk, or was it just that I was noticing for the first time? I could tell that Vanessa was looking at the fraught mothers and thinking 'That'll be me soon.'

Outside Kew Tube station was a flower stall selling really upmarket bouquets. 'Why don't we get one for Maya,' said Vanessa, 'as an apology for causing a scene last night? You could drop it round later, when I go to meet Judith for tea, and pick up my shawl at the same time.'

'That's not a bad idea,' I said, trying to conceal my delight that Vanessa had provided the excuse I had been looking for to check Maya was OK. 'I'm not sure what Dan might make of me pitching up with flowers, but I don't want there to be any ill feeling.'

We took a cab back to Hammersmith, and Vanessa set off to see her sister, excited to tell Judith about the baby and get the benefit of her advice on pregnancy, rather more useful than mine given her experience as a nurse. After she'd gone, I got in the car and headed to Maya's.

There is always a part of me that expects Sunday traffic to be lighter than during the week, but it never is. What with Sunday shoppers, family visits, and the usual sports and enter-tainment events, Sundays can often be the worst day of the week in London. It was 5.15 by the time I got to Little Venice. I parked round the corner from Maya's house, and walked the entire length of Blomfield Road, up to the bridge, partly to settle my nerves, also to see if I could spot Dan's car. I couldn't. No sign of photographers either.

Then I crossed the bridge and repeated the exercise on the Maida Avenue side of the canal. I stopped to look at the house with the blue plaque in honour of John Masefield. He'd lived there from 1907–1912. I'd never heard of him. It struck me that if I was a photographer, this was the place I would work from, rather than right outside Maya's house. Maida Avenue was slightly higher than Blomfield Road. There was a good clear view of the top of Maya's front door, and the windows upstairs. I was sure Dan's Merc wasn't there, which helped me gather my courage as I walked back over the bridge. But as I got closer to the house, I began to worry that it was Maya, not Dan, who had gone out in the car. I stopped to sit on a wall, four or five houses down, and tried to steel myself to ring the buzzer on the gate. As a jogger ran by, I felt self-conscious to the point of embarrassment holding a large bouquet. I could hardly walk back to the car with it, like some adolescent who'd been stood up on a date, or a hospital visitor who arrived after the patient had been discharged. Isn't it odd how you imagine random passers-by are somehow able to understand who you are, why you're there, what turmoil is going on inside you, and in the lives of people you know? As the jogger disappeared over the bridge, I realised he had not even looked at me. Is it only when guilt is lurking that you imagine this ability of others to look inside you? But why should I have been feeling guilty when all I was doing was retrieving a shawl, and trying to make sure no lasting damage was done as a result of the flare-up with Dan?

In the end, I decided just to risk it. If Dan was there, I'd face him out, maybe say the flowers were for both of them, act a little embarrassed at what happened. I walked slowly to the gate, pressed the buzzer and waited. It took a long time for someone to answer but, to my relief, it was Maya's voice that came through on the intercom.

'Who is it?' I didn't know if it was my imagination but her voice sounded shaky.

'Hiya, it's me.'

'Oh Steve!' she said, recognising either the voice, or my face on the video screen.

'Hope you don't mind me popping by, but Vanessa left her shawl. I was passing, so I thought I would pick it up. Is that OK?'

'Come in, come in. I found it on the sofa this morning. I'll bring it to the door.'

The gate pinged open and I scrunched up the gravel to the front door. After half a minute, Maya opened it. She was wearing the same sunglasses she'd put on when leaving La Forchetta. She had Vanessa's shawl in her hand.

'My my,' I said, 'you really are the movie star these days.'

'Meaning?'

'Sunglasses at home?'

I handed her the bouquet, which she took without much fuss, and I leant forward to kiss her on the cheek. She smelled different, somehow. There was the usual expensive perfume, but beneath it I could smell sweat.

'I'm resting my eyes,' she said. 'A late night followed by a day reading scripts always makes them tired.'

'Where's Dan?' I asked.

'Out playing poker with his friend Rudi. It's a regular Sunday thing. They go to this private men's club near the station . . .'

'I must say I'm relieved he's not here. Sorry about last night.'

'Oh well,' she said. 'These things happen.'

'Gonna offer me a cup of tea?'

She looked hesitant. 'Well, I was just going to have a nap, but . . .'

'OK, I get the message. I'll be on my way.'

'No, Steve . . .' She caught my arm. 'I'm sorry. I'm not myself. Come in.'

She led the way into the kitchen, a huge chrome and white-tile affair with a big Smeg cooker that would not have looked out of place in a small restaurant. She kept her back to me as she switched on the kettle, and appeared simply to be staring at it as it started to boil.

'Are you all right?' I asked. She dropped her shoulders a little, shook her head gently, almost imperceptibly, then turned towards me, removing her sunglasses as she did so.

'Not really,' she said, raising her left hand to stroke a cut above her right eyebrow. As I walked towards her, I noticed there was also a dark bruise around her eye. Then she fell into my arms, sobbing.

I held her up, hugging her close. The sobbing became something nearer to wailing, and her whole body seemed to be shaking. I stroked her back, trying to calm her, to reassure her that she was not alone. When the sobbing didn't stop, I couldn't help allowing my fingers to touch her hair where it fell on to her neck. That was unworthy. I knew that, but this was the first time, in the twenty years we had been friends, that I had held her like this.

'My God, the bastard,' I said.

She pulled away from me and looked into my eyes.

'It's not what you think, Steve. It was an accident.'

'Oh yeah? You expect me to believe that?'

'I swear to you, I fell.'

She had slowed the crying now, and was finding it easier to speak.

'I know what you're thinking, Steve, but you don't understand. It's difficult being Dan. There's so much pressure on him, and then there's this whole issue about whether or not to have a baby . . . I think the strain just gets to him sometimes.'

I was shocked. 'I can't believe you're excusing him!'

'Not excusing, just explaining why he behaved as he did.'

'OK then, explain some more.'

'It is so complicated,' she said.

'So just stick with what happened. Facts.'

'OK, I'll try, but don't butt in. Just hear me out before you rush to conclusions.'

'I'll try.'

And I did try, but it was hard. Her whole account appeared to rest on her belief that their argument was all her own fault. How it stemmed from the fact that she'd found the evening difficult having so many different aspects of her life together in the same room: me representing her past, where she came from, the things she felt safe with (I smiled at that); Dan representing the future, the man she wanted to have kids with; and then Sheldon and the journalist woman – the public side of her life, the bit she was getting more and more uncomfortable with.

'I guess I should have gone to Dan and talked it through after you'd all left, but I didn't. I just avoided him, pretending I had to supervise the caterers. Then, when I got into bed, he was fast asleep. I confess I was relieved. I didn't want to have to talk about his argument with you. And I think he was avoiding me too, because when I woke up, he was already in the gym.'

'Looking at his body double,' I said. It was a cheap shot. She did her best to ignore it. Just a momentary wince of irritation before she carried on.

'Working out. Like a madman. Two huge great silver dumbbells and he's pumping them to his chest so hard he looks like his face and his neck are going to explode. I knew he could see me in the mirror but he said nothing, and I went over to him, asked him if he wanted breakfast. He just carried on pumping the weights, didn't even look at me, said nothing.'

'Sulking.'

'Sulking, yeah, but sulking with menace. I was scared, so I left. The next thing I knew, he was behind me – shouting.'

'Shouting what?'

'Don't know where to start. I took him for granted, I didn't respect him, I only thought about myself, I thought I was superior to him, my career had always come first and now I wanted to have a family even though he didn't, and he was sure I was going to get pregnant anyway, and it was wrong for me and wrong for him, and if it happened he'd feel exploited and how fucking stupid was I even to think about not doing this new film and if I didn't do it, it would screw up his plans.'

'*His* plans?'

'Then he went into a big thing about how I should have stood up for him against you, and he couldn't believe that I confided in you about things that were personal to him and me, and who the hell was Steve Watkins anyway and just stuff like that.'

'Like what?'

'He said some pretty nasty things.'

'Like what?'

'It doesn't matter.'

'It matters to me,' I said, but it was not clear she heard me. She was in full flow.

'Anyway I didn't know what to do or say so I'm thinking it's probably best just to disappear for a while, and I make for the stairs to go back to the bedroom, but he comes up behind me and grabs me by the shoulder and he's into my face again and he says "Don't you ever walk away from me again," and I say "Well can we talk in a civilised manner please?" and every time I try to calm things, it just makes it worse and eventually I try to walk away again, up a few stairs and he grabs me and hauls me back, really pulling on my arm, then he yanks me so I go flying down to the floor and catch the side of my head on the banister post.'

'And then?'

'And then, nothing. It was as if he'd suddenly woken up. He just stood there looking terrified. And then he picked up his keys, and left.'

'Why didn't you phone me?'

'Think about it, Steve. What good would that have done? This was all about you in the first place. It would only have made Dan more angry.'

'And why the hell would that matter? You can't stay with him after he did something like that to you!'

'It was an accident, Steve. He didn't mean me to get hurt.'

'Oh bullshit, Maya. Sounds to me as if that was exactly what he meant!'

'Listen, I was there and you weren't. He lost his temper, that's all. I'm sure he and I can sort things out once he has calmed down and we can just talk sensibly.'

'Maya, you're deluding yourself. The guy's a maniac.'

'No, Steve, you're the one who's deluding yourself – because you don't like him, and you never have and you never will. I've said it before. I get the feeling you're always waiting for him to mess up.'

'*Schadenfreude* . . .' I muttered.

'Sorry?'

'It doesn't matter.'

We talked some more, but it was clear that I wasn't going to get Maya to change her mind. I could just about believe the cut came from her falling on the stairs. But the bruise looked to me like it had been punched in there. I asked her if she was sure he wasn't still on the cocaine. She assured me that she'd know if he was.

She was eager for me to leave in case Dan came back and I certainly didn't fancy being there with her when he did, but I was worried about leaving her alone with a violent man.

'I'll be fine,' she said.

'I'm not so sure about that,' I replied.

We reached an agreement. I would park my car opposite the house, on the Maida Avenue side of the canal, and keep watch until he came home. When he did, I would stay outside for an hour. If she needed me, she would turn one of the lights on and off a few times as a signal.

'How do I get in if you need me?' I asked.

'Oh this is ridiculous,' she said. 'He is not going to hurt me.'

'He has done it once. He can do it again. And I am not taking the risk.'

She took a pen and a piece of paper from the table close to the front door, and scribbled out a five-digit number. She then took a key from a drawer.

'The code gets you through the gate. The key gets you through the door.'

'Thanks.'

I had not even reached the car when she called me.

'I forgot to say – don't tell anyone. Not even Vanessa,' she said.

'Oh fuck,' I said. 'Vanessa! I've come away without the shawl.'

I hung up, retraced my steps quickly to the house, and let myself in through the gate. As I tapped in the code – 2-1-1-7 7 – I realised it was Maya's birthdate, 21 January 1977. It seemed very intimate, somehow, knowing her secret passwords. And I felt the same intimacy in taking the key from my trouser pocket and opening the door. It had a blue felt elephant attached to it with 'Don't forget' embroidered on one side. Maya was standing just inside the hallway, holding the shawl.

'Not a word,' I said. 'Not even Vanessa. Promise.'

I moved the car to Maida Avenue, and settled down for a long wait. After about ten minutes, I noticed Maya at one of the upstairs windows. It wasn't clear if she was looking for me, or for Dan, or for photographers. At 6.30 I called Vanessa to say I might be late back for supper.

'What's going on?' she said.

'Maya wants a heart-to-heart about whether or not she should do the film.'

'Where's Dan?'

'At his club.'

'Well I guess I should just be grateful that you don't go to your club on Sunday afternoons,' she said with a laugh. 'But Steve, be careful. If you give her advice and it turns out to be the wrong advice, you might find yourself in a tricky position.'

'Understood,' I said. 'Back as soon as I can.'

Just after 7 p.m. Dan's black Mercedes drew up in front of the house. He got out, slammed the door behind him, clicked the car shut, then tapped in the code to get through the gate. I thought about driving over to Blomfield Road immediately and letting myself in. What if he started laying into her as soon as he walked through the door? What if she couldn't make it to a light switch in order to signal to me? I felt a coward for having left the house. I should have insisted on staying, despite what Maya wanted. I should have risked his fury, no matter the danger to myself. It would have been worth it just to let him know someone else knew what he had done, what he was like.

I stayed where I was. Every minute felt like an hour. There was no movement, no sign of life within the house. I found myself fearing the worst, imagining all manner of horrible scenes unfolding behind that big black fence. But then at 8.15 Maya sent me a text: 'All fine. Talk to you tomorrow. Remember no telling. Thanks for your support xxx'.

I felt sick. Mixed in with the relief that she was all right was disappointment that she wasn't going to walk out on Dan there and then. She knew I was here, waiting and ready to take her from danger and keep her safe. Yet it was him she wanted to be with, even after he had beaten her up. I drove back to Hammersmith thinking Maya was sleepwalking to disaster and it was my responsibility to wake her up, make her face reality.

Chapter Eight

I sent Maya a text the second I got to work on Monday. I told her Jerry had the day off so it was safe if she wanted to call me. She phoned right back. I didn't like the sound of her voice. It was weak and tearful. Things weren't good with Dan, apparently, but they were being courteous to each other.

'Do you think he'll hit you again?' I was whispering, even though Jerry wasn't there to hear.

'He didn't hit me.'

'OK, do you think he'll *push* you again?'

She was adamant that he wouldn't. 'He was very repentant last night,' she said. 'I think in some ways he was more shocked by what he did than I was.'

'So what does the future hold?' I asked.

'I don't know. Hopefully we can try to work things out.'

'You can't keep all this bottled up inside you, Maya.'

'That's why I've told you.'

'What about your parents?'

'I phoned Mum after it happened but when it came to it, I couldn't bring myself to tell her. She wouldn't know how to handle it. She loves Dan and couldn't bear to think of us fighting.'

'What about Sheldon?'

'There's a problem there,' she said. 'He also works for Dan, remember?'

'I really don't think you can stay with Dan in these circumstances Maya.'

'There's a problem there too.'

'What?'

'I know you think I'm crazy, Steve, but I do love him.'

'Perhaps you should go on the misery slot on Dan's show?' I asked.

'What's that supposed to mean?'

'I'm sure he once did battered wives who stand by their men,' I said, immediately regretting that I had.

'That's beneath you, Steve. Take it back.'

'OK. I take it back.'

'Thank you.'

She went quiet on me for the next couple of days. Didn't call or email. Sent one-word answers to my texts. Then on Wednesday I could stand it no longer. I broke all the rules and dialled her number. She picked up but I could tell she was reluctant to talk. Dan was shouting something in the background. All I could hear was 'fucking this' and 'fucking that'. She said she'd call me back, but she didn't. I became so tense I could hardly type, which wasn't good since Jerry and I were working all out on the pitch for the contract with Qatar Airways. Jerry kept having to ask me questions twice. I could see he was puzzled. It wasn't like me to be so distracted. Usually I could trawl the internet for Maya gossip and hold a complicated phone call with a client at the same time. Now I was spending too much time staring into space. I wasn't on form. I was worrying about Maya the whole time.

On Thursday evening, Vanessa had an event to organise, a

dinner with the US board members and some of the bank's key London clients. She called me during the afternoon to check what I wanted to do food-wise and to say there was a ready-meal curry in the fridge. Before I knew it I found myself telling her I'd grab a sandwich from the canteen because I needed to work late on the Qatar pitch. A Vanessa-free evening meant I could do what I'd been wanting to do since Sunday: just get in the car and drive, nowhere in particular, in the hope that the speed and the freedom would somehow clear my head. That was the intention anyhow. But it didn't quite turn out like that because, at seven o'clock, having spent an hour sitting in traffic on the M40, I found myself heading towards the village of Taplow.

I don't know what made me think of going to see Frank and Anna Lowe. I suppose I thought they would understand the burden of carrying around private details of Maya's life knowing that, should they slip out into the open, vultures were hovering. The press could get days of coverage out of Maya not tipping a waiter in a restaurant, as happened once when a young Russian had been rude to her, or changing her hairstyle, or saying as she left a theatre that she did or did not like the play she had seen. I felt a sharp stab of panic thinking about just how gargantuan a media orgy the information I knew could unleash. Perhaps I was hoping I could confide in her mum and dad.

I'd never visited the Lowes in Taplow before. We had an annual dinner together with Maya, usually in the West End, and Mr Lowe and I would meet every few months for a pint at the railway workers' club in Ealing when he went to see his old mates. He'd never invited me to their house. I think he liked the opportunity to come into London. I wasn't even sure of their address.

All I remembered from what Maya had told me at the time she helped them move in almost two years ago was that it was just off a main road, up a little lane. A more important clue, I knew there was an identical black fence to the one outside her house in Little Venice. They had used the same builders as in Blomfield Road and I remember her saying some of the villagers had been upset at the new fence, thinking it was a bit of an eyesore in what I quickly saw was a very pretty, affluent Buckinghamshire village. Taplow was bigger than I expected it to be and there were more little lanes than I had anticipated. And by the time I got there it was almost dark and there wasn't much street lighting. I saw a couple of fences that looked possibles. I drove in through the gate by one of them, but then saw a woman lifting boxes from a car boot. It was not Maya's mum.

She looked at me suspiciously and as I was now on her land, I felt compelled to speak to her.

'Sorry to bother you,' I said, winding the window right down. 'I'm looking for the Lowes' house, Frank and Anna Lowe.'

She looked at me even more suspiciously now. She was about 70, evidently well-to-do, with very sharp blue eyes, and an odd dark purple colour plastered on her lips.

'You're not press are you?'

'Certainly not. I'm an old school friend of their daughter's and they always said to pop in and see them if I was in the area, but I'm lost to be honest.'

'You're a friend of Maya's?'

'Yes.'

'We don't see her.'

'I think she visits them a fair bit,' I said, feeling I had to defend her. 'And they go to see her a lot. They're a close family.'

'Yes, I'm sure,' she said, condescendingly. 'Don't see them often though. Not really of these parts, are they? We've been here forty-five years now.'

'I see. Anyway, if you could help me with directions, that would be great.'

The woman reluctantly drew me a map and I found myself driving back to a house I had already passed. The black fence was barely noticeable amid the huge conifer trees towering over it and the gates looked as if they were always left open. I drove up the drive and parked in front of a large mock-Tudor house.

As soon as Mrs Lowe answered the door, I realised I had been very rash. She looked as if she had seen a ghost. As I quickly learned, she could only assume that as someone from their past, someone they had not seen since moving out here, I was a bearer of bad news, and of course to a parent, the instinct on thinking it may be bad news is to think the worst news of all. She lived for Maya, and since she and Frank had both given up work, in many ways they lived their lives through her.

'Steve, what is it?' she asked.

'No, no, it's nothing,' I said, desperately trying to look reassuring. 'I was just passing through and I remembered you lived in Taplow and I thought it would be great to see you.' I let out a nervous laugh.

I could see the relief coursing back into her face, then she laughed too and said, 'My God, you gave me such a fright there. Come in, come in. I just saw my whole life flashing before me. I thought it must be something terrible that I couldn't be told over the phone.'

'I'm really sorry. I didn't mean to alarm you. But I didn't have your number on me and I couldn't get hold of Maya and to be honest, it was all a bit spur of the moment.' As I spoke, I was trying to untangle in my own mind which parts of that sentence were true, and which were false.

We were in a spacious lounge now. Even in February it felt light and summery. Maya's touch was pretty clear to me in the colours and some of the paintings. On two sides of the room, they had replaced the old brick walls with glass, better to see the beautifully tended garden, dominated by a lovely weeping willow, next to a little pond with a statue of a young girl at the centre, water gurgling from her mouth. I spotted Mr Lowe, wearing a check shirt, brown trousers and thick green gloves, illuminated by the single light inside his green-house. He had a cigarette hanging from his lips as he tidied everything away.

'Bit dark to be gardening isn't it?' I said.

She smiled. 'You know Frank. He'd be out there all night if I didn't make him come in. He misses his allotment though. Funny, isn't it? He has this great big garden to take care of, but I sometimes think he actually spends more time in that little greenhouse than he does in the garden itself. What he liked about the allotment was that you always bumped into people, people who were a bit the same but also all different, had their little plot of land and loved to talk about it. It's nice out here and the house is lovely, but I think sometimes he feels a bit lonely, a bit cut off.'

'Better than driving trains though, surely?'

'Well I suppose so, but all the years he was on the trains, he always left for work with a spring in his step.'

She switched off the TV, where she had been watching an early evening soap, slid open one of the glass doors and shouted across the garden.

'Frank . . . a visitor.'

Mr Lowe drew a final, heavy drag on his cigarette, stubbed it out on his shoe and put the stub in his pocket. He spotted me as he stepped up on to the patio.

'Well I never,' he said. 'It's young Steve. What a lovely surprise.'

'There's some wine open from when we were having our tea,' Mrs Lowe said. 'Would you like a glass?'

'Better not,' I said. 'Driving.'

She made some tea instead as Mr Lowe showed me around the garden, with an enthusiasm that belied the mood I had been led to expect by his wife.

Though they had already eaten, Mrs Lowe offered to make me dinner, as she had many times during my teenage years, but I made do with some cakes and biscuits she brought through with the tea.

I managed to keep up the pretence that I had just been passing by. And to be honest, I really enjoyed the chat. Parents sometimes seem to remember more about their kids' school-days than the kids do, and they were full of recollections of people Maya and I used to know and things we got up to, some of which I had completely forgotten. After the tension of the past few days, I found myself relaxing in a warm, comforting atmosphere. What was it about the Lowes that made them so easy to be with, I wondered?

Vanessa's parents were, if anything, too nice. They gushed

at each other the whole time and they were so enthusiastic they left you drained of energy. I could cope when it was Vanessa being so up about life, in fact I loved it, but when you had a whole family of enthusiasts, it all got too much. I think that's why I liked Mr Lowe. He got the balance right. He was upbeat about life. But, unlike Vanessa's parents, he didn't leave you feeling inadequate because you couldn't go into raptures about assembling a new piece of Ikea furniture.

'Did you ever think you'd end up in a house like this?' I asked.

'Not really,' said Mrs Lowe. 'The whole thing has been incredible. When you become a parent, you imagine you'll be looking after your child to a greater or lesser degree for most of your life, until, when you're getting old and doddery, they return the compliment. That's the deal, isn't it? So it's odd really, that the roles have reversed. We're in our 50s, pretty much retired so far as work goes, in a nice house, savings in the bank, and it's all down to her success. To me, she's the same little girl she always was, but she's so big now, as a phenomenon I mean. It's sometimes hard to get your head round it.'

'It's fabulous in a way,' said her husband. 'She had a dream, didn't she, and she went for it. And nobody can take it away from her – she's a success. But it can be very strange for us, you know. The kind of life she leads, the sort of people she knows, what her work and her existence actually involve now, it's just not what we know, is it? It's like a different world and sometimes I look at her, and I can't quite believe that Anna and I raised her. And it doesn't matter how rich or famous she is. As a parent, you always worry about her.'

I got the feeling they were enjoying sharing these concerns

with someone who went right back with them, as far back as the grimy brick of their house in Winchester Road and its shiny red front door.

'It's hard not to get angry sometimes,' Mrs Lowe said. 'All the rubbish in the papers. Telly's just as bad sometimes too.'

'Maya tells us not to read them,' chipped in her husband, 'but it's hard to escape from it isn't it? You go into the shop to buy your smokes and she's there, on the front pages of the mags or the papers and the headline says something about her you don't know, and it's very difficult not to want to know more. But then you're thinking "Well I don't want the newsagent looking at me like I'm a cheapskate," like they know who I am in there, and they could think "Look at him, Maya Lowe's dad and he's too tight-fisted to buy a mag so he comes in here and reads them and buggers off with his twenty Benson and Hedges." So you find yourself buying them, then reading them, then it's usually something that worries you, like she's had a row, or she's lost weight, or someone has said something bad to her, so you phone her up and of course then it's full circle, because she says "Dad, I keep telling you, don't read them. It is not worth it." She says if anything important happens in her life, she will tell us and to be fair, she does.' It was clear from the tone, relaxed, detached even, that recent 'important' events had not been reported to them at all.

'The other thing that happens,' said Mrs Lowe, 'is that even when you do avoid it, other people tell you. You'll be walking down the road and a neighbour will say, "I see Maya's in a bit of bother again." You know, last summer, when there was a big piece about whether she had the beginnings of cellulite at the top of her thigh in a picture the *Daily Mail* got when she and Dan spent the weekend on the yacht of that hedge-fund friend of his in the Med, three different people popped round with it for me, said they thought I would want to see it.'

'They're obsessed with cellulite those people. As if there aren't more important things to think about,' said Mr Lowe.

'The papers doctor the pictures anyway. There's no way she has cellulite,' I said.

'Of course what happens though,' said Mrs Lowe, 'is people believe what they read, or some of them believe some of it anyway.'

Mr Lowe told a story of a conversation he heard between two women last week, as he travelled back by train from London, where he had been for a railways reunion lunch. 'These people talk like she is part of their lives,' he said. 'I mean really involved with them. They were arguing about something they'd read in a magazine, something she's supposed to have said, which didn't sound like Maya at all, slagging off a load of other actresses, Halle Berry, Angelina Jolie, Keira Knightley, the usual lot, and these women were just unbeliev-able. One liked Maya, the other didn't and I thought they were going to come to blows and you're sitting there wanting to say "Shut up, it's my daughter you're talking about."'

'Which he did in the end,' said Mrs Lowe.

'Because then the one who doesn't like her is just really going for it. First she says Maya's had a facelift and a boob job and the other one is saying "You have no evidence for that" so she says she saw it on a website, and Maya's never sued so it must be true, and the whole bloody carriage is listening to this and then she keeps going and says something that was so over the top I did step in and told her to shut up.'

He paused, and shook his head. He left Mrs Lowe to finish the story.

'She said there had been a discussion on one of the Maya chat rooms that you have on the internet. Can you believe it, they have websites and chat rooms where the only thing they're talking to each other about is Maya, and apparently they've had millions of hits because of course they put pictures on there and cuttings and videos to get them all going, and this woman on the train said she'd been in the chat room and told people that Maya's marriage to Dan was a sham, that the whole thing was just a PR stunt so that they became a kind of new Posh and Becks, rather than just her being a star on her own and Dan a TV person in his own right.'

'So what did you say?' I asked Maya's dad.

'I counted to ten first, trying to tell myself to ignore it. Then I thought I would move to a different carriage but as I got up, I couldn't stop myself. I went over to her and I said "Excuse me madam, or miss, but you do not know what you're talking about." She was really taken aback, but only for a few seconds and then she starts saying "Well I'm entitled to my opinion," so I said "Not when you're telling lies about my daughter you're not."'

Mrs Lowe was beaming with pride.

'And do you know what she said?' he went on. 'She said "You don't look like her, so how do I know you are who you say you are?" And I'm getting my railway pass and my old union card and a credit card out, and I'm thinking "Why the hell am I having to prove myself to these low-lifes?"'

He looked troubled. 'Anyway she shut up and they got off at the next stop. And the other people were really nice, made a point of saying how they were pleased I'd stood up for Maya. But it's like – what business is it of anyone's? Why can't they just watch her films and watch his programmes and leave them alone?'

I mentioned the chat I'd had with Maya, and her concerns about taking on another big project. I was keen to see if she had mentioned it to them. She clearly hadn't.

'Wouldn't surprise me,' said Mrs Lowe. 'She always takes her time on big decisions. She'll think it through, talk it over with Dan, she'll make the right decision in the end.'

'I think Dan's pressing her to do it,' I said.

Mr Lowe asked when I last saw them. I gave them a totally sanitised version of Saturday's dinner party, said how beautiful the house was, how great Maya looked, how funny Sheldon was about some of the other actors and the sports stars he looked after, what wonderful food we had. I was trying to pick up on the slightest concern about Dan. But there was none. They clearly liked him a lot, especially Mrs Lowe.

'Do you think he ever feels he's too much in her shadow?' I asked. 'Must be hard, for a man, to be so obviously second fiddle to a more famous wife, if fame is your game. That clearly is the game for Dan, isn't it, even if some of it is on her back?'

'I think he just loves her to bits,' she said. 'Probably can't believe his luck in some ways. But I think he respects the fact she has her career, he has his and at the moment they're both doing brilliantly, aren't they? I'd worry even more for Maya if Dan wasn't there.'

I wondered if it was me who had the blind spot. I saw so clearly that he was the one exploiting the situation. I now knew he treated her badly, really badly. Yet the people who had known her longest, knew her best, saw only good in the man she had chosen to live with. It was worrying.

'So what about becoming grandparents? When will that

happen?' I asked, as casually as I could. 'You know, Vanessa and I are trying to start a family.'

Mrs Lowe smiled enigmatically. 'Well, I'm sure it's the right time for you and Vanessa to be thinking about it,' she said, 'but Dan and Maya don't need to rush. After all, they've only been married a year.'

'A year and a half,' I said, 'and I think Maya is keen.'

'They'll be great parents when the time comes,' said Mrs Lowe. 'I'm sure of that. Dan was so good to her when they first met. She was hurt when she split with Mike. Really hurt. Not like it said in that awful biography. That dreadful *Sunday People* journalist who wrote it made out the split was mutual, but it wasn't. He left Maya, and it tore her apart. It annoyed me that book. Do you know the writer had never even met Maya, not once? Not met us, not met you I don't suppose, not met anyone who really knows her, and she writes a book, *All About Maya*, with that fabulous picture of her on the front. And of course people think it's Maya selling herself, and that writer makes out she knows Maya inside out and she knows nothing, not a thing. Just making a few bob off her back, like a parasite really, never off the radio and the telly talking about her, like she is an expert, all because she wrote some trashy book, which she keeps saying she put together with the help of the people who know her best. Liar.'

'Not many people bought it, love,' said Mr Lowe. 'So she can't have made that much.'

'Yes, but the papers were full of it. And her big story if you remember was that Maya and Mike recognised that her talent was taking her into a world in which he couldn't keep up and so they agreed to separate. And we know it wasn't like that. She loved Mike a lot, so much she wanted a bigger commitment, and he just wasn't ready. His work came first, and he was very honest about that. And I think Dan has always put Maya first.'

'Do you really think so?'

'Yes, I do, no doubt about it.'

I was getting nowhere on the road to wherever it was that I thought I was going. When the conversation started I'd been determined to find a way to tell them about Dan's assault, but when Mrs Lowe made her comment about not feeling so worried about Maya because Dan was there, I realised I couldn't face destroying her illusions. After another half-hour of chat, I stood to leave. Mr Lowe and I arranged to meet up at his railway club in a few weeks' time and they were insistent that I should come over with Vanessa in April to see the spring bulbs in the garden. He walked me to the car. When we got there, he put his hand on my shoulder and said something that made my body turn cold. 'You keep an eye on her for us, Steve. Tell us if anything's wrong. You're not like all the other people around her. You go way back. We know we can count on you.' As I drove home, his words played around my mind and made me feel even lonelier, even more weighed down by a problem I could share with nobody, which was mine alone to resolve.

Chapter Nine

I had just got out of the shower on Friday morning when Brandon's PA called. Apparently the boss was already in the office and he wanted a planning meeting on the Qatar Airways pitch at 8.00.

'See you then,' she said, and hung up. I looked down at the small puddles of water that had collected at my feet, and cursed. Brandon was always doing this, forcing the pace, putting Jerry and me on edge. The calling of the sudden meeting was a pretty brutal management technique, which he used every few months on us, sometimes twice in the same week. It was a way of making sure he stayed in our minds at all times. 'If Brandon called a meeting now, would we have all the answers to all the questions?' It had become a mantra between Jerry and me. But the truth was that, in the past few days, Maya had supplanted the mantra and because of my distraction, Jerry had been doing the heavy lifting. I had specifically been charged with the task of analysing, and devising arguments to undermine, our main competitors for the contract with Qatar. There were eight companies going for it in all, but Websters were our main rivals. There was another smaller company, K&L, that was building a good reputation for itself, but I was less worried about them or any of the others. Websters was the one. I had barely got beyond Google and a skim-read of their marketing materials and annual reports. Brandon was no fool. He would realise I had not done the work.

I dressed as quickly as I could, shouted down to Vanessa to make me a flask of coffee, which I took with me in the car. Jerry was usually in by eight. Brandon knew I was more likely to be there at 8.30. That was why he had called the meeting for eight and why he had got his sour-faced PA to call us first thing. Bitch. Bastard and bitch.

I called Jerry from the car.

'Bastard,' I said. 'Why's he doing this today? It's Friday for God's sake.'

'He'll be wanting to work on it over the weekend. We've got that big strategy meeting on Monday.'

'Well I've not done the analysis on the other guys.'

'I know. We'll have to try and wing it.'

We did, but Brandon was having none of it. Jerry did a good pitch answering the question 'Why Globus?', a mix of the material we had used time and again to win new contracts, setting out very simply what we did and how, plus some good stuff showing our understanding of the special needs of the Gulf region, and though Brandon put Jerry through his paces, I could tell he was pretty impressed.

I had been asked to fill in the answer to the question 'And why not the others?' and I was barely three minutes in when Brandon stopped me.

'Are you waffling?' he barked.

'No,' I replied.

'Yes you are.'

Jerry tried to help me out. 'Steve has been doing a lot of the work on my side of the pitch too,' he said. Even if well meant, it had the effect of winding up Brandon even more.

'Jerry, I asked you to give me the positive side of the argument. I asked Steve to give me the negative. That is how I work. You know that. I could not have been clearer. So well done for trying to help out a mate, but it doesn't wash.' He asked Jerry to leave. I was sure he was going to sack me, and I had a momentary sensation of panic about not having enough money to raise the baby properly.

'Not good enough, Steve. Not good enough. You've had plenty of time to get this done, and you haven't done it. I don't need to tell you that this is the biggest deal Globus has ever been near. Do you know what the word "priority" means?'

'Yes, I do.'

'Right, well that is the word that applies to this. Priority. Now fucking well get on with it.'

He's an odd man, Brandon. I remember him saying, at one of our strategy meetings, that whenever you introduce yourself to someone, that person forms an instant impression of you that can be summarised in one word. 'A nanosecond, that's all it takes to label you,' he said, drawing some diagram on the whiteboard. He said we had to decide how we wanted to be seen when we were out selling, and then *be* that word. When I first met him at my interview for the job, 'geek' came into my mind as the one word I would use to describe Brandon. I have never been able to banish it. If you asked him what his word was, he'd say 'leader' or 'visionary' or some such. But all I could see was geek. He has managed to climb fairly high for a geek, mind you. He's brilliant at negotiating deals and planning travel routes for inanimate objects, but not so good at human interaction, as illustrated by the way he gave me an earbashing. It might have made me feel I had to work harder, but my company loyalty dropped ten notches.

'I hate that man sometimes,' I said to Jerry, once we were back at our desks. 'If he'd given me a couple of hours to prepare I could have got through it.'

'Yeah, but you know that's not how he works, is it?'

'You're going to have to help me,' I said. 'I've got a lot going on at the moment.'

'Vanessa?' Jerry had met Vanessa a couple of times, and liked her, made jokes about how I was 'batting above my average' in landing a wife as pretty and fun as her.

For a moment I contemplated telling him about what had happened to Maya, but then I realised I was being idiotic. It wasn't that I worried he would go snitching to the press. But I'd seen the glint in his eye whenever I let him in on secrets about Maya. Tell him this and he'd get so excited about being 'in on the story', he wouldn't be able to give sensible advice. No, I decided to divert him by telling him about the baby. After all, he was a family man himself. He was always going on about his kids. He'd be sympathetic.

'Hey, you're finally joining the real world! That's fantastic news.'

'Vanessa doesn't want people to know yet.'

'Sure, I understand. I'll keep it to myself. I'm going to enjoy watching you negotiate your paternity leave with Brandon though!'

For the rest of the day he kept looking up from his computer and grinning at me in some kind of attempt at moral support.

I suppose Brandon's tactic sort of worked because I did more good work in the next few hours than I had done the whole week. I modelled the presentation on one Brandon had done last year when he had knocked out an Irish company which had till then been sharing with Globus the logistics load of a car-hire firm. He had taken the Irish firm's own pitch, based on ten strengths, and turned every single one of them into a weakness. 'Leadership' became 'unconcerned by client interest'. 'Experience' became 'tired and stale'. 'Innovation' was turned into 'lack of clear principles', each claim fleshed out with evidence of fly-by-night tactics and personalities. He was incredibly proud of it and, rarely for him, had decided to throw a little bash in his office to celebrate when the whole deal came our way. I remember thinking that he was being completely disingenuous about the efficacy of the report because, after a few drinks, he admitted he had asked the corporate intelligence firm that sometimes did bits of work for Globus to dig up a bit of dirt on one of the Irish directors. 'So that's what clinched it,' I had whispered to Jerry. Nevertheless, the dirt-digging was swept under the carpet and for the next few months, Brandon went on endlessly about his contract-winning report. I knew my use of the format would flatter him.

I wrote up my notes, then called through to Brandon's PA. to ask if I could have five minutes with the boss before he left the office for the day. After conferring with him, she said he would see me at 6.30. Another bastard trick. Got me in early and now he would keep me in late. But at least it gave me a few more hours. Perhaps by then, I would have something vaguely approaching the kind of presentation he had been expecting ten hours earlier.

After lunch, I couldn't resist watching Dan's programme on my computer with the sound down low. Jerry raised his eyebrows. 'Fuck's sake, Steve,' he muttered.

'Last time, Jerry, I promise. I need to check something.' But Dan looked as cheerful as ever as he interrogated a stick-like single mum about how she'd got over her obesity. 'Why aren't you doing domestic violence as your big talking point, big talk big guest man?' I muttered at the screen. I felt power-less, and frustrated at my inability to help Maya. I wondered if she was watching her husband carrying on as though nothing had happened. I felt in my trouser pocket and quickly located Maya's house key. I ran my thumb along its edges, fingered the soft felt of the key ring. It felt comforting to know it was there – that if she was in trouble, I could get to her.

Jerry left at 5.30 with a sympathetic smile and a 'good luck' thumbs-up. I felt he could have waited to see how it went but he had to go to some event at his daughter's school. By 6.30, I had a fully-fledged PowerPoint presentation which I took, proudly, to my meeting with Brandon.

'Sorry about this morning,' I said. 'Hope this will make up for it.'

'Hope so too,' he said. 'I don't know what's been going on with you, but just remember, if it's not business, it's none of my business. But if it affects business, it is my business.'

'I understand.'

He could tell I had modelled the presentation on his own, and he seemed to like that. I felt confident in what I was showing him. Jerry and I had also done an analysis of our own pitch for Globus and tried to turn our own claimed strengths to weaknesses. Brandon watched attentively and then gave a loud handclap. 'Test to destruction,' he said. 'Good. I like it.'

I breathed a sigh of relief and was about to say 'Thanks . . . Great' when he continued speaking.

'Problem is, Steve, this is all very well but it's not exactly earth-shattering is it? I mean anyone can put together neat little PowerPoint displays. Websters are going to have all their top bods going at it. We need to do something different. Something to show we're not like the rest of the pack.'

I almost gasped at the hypocrisy of it, but then I had a brainwave. During my internet trawls I had noticed a number of articles about Websters, two of which (from *Private Eye* and the *Sunday Telegraph*) alluded to their role in a Department of Trade inquiry into price fixing, and another that came from a website called Businessgossip.com and suggested that one of their directors had got himself involved with underaged rent boys. Remembering Brandon's boast about his use of a private eye for the Irish deal, I mentioned them now.

'Gulf clients attach extreme importance to the moral standing of any company they do business with,' I said, parroting something Jerry had mentioned earlier in the day. 'I don't think they will like this sort of thing.'

'No, they will not,' said Brandon, looking pensive.

Delighted to have got one up on him, I pursued my advantage.

'I was wondering if we shouldn't call in your private investigation people.'

'You mean our commercial intelligence analysts.'

'That's it, yes, our commercial intelligence analysts.'

He laughed, or at least it was the nearest he ever got to a laugh, and said he would think about it.

'OK, thanks for seeing me,' I said, conscious as I said it of how pathetic that must have sounded.

'No problem. Good work.'

'Thanks.'

'And all because I gave you a kick up the arse this morning.'

'I guess so, yes.'

'You shouldn't have needed it. And I don't want to have to do it again.'

He really was a pillock. He couldn't bear to have the words 'good work' as the last message I took from our meeting. In Brandon's world even praise had to be turned into a bollocking, or a boast of his own skills.

It was freezing when I walked out to my car, and the car-park lights had been turned off. My Peugeot was the only car left, apart from Brandon's Volvo. Lowering myself into the driver's seat, I took my car key from my coat pocket. Maya's key had got entangled with it. As I started the engine, turned on the headlights and tried to get the heater going, I put her key on the passenger seat. It sat there, looking forlorn with its little elephant key ring and the slogan 'Don't forget'. It seemed like an accusation. I couldn't bear the prospect of a whole weekend of not knowing and anxiety. I decided to drive home via Little Venice and see if I could get a glimpse of what was going on at Maya's house. Vanessa knew I was seeing Brandon. She'd simply think my meeting had gone on longer than expected.

I couldn't find a space in Maida Avenue, so reluctantly ended up parking in Blomfield Road itself, about five houses down from Maya's. The chances of being spotted were greater than on the other side of the canal, but it was a risk that had to be taken if I was properly to see any comings and goings. Three photographers were leaning against the canal-side railings directly outside Maya's house. Being a paparazzo must be such a bizarre way to live your life, I thought. Hour upon hour standing around chatting, just waiting for another human being to emerge so that you could take a photo. I wondered if they ever stopped to question why they did it. One of them was drawing on a cigarette which he flicked over a barge into the water. He was wearing a green fleece, baggy jeans, thick socks and boots, like he was about to hike up a mountain. All the lights were on in Maya's house and a caterer's van was parked alongside Dan's Mercedes, from which a young man was unloading steel boxes while someone else carried them into the house. Clearly they had guests again, and clearly the media knew about it this time.

Keeping the engine running so that the heating stayed on, I sat back and tried to think things through. Did Maya really love Dan so much that she was prepared to forgive him domestic violence? Or was it that, deep down, she was afraid of the media frenzy that would ensue if she faced up to leaving him? Even for Mr and Mrs Joe Public splitting up was a nightmare. There were so many things wrapped up in that central relationship. Feelings. Money. Families. Friendships. Jobs. Houses. Kids often. But for Maya and Dan, there was all the other stuff on top. It wouldn't only be in Britain that the story would be major news. *Fast Track to Safety* had been number one in Australia for several weeks. She'd done a mini tour of Asia last spring. Italy was not the only European country where she had won awards. She was big in Spain because of the family connection. In America she was becoming mega. 'Maya splits from Dan'. Big story. 'Maya's agony as Dan beats her up'. Massive. This oh so chic street would be heaving with media. TV cameras as well as casual lurking photographers. Internet reporters as well as press. I had a vision of them all lined up on top of the canal barges, some up in the trees on both sides of the road, cameras trained twenty-four hours a day on the front door and the upstairs windows. It would be hell for

Maya, hell for her parents, a nightmare for the neighbours.

The film companies wouldn't like it either. Maya's image mattered. Girl next door who made it big. Never forgot her roots, family girl, didn't do the drugs thing, clean-living, happily married, sensible, beautiful but not a show-off, always helping good causes, breast cancer care patron, ambassador for UNICEF. Would a broken marriage and the sense of Maya as victim, rather than charismatic creator of her own glittering destiny, affect her career for good or bad? Even if I didn't know the answer, there would be plenty of highly paid, sharply dressed execs forced to work it out, if this thing ever became public.

Just before 8.30, as I was beginning to think I ought to call Vanessa, a Range Rover came to a halt outside the house, a couple jumped out and suddenly they were swarmed not just by the three lurking photographers but another half-dozen or so who had leapt from their cars. I wound down my window in an effort to see and hear better what was going on. The couple paused at the gate, where the young man I had seen at the caterer's van was waiting to show them in. I couldn't make out who they were but they seemed happy enough to give the photographers what they wanted. He was tall and dark, possibly mixed race. She was blonde and dressed in red. A contented murmur wafted down the street towards me as the photographers looked over the pictures they had taken. The guy in boots went straight to his car, put his laptop on the roof and started emailing off his snaps straight away. Next came a Jaguar and out stepped another couple, this one less keen to pose, and I couldn't get a good view. 'Mick, Mick, Mick, this way, this way, just one, just one,' but Mick, whoever Mick was, was having none of it. The most famous Mick I could think of was Jagger, but the Mick they were all shouting at was too well built to be the Rolling Stone. The next prey for the snappers was a couple arriving on foot. At first only one of the photographers spotted them but as the others followed the first flash, they were lost in a blitz of flickering light.

The photographers seemed to know that the dinner party was now complete.

'That's it I think,' I heard one of them say.

'You coming back for departures?' asked Bootman.

'Depends on what else I get. I've got a tip on Nicole Kidman tonight.'

Most of them returned to their cars. Some drove off, and I was able to move my Peugeot a little closer to the house. I thought about letting myself in at the gate and trying to get a glimpse of the party through the dining-room window. But not all of the photographers had gone and there was a danger of being snapped so I just sat there, watching as the street gradually emptied of people and resumed its usual calm. I'd been there for over an hour. I was beginning to feel stiff from the cold, and from sitting tensely in the car, so I got out and paced up and down the street. The windows of Maya's house were like a blank face, their drawn blinds firmly shutting out the hoi polloi. But then I noticed, in an upper room, shadows passing across the blind. Two people. It looked like a man and a woman – touching. Were they embracing? Wrestling? Was it Maya and Dan?

I stood rooted to the spot until they disappeared from view, and then for a long time after that. What should I do? I couldn't burst into a dinner party. And presumably if other people were in there for the evening, Maya was going to be OK. It was odd to think that last weekend Vanessa and I had been in there ourselves, as guests in our glad rags. I reflected how nervous I had felt, yet that was as nothing compared with the work-induced, caffeine-overdosing, Maya-protecting anxiousness that seemed to worsen with every minute of my spying mission.

Eventually I forced myself to drive off. I was glad to get away. As the lights of poshland receded in the rear-view mirror, I felt like I was leaving an alien land for my own. Yet someone I loved remained trapped there, and I didn't know what I could do to help her.

Chapter Ten

Vanessa was deep in sleep when I eventually went to bed that night, but I was unable to join her. I must have been awake for a couple of hours, my mind still racing. When finally I dropped off, I dreamt I was standing at the foot of the staircase in Maya's house, only the staircase had become an escalator which was moving the wrong way, so that with every step I made, I progressed no further forward. I tried to run but my legs felt like they were filled with lead and wouldn't carry me. I moved across the hallway, tried to summon one last burst of energy, ran towards the escalator which took me a few yards, far enough to see Maya on the landing at the top, arms whirling, trying to stop herself from falling, before my legs gave way and the escalator took me back to the hall. I woke up just after four in the morning. Vanessa's head had disappeared beneath one of her pillows. I tried to get back to sleep but quickly realised it was hopeless and after half an hour or so, I gave up. I went downstairs to make myself some coffee. For want of anything better to do I picked up Vanessa's laptop and logged on to We-know-the-stars.com. There, already, were the photographs of the guests arriving at Maya's dinner party. It turned out Mick was the TV impresario who had recently taken over the production of Dan's show. The mixed-race guy was a rap artist and his girlfriend a former model turned dancer. There was also mention of a US film financier, Jim Elliott, who must have arrived before I had. Alongside a picture of Dan stepping from his car, they had a mock-up menu complete with the wines they'd had. Obviously they'd been tipped off by the caterers. She could trust nobody, I thought.

I knew I needed to get some proper rest at the weekend so I would be back on form in time for Monday's meeting on Qatar, but I just couldn't stop thinking about what I'd seen at Maya's window, and wondering why she hadn't been in touch with me. Was Dan stopping her? Holding her some kind of hostage in her own home? Terrible images of what he might be doing to her kept passing through my mind. The more I thought about them, the more I knew I couldn't just sit around all day without doing something. In a flash, I was upstairs, dressing quietly, then back downstairs to fill a flask with coffee before sneaking out of the house. I left a note for Vanessa on the kitchen table: 'Brandon texted late last night. He wants me to go into the office today to work on the Qatar project. Call my mobile when you wake up. Sorry! X'.

This time I found a space right outside John Masefield's house, on the Maida Avenue side of the canal. By 6.30 I was parked up, looking across the water at Maya's house. The blinds were still drawn on every floor.

It was so dark it seemed almost like the middle of the night. It was as if I hadn't been home but had spent the last ten hours slouched in my car. This must be what it feels like to be a policeman staking out the home of a terrorist suspect, I thought, pouring myself a coffee. Police. Paparazzi. All that waiting. Perhaps my job wasn't so bad after all. It certainly wasn't as boring as this.

I had brought my Qatari work with me and was able to do a little, rereading the files on the rival companies, but it was important to keep an eye on the house, not lose my concentration. There was no one in the street until shortly after seven when a solitary jogger appeared, breath steaming. He looked at me slightly suspiciously and I immediately pretended to be consulting an *A to Z*. After that there was no one else until about 7.30 when the dog walkers started to show up. A young woman in dungarees emerged from one of the canal barges, took a look around, then went back inside. The curtains in Maya's bedroom opened at 8.35 just as my mobile trilled with Vanessa's call.

'Jesus, Steve, where are you?'

'Didn't you see I left a note? I'm at the office.'

'I didn't mean "where are you?" literally. I meant where are you when I need you? I've just spent the last half-hour throwing up!'

'I'm so sorry,' I said, feeling stricken. 'I'll leave now. I can be back in half an hour.'

'No, no, don't worry. I know this Qatar deal is important. I'll be fine. I might go to Judith's and spend the day on her sofa. She said she wasn't doing anything.'

'If you want me to come, just call.'

I felt a complete bastard. I was being ridiculous, I thought, worrying about a friend when my wife needed me more. But at that moment, Dan and Maya emerged through the black gate.

Dan was wearing red running shorts, and a gold sweatshirt. Maya had a light green tracksuit, and a white bobble hat. They stood on the pavement and talked for a few moments as Dan stretched. I was transfixed. Over the past week I had thought about them so much, they had fuelled my imagination, and it was somehow startling to see them in the flesh. Dan reached over to touch Maya's arm, said something to her, then ran off towards the bridge. Maya followed him a few moments later, jogging with ease and elegance.

It was hard to stop myself from trailing them, but I sat tight. While I waited for them to come back, I played over and over in my mind the image of Dan touching Maya's arm. Was it a loving touch? If so, why did they not jog together? Clearly, he could run faster than her. But surely, if they were going out for a run at the same time, they would run together? Maya had told me they did.

Maya was back first, after half an hour. She had removed the tracksuit top and tied it around her waist. Her neck was glistening a little. Dan, who appeared about twenty minutes later, was red-faced and sweating, as if he'd been running hard.

At that moment Vanessa sent a text to say she was on her way to Judith's in a cab, and would I pick her up when I'd finished work? Judith lived in Paddington, close enough to St Mary's Hospital to be able to walk to work, and near enough for me to swing by easily on my way home so I texted back to say fine. I stayed in Blomfield Road for the whole day, not even leaving the car to get a sandwich for fear that either Maya or Dan might spot me on the move. Maya stayed in, but Dan left the house twice during the day, first for half an hour at around eleven, the second time for two hours over lunch. Each time he looked a bit hassled and dishevelled. By the time I was listening to the five o'clock headlines on the radio, it was getting dark and I realised that I couldn't expect Vanessa to believe that Brandon would make me work through Saturday evening when the presentation was still some weeks away. I wondered how Maya was feeling, cooped up in the house, her husband dashing about. I sent her a text. 'Doing OK?' Unusually, she texted back almost straight away. 'Fine. Got evening to myself. Dan playing poker at club. Staying in with book. What r u up to?'

It is possible to read too much into a text, but she sounded pretty laid-back. How should I answer? 'I'm staking out your house, sick with worry that your husband is holding you hostage'? I was pondering my reply when Vanessa called to say she was ready to go home, and then something else happened that made me forget about answering altogether. I was just telling Vanessa that I was on my way when Dan appeared at the gate, and headed to his car. 'I'll call you right back, Vanessa,' I said. 'Just give me a minute.' I started the engine, did a quick three-point turn and managed to catch up with Dan's Mercedes just as he was turning off Maida Vale into St John's Wood Road.

'This is weird,' I thought. 'I'm actually in a car chase.' It was both exhilarating and terrifying at the same time. I had to risk a red light to get within sight of him, and tried to stay one or two cars behind. It was hard, and twice I feared I had lost him. He seemed to be driving aimlessly but fast, and must have covered three or four miles to complete a distance of less than one, eventually pulling up outside a church opposite a cul-de-sac, Abercorn Close. I stopped less than forty yards behind him, far too near, and tried to sink into my seat as he locked his car and walked into the Close. Fortunately, he didn't spot me. I inched forward and managed to see him ring the bell of a house almost halfway down. I didn't get a glimpse of who answered it, but he disappeared as soon as the door opened.

Vanessa had called twice during the time I was driving. I called her to apologise for hanging up, said I was on my way.

'What's the matter, Steve?'

'Nothing. Brandon called me in when we were speaking. But it's fine. He says I can go.'

I was afraid Vanessa would hold my day away against me but she was embarrassingly sympathetic when I arrived at Judith's flat just off Praed Street.

'I can't believe Brandon's making you work so hard,' she said, giving me a big hug as she got into the car. 'You look shattered.'

'Well, at least I haven't had morning sickness,' I said, trying to divert the attention back to her. 'How long do you think it'll go on?'

'Judith says there's no way of knowing. Some women don't have any sickness, some get it right through their pregnancy. Let's hope I'm somewhere in between.'

'Yeah, let's hope so.' I turned on the radio in the hope the music might stop the conversation. I needed to think.

Whatever it was, the house where Dan was spending the evening did not look much like a gentlemen's club to me. The shame was that because I'd had to collect Vanessa, I didn't have the time to discover more. Not right now anyway. But I would. If Dan was up to no good, I was determined to find out what it was.

Chapter Eleven

I was glad to get to the office on Monday morning. Sunday at home had been a day of ever tightening claustrophobia. Vanessa vomited again in the morning, and I felt irritated by my inability to say or do the right things to make her feel better. If she had been a less nice person, I think she would have told me to piss off so that she could rest quietly on the sofa and leaf through the baby books that Judith had lent her. Instead she tried to make conversation, asking questions about how everything was going with Qatar. I couldn't find the answers, somehow, and got edgy. Partly it was lack of exercise. A long walk was built into our Sunday routine and without it I went a bit stir-crazy. Mostly, though, it was because my mind kept framing and re-framing pictures of Dan walking into that house in Abercorn Close – and trying to work out what they meant. Something weird was definitely going on, but I didn't know how I could find out more. I'd had my fill of sitting looking at curtains and canal barges, and I certainly wasn't cut out for car chases. Even those few minutes spent trying to follow him the previous day had been much too nerve-wracking. Dan was an aggressive character. I shivered a little on reflecting how close I had been to him, therefore how close to being spotted, doubtless dragged out of my car and given a battering. The phone call to Vanessa from A&E would not have been an easy one.

I enjoyed the solitude of my Monday-morning drive to Heathrow. For once, I had reason to look forward to the afternoon's strategy meeting. I thought it would be enjoyable to watch my colleagues' faces when I announced that I had uncovered evidence of misdemeanours by Websters. As it was, Brandon denied me the chance. There was a note from his PA, stuck to my computer screen when I reached my desk.

'Join the boss in the private dining room as soon as you get in.'

I showed it to Jerry.

'Any idea what this is about?'

Jerry shrugged. 'Not a clue. Perhaps he wants to buy you breakfast in celebration of Vanessa's pregnancy.'

'Ha, ha,' I said, dumping my coat and straightening my tie. 'There's no way I'm telling him about that till the last possible minute.'

He could see I was nervous. 'I wouldn't worry. It'll be something about the Qataris.'

'Why just me then?'

'You know what he's like. Talk the talk on teamwork; in reality divide and rule.'

I walked down to the ground floor rather than taking the lift, to give myself a chance to compose myself. The 'private dining room' – the words had been underlined on the note – was a grandiose description for a cordoned-off corner of the main canteen, used mainly by executives for working breakfasts and lunches. There was little to distinguish it from the canteen, other than tablecloths, table service and fewer health and safety notices. When I got there, Brandon was energetically spreading a pat of hard butter across a tired piece of toast. Beside him was Brian McCann, the head of a chemicals company we frequently did business with.

'Ah, Steve,' Brandon said. 'Come on over and sit down. We're just finishing up.'

Usually he'd make me stand. The friendliness was all an act, to persuade his guest that he was the gregarious team leader of happy, motivated individuals. It didn't extend to offering me a cup of coffee.

'I thought we'd meet in here because I wanted a quiet word,' he said, after he had shaken McCann's hand and seen him out. 'I've been mulling over that information you dug up about Websters and I've decided I want you to go and brief Tim Waller, the boss at Swift International. Tell Waller what you want, pursue it at your discretion and let me know if costs start mounting up. I'm putting you in charge of this, Steve, because I think you're thorough and basically trustworthy. Don't discuss it with any of your colleagues, not even Jerry, and don't let me down.'

It was clear from the way Brandon knocked back the rest of his coffee in one large, noisy gulp that the conversation was over. He told me his PA would set up the meeting with Waller and email me details, along with information about how Swift invoiced us. Then he stood up and left. I sat at the table for a moment trying to take in what had just been said. I knew Swift was the corporate intelligence company that Globus used, but I'd never had anything to do with them. That was always Brandon's territory. I felt a strange warmth knowing that he was trusting me. It suggested my prospects at Globus were better than I had been fearing. On the other hand, dealing with espionage companies was way outside my comfort zone.

Still, I thought, it was good to be stretched. Frankly Maya wasn't the only reason I hadn't been concentrating on the Qatar pitch. I was bored. I needed a new challenge, new excitement. Perhaps this was it.

I spent the rest of the week in a state of nervous anticipation. Brandon's PA had arranged the meeting with Waller for Thursday at four, and I was finding it hard to concentrate on other things, or talk properly to Jerry. I kept being drawn back to Swift's website. It was an impressive, slightly scary affair, their logo a white-headed, black-feathered bald eagle, its huge curved wings appearing to embrace a red globe, cartoon skyscrapers fading into a gloomy mauve background. The home page boasted of global reach, with networks in every major economy in the world. It spoke of former police and military personnel experienced in fighting organised crime and international terrorism. It promised 24/7 commitment and absolute discretion. A series of button-style headings directed me to brief descriptions of their core work – corporate intelligence; mergers and acquisitions; due diligence; debt recovery. On one particularly boastful page, they came close to claiming they could get inside any government department, company account, bank or phone system anywhere in the world. I wondered what kind of a man Waller would be, and whether my paltry enquiry about allegations of inaccurate accounting and sexual shenanigans would be something that interested him. It looked as if he might deal with grander things.

I also did my usual internet trawls for Maya and Dan coverage. Tuesday had delivered a glut of pictures of Maya arriving at JFK airport in New York. There was lots of speculation about why she was there, with all sorts of wild guesses about which producers she was talking to, and about what film. While I was pleased that she was away from Dan, and therefore safe from harm, I felt a little hurt she hadn't mentioned the NY trip to me. But then the next day I got a sweet email: 'In the Big Apple discussing "the big movie". Wish you were here to advise. They are piling on the pressure but I still can't feel enthusiastic.'

I replied immediately: 'Follow your own instincts and don't be bullied. I'm here if you want to call xxx'.

I thought of driving over to Little Venice on Wednesday evening to do some Dan-watching, since Maya's absence might tempt him to be less circumspect about his movements, but I couldn't face it. And anyway, I felt I had to be on top form for my meeting with Waller.

The offices of Swift International were right in the heart of the City, off Bishopsgate, so I gave myself a good hour and a bit to drive there. When Jerry asked why I was leaving early, I spun him a line about a hospital appointment with Vanessa.

It took me a while to find the right building. A Canadian bank took up the first six floors, and had the most dominant branding – there was no mention of Swift – so I walked past the entrance a couple of times before I worked out it was the one I needed. In the lobby, an attractive though stern young receptionist asked me to fill in my name and company and gave me a day pass on a wire chain. She pressed a button to let me through a turnstile and said someone would meet me on the ninth floor. A slightly older but equally attractive woman met me when I came out of the lift and showed me into a glass waiting room with two chairs, a set of neatly laid out newspapers on a mahogany table, and a water cooler. She asked me to wait while she contacted Mr Waller's secretary. I noticed that all the people who passed me kept their eyes down. I wondered if it was because secrecy was important in such places, or just that they were very busy. I tried to be similarly discreet myself, but I couldn't help staring. Within a few minutes the woman came back and led me to Waller's office.

I don't think I had ever seen a tidier desk. It was ebony-coloured, with a closed laptop at the centre, two telephones, a silver fountain pen and one sheet of A4 paper lying neatly beside a framed photograph of wife and children. The man behind it was similarly immaculate, almost totally bald but with striking blond eyebrows above healthy blue eyes which narrowed deliberately to appear intense.

'So how can I help you, Mr Watkins?' he asked, indicating that I should sit down in the leather chair facing him.

I laid out printouts of the articles from *Private Eye*, the *Sunday Telegraph* and Businessgossip.com – they looked embarrassingly tatty and dog-eared next to his clean, flat piece of paper – and launched into a speech I had been rehearsing on the drive over about the suspicious nature of Websters' involvement in a property venture in Dubai, and the innuendoes in the media about the sexual proclivities of its finance director, Francis Parry. Waller listened carefully, took a few concise notes and then stood up.

'Well, that all seems straightforward enough. We should be able to give you a report on the Dubai business in a week or so. As for what Mr Parry has been up to in his spare time, you'll have to talk to my colleague, Warren Stafford. That kind of stuff is not actually done out of here. We have a separate office in West London which does marriages, divorces, private lives. We're the same firm, but we try to keep ourselves a bit separate. They do sex, we do power and money. When people come in here, I like them to think "City analysts", not "gumshoes trailing lovers and mistresses around the place". If you've got time, I could see if Stafford can fit you in this afternoon?'

I mumbled my assent. I'd had thoughts of paying Vanessa a surprise visit at her office, which was about four streets away. We could have gone for a drink at the Half Moon, where we sometimes went when we were first going out, and then driven home together. It would have saved Vanessa a tiring Tube journey. But instead I found myself driving to Shepherd's Bush to meet a 'gumshoe'. I pondered Waller's words as I drove. There was something about his suave assurance that made me feel shabby and inadequate, as if I belonged with the gumshoes rather than the City analysts. I began to regret that I had ever tried to impress Brandon with my dirt-digging, and longed to get the whole business over and done with. But as I got nearer to Shepherd's Bush, a plan began to form in my mind that changed my mood entirely. I wanted to follow Dan but didn't have the nerve. The man I was going to see specialised in following people. Perhaps his expertise and my needs could meet somewhere.

The office was on the main road just down from Shepherd's Bush Tube station, between a 24-hour convenience store and a dry cleaner's. A middle-aged receptionist with thick glasses sat behind an imposing grey counter to the right of the entrance, a messages board the only adornment on the wall behind her. The main office was a floor up, behind a coded entry pad. The receptionist tapped in the code, shielding the number pad from me with her spare hand, like she was taking money from a cashpoint, and showed me through. Twenty or so men, and a handful of women, were working in a quiet, rather stuffy atmosphere. Several wore headphones.

There couldn't have been a greater contrast between Tim Waller and Warren Stafford. Waller had said that Stafford was ex-Special Branch, but he struck me as more military than police. He had a big square face, thick dark eyebrows over brown eyes surrounded by wrinkles. Close to his nose was a small but serious-looking scar. He was wearing a creased white shirt undone at the top, with his tie loose around his neck. The two men's offices were pretty different too. Whereas Waller's had been tidy and clean, Stafford's was a tip. There were the remnants of a lunch served in a polystyrene box on his desk, a scattering of shoes and discarded clothes on a couple of armchairs behind him, and, instead of a silver fountain pen, he had an old biro stuck in a mug.

'Excuse the mess,' he said. 'Fucking cleaner's off sick. Everyone goes on about how reliable the Poles are. Not this one.'

'No problem,' I said, trying to ingratiate myself. Though I'd taken an instant dislike to him, I was eager to form a rapport so that I could find a way to raise the subject of Dan – or at least sound out whether I could trust him enough to do so.

We spent ten minutes or so discussing Websters' finance director, and how Stafford might go about confirming the story – perhaps story was too strong a word, 'hint' was more accurate – that Parry used rent boys. He explained to me how, if talking to people didn't turn up the evidence we were looking for, then he could, if necessary, mount a surveillance oper-ation on Parry himself.

'Might need to catch him at it, eh?'

'Right, I see.'

'They're not too fond of poofters in the Middle East, are they?' he said, giving me a wink.

He could see I was taken aback by the crudeness with which he expressed Parry's sexuality.

'You're not a poofter too are you?'

'No.' I could see why Waller liked to work separate from this side of the house.

'Good. Nothing wrong with it of course. Just don't want it anywhere near me. Now, leave this particular nancy boy with me Mr Watkins and I'll see what I can do.'

He started to get up, but I was eager to prolong the conversation, and asked about costs.

'Let's discuss that when we come to it,' he said. 'Your retainer will cover the asking of a few questions. If we need to do more, I'll let you know.'

'But what are we talking?' I insisted. 'Thousands? Tens of thousands?'

'Depends how important it is for Globus to nail this man,' he replied. 'A few grand if the story checks out quickly. A lot more if I stick him under surveillance. It could be tens then.'

'Not cheap.'

'No. If you want round-the-clock surveillance for a couple of weeks, which is usually the minimum it needs, I use teams of eight.'

'Eight!'

'At least. Two teams of four, twelve-hour shifts. It is not easy sticking with someone, especially in London. Plus we incur a lot of expenses. Where the target goes, we go. They walk, one of us walks. They drive, we drive. They hop on the Tube, one of us hops on the Tube. They fly, we fly. And we do electronic surveillance too, which can be costly because we have to recoup the investment on the gear we use, which gets more sophisticated all the time.'

'Electronic surveillance?'

'Phone calls, bank statements, that sort of thing.'

'All legal?'

He leaned towards me, laced his hands together and plonked his elbows hard on his desk.

'There are two ways of doing this, Mr Watkins. I can tell you all the things we do, and you and your conscience can lie awake at night worrying about civil liberties. Or you can just let us get on with it. If occasionally we do things we shouldn't, then nobody can ever say you knew about it. But understand this – we have done hundreds of personnel watches, and I have not been in court once, other than as a witness. So relax.'

I tried to relax but my mind was buzzing. I'd already decided that, even if Stafford couldn't get proof of Mr Parry's escapades, there was no way I was going to involve Globus in further investigations of him. It was too risky. Stafford might not find anything, and I'd have wasted company money in the process. Hardly the way to endear myself to Brandon. When it came to my own personal dilemma, however, the 24-hour surveillance that Stafford had described seemed perfect, even if I had no idea how I'd pay for it. Perhaps, I thought, I could just see if he'd give me a bit of advice. I took a deep breath and asked if I could rely on his discretion.

He gave me a knowing smile and passed me a company leaflet on which the Swift International 'service pledges' were listed, the last and most prominent of which was 'TOTAL DISCRETION'.

'Have no worries on that front,' he said. 'I know things that would make your bloody eyes fall out. You want to know my motto? "We gather the secrets, we give the secrets, we keep the secrets." That is our work. So long as me and my boys get paid, what the client does with the secrets is their concern, not ours.'

I paused, looked at him closely, tried to get the measure of him.

'Don't tell me,' he said. 'I've got a hunch born of seeing many people like you sitting in that chair down the years . . . You're worried your missus is playing away?'

'Not at all. I know you can never be a hundred per cent sure of anything in this world, but I'm at ninety-nine on that one.'

Now he was the one staring more intently, trying to get my measure.

'Let me guess again then. You've got a *friend*?' He raised two curled fingers on each hand to drop a sarcastic quotation mark around 'friend'.

'Correct.'

'And *he*'s worried his missus is playing away?'

'It's a she.'

'And what's your interest? Trying to blow out a rival are we?'

'I said I was happily married.'

'Just because your missus is on ninety-nine per cent, it doesn't mean you are.'

'This lady is a genuine friend, nothing like that. We go back to childhood.'

'Aw sweet. And she's a *lady*. So what's the issue . . . your friend's husband shagging someone else?'

I didn't like him much when I first met him and I liked him even less after a few minutes in his company. He knew that he emanated intimidation. Yet the more he seemed deliberately to offend and annoy with his jibes and his political incorrectness, the more I felt myself being propelled towards confiding in him. Perhaps it was simply the relief of finally being able to talk to someone about my worries. Whatever it was, I found myself telling him Maya's story, although I didn't of course mention her name. When I'd finished, he gave a low whistle.

'Domestic violence,' he said. 'I fucking hate that. No matter how much a woman provokes you, you never ever hit her. First rule. And you say she's a celeb, this friend of yours?'

'Big.'

He looked me in the eye. 'So what are we talking here? You want to hire me to check out this husband of hers?'

I hadn't expected this question to come so quickly, and now I thought about it, the idea was absurd. He'd talked of bills possibly running into five figures. I'd only be able to find a sum like that if we won the Qatar contract and I got paid my bonus . . . And then I had a thought. It was obvious we were going to win the contract – Brandon was just fretting to get us to work harder – and I didn't have to tell Vanessa exactly how big the bonus was: I could knock ten or even twenty grand off and she would be none the wiser. If I could only get Stafford to delay his invoice for a few months, until the Qatar deal was signed, I'd be well able to pay him. The important thing was that I would finally get to know whatever there was to know about Dan. On the other hand, if I didn't take this opportunity, Maya would come back from New York and I'd be plunged right back into a state of chronic anxiety about her.

'Mr Stafford,' I said, 'how would you feel about folding

the invoice for this separate job into the Parry invoice for Globus?'

He looked at me hard. 'As I said, so long as me and the boys get paid, it's up to the client how they behave. But I suggest you think carefully about what you're getting into.'

I stared at the floor, then up at him again. 'I don't think it will be a problem, Mr Stafford. I've got clout at Globus. I can square things there. I just need a little time.'

I was sure I would be OK. The retainer that Globus paid Swift might well cover some of the surveillance and by the time the invoice needed to be paid, I would have the funds to cover my share. I knew it was a risk but it seemed one worth taking if I could help Maya.

'All right,' said Stafford. 'So why don't you tell me who it is.'

He sat back and stared at me. He knew I had nothing more to go on, no more questions to ask that would help or hinder my judgement. I was going to have to follow my instinct, and decide. Not doing a hard sell was a part of his hard sell. Despite his slovenly appearance and his cynical view of the world, I sensed he knew what he was doing, and that he was as good at keeping secrets as he boasted. But as the moment came to tell him, my guts were raging. I wanted a glass of water. He was clearly not going to utter another sound until I said the name. I looked him in the eye and said quietly 'Maya Lowe and Dan Chivers.'

He let out an audible gasp. 'Fuck! I see what you mean about being discreet.'

'Yep.'

'Wow. OK. Well, first of all, thank you for hiring us.' Christ alive, I thought, Maya even affects people like him. Manners all of a sudden. Or was it the seriousness of the assignment that inspired the change?

'Second, let me assure you of something – all those cowboys and Indians out on the shop floor report only to me. Only the ones I assign to the case will know who it is. They will talk to nobody about this. They need not know who you are or why you're interested. When I brief them, they will probably think we're working for a newspaper, and we can allow them to live happily under that illusion, OK?'

I nodded.

'You need deal with nobody but me. I will deal with nobody but you. My guys will see only those parts of the report they compile. Nobody will see the full reports but us. I will stay very hands on at all times.'

'What about Waller?'

'He won't know a thing. He fucking hates this stuff. I love it.' And he laughed.

'And you'll let me know how the costs are going?'

'Sure.'

'And we can agree language for the invoicing?'

'Easy.'

His demeanour changed, became more focussed, less flippant as I spent the next half-hour filling him in on where and how Maya and Dan lived. Phone numbers. Family. Cars. Favourite bars and restaurants. Rudi, the poker club and Abercorn Close of course. He loved that, let out a little 'oo' as if someone had gently pinched him. He wrote it all down in a black leather notebook. When I'd told him everything I could think of, including the code to the gate, I reached into my pocket and pulled out Maya's key. 'You might need this,' I said, and laid it on the desk. It looked small and vulnerable lying there, its cutesy blue-felt elephant out of place in the hard masculinity of Stafford's office.

'Ta very much,' said Stafford, picking up the key and putting it in his desk drawer. 'Not sure I'll have to use it. But every little helps as the man from Tesco says.'

He seemed energised by the brief, as if suddenly some fresh impetus had been injected into his life. He threw his polystyrene lunch box into a bin, tidied up the clothes and shoes on the chairs behind him, shook my hand warmly and said he looked forward to working with me. 'Two weeks is all we need,' he boasted. 'You can find out pretty much everything about anyone in two weeks.'

As I walked out into the busy streets of Shepherd's Bush, even though I had a parking ticket, I too felt a new enthusiasm. Ever since the dinner at Maya's I'd been feeling powerless, ground down. But I felt like my hands were on the steering wheel now. Like it was me, not Dan, who was in the driving seat of a black Mercedes on the way to a secret assignation.

Chapter Twelve

When you start thinking a lot about the idea of surveillance, strange things happen to your mind. At least they did to mine, after I'd done my deal with Stafford. By the weekend, there had been a change — subtle, but strong enough for me to be aware it was taking place — in the way I was interacting with the world around me. Paranoia is too strong a word. It wasn't that. But it was the feeling that I was being watched.

Can you tell if you're being watched? Sometimes I've felt a prickling sensation in my back, and sweat on my neck, and I've turned round sharply to find someone behind me who I didn't realise was there. I remember being in a library once, head bent over a book, certain that someone was watching me and, sure enough, when I raised my eyes, a pretty girl opposite looked away quickly, immediately pretended to read her magazine. Maya talked too of having a sixth sense that alerted her to photographers hidden behind cars or trees even when there was nothing to suggest they were there. She'd once gone over to a bush with a large watering can and given the paparazzo inside it a cold shower. It made for some great pictures, and she regretted it later.

Would her sixth sense pick up Stafford's men, I wondered? I had to assume that if they were following Dan, at times they'd be following Maya too. Would she feel spooked? Would she discover someone was tailing her and want to know who had put them up to it? Would Dan? As a result I started to feel spooked too. Even though I could see no reason why Stafford's men would be the slightest bit interested in my movements, I felt like they were observing me. It was as if I was starring in a film that I was also watching. I watched myself driving to the supermarket on Saturday morning, having told Vanessa to take things easy and let me do the food shopping for once. I watched myself waking Vanessa from an afternoon nap so we could go for an early dinner at our local Italian. I watched myself watching Maya arrive back at Heathrow on Sunday morning after her New York trip: there was a short clip of it on the *Entertainment Hour*. I didn't like the feeling of being disassociated from myself. It made me eerily self-conscious. Suddenly I became aware of the way I walked, the slightly fake tone of gentleness when I spoke to Vanessa, the authority I tried to paint on to my voice when I answered the phone. This must be what it was like to be Maya, I thought. Her life was one big film in which she was both performer and spectator. Everything she did – from brushing her teeth in the morning to removing her mascara at night – was of interest to people. I could see the appeal of having a life like that. So often I felt like some insignificant insect, toiling un-noticed amid billions of others. How would it be if, when *I* walked into restaurants, they changed shape and temperature? Would I have liked it more if that young woman in the super-market car park hadn't just said 'Thanks' when I moved my car to let her into the space but had opened her eyes wide, put her hand to her cheek, shrieked 'Oh my God, it's Steve Watkins' and taken a picture with her mobile phone? It was so far from my experience, it was difficult to know whether I'd like it.

Maya called me unexpectedly just after lunch on Sunday.

'Hey,' I said. 'How was New York?'

'Great, as usual. I love my apartment there, Steve. I wish you could see it.'

'Just say the word and I'll be on a plane,' I said. I'd always wanted to visit New York but somehow the right circumstances had never presented themselves.

'It's difficult to deal with the jet lag,' she said. 'In fact, that's why I'm calling. Dan's out at a poker tournament at his club and I need help staying awake until this evening, so I don't get my sleep patterns all messed up. Do you want to come over and keep me company? I've lots to tell you about the film.'

I glanced over at Vanessa who was snuggled up on the sofa.

'Hold on,' I said, 'I'll have to consult.'

I pressed the mute button on the phone and asked Vanessa what she thought. She seemed fine about it.

'I was planning to have a sleep anyway,' she said. 'You go. Pregnancy's boring. No point in both of us being bored.'

Forget paranoia – when I arrived at Little Venice I was sure I was being watched. Yet when I tried to work out which of the cars parked along Blomfield Road might belong to someone from Stafford's team, they were all empty. I drove slowly the entire length of the street, then checked Maida Avenue too. There weren't any photographers either, as far as I could tell. Before I got out of the car, I texted Stafford to suggest he have someone check if Dan was at Abercorn Close. A text pinged back immediately: 'From now on you just assume I know where he is.'

Something held me back from using the code to open the

gate. I rang the buzzer instead. The gate clicked open and Maya was at the door by the time I got there.

'I should give you the code to get in,' she said, kissing me. She seemed to have forgotten that she already had, and I didn't want to remind her in case she asked to have the key back.

For a woman who had spent the night on a transatlantic flight, she looked great. Her skin was perfect, her hair lustrous, her eyes alive and full of energy. I complimented her on it.

'I'm not the face of Europe's fastest growing upmarket skin-care product for nothing, you know,' she said, giving a mock toss of the head. 'Although, actually, I'm not renewing the contract when it comes up next month.'

'Why not?'

'Dan, Nick and I did a review of all the different things we're involved in, and that one bit the dust.'

'What kind of review?'

'Just went over everything. First me and Dan, talking it all over, sorting a few things out, then we got Nick in to go over the stuff that affected work.'

'And?'

'The top line is – we've sorted out our differences. I do the movie. We try for a baby.'

I was taken aback. Reconciliation was not what I'd expected.

'That sounds like a cosy little deal,' I said.

'Don't look at me like that!' she said.

'Like what?'

'Like I'm somehow caving in. Yes, Dan and Nick wanted me to do the film, but now we've sorted everything out, I want to do it too. It took lots of soul-searching and long phone calls between here and New York, but the main thing so far as I'm concerned is that we start trying for a baby. Plus I'm cutting right back on product endorsements, though we agreed we might do some advertising stuff together.'

'Lucky Dan.'

'Come on Steve, he's my husband. We talked a lot about all the anger and stress he is bottling up, and he has promised to go and see someone about it. That's part of the "deal" too. So you see, Dan's outburst actually helped solve our problems by getting things out in the open. In a way, I'm glad you helped bring it all to a head. It wasn't good for him to keep things hidden from me.'

I almost choked. How could she imagine Dan was no longer hiding things from her? The whole deal stank. Basically Dan had been rewarded for hitting her. She did the film. She helped him with his commercial tie-ups. And they had sex night after night no doubt, maybe mornings too.

Seemingly oblivious to my disgust, Maya went off on one about how she needed to show greater understanding of what it was like for Dan to be married to her, still a little bit in her shadow. She even said she was going to help him get some A-list guests from the States for his show so he could 'take it to the next level'. That was too much.

'For God's sake, Maya,' I said. 'Can't you see he is using you?'

'Don't be ridiculous Steve, it's nothing to do with being used. This is how it works in show business. People help each other. You don't understand because you're not part of it.'

'OK, OK, I'm not part of it, but I'm not stupid either. If Dan's so loving and loyal, why isn't he here with you this afternoon? You only just got home, for Christ's sake. Why is he out playing poker with his friend rather than here with his wife?' I felt like adding 'poker my arse' but it was important I stayed patient, let Stafford do his work.

'I could ask why *you* are seeing a friend today rather than staying home with Vanessa,' she said. 'You could even ask yourself.'

'It's totally different,' I shouted, outraged. 'Vanessa encouraged me to come out. She likes me to have an independent life.'

'I don't see any difference,' Maya said quietly.

We were silent for a few seconds, but we have always been able to move on quickly from little flare-ups, with each other at least.

'Sorry for going over the top,' I said. 'You're right. There's no difference. I just worry for you, that's all.'

'You've got Dan all wrong.'

'Yeah, I'm sure I have. Listen, I'm really glad you've worked things out.'

She went into the kitchen to make some tea and then called me through to the more lived-in of the two main sitting rooms downstairs. A giant TV screen dominated the far wall. The furniture was a little less glossy magazine. We sat on a low, wonderfully comfortable dark blue sofa, and she told me more about the film. It was called *The Hunter Hunted*, which I thought had a good ring to it. And I had to admit the plot made it sound like the kind of film I would want to see. Apparently it was about a New York-based hit man and his girlfriend. The girlfriend, who worked as a PA to an advertising executive, didn't know her boyfriend was a hit man. She thought he was an undercover cop with the NYPD. The two of them had this nice, romantic New York life until the son of one of the hit man's victims, a big underworld figure, discovered who had killed his dad. The hit man had to go on the run, and he took the girl with him. As they crossed America, she found out who he really was, and the relationship was thrown upside down.

'So *Bonnie and Clyde* meet *The Sopranos*,' I said. She laughed. I asked her who played the hit man and she let out a little squeal of excitement.

'Three guesses?'

'You know I'm no good at guessing.'

'Go on, you have to.'

'George Clooney?'

'A bit old!'

'Adam Sandler?'

'A hit man! Per-lease!'

'Oh I don't know, Danny DeVito.' She laughed, then leaned over and whispered.

'Matt Damon, that's who.'

'Oh my God. Vanessa will be beside herself.'

'Isn't it great? I have to say, that's what swung it. Don't tell Dan though.' And she let out one of her wicked laughs.

'So how long will you be away do you think?'

'Minimum eight months. I reckon more. I'll be in on all the pre-production stuff because of the money I'm putting in.'

'So you're producing it too?'

'Not exactly, but I'll be on the credits for more than just acting.'

'Great.'

'We're filming a big block in New York, and then we literally go all over the States, then Mexico, then over to the UK. There's a big final shoot-out on the London Eye. It's going to be so weird, me being an American in London. We don't start till September though.'

'Away for Christmas?'

'I'll be back and forth.'

'And if you get pregnant?'

'The producer and director are aware we're trying. They're fine with it.'

'What, just write in a pregnant girlfriend on the run?'

'Or hide it. Or it may not show. Or it may not happen.'

'Well, I hope it happens,' I said with all the enthusiasm I could muster.

She came towards me, and planted a kiss on my cheek. 'Thank you, Steve.'

A warmth had come back into Maya's voice. It felt like old times. When she first started getting work she would always call me first when she found out she'd got a part in an exciting new project. I thought of all the walks we'd gone on, with Maya babbling enthusiastically about this director, or that lead actor.

It was a beautiful, crisp afternoon, with a hint of spring in the air, and the sun was just beginning to go down. I took Maya's hand.

'Let's go for a walk by the canal!' I said.

'Are you joking?'

'No! Let's go for a walk. It's gorgeous out there, and the fresh air will help stop you nodding off when I've gone.'

She looked tense, undecided.

'I didn't see any photographers,' I said.

'Everyone is a photographer these days,' she said. 'I went for a quick walk round the block to stretch my legs when I got back and in ten minutes I had maybe six or seven people stop me and ask if they could take a picture on their mobile. That's in posh Little Venice. So you can imagine what it's like once you get closer towards the *Heat*-reading classes of the Harrow Road.'

'So what?'

'Well, it just takes one of them to snap you and me out together and before you know it it's been sent online or to a paper or magazine, and Dan sees it and goes ballistic. They pay readers to send in celeb pics on mobiles.'

'So Dan has banned all contact with me?'

She seemed embarrassed.

'Photos of me reflect on him too, you know. It's not just my own image I'm managing.'

'Ah yes, I forgot,' I said.

Maya noted the sarcasm in my voice and it seemed as if we were going to get back into the same row again, but then she stood up, clearly deciding she'd had enough of arguing with me.

'OK, let's go for a walk,' she said. 'Wait there while I get a disguise.'

I adored every second of it. I sensed she did too. She put her hair up in a bun under a baseball cap, the peak pulled down over her eyes and wrapped a big scarf round her neck so it covered her mouth. Each time we walked past someone who didn't recognise her we laughed and did our secret hand-shake. Soon we stopped worrying about it and just enjoyed being outside together. There was a reddish glow in the sky, which was reflected on the water, and the smell of woodsmoke from some of the barges felt warm and comforting. As we reached the footbridge to Harrow Road, she put her arm in mine, and squeezed it.

'Glad we came out,' she said.

We walked on as far as a small park, where a few kids were hanging out, close to a bench where two winos were working their way through a pack of strong lager.

'I think we should head back,' she said. 'Dan might come home.'

'OK, but first I want to say something.'

'Sounds like you're about to make a speech.'

'Come over here,' I said, leading her to the play area where a couple of dilapidated swings were hanging from a chipped metal frame. We sat down on them.

I cleared my throat. 'I know there have been a lot of things driving us apart,' I said. 'You think I'm not being supportive about Dan, and then there's Vanessa being pregnant and the baby, which will take up a lot of my time. And then maybe you'll get pregnant and be caught up in that. But I just want to say that, no matter what, whatever happens, I'll always be here for you. There's nothing I wouldn't do for you. You know that, don't you?'

She leaned over and put a hand on my knee. 'I do know that, Steve, and I'm very grateful. We'll always stay friends. I need you. You keep my feet on the ground.'

And, with that, she kicked off and started swinging as high as she could, and I pushed her even higher. We were giggling as we set off for the house. It felt as though we were 15 again.

After a while, we stopped talking and just walked, arm in arm. I wanted to stay in the moment, bottle it, keep it for ever. Even the presence of what looked like a lone hack in a white Audi, staking out the house from the other side of the canal, could not diminish the magic.

We had a final cup of tea together before I set off for home.

On the way back it dawned on me that the lone hack hadn't bothered to take a picture. It must have been one of Stafford's men. The thought troubled me, diffused the pleasure of the last wonderful hour.

'Must be horrible,' I said to Vanessa later that evening, after I'd told her about Matt Damon.

'What?' she said. 'Getting to snog one of the sexiest film stars on the planet?'

'No, being followed the whole time.'

Chapter Thirteen

Stafford was true to his word that it only took a couple of weeks for him to get what he needed on someone. I'd told myself that if, on the third Friday after our meeting, he hadn't been in touch, I'd call him. I didn't have to. He was in touch first thing that Friday morning.

'Can you talk?' he asked.

'Yes,' I said, trying not to sound too eager. I was sitting in my car in the Globus car park, having just arrived.

'We should meet.'

'OK,' I said. 'What have you found out?'

'Not a good idea to discuss it over the phone, Mr Watkins. Are you free tomorrow morning?'

'Yes,' I said, trying to remember if Vanessa had any Saturday plans for me.

'Ten o'clock. There are some parking bays right behind the Kensington Hilton. I'll see you there. I'll be on foot, so make sure your car is nice and tidy for me.'

With that, he chuckled, and put the phone down.

I suddenly noticed a slight tremor in my hands, caused partly no doubt by humiliation at being rebuked for my naivety about how such information is handed over, partly from nerves and excitement about a secret assignation in a parking bay.

Stafford's brief, enervating call turned Friday into a washout as far as work was concerned. All I could think of was what he might tell me in the morning. He knew already, whatever it was. I knew nothing. The power was with him. Jerry kept flicking elastic bands at me in an attempt to drag me back into his world.

First thing Saturday, I gave Vanessa the same old story about needing to go to the office to work on the Qatar project – the believability of which was enhanced by the fact she already knew that Brandon *was* actually due to fly out there the following week for the first presentation.

There were several empty bays behind the Kensington Hilton hotel, but as I drew up just after 9.45, I decided to park close to a builder's van. I had a coffee with me, which I'd bought in a café on the Goldhawk Road, but it was bitter and in any event, my stomach felt like a thick layer of air was swirling around inside.

With every passer-by, I felt a ratcheting up of the anxiety that had been with me since waking. None of them had a clue who I was, let alone what I was doing there, but I felt that they knew exactly what I was up to, and disapproved.

Stafford was bang on time, carrying a little leather attaché case and a brown sports jacket under his arm. It was surprisingly warm for the time of year and sweat rings were pushing their way out from his armpits. I was about to signal to him but he had clearly seen me already – I imagined they were trained in seeing before being seen – and once more I felt idiotic, and vulnerable. He opened the door and got into the passenger seat.

'We gather the secrets. We give the secrets. We keep the secrets. For you to decide what to do with them.'

With those words, he passed me a yellow folder, marked 'FAO client 532f, re Target 96c, personal'.

I stared at it with incomprehension, unsure what I was supposed to do next. I felt like a trainee bomb-disposal expert facing his first explosive device. As the yellow folder lay on my lap, I surmised, both from the way he had handed it to me, and his cocky demeanour as he had strutted towards my car, that he had unearthed genuine secrets. Secrets that could affect Dan's life, Maya's life, maybe mine. He was enjoying his moment of knowledge as power.

For the first time in our relationship, Stafford tried a bit of small talk.

'How do you like the Peugeot then?'

'Good.'

'We had one a while back. I found it a bit cramped. Switched to Saab. Then BMW. Now the wife is trying to get me to get one of these Prius things, save the planet and all that.'

He did not strike me as an environmentalist.

'This is a company car, so I don't have much choice really,' I said.

'Anyway,' said Stafford, resuming his professional tone, 'how do you want to play it? Read it now, with me here, or read it alone and see you later? I think you will find the money well spent. Very, very interesting. Better than the usual bollocks I deal with.'

The folder was held closed by two orange elastic corner bands across the top right and bottom right. I flicked them back, and opened it. There was a lot more than I expected. Maybe forty pages of text on plain white paper, not a bald eagle nor a red globe anywhere to be seen. The anonymity of the deniable document.

'Read the first page,' said Stafford, sensing as I leafed through it that I didn't know where to start. 'There's a summary.'

And so I did. No matter how badly I thought of Dan, what I read made me feel sick.

Main points

- Clear evidence of extramarital relationship.
- Clear evidence of drug abuse (cocaine).
- Inappropriate media relationships (clear use of partner for image building, including tip-offs re movements).
- Target's wife unaware of all of above.
- Finances strong.
- Professional position secure.

I laid the file on my lap, sat back and stared out at the dark grey, windowless building in front of me.

'How do you know all this?' I asked.

'It's in there, sir, in black and white. Movements. Meetings. Phone calls. You'll see.'

'*Clear evidence* of an affair?'

'Not a doubt. He goes there every couple of days at least, sometimes just for a quick one, other times he's there for hours. Second time round, we had inside covered for sound, outside covered for film. Page twenty-three I think.'

I turned to page twenty-three. Stafford pointed to the relevant entry.

'Target left Blomfield Road 1410hrs. Some evidence of fear of being under surveillance. Parked close to Lord's cricket ground. Walked to Abercorn Close. Entered private residence, Abercorn Close, 1440hrs.'

I felt seedy and dirty, like I was gorging on pornography, and Stafford felt like a dirty, seedy presence alongside me. His heavy breathing and faint smell of bacon added to the sense I was at the centre of a scene I should never have entered.

'Target and companion engaged in conversation. Subjects covered included Wayne Rooney, Target's programme ratings, Chinese restaurants, companion's argument with colleague, new Sean Penn film, a party Target's companion due to attend later, state of Target's marriage, plans for future meetings. (Transcript file 532f-qm6.) Target and companion moved to bedroom. Sexual intercourse took place. Target had shower. Target and companion returned to lounge area. Conversation returned to state of Target's marriage, partner's career plans, plans for future meetings. Target and companion had sex again. Target left 2150hrs. Walked to main road. Made phone call from outside St Mark's Church. Hailed cab. Returned to car, then Blomfield Road. Target arrived home 2202hrs. Target's wife at home after canal-side walk with unidentified male. (Some signs of intimacy. No evidence of sexual relationship.)'

He saw my wry smile. 'That you?'

'I thought I spotted one of your men,' I said. 'White Audi?'

'Couldn't say,' he said, winking.

I didn't want to read on. A man was walking by now with a young black Labrador, which had stopped directly in front of the car and was sniffing around for somewhere to pee. Walking the dog. What a wonderful simple thing to be doing, I thought. I wondered what kind of dramas and complications the man had in his life. Surely nothing like this.

'So?' said Warren Stafford. 'What do you make of it all?'

'Who is she?' I asked after a short pause.

'Turn to page three,' he said. 'Most fitting, don't you think, that the bird should be on page three of my report?'

I opened the folder again. Summary. Paragraph one. 'Target is conducting an illicit and sexual relationship with Sheila Hegarty, founder and owner of show-business website, We-know-the-stars.com. Phone records and private conversations indicate this has been going on for several months. Miss Hegarty was previously employed by Mr Nick Sheldon, show-business agent, who represents Target and Target's wife. Texts, phone calls and private conversations reveal that Target is passing Miss Hegarty information re Target's wife and others in her circle. Target's motives here are uncertain. He is not getting paid. There is no evidence that Target wishes to end marriage and put relationship with Miss Hegarty on a more permanent footing. Limited research leads us to believe Target may not be Miss Hegarty's sole companion. No firm evidence of this yet. She leads busy and varied social life, which may merit further investigation.'

'So Rudi doesn't exist?' I said.

'Nope. And the only poker game he is playing is with Miss We-know-the-stars.com.'

'Very funny, I'm sure.'

My head was numb. The facts of it were bad enough. But what was I to do with them? Could I trust Stafford or the people in his team not to go to the press? They might find it impossible to resist the huge sums they could make – far bigger than anything Globus was going to be billed for. And what was I going to say to Maya? Everything, or nothing?

'Don't you want to know about the drugs?'

'I suppose so.'

'Page eight.'

'Circumstantial evidence of drug abuse. Tuesday 1450hrs, operative 42 penetrated dressing-room area of Target's TV studio. 42 noticed significant mood change in Target between arrival at studios and broadcast, noted also nasal activity consistent with post-cocaine use. 42 penetrated Target's personal dressing room during transmission. Evidence of recent use of cocaine. (Trace filed in sealed envelope 532f-ev2.) Thursday. Recording of Target's visit to companion, Abercorn Close, indicates shared use of small samples of cocaine prior to sexual intercourse. (Tape 532f-ss3.)'

'Sex, drugs – just the rock and roll missing,' I said bitterly.

'You surprised?'

'Not really. The man's a bastard.'

'Yeah.'

'So he's telling this Hegarty woman what Maya's up to?'

'And what *he*'s up to. And their friends.'

'But not for money?'

'Nah. Because he's screwing her, and because he knows she'll put him in a good light, and because hers is the site the papers are tracking all the time. So it's a win-win for him. Shag whenever he wants. Great PR all over the fucking place.'

I tried to reply. No words came.

'Do you want to see what she looks like?'

Before I could answer, he took a hardbacked envelope from his briefcase.

'FAO 532f. Photofile 1' was typed just below a red 'Do not bend' graphic.

Inside were dozens of photos, some clear and sharp, others which looked like fuzzy copies of video footage. They were mainly of Dan. Leaving home. Walking down the street. Getting into a cab. Out of a cab. Getting into his car. Out again at the studio. Signing autographs. More cab rides. More walks. Arriving at Abercorn Close. And leaving. Then there she was. It was hard to tell from pictures, but in the ones they had of her walking out of her house, she looked tall. She had long brown hair. She was stylishly clothed in a simple grey dress with a little black bow and matching belt. Prada bag. Dolce and Gabbana shades. Not quite in Maya's league, but not far from it, and very Dan. She was good-looking, sexy, a few years older than Maya.

'Not bad eh?' said Stafford. I nodded.

'I've got moving pictures too, if you want to take a look.' He pulled out a small video camera, with its own built-in screen, and showed me a short film of her walking from her house, locking the door, clip-clopping in high heels over the cobbled close, down to the end of her little road, then getting into a waiting car.

'Very ladylike the way she swings her legs in . . . here you go . . . watch this bit.' There was something mildly perverted about the way he said it, but I had been right about Stafford's brutal efficiency. He had covered every angle.

'It's great that Abercorn Close is a cul-de-sac,' he said. 'Very useful for watching any comings and goings. And handy having the church nearby where my boys can go and pray to be forgiven for all the terrible things they do to dig up these secrets.' I looked over at him. He was smiling.

'Do you like your work?' I asked.

'It does me fine. I was a cop for most of my life, crap money, OK pension, dangerous at times, some nice easy periods. But the point was I had no control. My life was dictated by other people, a lot of them bad. Now I still work for other people, good and bad, but I do it the way I want to do it. I run my side of the business and it is successful and it means I have a nice house, nice holidays, and I give youngsters a chance to learn the ropes. So yeah, I do really.'

I nodded.

'One other thing,' he said. 'Page thirty-one. You'll see she's not the only media contact Maya doesn't know about. It looks like he's only shagging one, but he talks to plenty more. Tabloids especially, but some of these showbiz programmes too, and the mags. And if there is one thing these hacks love, it is someone who makes news talking to them about someone who makes even bigger news.'

Bright sunshine was hammering directly through the windscreen and I felt the beginnings of a headache. Stafford was suddenly a rude and unpleasant presence and I was desperate for him to get out of the car, to give me the space I needed to think.

'Well, that's that,' I said. 'Thanks very much. You can call your men off, now.'

Stafford bowed his head, in mock submission, but said 'I don't think we've got the whole truth about his philanderings yet.' He then threw me by asking 'Don't you want to know if there are any other women in his life?'

'Why would I think there might be?'

'He's booked a suite at the Savoy for next Thursday night. Now, why would he do that? He can bonk Miss Hegarty in Abercorn Close, he can bonk his missus at home. Perhaps there's someone else.'

I felt nauseous. Maya had told me she had a meeting in Paris on Thursday, and was staying overnight. Was there no depth to which Dan was not prepared to stoop?

Obviously I couldn't call a halt to the surveillance yet but

I was worrying about the costs. 'Are we inside the retainer?' I asked.

'I'm afraid not. What's more, your Mr Parry from Websters is coming up squeaky clean. Whatever he gets up to with young boys, he has got his tracks well covered. No one's talking. And I think that might mean there's nothing to say. We can't find any other interesting leads. Your man lives with a bloke, sure, a computer technician, but they've been together for seven years, got one of those gay marriage things. He is the main breadwinner, finances in order, no bad habits apart from the obvious, loves his mum clearly, boring old fart really. Now, there are two options: start a little surveillance of Mr Parry too, or drop the matter entirely.'

'Drop it,' I said, hastily. It seemed bizarre, and irrelevant, suddenly to be discussing Globus business in the midst of a Maya crisis, but I had to remind myself that this was the reason that I was involved with Swift International in the first place.

'You're the boss,' said Stafford. 'And Maya?'

I hesitated for a moment. 'One more week,' I said. 'Then we'll stop.' Despite all the risks, if there was more to know about Dan, I wanted to know it.

'Okeydoke,' said Stafford, stepping from the car. 'I'll see you later.'

Before leaving, he put his head back inside, looked at me, and laid the folder on the passenger seat he had just vacated.

'Your copy, sir,' he said. 'Careful where you leave it.'

Chapter Fourteen

'So Steve, you got all your Qatar stuff honed and ready to go?'

Jerry was looking his usual spruce self. Button-down collar, trousers with a fine Monday-morning crease. Shiny shoes, too. Apparently his son offered to polish them for him every Sunday night, for a pound. I, on the other hand, looked like shit. My eyes were tired and baggy from not sleeping. My shirt was all wrinkled because Vanessa was feeling too unwell to do the ironing.

'Wish we could be there to see Brandon hitting them with it in Doha . . .'

I didn't engage beyond a non-committal grunt. I needed Jerry to hurry up and go into his meeting with Brandon so that I could call Tim Waller at Swift International. The Qatar presentation seemed insignificant in comparison to the revelations about Dan that I'd been struggling with over the past forty-eight hours, but I was aware that I desperately needed something to give Brandon, now that the press rumours about Websters' finance director had turned out to be a dead end.

Jerry was in an irritatingly good mood, and insisted on showing me dozens of pictures of his daughter's seventh birthday party on his phone. Eventually he sauntered off and I immediately dialled Swift International and asked to be put through to Waller. After what seemed like about five minutes, an officious secretary told me that Mr Waller had assigned the case to his assistant, Luke Morgan, and it was he who would be talking to me. It was a nervy conversation; Morgan was clearly much younger, and new in the job. He seemed eager to make a good impression, but he was rambling and it made me anxious that Jerry might come back before the call was finished. Still, in the end I was glad I wasn't talking to Waller because it was evident I'd made something of a fool of myself. According to Morgan, if I'd read the issue of *Private Eye* that came out two weeks after the one I'd talked to them about, I would have seen that, far from being under investigation themselves by the Serious Fraud Office for accounting irregularities on the building project in Dubai, it was Websters who had drawn the irregularities to the attention of the SFO. And there was worse. Apparently I'd failed to see an 'Apology' printed in the *Sunday Telegraph* three weeks after they'd broken the original story. The young man read it out to me with exaggerated clarity:

In our issue of 19 January, we may inadvertently have given the impression that Websters, a logistics company based in Harrow, Middlesex, was investigated by the Serious Fraud Office over allegations of improper accounting. In fact we now understand it was as a result of Websters' alertness and public-spiritedness that the SFO were to mount a successful investigation into corruption concerning a building project in Dubai. We apologise for any misunderstanding. We have paid Websters' costs in this matter and have made a substantial donation to their partner charity, Leukaemia Research.

There was a short silence after he'd finished, during which he was clearly relishing his performance while I was feeling ever greater dismay.

'Right,' I said eventually. 'I'm sorry for wasting your time.'

'No time wasted,' said the young man pleasantly. 'It's what we're here for.'

'And there's nothing at all to implicate Websters?'

'I'm afraid not, no.'

'Then I'm fucked,' I said. The words slipped out without my meaning them to. They were a reaction to my state of nervous exhaustion and intense disappointment that what had seemed a pathway to Brandon's heart had in fact given him yet another stick with which to beat me. I immediately tried to back-pedal and put an end to the conversation via a succession of garbled apologies.

'May I make a suggestion?' said Morgan, interrupting my mumblings.

'Please do,' I said.

'Well, I happened to notice that Websters have failed to complete a couple of jobs on time recently. Perhaps you could get them for inefficiency rather than scandal?'

I leapt at it like a hungry bird pounces on a speck of discarded bread. 'Oh, that's great,' I said. 'That could be just the thing. Get me everything you can on it. As soon as possible.'

Suddenly I felt in control again. Like a man who had all the information resources of the world at his fingertips, and could wipe out his competitors by getting the right information into the right ears. But the feeling vanished as quickly as it had arrived. The second I had put the phone down on Morgan, I thought again of Stafford's sordid little folder, and the euphoria gave way to anger. I had no idea what to do with it.

I was trying not to be consumed by hatred. Why was it that Dan, who had never done a decent thing in his life, had everything going his way: Maya back onside through their dirty little deal, a job he loved, and a mistress who was happy to share him with his wife provided she could help him promote his career? It was disgusting. He needed to know that just as things could go right for people, so they could go wrong too.

What appalled me as much as anything was that he treated Maya with such little respect. Could he not see how special she was? It was as if fame had turned his life into a stupid game where all that mattered was how high up the celebrity pecking order he was, not the fact that he had the trust and love of one of the most beautiful, intelligent and talented women in the world. Well, it was about time Dan was taught a lesson. He needed to learn to value Maya by seeing what it might be like to lose her. He needed to know how it felt to be alone and friendless in the world, with no one to turn to.

I had buried Stafford's file at the very bottom of my briefcase. Now I took it out, looking around me to make sure I could read in peace, then turned to the page that summarised Hegarty's career path. 'You think you know the stars,' I muttered. 'Well I fucking know things you don't.' There was a telephone number for Hegarty's office listed. I was just about to dial it when Jerry came back into the office and I had what I thought was an inspired idea. Hastily packing Stafford's folder back into my briefcase, I painted on the gloomiest expression I could muster, and sighed loudly.

'Brandon wants to see you at 10.30,' said Jerry, as he sat down at his desk. Then he noticed my mood. 'Bad news?' he asked.

'Yeah.'

'Vanessa?'

'No.'

'Maya?'

'Yeah.'

'Shit, Maya again. If anyone had told me that by working at Globus I'd get inside information on the ups and downs of Maya Lowe's day-to-day life, I'd have thought they were barking! What's the problem this time?'

'She's in a very difficult situation. Apparently some bastard is tipping off the media about her movements, business decisions, all sorts of things that shouldn't be getting out.'

'God. How does she know it's one person?'

'Because it's happening so regularly. And there's a consistent pattern. She has a confidential meeting and the next day she's reading about it in the press. She goes out for lunch, the press know where she is.'

'Poor woman. It must be hell having to worry about things like that. Still, it's bound to happen. She's big news. Big news sells.'

'Yeah, but surely even if you're big news, you should be able to trust the people close in.'

'Real trust, Steve?' Jerry put on his 'I'm gonna dispense words of wisdom' face. 'Not easy. Not in any world, but certainly not in hers.'

I seized my moment.

'Could I trust you, Jerry?' I asked quietly.

'What do you mean?'

'She's asked me to do something for her, and I was hoping you might be able to help . . .'

I could tell he was excited. His chin jutted forward and his eyes widened.

'Shit, you know what a fan I am, Steve. What's she asked you to do?'

'Just make a phone call – one phone call that might help her find out who's doing this to her.'

His expression changed. Doubt crossed his face.

'Sounds a bit dodgy . . .'

'I promise you it's not. It's one phone call, that's all. The person on the other end of the line will have no idea it's you.'

'Are you sure this is not going to get me into bother?'

'I swear. It's just that you are the only person who even knows how Maya involves me in her life, and I want to keep the circle of knowledge as small as possible.'

'Why don't you do it?'

'Because the person knows my voice.' Though this was not strictly true, it was not impossible that Hegarty would be with Dan, who did know my voice. She might let him hear, or she might keep tapes of her calls, and play this one to him later.

'There's no risk to you. It's just a phone call.'

I could see he was hesitant. He needed to see I was adamant.

'Her next premiere . . . front-row seats, backstage passes, invite to the after-party, meet Maya, the lot. I promise you.'

'For the wife too?' he asked.

'Of course.'

He started to bob his head from side to side, indicating he was being swayed. 'OK,' he said, nodding. 'Who do I need to call?'

I wrote down Hegarty's number on a Post-it. Beneath it I wrote what I wanted him to say. My handwriting is not great, so I wrote in clear capital letters, which took me longer than I anticipated, and I could feel Jerry tensing and growing agitated alongside me.

'HI,' I wrote. 'YOU DON'T KNOW ME, BUT I'M INVOLVED IN THE DEAL FOR MAYA LOWE'S NEW FILM. YOU MAY HAVE READ ABOUT IT. ANYWAY, SOMEONE VERY CLOSE TO HER IS BETRAYING HER. SOMEONE

VERY CLOSE TO HER IS ALSO USING CLASS A DRUGS. I WONDERED IF YOU WOULD BE INTERESTED IN THE STORY.'

'Is that it?' asked Jerry.

'That's it.'

'And what do we expect him to say?'

'It's a her. Sheila. And we don't care what she says. You listen. Then see where it leads. I'll be here. Are you up for it?'

'Are we not better doing it from a call box?'

'It'll come up as a withheld number. When you call me at home it always does. Come on, I'll put it on loudspeaker so I can hear what's going on and give you a steer if necessary.'

'All right,' he said, taking a deep breath. 'But only because it's Maya . . .'

As he leaned towards the phone, dialled the number, and waited for the connection, I was sure it would go into voice-mail, or she would reject the call because she couldn't see who it was from. But she picked up after two rings, answering in a very clipped, South African-sounding voice. 'Sheila Hegarty.'

Jerry read his words to perfection. He sounded natural, at ease.

After he'd finished, there was a long pause, then Hegarty said, 'Who is this?' She was clearly rattled.

'It doesn't matter who it is. Do you want the story?'

Jerry was looking at me, ready to take direction, but he was doing fine and I nodded my approval.

'Who are we talking about?' she asked.

'What do you mean?'

'Who is this person who's supposedly so close to Maya?'

I leaned over and pressed the button on the console to end the call.

'Well done,' I said. 'That was perfect.'

Jerry was breathing hard. 'I don't know who or what Sheila Hegarty is but she was panicking big-style, I would say. I could hear it even before she spoke. Is she the one you suspect?'

'No. She's the one who gets the tip-offs from the suspect. Hopefully this will lead us there.'

After his initial nervousness, Jerry seemed energised by being involved. He dropped his fists hard on to the table and laughed, then rubbed his hands together as his laugh reshaped itself into a mischievous grin. I asked him to promise me he would not discuss it with anyone, including his wife. 'Don't worry,' he said. 'And if you need someone to bounce things off, just let me know. But don't lose sight of the main picture Steve – it's got a camel in it, and it begins with a Q.'

'You bet,' I said and tried to settle back down to work. It was difficult, though. I was conscious of feeling wired. In an effort to calm down, I went to the toilet to wash my face. As I stared in the mirror, I saw unrested eyes staring back at me, and spoke to my reflection. 'Stop doing things without thinking them through, you fool.' I nodded. 'Be strategic. That means work out the strategy first, and let the tactics follow. That was a fucking tactic. But does it fit the strategy? Answer? You don't know, Steve, because you haven't thought it through.'

Someone came in. I stopped talking to myself, went to the roller-towel and dried my hands and face. I walked back to my desk.

'Maya called,' said Jerry. 'Literally ten seconds ago. First your mobile went, then your landline. I hope you don't mind. I answered it for you in case it was urgent.'

'Shit – you didn't say anything? About the call I mean?'

'No. Why?'

'That's good.' Across my mind the narrowly avoided worst-case scenario was racing — Maya calls, asks for me, I'm away from my desk, Jerry says he's just called Sheila because he's trying to help Steve find your mole, Maya, and she thinks what the fuck is he talking about, and asks him, and he blunders on, and in one stupid phone call, I get completely found out and done in.

'It's just that I never mentioned I was going to get someone to help me.' I felt my heart slowing.

'It's bloody weird hearing her voice,' he said. 'Even now, when I should be used to it, if it's her on the line, I find it very odd.'

I hated lying to Jerry almost as much as I hated lying to Vanessa. He was my closest colleague, like a partner. What really troubled me was the ease with which I seemed to be able to do it. And soon, I was probably going to be lying to Maya too.

I decided to wait before calling her back. I really had to sort in my own mind where all this was going.

I went back to the toilet and this time locked myself inside one of the cubicles. Then I stood against the door and tried to think through what I knew. I knew that Dan was having an affair with a showbiz journalist. I knew that he was taking drugs. I knew that he was tipping off the press about things Maya thought to be secret, not just her movements but also her business and professional dealings. She had shown herself capable of forgiving his violence against her, but could her understanding extend to betrayal on this scale? I could imagine Maya thinking that one of these issues could be dealt with, if Dan was repentant enough. But all three? It seemed highly unlikely. I had the power in my hands, if I wanted to use it, to destroy the marriage. But was that what I wanted? To what effect? If all it created was a media battlefield strewn with bodies, and Maya hurt and saddened, did I really want to be responsible for that? Wouldn't it be a case of 'shoot the messenger', and my friendship with Maya ending up as one of the battle casualties? No, I needed to slow down. I couldn't simply rush towards the pleasure I could get in hurting Dan, seeing him crumble, maybe driving him from our screens. I had to reflect more deeply.

Meanwhile I had to call back Maya. I stayed in the toilet and rang her from my mobile.

She answered after one ring, and she sounded flustered.

'Sorry to call you at work, Steve, I just needed to get something off my chest.'

'No problem,' I said, heart racing a little, wondering what it could be.

'It's just that Dan's let me down over a charity dinner we were supposed to be going to tonight, a big fund-raiser for breast cancer. I have to make a small speech, do the raffle. It's not a big deal but I wanted some moral support. Now Dan's just phoned to say he's really sorry, he completely forgot, he and Rudi are in a poker tournament tonight, one of a series, he can't get out of it. It's strange that he should prioritise poker over this dinner. I mean it's a good PR event for him too . . .'

'Fucking hell!'

'What?'

I didn't routinely use such strong language around Maya, but I was reeling from the realisation that Jerry's call to Hegarty had had just the impact I had wanted. Hegarty had clearly called Dan as soon as she got the anonymous phone call. Dan must then have decided he had to go to see her, after filming his show, to find out more. So he had called Maya with the old Rudi lie.

But now I had a different problem to deal with. Maya was no doubt wondering why a fairly routine statement that Dan was standing her up for a game of poker had provoked such a strong reaction.

'Sorry for swearing like that,' I said. 'A colleague just showed me something while we were talking. A work thing. Bit of a shock. Nothing important. Sorry. Yes, a last-minute poker tournament does seem a bit odd. Maybe he's just not into breasts – cancer I mean. Or maybe you should be sending him to Gamblers Anonymous.'

Maya sounded pissed off. 'I don't see what there is to joke about. I called you for a bit of sympathy.'

'I'm sorry,' I said, 'but is it really so bad? You know you can handle dinners like that on your own. You've done it plenty of times before.'

'It's not so much the dinner, it's the fact that he's spending so much time playing poker. You joke about Gamblers Anonymous but it's like it's becoming an obsession. I'm worried he's hiding something from me – like it's not really about the poker at all.'

I was close to blurting out the whole story, but clenched my right fist tight and told myself it wasn't the moment. If I was going to tell her, I had to know what I was going to do next.

'You know my feelings about Dan,' I said, 'but things may not be as bad as you think. Discuss it with him in the morning,' I suggested. 'See if you can work out what's going on. It's probably what he says it is.'

'Yeah, you're right. Maybe he just doesn't fancy another evening as Mr Maya Lowe. It's very hard for him, you know.'

'Sure,' I said. 'I know.'

I looked at the time and realised that I was already three minutes late for Brandon. Trying to give Maya some final words of reassurance while straightening my tie, I rushed out of the toilets and ran straight into Brandon himself.

'Going somewhere in a hurry, Steve?' he asked, smirking.

'Sorry Mike,' I said. 'It's just that I was on the phone to Waller. It seems we're on to something.'

He took me to his office and I proceeded to give the speech of my life, telling him how I'd asked Swift to follow up on a tip I got which suggested they had screwed up some big contracts, and that this was now proving a more fruitful line of enquiry than the SFO probe. Brandon looked, for him, quite impressed. Between us, we devised a medium-term strategy. It would be a few months before the Qataris made their decision. Brandon's meeting in Doha at the end of the week was simply to present Globus to the Qataris as a contender for the contract: a question of describing the company, its achievements and capabilities, then doing a lot of non-alcoholic socialising. If he got through that – and we were confident – the Qataris would outline their requirements and then fix a date for Brandon to return with a more concrete pitch for the specific business, currently being done by a Dutch firm the Qataris had fallen out with. By then, Swift would have done all their research and Brandon would be in a position to campaign aggressively against our competitor, as well as set out our own stall. I left Brandon's office feeling a renewed confidence. Strategy. That was what it was all about. I could do this.

I was halfway along the corridor when Stafford called my mobile. There was no small talk. Not even a hello. He sounded cross.

'Have you been talking?'

'What do you mean?'

'I mean what I say. Have you been telling people what you saw in the file? It's your info and you do with it what you want. But if you want us to keep proper tabs on this feller, for fuck's sake don't alert his fucking bird.'

'I didn't.'

'Oh really? Well, she gets an anonymous heavy breather saying someone close to the Target's wife is betraying her and taking drugs, and immediately she calls your man and tells him she thinks they may have to go easy, not see each other so much for a while. Doesn't exactly help us, does it, if they kind of half suspect someone is spooking them?'

'I told nobody,' I said.

'Well, in which case there's someone in your office who's doing it, which is a bit fucking unlikely, is it not?'

I said nothing.

'Listen,' he said, 'you're the client, so you're always right. And you will have your own reasons for what you're up to, and that's fine. But while we are on the case, it is honestly best that you just leave it to us. If you want to tell me what you plan to do with the information, fine. If not, also fine. But you will get a better job done by us, if you let us do it properly. Have you got that?'

'Yes, I understand.'

I looked hard at my mobile. Were they bugging my phones too? How did they know the call to Sheila came from Globus? It was important not to get paranoid, but it was difficult not to feel it, especially as I reflected on Stafford's parting homily before he hung up.

'There's a saying in my world, Steve, and you'd do well to learn it: know your own depth, because if you don't, you'll end up out of it.'

Chapter Fifteen

I had another Dad dream that night. It was unlike any I'd had before. Normally I'm in the dream too, but this time he was alone, and tranquil, sitting cross-legged on a darkly creosoted bench in Mr Lowe's garden. He was wearing clothes of my era not his – denim jeans, a polo shirt and trainers – and smoking a cigarette, smiling as he surveyed the landscape. In my dream I knew it was Mr Lowe's garden, even though it was my dad sitting in it, because I recognised the greenhouse. Other things in the garden were unfamiliar – the bench, a little stone statue of a rabbit – but every detail of the church-shaped greenhouse was exactly as I had seen it, from the lavender paint on the timber frame to the clutter of plant pots inside. The scene was so vivid that it woke me up.

The only illumination came from the bedside clock. It was 4.24. On empty roads, I could be in Taplow in half an hour, even less if I went for it. I could be in the Lowes' garden before it was light, certainly before they were up. I could be back home before Vanessa was awake. 'We give the secrets, we keep the secrets.' Stafford's words seemed to wake with me. I was grateful to the dream. I'd been torturing myself about how to get Maya the information she needed without her knowing it came from me. Now I knew how I could do it. Stafford was right. I was out of my depth. Far better to let someone else take over.

I slipped out of bed. I wished I could cleanse the grime from my teeth but worried about waking Vanessa, whose gentle breathing I could hear as I grabbed my clothes and made my way, as quietly as I could, downstairs. My briefcase lay at the foot of the ornamental umbrella stand in the hallway. I took my key and opened it, removed the yellow file, and crept out, stopping only to take a straw hat from the old box filled with clutter beside the umbrella stand. Furtiveness amplified every little sound I made. As I pulled the front door closed, I realised I needed an envelope in which to put the file. The beauty of the report itself was the absence of any markings. It could have come from anywhere. Stafford's yellow file, with the client and Target number on the front, gave an unnecessary clue. The chances of finding an open shop selling envelopes en route were small, so I endured the torture of more noisy, nervy blundering around in the dark as I went back into the house, and found a fresh A4 brown envelope in Vanessa's bits and bobs drawer in the kitchen.

The biggest risk now was that she would wake on hearing the car engine starting. It was parked directly beneath our bedroom window. I found myself trying to turn the ignition key slowly, as if it made the slightest difference to the volume. The engine started up first time, and immediately REM blared into action on the radio, which I hurriedly switched off. If she had woken on hearing the car choking into life, her immediate fear would be theft; she would reach over to me, see I was not there, jump up and come to the window. I waited for almost a minute. Satisfied she was still sleeping, I set off.

There were more cars on the road than I expected, and a

hint of dawn in the sky that made me nervous. The curious light appeared to be taunting me. It was as if nobody was quite sure whether it was day or night. The hazy grey sky, and the headlights coming towards me as I crossed Hammersmith Bridge, belonged neither to one nor the other. By the time I reached the motorway, the inside lane was almost as busy with vans and lorries as when I drove to work. As I passed Heathrow, the first planes of the morning were queuing to land. It had taken a journey out of my usual time zones to see what '24-hour London' really meant. There were lots of places open where I could have bought an envelope.

Just before I got to Taplow, I pulled into a lay-by. I had to decide how much of Stafford's file to hand over. I already knew I didn't want to give the transcripts. Too much information. Stafford had kept the envelope with the cocaine trace. It was the photos I wasn't sure about. There were so many. Tipping them out on to the passenger seat, I sorted through them. They needed to tell a story. I selected four in which Dan looked shifty, and laid them on the dashboard. Then I found one of him entering the house in Abercorn Close, and another of Hegarty leaving. Finally I added a couple in which she looked particularly glamorous. I realised there were none showing the two of them together. So the disc which contained the recording of them taking cocaine and having sex would have to go in too. By the time I had put what I wanted into the envelope, and the rest back into the yellow folder, it was starting to get properly light. I needed to get a move on. I had one last conversation with myself. Was this the right thing to do? Would Mr Lowe definitely see the envelope? Would he know what to do with it? Would he know how to play a CD? Would it definitely get back to Maya? Who would they think could have done this?

I couldn't be certain about the answer to any of those questions, apart from the first one: it *was* the right thing to do, I was sure of it. I put on my straw hat, and drove to within a couple of hundred yards of the Lowes' driveway. Then I stuffed the envelope inside my jacket and got out of the car.

If anyone had asked me to describe the entrance to the house based on my earlier visit, I'd have said it had a thirty-yard concrete driveway broadening out into a pebbled parking area. In fact, the pebbles started as soon as I walked off the road. I stepped on to the grass verge beside the drive to avoid the scrunching sound they made, then wove through the apple and cherry trees at the side of the house before halting beneath a giant conifer. I was now at the edge of the lawn and faced a choice. I could walk straight across it to the greenhouse, about a cricket-pitch length away, or continue to work my way through the trees and shrubs at the edge of the garden, which seemed three times larger than I remembered it. I was sweating, and the occasional snatch of birdsong disturbing the stillness made me even more aware of the sound of my own breathing. It also spoke to me of passing time, and the day beginning. I pulled my hat down further over my eyes and strode out across the lawn, resisting the urge to turn round and look at the house, to see if any curtains were open upstairs. I needed to focus on one thing: getting to the greenhouse and putting the envelope in an obvious place for Mr Lowe to find it.

In my isolation, the swish of my feet in the grass and the rustle of my arms rubbing against my sides sounded deafening, but eventually I was there. The greenhouse door was ajar. I pushed it open, slid through. There was a shelf immediately to the left, covered in plant pots. I placed the envelope between two of the pots. But it did not stand out there. Looking around, I spotted a green electric lawnmower tucked into the far corner, beneath a hanging basket and a coat rack full of old jumpers and jackets. I lifted out the mower, and placed it just inside the door. Anyone going in would virtually trip over it, I thought, so I propped up the envelope where the handle joined the mower. Then I ran, head down, back across the grass.

As I drove away, I found myself gagging, as if bomblets of air were gathering in my chest then forcing their way through a throat that didn't have room for them. I worried I was about to vomit, and wound the window right down. I had no water, and no time to stop to buy some. It was 5.41. I was determined to be back in bed by six. Luckily, by the time I reached the motorway, I could feel a little moisture and normality coming back to my mouth. I put my foot on the accelerator and managed to get home within the time I had set myself. I replaced the straw hat in the box, took off my shoes and crept upstairs. Unfortunately, when I was halfway up, a light went on in the bedroom. Vanessa must have heard me.

'Hello?' I heard her say, the voice a mix of straightforward enquiry and burgeoning anxiety.

'Hiya,' I said, trying to inject normality into the situation.

'Where've you been?' she asked, unsure whether to be angry, or fearful.

'I woke up in a total panic about the Qatari job,' I said, finally reaching the bedroom and seeing her, sitting up, agitated.

'Why?'

'I was convinced I'd left all the papers on my desk.'

'So what?'

'Brandon would have gone mad. There are some real security issues on this one.'

'So you've been to the office?'

'Yeah. Sorry. I didn't want to wake you.'

'And?'

'They were in my briefcase. Idiot or what?'

I couldn't tell if she believed me or not. 'Steve, you're doing too much. You're getting stressed out.'

I sat down on the bed and put my arm round her.

'I know,' I said. 'But if this deal comes off, it'll be worth it, believe me.'

Chapter Sixteen

There were some beautiful pictures of Maya in the morning papers. I hadn't realised the fund-raiser had been a big black-tie ball, and she was wearing a stunning evening gown, full-length, with just the hint of a train, so in one of the pictures she was delicately holding her dress up after getting out of the car. It was light cream, worn off the shoulder, with a slight pelmet at the top, and a jewel effect patterned down one side, curving over from the back to the front of her waist, and over her thigh. The picture most of the papers used, though, several of them big, on the front page, was taken as she was doing the raffle. She had to lean forward low into a tombola drum to draw out the winning tickets and as she did so, the photographers got a clear shot of her breasts as the top of her dress hung away momentarily from her skin. I could tell looking at her face that she was shocked at the sudden explosion of flash bulbs, so the picture was a wonderful mix of innocent eyes and alluring flesh. Even the *Daily Telegraph* had her on the front, under the headline 'Maya does her bit for breast cancer'. The tabloid captions were less subtle. 'Maya pops out for breast alert' was the *Daily Star*'s effort, complete with a plug for their website 'to see Maya's *oops* moment in full-colour video'.

I was leafing through the papers in the foyer of Globus when Brandon came in, pulling a suitcase on wheels.

'Flight leaves at seven this evening, Steve,' he said as he strode towards the lift. 'Come to my office with Jerry at 3.30 and we'll have a little team drink before I set off.'

'Sure, Mike,' I said, surprised. 'We'll be there.' I hoped he clocked that, for once, I was in before him.

With the first stage of the Qatar presentation up and ready to go, things were quiet in the office. I desperately sought to distract myself from thinking about when Mr Lowe might find the envelope, and what he would do when he did, by checking out the internet for pictures of Maya and her breasts. There was blanket coverage.

'Bloody hell,' said Jerry, catching a glimpse over my shoulder. 'That body is something else.' When we went down to the canteen for a coffee mid-morning, we stood in reception and watched Sky, which was running a loop of Maya leaning down to draw out the raffle ticket, along with a red button/green button survey asking whether or not she had done it on purpose. They also had an interview with the showbiz editor of the *Mirror* who said they'd had more hits on their site than when Britney shaved her head. Although I was sure Maya would be annoyed with herself for giving the media such an easy shot, I imagined the charity would be pleased about all the attention they were getting, and that would probably please Maya. She was selfless that way. Thinking about her generosity to others made me nervous again about Mr Lowe and the envelope and what he would say to his daughter. I couldn't bear to see her suffer.

'You all right, Steve?' asked Jerry as he headed out for a meeting in town. 'You look pale.'

'Fine,' I said, trying to buck myself up. 'See you at Brandon's drinks do.'

He hadn't been gone long when Maya's number flashed up on my mobile. I looked at it, lying on my desk, and I went cold. This was it, I thought. She'd found out.

'Hi there,' I said, but I knew my voice was weak and reedy. Her voice was stony, distant. It made me even more convinced she'd had the bad news. In fact it turned out that I was wrong about her being pleased for the charity. She was furious with them for their mispositioning of the tombola drum, convinced the organisers had set it up deliberately that way, and furious with the general public for being so interested in her anatomy.

'I can't believe people think I would do a thing like that on purpose,' she moaned. 'I mean, what do they think I am? Some kind of reality TV publicity junkie?'

'They don't think you did it on purpose,' I said, citing the result of the Sky survey in which a clear majority had voted to say they thought it was an accident. 'The public love you, Maya. They're always sticking up for you.'

'Well I wish Dan agreed with you. He hit the roof, talking about how I only did it to embarrass him because he didn't go with me.'

I suddenly knew what gobsmacked meant. I felt like the air had been punched out of my lungs. What was it with Dan? The guy went off to screw some showbiz hack and snort cocaine and then had the nerve to upbraid his wife for doing something he was constantly nagging her to do in the first place – namely get herself on the front pages even when she had no film to promote. It seemed my attempt to put the wind up Dan, and get him to cherish Maya a bit more, had had absolutely no effect whatsoever.

'Did you ask him about his poker playing?' I asked, trying to suppress all the rage I was feeling.

'It didn't seem like the right time,' said Maya. 'In the middle of our conversation, his producer called to say they were switching the misery slot from teenage parents to breast-cancer survivors, and he went into this great rant about how the world was conspiring against him.'

I shook my head in wonder at his ability to be both sinner and victim at the same time. 'So how did you leave it?'

'That we'd talk about it tonight. I'm dreading it though. I just don't know how to get through to Dan at the moment. He promised things were going to change, but nothing's different. He is so het up all the time, like stressed. I know live TV every day is not easy, but it really seems to be getting to him.'

'Not helping the sperm count either, I imagine.'

'I'm so glad you're concerned. I'm afraid there's not been enough of that going on for the sperm count to matter.'

'That's the first good news I've heard.'

'Now now, you were doing very well till then.'

There was a pause as we both wondered whether the conversation was going to tip into an argument. Then I had an idea. Brandon was going away. It would be easy for me to nip into town for a long lunch tomorrow. I should suggest to Maya we meet. That way I would be able to find out if Mr Lowe had said anything to her between now and then.

She seemed really pleased at the idea. 'That would be great. Not in a restaurant though. I can't face going out. Come to the house, and I'll get some food brought in. I could maybe even make something myself. But no facetious comments about Dan, OK?'

'Promise.'

'Perfect, see you then,' she said, and rang off sounding much happier.

When I wandered along to Brandon's office that afternoon, I was amazed to see he'd opened a couple of bottles of champagne. Alan Thompson from accounts was there, and a few people from contracts.

Brandon made a little speech. 'Maybe this is premature, folks,' he said, 'but as I prepare to set off on this journey, I've got a good feeling about the deal, and I want to thank you all for the hard work you've put into this first stage, particularly you two.' He nodded towards Jerry and me. There was a faint murmur of 'Hear hear'. 'You know my approach: you set the objective for the operation, then you build the strategy, then you perform the tactical execution. For Operation Qatar, so far so good. It's been hard work. There have been ups and downs, but I think we are getting there. And seeing as I'm not going to be offered a drink for a while, I thought I'd call you in for a toast.'

We were all raising our glasses when suddenly there was a commotion outside in the corridor; the sound of running and then a lot of shouting. Finally Brandon's PA put her head round the door and said, 'I'm sorry, Mike, but there's someone out here who insists on speaking to Steve. Somehow he managed to bust his way past reception. I'm terribly sorry.'

I felt the chill of fear. My first thought was it was Dan. Brandon gave me a quizzical look.

'Work related, I hope.'

'I'm afraid I don't know,' I said, aware of everyone in the room scrutinising me as the atmosphere suddenly fell flat. 'If you'll give me a minute, I'll find out who it is and be back as soon as I can.'

As I turned the handle of Brandon's door, I could feel sweat beads pricking through my neck.

It was Mr Lowe. He was sitting on one of the leather armchairs in the breakout area, his head in his hands. He looked up as I went over.

'I'm really sorry about this, Steve, but I had to see you. Something terrible has happened and you were the only person I could think of. I just don't know where to turn.'

'Don't worry about it, Frank,' I said, throwing a glance over my shoulder to see if anyone was watching me. But the champagne drinking had recommenced and there was a reassuring hubbub coming from Brandon's office. 'Let's go down to the canteen. I'll get you a cup of tea and we can talk there.'

I was grateful for the queue at the tea counter. It gave me a chance to think about how to react to what I knew Mr Lowe was about to tell me. It was at moments like this that I appreciated Maya's skill all the more – her ability to cry or laugh to order. I was going to have to pretend that everything Mr Lowe was divulging was completely new to me.

As the queue shuffled along, and I made the occasional friendly nod in the direction of Mr Lowe, waiting for me at the corner table near the vending machines, I put into my mind the notion that I was a boxer. I thought of the big Joe Calzaghe fight I'd been to with Jerry last March at the Manchester Arena. I wasn't a big boxing fan but Jerry had got tickets through a contact and it was just a fun thing to do. Calzaghe was up against an American, Jeff Lacy, who was favourite to win. But Calzaghe absolutely battered him. The papers the next day said he threw more than a thousand punches in twelve rounds. Lacy's face at the end was a mess of cuts and bruises. As I paid for the two teas, I decided that was how I'd play it: like an exhausted Lacy taking blow after blow from Calzaghe as he hung on to the ropes.

I took the cups of tea over to Mr Lowe. He added a spoonful of sugar and began to stir it in. He looked tired and old.

'Is Mrs Lowe all right?' I asked, trying to start a conversation, but also to cement the idea in his mind that I knew nothing of what he was going to say.

'Anna? Oh yes . . . It's nothing to do with Anna.'

'Maya then?' I pretended to be alarmed. 'She hasn't had an accident has she?'

'No, no, she's fine . . . Or rather, she is now, but she may not be soon.'

'I'm sorry, Frank, it's hard for me to know what you're saying . . .'

'Well, it's like this. I've found something . . . awful. And I don't know what to do with it.'

'Found what?'

His story was so long-winded that it was difficult to concentrate, since I already knew the punchline.

'Well, I was out shopping with the wife this morning, then we thought we'd go into Reading for a cup of tea and a look around, but I fancied getting back to the garden, it being such a lovely spring day. I've got some new stuff for the borders, and I'm thinking I need to get on with it. So the thing is, you see, I have this little routine when I'm doing the garden. I get my tea, I walk around the place having a fag, deciding how I'm going to spend my time, then I go into the greenhouse, and I always change into one of the pullovers or coats in there. Daft really, but it's a way of making the garden separate from everything else, I guess. So I finish my fag, I walk into the greenhouse and I can see straight away, someone has been in there. I always have my lawnmower in the same place, right in the corner, and it's been moved out to the middle. So I'm thinking what the hell, burglars or something, and I'm looking around . . . and then I see there's an envelope, sitting on the mower, so now I'm really thinking this is all a bit strange, you know, so I pick up this envelope, just an ordinary brown envelope, I open it, and it's like a big document, lots of pages, with photographs . . . pictures of Dan, and some woman, and there's one of those CD things.' He paused to take another sip of his tea. 'So I start reading the stuff and . . . and . . . oh my God Steve, I can't tell you . . .'

'Can't tell me what?'

'It's here,' he said. 'Read it.' And he pulled out my envelope from the bag he was carrying and laid it on the table.

I stared at it. It was bizarre to be looking at something so horribly familiar and have to pretend that I'd never seen it before. I pulled out the pages of the report, and started to read, all the time reminding myself to think 'Joe Calzaghe, Jeff Lacy, Joe Calzaghe, Jeff Lacy, punch, punch, punch.' I felt as though I did a pretty good job. As I read Stafford's main points, I took the first blow – extramarital affair – like a hit to the side of the face; my eyes opened wide, I jerked my heard towards Mr Lowe, then shook it back. The second – drugs – was the follow-up shot, and now my mouth was gaping open. At the final pummelling – Dan was tipping off the press about Maya left, right and centre – my head fell forward.

'What the hell is this?' I asked.

Mr Lowe let out an enormous sigh and stared into my eyes.

Then he looked down as though consciously trying to regain composure and stay calm, not cry.

'I don't know. Just arrived, like I say, in the greenhouse.'

'But who put it there? Why?'

'I don't know. I just don't know.'

'Do you believe it?'

'I was trying not to, but then I listened to this.' He held out the CD. 'You can listen to it if you want, but I don't advise it. It's a load of grunting and snorting and generally foul language, but it's definitely Dan talking to some woman who is not Maya.'

I knew it all too well. I had listened to it several times: Dan saying 'You go first', then the sound of first one sniff, then another, then a female voice saying 'Good stuff', then Dan saying 'Not as good as the stuffing you're gonna get', then her saying 'You're all talk', him saying 'We'll see about that', then laughter and the voices becoming weaker as they moved somewhere else, then stronger again, kissing and groans and Dan saying 'Aw Sheila, I just love this, I love it' and her laughing again, more kissing, more moaning, on to the end.

'Jesus,' was all I could think of saying.

'This'll kill them both,' he said. 'Not just Maya, Anna too. Anna adores Dan.'

'What a bastard,' I said.

'Yep,' said Mr Lowe. 'I think you can safely say that's exactly what he is.'

'So what are you going to do?' I asked.

Mr Lowe put down his cup of tea. 'That's what I was going to ask you.'

We both looked down, and then looked up again, and saw the fear in each other's eyes.

'I have to tell her, don't I?' said Mr Lowe, clenching his fists.

'You could talk to her agent,' I suggested.

'Sheldon? No fear,' he said. 'This is about her now, nobody else. The rest can fuck themselves.' I had known him on and off for twenty years. I think it was the first time I had heard him swear. His face was returning to its usual, pinkish colour. There was a determination and a clarity in him that I had seen from an early age in his daughter.

He stared out of the canteen window, lost in his own thoughts for half a minute, then turned to me and said, 'I know what to do about this. I'm going to tell her straight. And I want you there when I do it. I value your friendship with Maya and so does she. She will need it more than ever once this hits her.'

I don't know what I had imagined when I crept across Mr Lowe's garden at dawn, but I hadn't expected that it would lead to precisely the thing I was trying to avoid: me being present at the breaking of the news.

'Do you think it's really appropriate for me to be there?' I asked, hesitantly.

'Sod appropriate,' Mr Lowe said. 'It's necessary. I don't think I can do it without you.'

There was no escaping. I was back into something I had hoped to be out of, although at least with a cover story.

'OK,' I said. 'Of course if that's what you want, I'll be there. As it happens, Maya and I are due to have lunch tomorrow at Blomfield Road. Dan will be filming his show. You could come with me, and we could do it then.'

'I don't think I can wait that long,' he said. 'I can't bear the idea of that man spending another night next to my daughter.'

'I think you have to wait,' I said. 'It's really important that Dan isn't there when we talk to her, and the only way to be sure of that is to do it while he's at work. Just be strong. We'll get through this, I promise you.'

I was patting Mr Lowe's hand when suddenly Mike Brandon's voice boomed across the near empty canteen.

'So, business or pleasure?'

He was standing in the doorway, wheelie suitcase at his heel.

'Neither, I'm afraid,' I said grimly, looking apologetically at Mr Lowe.

'Well, hopefully it will be resolved by the time I'm back,' said Brandon. Then he marched off to catch his plane.

'Good luck,' I said. But I don't think he heard me.

Chapter Seventeen

'As big days go, this is a biggie,' said Vanessa into the mirror as she made herself up before work. I was putting on my tie, just flicking the long bit over the short bit, and I stopped, shocked at what she was saying. What did she mean?

'I'll meet you in the foyer of the hospital at half three,' she continued, and I suddenly remembered. We had an appointment for our first scan.

'Yeah, great,' I said, 'big, big day.' I had completely forgotten about it. 'See you there.' I hadn't thought through what might happen after Mr Lowe and I had broken the news to Maya, but I figured I should be able to get away by three and be at the hospital in time. I had to really. It was one of those moments.

Mr Lowe and I had arranged to meet outside John Masefield's house. It was a quiet Wednesday and I hoped there wouldn't be any photographers about. As Mr Lowe pulled up behind me, I got out of my car and went to sit in his, where the offending brown envelope was lying, accusingly, on the dashboard. He looked dreadful when he arrived, more dishevelled than ever. He clearly hadn't slept well.

'How should we play it?' he asked. 'Should we go in together?'

I'd thought about this and I much preferred the idea that Maya should think I was hearing the news for the first time too, but I wasn't sure Mr Lowe would want to participate in this kind of deceit on his own daughter.

'Won't she think we're ganging up on her?' I asked. 'If we both pile in with a folder full of evidence?'

He seemed swayed by this.

'Hmm. Maybe you're right. Perhaps you should go in, as if you're having lunch as planned, and then I should turn up, sort of unexpectedly? There's no need for her to know that you've already heard about all this . . .'

'Yes!' I thought. That was exactly how I wanted it to go.

'I think that's right,' I said to him. 'I can assess her mood before you arrive, then I'll be better placed to help you both when you tell her.'

I left Mr Lowe sitting in his car, staring gloomily at the brown envelope. Crossing the bridge over the canal, I couldn't see any photographers. There were a couple of guys leaning against the railings a few houses down from Maya's who might have been pressmen, though neither of them took pictures of me. As I was pressing the buzzer on the gate, I heard one of them speaking Russian. Russians – there's something else my dad wouldn't recognise. London is full of them now, either working men doing up houses, or the super-rich buying them, along with Dad's football club. But at least they weren't press.

Maya was wearing denim jeans, flat black shoes and a red zip-up top.

'It's so good to see you, Steve,' she said, leading me into the dining room where lunch was laid out – a lavish plate of charcuterie (lots of salami I noticed), expensive bread and a fantastic-looking salad. 'I hope this is going to be enough food.

I sent the maid out to get stuff and she seems to have been in a frugal mood.'

'It looks great,' I said, 'and anyway, I'm not that hungry.'

It was true. If it's possible for a stomach to feel light-headed, that's how mine was feeling, and my throat was dry, the top of my mouth crusty. The dining room looked different from when I'd last been in there. Maya had replaced some of the paintings with a series of classy black and white photographs, each with a tiny plaque at the bottom of the frame, inscribed 'London life, to Maya and Dan, from Patrick'. Maya had worked so hard to build this perfect, beautiful life, and I was about to throw a bomb into it.

'So, did you talk to Dan?' I asked, barely managing to get the words out.

'I did. We had a long chat last night and he was amazing. Very open about his problems and really apologetic. He recognised the poker playing has been getting out of hand and he said he was going to have a break from Rudi for a while.'

'Right, OK . . .'

'And he admitted that sometimes he finds it really difficult dealing with the fact that I'm so much more famous than he is. He was very honest about it.'

'So you think you two can work things out?'

'I'm sure of it. I feel if we can just be honest with each other, we can get rid of the things that are coming between us.'

I was sitting with my arms crossed and I could feel my pulse in my armpit, going way too fast. I thought to myself, I cannot do this, I cannot be responsible for making Maya so unhappy. I'd always thought 'Ignorance is bliss' was a stupid saying, just an excuse to sweep unpleasant facts out of sight. But right now it seemed the best, the wisest course of action. I needed more time to think about this. I had to call Mr Lowe, stop him from coming.

'Maya, can you give me a second to make a call?' I asked, making for the door. 'I've got to meet Vanessa later – for our scan – and I've just remembered I need to arrange the time with her.'

'Sure,' she said. 'Stay here and make it. I have to go and fetch the wine from the kitchen.'

But just as she was walking down the hall to the kitchen, the doorbell rang. I was too late. Shit.

'Dad!' I heard her say, as she looked at the video screen inside the door. There was shock in her voice. She pressed the button to let him through the gate, then waited by the open door as he walked towards her.

'What is it? What's wrong? Is it Mum?'

'No, no,' said Mr Lowe.

'What then? Something's up, I can tell. I've never known you just turn up without telling me you're coming.'

'There's something I need to talk to you about, love,' said Mr Lowe. 'Can we go and sit down?'

'Of course,' said Maya, sounding more and more worried. She was talking fast. 'But Steve's here for lunch. He's in the dining room. What should I do? Shall I tell him to get started without me?'

I'd worried about Mr Lowe's acting abilities, but I needn't have.

'Steve? Oh . . . well, that's good I think. It might be an idea for him to be there when I tell you this.'

'Tell me what, for God's sake? Dad, will you please explain what is going on?'

I went to stand in the doorway of the dining room so that Mr Lowe could see I was there.

'Steve,' he said. 'I've got some bad news for Maya and I think it might help if you could be with us when I tell her.'

Maya had gone white.

'It's Mum, isn't it? You're lying to me. It's Mum.'

'No, love, honestly. Let's go through here.'

I took her arm and led her to the sitting room, where I guided her and her father towards the large white sofa and then went to stand close to the window.

'So?' said Maya, looking at her father with large, scared eyes.

'It's about Dan, love.'

'What about Dan? God, has he had an accident?' She raised her hands to her cheeks.

Mr Lowe had the look of a man about to dive through ice into freezing water.

'You need to see this,' he said finally. He had a B&Q shopping bag with him, from which he took the envelope, removed the report and handed it to Maya.

'This arrived in my greenhouse yesterday. No explanation. You should read it.'

'Why do I have to read something? Why can't you just tell me?'

'I can't. Please, read it.'

I stepped in. 'Maya, you're going to have to be strong, whatever it is. You should do as your dad says.'

Maya looked as if she was about to carry on arguing, but then with slightly trembling hands she took the papers and began to read. It was unbearable to watch. I knew those pages so well. I watched her eyes fall upon each dire revelation, watched the pain etch more and more into her brow, watched the incomprehension spread across her face. After four pages, she looked up.

'Is this from a newspaper?' she asked, handing me the pages so I could read them.

'I have no idea, love. It just arrived in a brown envelope.'

'But it could be nothing,' she said. 'It could be some lunatic fantasist just messing around.'

'There's pictures love, and sound.'

'*Sound*? What do you mean *sound*?'

'Darling, believe me, you don't want to know. But I know. I don't know where it came from, or why, but I know it's true.'

'What do you mean *sound*?' Maya insisted with a steely glare.

Mr Lowe looked like he had been punched. With huge reluctance, he reached back into his bag and pulled out the CD.

'What is this?' she asked.

'*Sound*,' he said. 'Sound of him and his fancy bit, snorting cocaine and having sex.'

She held it, a plain silver disc with a hole in the middle, through which she slipped her little finger, then spinning the disc round and round with her thumb, she stood up and walked to the door.

'Where are you going, love?'

'To listen.'

'Please Maya, don't. Reading about it is bad enough. You don't need this.'

But she walked out, CD still stuck to her finger.

'Go with her, Steve,' said Mr Lowe. 'Try to make her see sense.'

I followed her up the stairs to her study, calling to her that she should take her father's advice. But it was pointless. She was determined. She had to know.

She put the disc into a laptop on her desk, then went to stand at the window, looking out over the canal. When she heard the snorting of cocaine, she shook her head gently from side to side, and her shoulders sagged a little. When the word-less noises became those not of flirting and foreplay but of a couple making love, him groaning, her screaming, the sound of a slap from time to time, she banged her wrists against the window frame. And when the voice of Dan said 'I love you, Sheila', she turned towards me, tears rolling down her face, and said simply – 'Bastard.'

'My God!' I said. 'I never liked him but I can't believe he'd do something like this to you.'

I walked over to her, put my hands on her shoulders, and pulled her towards me. Her hair smelled of honey. Her sobs were now spasms of pain and loss, a woman in grief. After a few moments, she pulled away from me and slumped into a chair.

'It can't be true.' She clasped her hands tightly together and held them in a reddening knot just under her chin. Mr Lowe appeared in the doorway. 'I can't believe this, Dad. I can't. I just can't.' And she started to cry again. He walked to her, put an arm around her shoulders, and she collapsed in towards him, sobbing. 'This cannot be happening,' she said through the tears. 'It cannot be happening.'

Eventually she calmed down, and I went to the kitchen to make some tea. I came back to find her sitting staring at a picture of Sheila Hegarty.

'She is the scheming bitch who was crawling all over me after last year's Baftas,' she said. 'It's why the press always know where I am and what I'm up to.'

'Like at our lunch at La Forchetta,' I said. 'Jake whatsis-name, We-know-the-stars.com.'

'Bloody Rudi! I was right. It wasn't about poker. I thought he was having a good time with his mates, and actually he was being led astray by some star-fucking bitch. What an idiot I am. I should have been more, I don't know, more alert. Women like Sheila Thingy zone in. It happens. I should have seen it. I should have done something to prevent it.'

'Maya, you've done nothing wrong. He has,' I said.

'You don't know him, Steve,' she snapped. 'He's so vulner-able. I could have protected him, if only I had seen what was happening. He needs me.'

Mr Lowe took her hand.

'I think Steve's right, love,' he said firmly. 'I don't think he's got any excuse.'

'Does Mum know?' Maya asked. He shook his head. I watched a tear fall from the corner of her eye, roll slowly down the little line on her cheek to the left of her nose. She put out the tip of her tongue to catch it and rolled her tongue along her top lip. The beauty was still there, but she was in pieces.

'Mum'll be devastated,' she said.

Mr Lowe nodded. 'I know, love. We all are.'

She stood up quickly, and stomped towards the TV, newly discovered anger driving out the calm of the last few moments in every step. 'I want to see what he's doing,' she said. It seemed an odd reaction, but she switched on the TV, and flicked the remote to channel three. Dan was standing with a big smile on his face, holding his clipboard, interviewing two bikini-clad pole dancers. A tickertape ran along the bottom of the screen 'after the break . . . Big Guest . . . M&S boss on why he wanted Dan's Maya on his posters . . .'

'I refuse to believe he'd use me like that, Dad,' she said. 'He's been put up to it. Drugs do that to people. That bitch got him hooked, then manipulated him. Don't you think, Steve?'

It was a hard question for me to answer. Also I was pre-occupied by time. It was getting on. If I was going to be able to leave for the hospital, we had to get the situation sorted as quickly as possible.

'Maya,' I said, trying not to sound rushed. 'Why don't you put a few clothes into a bag and then your dad can drive you back to Taplow. You'll have some space to think there.'

'Good idea, Steve,' said Mr Lowe. 'She'll need to plan the divorce very carefully. Someone like Maya can't leave her husband without the whole world knowing about it.'

'Divorce?' She looked thrown, as if she was only just thinking about the idea. 'No! I want to stay here. I want to confront him about everything.'

'Is that wise?' I said. 'Think about what happened last time you two had a row.'

Maya seemed overcome by uncertainty. Mr Lowe wanted to know what had happened.

'I guess I might as well tell you, Dad,' she said quietly, 'since you're involved in all this now. We had a fight a few weeks ago, and Dan . . . he pushed me. I fell and hurt myself. I thought we resolved things but, anyway . . .'

I watched Mr Lowe's face turn from pink to red. I'd never seen him so angry. He looked as if he wanted to punch the walls down.

Maya got up and started pacing the room.

'Nick. I need Nick,' she said. 'He always knows what to do. And he'll have some idea what sort of creep is behind this disgusting document. It's scary, Dad, to have someone getting that kind of detail on your life, following, taping, taking pictures. We're talking criminal stuff.'

Mr Lowe nodded. I said nothing.

Maya had suddenly flown into manic mode. She was desperately searching for her mobile, which I remembered she had left downstairs on the dining-room table. I put my hand on her arm. 'If you really feel you need Nick now, let me drive you to his office,' I said.

'Are you crazy?' she practically screamed at me. 'I can't deal with this in a fucking office, with God alone knows who else there, and people wandering in and out. Do you think I can risk his PA hearing me tell him my husband is betraying me, or one of his other clients? Do I want to be seen in the street like this? Sometimes I think you haven't a clue what it's like to be me, Steve! You just have no fucking idea.'

Mr Lowe gave me a sympathetic look but I covered up my hurt by trying to be efficient. Dan's show finished at 3.15. I pointed out that assuming Dan was coming straight home – admittedly not certain – he could be here pretty soon. End of programme. Make-up removal. Change. Maybe have a drink and a chat with the guests. Home by 4.30.

This panicked Maya even more.

'Nick needs to get his ass over here right now,' she said. 'Fast. Where the hell is my phone?'

I ran downstairs to fetch it for her. The dining room looked forlorn, with its untouched lunch and empty wine glasses. The maid was hanging around the kitchen looking confused. I told her she should go home.

Nick was in a meeting when Maya called. His PA informed her he was at the Lanesborough hotel, which Maya told us was his favourite place to meet clients, just down the road from his office off Hyde Park Corner. She knew not to bother calling his mobile because he always switched it off when he was seeing people. She told his PA it was triple urgent and ordered her to go round to the hotel immediately and tell him to call. She reckoned it would take the girl three minutes to get to the hotel, almost as long to puncture Nick's irritation at being interrupted and then another couple of minutes for him to extricate himself from his meeting. She was pretty accurate. Ten minutes later her phone rang.

Maya put on her 'listen to me, no nonsense' voice, and though I could sense in the silences Nick's questions and protestations, he was clearly having trouble holding out against Maya's determination that he should do as she said. She was still, after all, his most lucrative client, even if some of his footballers were catching up.

'I'm sorry to disturb you, Nick, and I wouldn't have sent Carol round if it wasn't important . . . I understand that but listen . . . I have to see you, and I mean now . . . I have to see you and I have to see you without Dan . . . So you need . . . listen to me Nick, you need to get to him and I don't care what it is but you have to give him a reason why he has to be somewhere else till say half six at the earliest, maybe seven is better . . . no Nick, I can't say, but believe me, you have to do this . . . Yes, there is a problem . . . yes, a big problem . . . no, you can't talk to Dan . . . I want to talk to you first, nobody else apart from the people I'm with . . . That doesn't matter Nick . . . Look, the longer we talk now, the more time we waste. Please, get over here and find a way of stalling Dan . . . OK, bye.'

She came off the phone, looked at her dad, and said,

'Sometimes even the ones who aren't wankers can behave like they are.'

'You need to decide what you tell him,' I said.

'Everything, I think,' said Mr Lowe.

She nodded.

'Probably.'

I glanced at my watch. I had to go.

'Listen Maya, you probably don't want me around now, so I'll head off . . .'

'What?' She looked distraught. 'You're leaving me alone in the midst of all this?'

'Not alone. Your dad's here.'

'*Us* alone, then. Don't go, Steve. I really need you on this one. I don't think I can face the rest of the day without you.'

'But Nick . . . He might not want me to—'

'Sod Nick,' she said with surprising force. 'Nick does what I say.'

I explained that Vanessa had her scan, and was expecting me, but she was adamant.

'Vanessa will understand. It's only a scan. It's not as if she's giving birth.'

'I'd better go and call her,' I said quietly, and walked into the upstairs sitting room, a small cosy den where Maya tended to hang out if she didn't have guests. There was no way I could admit to Vanessa that I had to miss our first scan because I was with Maya. I told her that Brandon had called from Doha demanding urgent last-minute information for his presentation, and Jerry and I would have to stay late to get it for him. She was calmer than I expected about it. 'I think they give you a photo,' she said sadly. 'You can see it then.'

After she hung up, I stared out over the forbidding black fence with its security cameras, and watched a young couple who were sitting cross-legged on the roof of the barge moored directly in front of the house. They were sharing a cigarette, and laughing at a story the woman was telling. They looked so happy, so carefree. The woman's face was so animated, yet her demeanour so relaxed. I wished I was the man listening to her, particularly when I saw Nick Sheldon's cab pull up outside. He had a large brown briefcase with him and he was stuffing papers back into it even as he was paying the driver. He was clearly flustered, and emanated a gruff irritation with every step he took from the gate up to the door. I heard Maya greet him and ask him to follow her into the downstairs sitting room. He sounded surprised to see her father. He was even more surprised to see me when I went down to join them.

'Hello, Steve,' he said. 'I wasn't expecting to see you here again so soon.' He did not offer his hand. I guessed he was aware of Dan's views of me, even before the altercation he had witnessed at the dinner party. He threw his coat over the back of a chair, removed his jacket, walked to the far window and then turned to face everyone. 'So?'

Maya was very businesslike now, determined not to let her emotions overwhelm her, though I knew she was in turmoil inside, while her father made a point of sitting right by her, with his hand on her back.

'Sorry to drag you out, Nick,' said Maya, 'but we have a real problem and I need your advice on how we deal with it in the short term. I think you should sit down.'

'I'm fine. I prefer standing when I don't know what's going on. It gives me more options about where I go if I don't like what I hear.' He undid the top button of his shirt and loosened his tie. He looked much bigger standing up than sitting down, which is how I had mainly seen him when we were here for dinner. As the top of his shirt opened, a spare chin fell down to fill the space.

Maya put her hands in her lap. 'OK. Well, there is no easy way to say this so I will say it straight out. Someone left a brown envelope in dad's greenhouse. It had evidence inside that Dan is having an affair, still snorting coke, and tipping off the press about me.'

'What?'

'Which bit didn't you understand?'

'I understand it all. I was asking what you mean by "evidence".'

'What looks like a surveillance report. Page upon page of it, pictures and a nice sound-only tape of Dan screwing someone who's not me.'

'Is this some kind of joke?'

'Am I laughing?' she asked.

Mr Lowe took him the report. Nick stood by the fireplace, skim-reading, his demeanour becoming more grave page-turn by page-turn. When he had finished, Mr Lowe showed him the photos.

'Christ alive, it's Sheila,' he said. 'I never thought Sheila Hegarty would go that far.'

'You know her?' asked Maya.

'Used to work for me. Got a horrible feeling I introduced them.'

'Thanks.'

'Are we one hundred per cent sure this is bona fide? It is amazing what people can do with technology,' he said. 'I think we need to be a little careful here. Dan does not go overnight from good guy to bad guy.'

'Tell him about Dan's behaviour on the night of the dinner party, Maya,' I suggested.

'I know all about the dinner party,' Sheldon said, rather curtly. 'I was there, remember?'

'There's something else you need to know,' said Maya. 'After you'd all gone, Dan and I had a row. He acted aggressively. I got hurt. Black eye. To be honest, ever since then I've known something was troubling him, I just didn't know what . . .'

Sheldon scratched the side of his nose, then ran his finger along his bottom lip, giving himself time to think.

'You weren't kidding when you said it was urgent. Jesus, I'm sorry, Maya. This must be devastating for you.'

He paused again, looked at Mr Lowe, then at me. 'You're happy to have this discussion with others present?' he asked her.

Maya was crying again now, as if the smidgen of human sympathy shown to her by Sheldon had opened the floodgates. 'Yes. Steve is my oldest friend.'

'OK,' he said, going over to Maya and putting his arm round her. 'Here's how I see it, Maya my darling. First we have to work out whether or not it's a stitch-up. Yes, Dan may have lashed out at you in a moment of anger, but that doesn't necessarily mean he's an adulterer. Someone might be trying to set him up.'

He ruled out newspapers as the source of the envelope. 'If they had this kind of stuff, they would want it as a story. The only possible exception is someone inside the newspaper who is suffering a conscience attack and wants to tip you off that the story is about to blow. But I doubt that, somehow. There aren't too many people in newspapers who lie awake at night worrying how movie stars are going to feel about having their marriages wrecked. No, this seems more like the work of an enemy. Someone working up a story to get at Dan. Perhaps a TV rival, inside or outside ITV, trying to take him out. Or, it could be a love rival of course . . .'

'Me? Another man? News to me,' said Maya, wiping her eyes.

'Thought so . . . Anyway, leave it with me, Maya darling. I have a few cop friends, who know about this sort of thing, and I think I can trust them to be discreet.'

He wasn't looking at me as he said it, but I felt the words were directed towards me, and it made me nervous. I sipped lukewarm tea from the red and white striped mug in my hand.

'As for you and him, Maya,' he continued, 'what do you want to do if it turns out to be true?'

'She'll leave him, of course,' Mr Lowe said, speaking for the first time since Sheldon had arrived.

'Is that what you want, Maya?' said Sheldon, putting his hand on her arm.

'I don't know! I don't know what I want,' she wailed.

At this point Mr Lowe came over and put his arm protectively around her.

'If this turns out to be true,' he said, 'she's leaving him, and that's final. There's no way I'd allow a snake like that anywhere near my daughter.'

'The press will think they've died and gone to heaven,' said Sheldon, getting out his phone and punching in some numbers. 'Carol,' he barked. 'Where are we at with Chivers? Going OK?'

'Where is he?' Maya asked after he'd got off the phone. Her expression was a mixture of hurt and fury.

'I pulled one of my footballers from a visit to St Thomas' Hospital,' Sheldon said. 'Told Dan he had to stand in, talk to some of the kids, sign a few autographs. He'll be through by six-ish. We need to make a plan. Perhaps it's helpful that I'm his agent too, although of course, Maya darling, if all this turns out to be true, I won't be any more, don't worry about that.'

Maya was holding her father's arm now, clinging to it, as if he might be able to put everything right, like he did when she was younger. But he had the look of a man who knew he was powerless. Maya no longer inhabited his world. There was nothing he could do to help.

'I want Mum,' she sobbed. 'Get Mum!'

'I'll call her, love,' said Mr Lowe. 'Perhaps she could get a taxi here.'

'No!' said Sheldon, seeing the situation get out of hand. 'When you have a mess, the best thing is to clear it up, and this is what we have to do. We have to buy time. I need to check the veracity of these allegations. Maya needs to work out what she wants. If we have to go public, then we need to do so on our terms: take Dan and Hegarty by surprise, making clear Maya is the wronged party, and with enough detail for the media to go and bother other people rather than her. We say nothing about secret reports or private detectives. We say nothing about him hitting her. We let the drugs thing come out, but we say nothing about it once it does. We simply tell them that he has admitted to an inappropriate relationship with another woman who has used him to get information about you, and Maya has decided this is unacceptable behaviour. She is heartbroken, but sees no alternative except to make a clean breast of it.'

'At least they'll have the pictures to illustrate that,' I said, trying to lighten the mood. My joke fell flat. Maya smiled weakly. Nick ploughed on. I felt a fool.

'As for timing, my desire would be to sit on this until there is a day when the news is completely swamped by something else. I don't know, India and Pakistan go to war, or the Queen dies, I don't know . . . So the question is, Maya, can you live with it for a little while yet, not let Dan know what's going on?'

She snorted at him. 'You are kidding me? What, like he comes in and we eat together and sleep together and laugh and joke and generally have a nice husband-and-wife time, and then we wait for a war, or a bomb to go off in the Tube and only then do I say "Oh by the way darling, I hear you're screwing Sheila Hegarty and filling your nose full of drugs every time I'm not looking." I don't think so.'

'Fair point,' he said. 'I'm just thinking aloud here, and remember, none of us knows the truth for sure yet. OK – what about saying your mother's ill and you've gone to Taplow to look after her. You stay there for a few days, you have the occasional phone call with Dan, but you don't let on. Meanwhile, I get everything organised, and if necessary prepare statements, work out the parameters of a legal settlement, tee up a few people to say the right thing for when the shit hits the fan, and then we go for it.'

'There is something in what Nick is saying,' Mr Lowe said, clearly relieved that someone was taking charge of the situation. Maya looked at me. I nodded. 'It's only a few days,' I said.

'I've got that meeting in Paris tomorrow night,' she said to Sheldon.

'I can get it postponed,' he said.

'I know I am an actress, but I'm not convinced I can pull this one off.'

'Think of the alternative,' said Nick. 'He comes here tonight. We tell him. He confesses. You kick him out. He's straight off to Sheila. And maybe she is madly in love with him and she thinks "Hallelujah, I've got my man." But if Sheila is the same Sheila I know and don't much love, she thinks "Halle-fucking-lujah, I've got the biggest story of my life and I can get it out there on my website without anyone even knowing I've been screwing him, and I've hit the media big time all of a sudden. I'm getting asked on to every TV and radio chat show. I'm being inundated by the papers and the mags. I'm made." That's what happens, Maya. So we lose control. He can say anything he wants by way of defence. She will milk it for everything it's got, including if it comes out that she was the one having the relationship. What skin off her nose? She's a single woman. She's a showbiz journo, and she gets the biggest showbiz story of the year. Win-win for Sheila. It's what she's always been about. Sheila number one, two and three, with Dan and whoever else she is shagging a long way behind.'

Maya looked to be in pain now. 'I'll go and pack some stuff,' she said. Mr Lowe went with her to help.

'What a horrible world you live in,' I said to Sheldon when they'd gone. I knew it sounded pompous but I was both impressed and disgusted by his analysis of Sheila Hegarty's character.

'Yeah well,' he said. 'There will be some like her in your business too. Just that the stakes are higher the further up the fame-and-money ladder you go. All around Britain tonight, there will be people facing up to the end of their marriages, coming to terms with betrayal and deceit, telling new lies to cover up the old lies, worrying about the effect on their nearest and dearest, their jobs, image, reputation. The only difference for these guys is they have to do it in public, and the public think they have a "right to know".' He raised the first two fingers of both hands to mimic quotation marks, signalling his belief that the public had no such right at all.

'Live by the media, die by the media?' I asked.

'No, more that you've got to take the rough with the smooth, and just get used to the fact there is no longer much difference in the media's eye between the public interest, and what the public is interested in.'

He was over by the window, half addressing me, half talking to the air above the canal.

'The thing is, you're in the logistics business. I'm in the illusion industry. Films are an illusion. TV is an illusion. They parade as reality, but they're necessarily manufactured. And the industry's job is to feed the illusions people think they want to have. They want to think they know Maya and Dan. Like they're neighbours, or relatives. Why is she "every man's fantasy"? Because men want it to be OK to have the fantasy, and if everyone is having it, there must be nothing wrong with it. Look at what happened when Diana died. Millions of people crying their eyes out like they'd lost their own flesh and blood. And then getting all steamed up because they thought *her* flesh and blood didn't care as much as they did? The illusion they had was that their "love" for Diana, and her feelings for them, were real. And do they still lose sleep over Diana? Course not. They go and see the movie

The Queen, and have a good night out. They've found new objects of illusion. Leona Lewis – they think they could be her because she came from nowhere: one day nobody, the next a superstar. Jordan – a whole media industry made out of two manufactured tits. But millions of women and kids look up to her.

'These poor fuckers – they've lost faith in God, Queen and country, so they pour it into their illusions. And the punters are convinced that what they think about their objects of illusion matters because you've got all these damn fool TV and radio stations saying send us your views by text and email, and call in. I ask you, what kind of saddo has nothing better to do than phone a radio station and talk about Maya's and Dan's marriage? Well you wait, because the answer is all kinds of sad fuckers. They'll be calling and texting and emailing and the presenters will be jerking themselves off saying they're part of the great national conversation, but what's it about, Steve? Nothing really. They're in illusion land, and a few people get fat and rich creating the illusions for the sad fuckers to believe in.'

'Like you, you mean,' I couldn't resist saying.

'Yeah, like me. But it's different. I believe in talent – in helping talent. My dad worked in the fishing industry. Got laid off in the early eighties. I came home from school and my mother was sitting at the table looking like her family had been wiped out by the plague. And I said to myself there and then, I will never be dependent on a boss for my success or prosperity, I will make my own. I said I'm never going to do a tough physical job, I'm going to use my brain and my character. And I'm going to help others make the most of their brains and characters too. It paid off. My mum and dad now live in a six-bedroomed mansion at the other end of the country, overlooking the sea in Northumberland, which I bought for cash with the ten per cent I took from one year's salary on one of my Arsenal players. They go out walking with their dog Samba every morning and every evening. They go on holiday every summer to Florida and every spring to the Lakes and they are finally happy. That's what I've managed to do for them. After all, when it comes down to it, family's the most important thing.'

It was a touching speech for such a tough operator. Much as I disliked Sheldon, I couldn't help welling up inside. I thought of Vanessa and her scan, and the fact that I wasn't there, and I wanted to cry. Sheldon was clearly discomforted by the emotion in my face because it provoked a return to his hardbitten persona.

'Anyway, enough of this crap. We need to sort out this fucking mess.'

I followed him out into the hall. Mr Lowe was coming down the stairs with Maya's suitcase.

Sheldon called Dan.

'How's it going?' he said. He laughed at whatever came back in response. 'Well, thanks for doing it. Those footballers are so bloody unreliable. I owe you one. Speak tomorrow.'

'I don't know how you can still talk to him like that, Nick,' said Maya, who was standing at the top of the stairs pulling on a black woollen jacket and putting on her dark glasses.

'You of all people should know when a little acting is necessary, Maya my sweet,' said Sheldon. 'Now off you go to your mum, and let me sort all this out. I know it's horrible for you, but you also know, there's not much Nick Sheldon can't fix for his number one and only superstar.'

'A marriage?' asked Maya with a brittle smile.

'Well, maybe not a marriage, but I can fix how a marriage is perceived. And sometimes that can help.'

I thought Maya was going to cry again. But she strode down the stairs, buttoning her coat, her dad following on behind with her bag.

When she reached the door, she stopped to hug me.

'Thank you, Steve,' she whispered.

I kissed her cheek.

'You'll get through this, Maya,' I said. 'I know you will.'

Chapter Eighteen

In as much as I had prepared myself for my arrival back home that evening, I think I had expected to find Vanessa sitting at the kitchen table, looking proudly at a small black and white photograph of our clearly visible foetus. The scene that greeted me couldn't have been more different. She was lying on the sofa, weeping, with her sister trying to comfort her.

'Thank God you're home, Steve,' Judith said as I walked into the room. 'I came round as soon as I could, but Vanessa really needs you. She didn't want to ring you at work, because she said you were up against a deadline.'

As I rushed over to her, my first thought was that she'd had a miscarriage. Judith saw the panic in my face and tried to reassure me.

'No, it's not that. It's a little worry the scan threw up. There's something called a nuchal measurement and it wasn't quite what it should be, which can sometimes be an indication of a baby being Down's. They want Vanessa to go in for an amniocentesis test.'

'Honestly Steve, I'm sure it's going to be fine,' Vanessa said, unconvincingly through her tears. 'The doctor said it was just a precaution . . .'

I looked at Judith for guidance. 'Amnio-what? I've never heard of it.'

She passed me one of the leaflets that were lying on the coffee table.

'Take a read of these. But remember they always say the worst thing, so don't get alarmed.'

It was hard not to. The very first sentence – 'Amniocentesis is a diagnostic test performed on pregnant women to detect chromosome abnormalities' – had enough in it to start the panic. Chromosome was a horrible word. Abnormality was worse. The second sentence cranked up the alarm. 'In particular it can alert mothers to the possibility of Down's syndrome or other congenital problems in the child.' And by the time I had read the next paragraph, printed in a lovely and totally inappropriate pastel shade, I felt like my chest was going to explode. 'It is a commonly used, safe practice, but which carries a small – less than one per cent – risk of miscarriage. It is almost one hundred per cent reliable in detecting any chromosome abnormality, for which there is no treatment. It is therefore important for expectant parents to discuss in advance of an amniocentesis whether or not the mother would wish to terminate the pregnancy in the event of an abnormality being detected.'

'Christ, Vanessa, you mean we may have to decide if we want to keep the baby or not?' I said.

'It won't come to that,' said Judith. 'They just need to be careful, that's all.'

She stayed for supper during which she tried to reassure us with statistics about the number of women who have amniocentesis tests where no abnormality is detected and no miscarriage precipitated, but it was impossible to stop feeling anxious.

When she finally left, Vanessa and I sat and held each other. It felt strange – as if we hadn't been so physically close for a long time.

'I can't believe I wasn't there with you,' I said, stroking her hair. 'I feel awful about it.'

'That's OK, Steve,' she said. 'I know what work is like at the moment. And money's important too. I mean, God, if we end up having a disabled child, we're going to need every penny we can get.' And she started crying again.

I suddenly remembered the car drive when I took Maya to have her abortion. I hadn't thought about it for years. Like Maya, I'd buried the memory, as if by doing so I could bury the event and no one would ever find out. It was perhaps the only untold secret of her microscopically examined life. Even her parents still didn't know. At first I'd been terrified that a doctor or a nurse might think of making a few quid by telling the press, but as the years had passed and nothing happened, that seemed increasingly unlikely.

I remembered how calm Maya had been. Unlike poor Vanessa, currently sobbing into my shoulder. Or me. I'd been confused about this child, not sure if I was ready to become a father. Now, faced with the idea of losing it, I suddenly wanted it more than anything I'd ever wanted in my life. At that moment, as I moved my hand backwards and forwards absent-mindedly across Vanessa's back, I made a resolution. I would start putting Vanessa first, and I would never let anything stand in the way of my being the husband and father she and our child were entitled to. I'd done a lot for Maya. I'd been there for her whenever she needed me. I'd just rescued her from a bad marriage she was too blind to see. Now I could step back. She had other people to look after her. When the contents of the file were proved to be true, Sheldon would steer her through the nightmare of all the publicity. She would immerse herself in her work once more. With the help of her lovely parents, she would recover, and no doubt she'd soon find another, more worthy man. Of course I would miss being a central part of her existence, but I told myself it would be better like that. I needed to get back to my own life, start giving my wife some attention.

I had forgotten, of course, about Stafford. He called me on Friday morning just as I was pulling into the Globus car park. He was so far from my thoughts that I didn't even recognise his number on my phone.

'The eagle has landed,' he said.

'What?' I said. 'Who is this?'

'You don't remember? How quickly you move on, Mr Watkins.'

'Mr Stafford?'

'Who else?'

'I'm sorry, I—'

'No need to apologise. You've had a lot on your mind, I know that.'

I wondered what he meant. Whether he was referring to Maya or Vanessa. I hated the feeling that he had access to my private life. I couldn't believe that I'd had the balls to hire him. That first meeting in his shabby office already seemed like a lifetime away.

'Mr Stafford, I've been meaning to call to say there's no need now to continue the surveillance. We've achieved what we needed to achieve.'

'She's leaving him then?'

'Nothing's decided yet, but . . .'

'It looks that way?'

I didn't answer but he seemed to take my silence as a yes.

'Right, well I'll just drop the final file round to you, and we'll call it a day. It was worth it, though, seeing whether that Thursday-night booking at the Savoy would turn up something new. I think you'll find it all very interesting. One o'clock. Globus car park.'

'Couldn't we make it after work?' I asked. I didn't like the idea of him hanging around near the office.

''Fraid not,' he said. 'My grandson's playing in his school concert. My daughter will kill me if I'm late.'

'It's nice to know someone scares you.'

'Oh yes. And when I listen to Matthew playing his guitar very badly, I will be happier than Target 96c has ever been in his entire life. And what is really sad, you know, is that someone like Mr D bigshot C won't even understand why. He might *be* important, but he doesn't know *what's* important. I'll see you at one.'

And before I could say anything else, he rang off.

In an attempt to steady myself before I went into the office, I phoned Vanessa to see if she'd got to work on time and was feeling OK. She'd taken the previous day off to think about what she'd want to do if the amnio suggested that the baby had Down's syndrome. She hadn't come to any conclusions, though, and wanted to spend the weekend discussing it.

'I'm fine,' she said. 'What about you? You sound shaky.'

'It's just a lot to take in, isn't it? I'm not sure I'll stop sounding shaky until we've been and had that test,' I said. 'But don't worry about me. You just take care of yourself.'

Afterwards I rang the Lowes. I'd told myself that I'd make one phone call, to find out how Maya was, and then that would be it. I'd speak to Maya if she called me but I wouldn't let myself get involved. Mr Lowe answered the phone. Maya was still asleep, he said, and he didn't want to bother her. She'd been crying most of yesterday and she was exhausted. But there was nothing new to report anyway. Dan seemed to accept her story about her having to cancel the Paris trip and come to Taplow because Anna was ill. She'd had a brief word with him yesterday afternoon and felt it went fine. Mr Lowe sounded pretty exhausted too. Apparently Mrs Lowe was taking it almost as badly as Maya and had gone round the house taking down all the photos of Dan.

'If there are any developments, I'll let you know, Steve,' he said. 'And thanks for all your help.'

I was on a difficult and complicated conference call when Stafford's car pulled up beneath my window at exactly one o'clock. I sent him a text to say I would be down in ten minutes.

He had reclined the driver's seat a little and had his eyes closed when I arrived at his car .

'There's a little lay-by not far from here,' I said. 'Can we go there, away from the office?'

'Sure. Hop in. Scared of being seen with me are you?' He drove a Land Rover, immaculate inside, totally unlike his messy office.

'So you got a new car in the end?' I asked.

'Last weekend,' he said. 'Love it.'

'Hardly a Prius.'

'I know,' he smiled. 'Look at the skies, mate. Look at all those planes stacking up. I keep telling Mrs S – me changing my car can't compete with that.'

When we got to the lay-by, Stafford pulled over behind a parked-up lorry, tutting loudly at the litter in the hedge behind the van serving tea and coffee. He handed me a second yellow folder.

'Why don't you have a look while I fetch a couple of teas?' he said, and got out before I had time to protest. The idea of having to handle yet another folder filled me with dread, but at the same time I now felt something of a connoisseur of surveillance reports. I opened the folder.

'Client 532f/Target 96c Report 2'. There, in front of me, was the same summary of 'main points', laid out in the same way on plain white paper. But the contents, and their impact on me, were scarily different.

Main points

- Continued drug use pre- and post-transmission of Target's chat show.
- Continued contact, including sexual intercourse, between Target and SH at Abercorn Close.
- Target overseeing hire of electronic communications 'expert' to monitor SH phone traffic.
- Discussion between Target and SH of interference in Target's marriage by wife's friend, Steve Watkins, and Target's desire to hire an intimidation expert to 'put the wind up him'. Enquiry put by SH to communications 'expert' about rates for intimidation.
- Clear evidence of Target's sexual relationship with second media contact during a night spent at the Savoy hotel.

I closed the folder quickly, as if I'd been stung. Stafford was looking over from the van's counter where he was trying to fit unwilling lids to the tops of two polystyrene cups. He saw me looking towards him, and winked. I was determined not to seem scared, though my mouth was crusting up and when he looked away, I licked all around my lips and the inside of my mouth to try to get some wetness in there.

He got back into the car, handed me my tea, and held out a little sachet of sugar and a thin wooden stirrer.

'Who's the second affair with?' I asked, determined not to let my first question be about the 'intimidation expert'.

'Page seven. Affair's too strong I would say. Looks like an occasional encounter to swap sex for stories.'

I flicked to page seven. 'Target left Blomfield Road on Thursday evening at 1923hrs. Drove himself to Temple station. Got out and walked along Embankment to Savoy hotel riverside entrance. Clear concern of surveillance. Spent the night in room 312. Evidence of sexual intercourse. Confirmed by subsequent entry to room 312. Semen traces on sheets. Remnant of condom wrapping beneath bed. Target left 0812hrs for breakfast meeting with agent. Companion settled bill 0830hrs. Paid by Visa debit card 3363 4639 6651 6356. Cardholder Angela Cairns. Subsequent research established Miss Cairns is a freelance writer on show business and film for the *Sun, Heat* magazine, *Look* magazine and a number of US celebrity publications and websites. (54 articles over last five months on Target and partner contained in file 532f/m1.) Formerly at *Sunday People*, where wrote and published biography of Target's wife.'

'Jesus Christ,' I said.

'He would not approve, and nor would His Father,' said Stafford.

'So, even though he's worried someone's on to him, and he has promised his wife he is going to cut down on his poker, the moment she's out of the way, he's screwing her biographer in the Savoy hotel. It's disgusting. The man doesn't let anything get in the way of his own pleasure.'

'You call it pleasure? I'm not so sure,' said Stafford. 'Got it all going for him on the surface hasn't he? But drugs, extra-marital relationships, it's not just the pursuit of pleasure, you know. It's running away from your reality.'

'What about the monitoring of phone traffic?' I asked. 'What's that about?'

'That was your doing was it not? She panicked like buggery when she got that call you made, he legged straight round to see her, and once they'd calmed down and done what they normally get up to, he decided she had to get someone to monitor her calls. They hired a complete loser though. He's got nowhere. Just doesn't know how to track back, so he's relying on the guy calling her again, which of course he won't, will he?'

It was another gently undermining slap on the wrist. I decided I couldn't face asking about the intimidation expert. I'd read the file properly when Stafford was gone. I plugged in my seat belt, indicating that I was ready for him to drive me back. 'Right, well like I said, we can call it a day now, so thanks for everything. I'd better get back to work.'

He laughed. 'You're being a very bravey-wavey little soldier-wolja, but you would not be human if you had no interest in knowing more about the *intimidation expert.*'

I tried to play it cool. 'I assume he's just trying to impress Hegarty, making out that because he's interviewed a few gang-sters in his time, he can talk tough.'

'I hope you're right. But if you're not, you'll be pleased to know we do reasonable rates for a full close protection service, modelled on Diplomatic Group Protection for top politicians and Royals.'

'What did he actually say?'

'Page twelve.'

I flicked forward to page twelve, and he leaned over me as I read. I could feel his breath on my arm. 'In his conversation with SH, Target indicated he was concerned partner's male friend SW was deliberately seeking to interfere in his marriage. He twice referred, in very menacing terms, to the need to "put the wind up him". In subsequent conversation with tele-coms operative, SH made enquiries as to whether same firm did "scaring off" work. This led to casual conversa-tion/discussion of rates for different forms of intimidation, mental and physical.'

'A little more than "tough talk" isn't it?' said Stafford, seeing on my face the impact of what was happening in my guts. 'You need to take care.'

'Thank you, I will,' I said. 'Now shall we go?'

The next fifteen minutes were torture. Stafford drove me back to Globus, drumming his fingers irritatingly on the steering wheel whilst also whistling quietly to himself. I was willing the journey to end, desperate to be rid of his company. When we arrived at the car park, I started opening the car door before he'd stopped, I was so eager to be gone.

'Hold on, Mr Watkins,' he said, pulling me back. 'I need to return this to you.'

He fished Maya's key out of his briefcase. I grabbed it, shoved it in my jacket pocket and got out of the car, nearly tripping over in the process.

'Mind how you go now,' he said, cheerily, as I rushed off.

As soon as I got to the office, I dashed into the men's toilets next to reception. I turned on the cold tap and let the water run till it was icy, cupped my hands to gather in as much as I could, splashed it on my face, then ran my hands round the back of my neck. I enjoyed the sensation of one or two drips of water making their way down my spine beneath my loose-fitting shirt. I looked in the mirror. My face seemed grey. 'Don't worry yourself, you'll be fine,' I said to my reflection. 'Stafford was wrong. It *was* tough talk. Dan was showing off to Hegarty, and Hegarty and Mr Phonetap-merchant were just showing off to each other. Dan's not that daft, so stop worrying.'

I didn't convince myself, though. The bottom line was this – did I imagine Dan was capable of organising someone to beat me up, or worse? A few weeks ago, I would have said not a chance in hell. But since then I had learned a lot more about him. He hated me, possibly even more than I hated him. He was a liar, a cheat, an adulterer, a wife-beater and someone totally obsessed with his own interests, personal and professional. It was not that hard to imagine he could go a few steps further in the pursuit of something he wanted to make happen.

I think Vanessa's pregnancy, and the approaching test, sharpened my sense of vulnerability. I started to imagine the worst possible scenarios, up to and including Dan actually hiring someone to wipe me out. It was the logical conclusion of what he had been discussing. And no matter how often I told myself I was being irrational, I was unable to block from my mind the idea that Vanessa might have to raise our child alone. I had read only last week a big article in the *Sunday Times* magazine about British and American soldiers killed in Iraq and Afghanistan, who had left behind wives pregnant with babies who would never know them. I'd had three years with a dad. These soldiers' kids had nothing, not one day, just a mum who would have to explain why most kids had a dad, but not them, and why she just had their wedding photos and a medal he never got to wear.

Then I told myself to stop being ridiculous. What was I doing comparing the danger of going to war with my situation? It haunted me though. I was scared. I went back to my desk with all these fears buzzing around in my head. Jerry could tell something was wrong. He said I looked vacant and pale.

'I'm fine,' I lied.

'Maya stuff?'

I nodded. I thought about telling him I had just been told I was in physical danger, but I realised it would panic him. After all, he'd been involved in the phone call. He'd start thinking people were out to get him too.

'The phone call didn't work, then?' he asked, as if reading my mind.

'Too early to tell.'

'Well, try not to worry too much about it, Steve. She's got a good brain, that Maya. She'll sort out her problems. By the way, Brandon called. This'll cheer you up. The presentation went down a storm. The Qataris have announced a shortlist of three. It's just us, K&L and Websters now. Brandon said to tell you we'd definitely be in need of your Websters stuff, whatever he meant by that.'

'Great,' I said with as much enthusiasm as I could muster, and then buried myself in my work for the rest of the day so that Jerry wouldn't talk to me.

When he'd left — he always went home early on a Friday —

I pulled out the yellow folder. I just wanted to get rid of it as quickly as possible. What should I do with it? I couldn't possibly leave another envelope in Mr Lowe's greenhouse. Then I had an idea. A way of protecting myself, and covering my tracks at the same time.

I checked that there was no one around who could come in and disturb me. Not a soul. With Brandon away, the office was a Friday-afternoon desert. Going back to my desk, I clicked into Word, created a blank page on my computer screen, and started to type.

'Watkins . . . you don't know me . . . but I know you . . . and you know Maya . . . lucky boy . . . not so lucky now though . . . sorry to land this on you . . . Mr Lowe looked like he couldn't take another one . . . so it's your turn . . . see page twelve . . . be afraid, Watkins . . . be very afraid.'

I changed the typeface to Franklin Gothic Heavy, upped it to 24-point, then printed it on a sticky-backed, postcard-sized address label, which I stuck to a plain Manila envelope. I took the yellow file from my briefcase, removed the report, and placed it inside the envelope. Then I called Nick Sheldon and told him I needed to see him urgently about a package I'd received. 'What kind of package?' he asked. If there was one thing I had learned from Stafford, it was that there was no such thing as a secure phone call, so I tried to keep explanation to a minimum.

'Let's just say it's the Greenhouse Effect,' I said.

Chapter Nineteen

Four days later, I was listening to Radio Five Live on my way to the office when the Tuesday-morning phone-in about the cost of the 2012 Olympics was interrupted. 'Sorry to cut in on you there, Alison from Slough,' said the presenter, 'but we're just getting reports of dramatic events on Teesside. The Press Association is reporting an explosion at the refinery there. The report says fire services from several parts of north-east England have been called out. Like I say, details very patchy but reports of a major explosion . . . In fact I have just been given another agency report quoting what it calls police sources, unnamed, confirming – explosion at the Teesside oil refinery, blaze being tackled and – I quote – "terrorism clearly cannot be ruled out."'

This was not a declaration of war by India or Pakistan, let alone the Queen's death, but it was surely the kind of news story that Sheldon would seize upon to distract attention from the announcement of Maya's and Dan's divorce. I already knew it was going ahead. It had just been a question of when.

'Not sure I need another file to convince me of Dan's misdemeanours,' had been Sheldon's reaction when I took the second report round to his office after work on Friday. 'All I have to do is mention the name Sheila Hegarty and he starts sweating. Good of you to bring it along though, Steve.'

Sheldon's office was more like a luxury suite than a place of work. His desk, such as it was, was a delicately carved mahogany piece tucked beneath a row of bookshelves. There wasn't even a chair in front of it. He had two banks of phones and a computer screen on a low level glass coffee table in the centre of the room. A clutch of papers, folders and magazines indicated he worked from the sofa, a lime-coloured affair running the length of the room, with two matching light blue armchairs at either end. The walls were covered top to bottom with posters, framed cuttings and cartoons. Dominant among them, directly above the stone hearth, was a copy of the main advertising poster for *Please Miss*. Maya had signed, in large gold marker pen across the foot of the poster 'To Nick, who makes it all happen, love and gratitude, Maya'.

Nick settled on to the sofa, stirred the tea his secretary had brought in, told her as she left he would need a call with Maya in half an hour or so. He read the report, more slowly than he had the previous one, in total silence. He did not look at me once, until he reached the end. Then he set it to one side, looked up and asked simply 'Well?'

'Well what?'

'How did it reach you?'

'Just arrived. Like that. Inside another envelope marked private and personal.'

'Home or office?'

'Office.'

'First post or second?'

'Hand delivered. I called you as soon as I got it.'

'Why me not Maya?'

'She trusts you to deal with this kind of stuff.'

He picked it up again, leafed through more distractedly.

There was no sign of the sympathy I had been expecting. It was there in black and white – I was under threat. Yet Sheldon was saying nothing.

'What do you think?' I asked.

'About what?'

'What it means.'

'Who for?'

'Well, everyone.'

'I don't know. All I know is it's a mess.'

He buzzed his secretary. Maya's voice came through a few moments later on the loudspeaker. I wanted to say hello, but was excluded from the conversation. Sheldon made me feel like I wasn't there.

'Hi Nick.' She still sounded very low.

'Hi darling,' he said. 'How goes?'

'You know. Just keeping on keeping on.'

'Spoken to Dan?'

'Just did. I pretended it was a scene in a film. Even rehearsed a few lines before the call. I don't think he realised anything was up. I know I've been cold but he's probably thinking it's because I'm worried about Mum. I can't sleep though. Can't stop thinking about it. Panicking about the future. But plenty of people have got through worse. That's what I keep telling myself.'

'You'll get through it, love, promise. How did he sound generally?'

'More suspicious than yesterday. Have you talked to him?'

'We had breakfast together. At the Savoy. It was weird. On the way in I bumped into that woman who wrote that book about you. All I told him was there were rumours swirling around about him and some journo chick and he needed to be careful.'

'How'd he take that?'

'Freaked out.'

'So it's true then?'

'In a word, darling: yes. I'm very sorry.'

There was a long silence on the end of the phone. Then Maya said, with a new steeliness in her voice, 'OK, Nick, that's it. It's over. I've thought about it a lot. My dad's right. I can't stay with him after this. Do what you have to do.'

Nick's jowly face was a picture of melancholy.

'OK, Maya, just give me a bit more time. This thing needs to be cooked to the right temperature, so it comes out the best possible way for you. That's all I'm thinking about now. You.'

He replaced the receiver and sat back into the sofa, exhaling loudly.

'Why didn't you tell her?' I asked.

'I did.'

'About this new stuff I mean.'

'Was it necessary? No need to rub salt in the wound, is there? Jesus, Hegarty's enough to show Maya he's unfaithful. She doesn't need to know he's screwing every media bitch on the planet.'

He ushered me out after that. Didn't even let me finish my tea. I found myself standing, bewildered, amidst the Friday-night rush hour on Hyde Park Corner wondering what on earth to do next. But then I realised it was simple. I had to go home to Vanessa and try to forget all about it. Things were in Sheldon's hands now.

Hearing about the explosion on Teesside, though, brought it all back. I was confused about how I felt. Half of me wanted to be involved, at the centre of a major news story, standing at Maya's side; half of me wished it wasn't happening. Vanessa and I had gone into the hospital for the amniocentesis test the previous day and we were waiting for the result. I knew I should be focussing all my attention on that.

I did my best to do some work, just get my head down and wait, but I found it impossible to focus on anything but the drama I had been drawn into, and which was about to explode in directions that would be uncertain, no matter how careful the planning by Sheldon. I say 'drawn into'. Motives are always complicated, but I like to think mine were good. In my own way, I loved Maya, and what purer feeling is there than love? If I hated Dan, it was because of my love for her, and the fear ever since he entered her life that he was a bad person, and bad for her. That she could not see it did not make her a bad person too. It just meant she was blind to the reality of him, because of his skill at erecting a front for her to admire.

As I waited for the news to break, I thought this must be how terrorists felt when they were back at base knowing a bomb was about to go off, readying themselves to watch all the panic that ensued. I suspected they were better prepared, and better trained for the wait than I was. I felt a little cheated that I would not be there at the exact moment when Dan heard the news, and the front came tumbling down. Forget Jeff Lacy being pummelled in the ring. For Dan it would be like getting mown down by a firing squad. He deserved it of course. I felt no sympathy other than for the fact that he did not get what life was really about. There was still a part of me thinking he would glory in being such big news. But maybe that was an unworthy thought. He had parents too, siblings, fellow victims of fame, people who would have to share the same nausea Sheldon was soon to inject into him.

Lunchtime came and went without a whisper. Several times I reached for my phone to call Maya, but stopped myself.

Then, at 3 p.m., Mr Lowe called me. He sounded totally stressed.

'It's today isn't it?' I said.

'Press notice going out on the wires and the websites 3.15 p.m. So any minute really.'

'How is she?'

'Fine considering. Nick has done a good job on the statements, not many people know she's in Taplow though I guess they'll descend on us. But she'll be fine here.'

'Any news on how Dan reacted?'

'Have a word,' he said. 'Hold on, she's out on the patio.'

Before I could say no, he was calling to Maya. She came to the phone, sounding calm, but tired.

'You haven't phoned me,' she said, sounding accusing.

'I wanted to give you your space.'

'Dad tell you what's happening?'

'He did. Are you ready?'

'Can you be "ready" for something like this?' she said. 'I feel . . . I don't know . . . just so sad.'

'Dan knows now?'

'Yep. Nick saw him about eleven at home. He denied it all at first, but Nick told him the proof was one hundred per cent. He blustered for a while, said he didn't believe it, but after a bit, he just asked Nick straight out "How did she find out?"'

'And what did Nick say?'

'Dunno, guess he said it didn't matter, what mattered was what we did about it. He told him what I had decided, and then showed him the statements he'd drafted. He said Dan realised then that he didn't have a leg to stand on, just sat down, and looked like he was going to cry.'

'Did he?'

'Cry? Not when I spoke to him.'

'You spoke to him?'

'Yeah. Nick called first, said he had told Dan everything, and he wanted a word.'

'You didn't have to speak.'

'True, but I'm glad I did.'

'What did he say?'

'Sorry. He just said sorry.'

'What? Literally – just sorry? Nothing else?'

'What else could he say? He said he was really sorry for everything he had done, he knew he had hurt me, but that had never been his intention. He loved me and he wanted me to know that.'

'Christ what a nerve.'

'It wasn't like that, Steve. I know he loves me. It's just that he hasn't been able to handle his fame the same way I've handled mine. He has allowed it to take control of him, to give him a feeling of invulnerability.'

'I can't believe you're excusing him for sleeping with other women! The cocaine, that's one thing, but screwing Sheila Hegarty!'

'I'm not excusing, I'm trying to understand. That's what my work is all about. Understanding.'

'Well, you're a saint if you can be understanding towards someone who has treated you as badly as he has.'

'Saint Maya. I like it,' she said, trying to drive the conversation on to a lighter level. 'Maybe that's what they'll call the next book.'

She seemed eager to get off the phone after that, presumably in case Nick called again. She quickly ran through the other issues, saying that Nick had already informed Dan that he could no longer be his agent. He was going to help him through the announcement, but after the statements went out he would represent Maya only. She was just telling me that the drugs allegations were being briefed to the *London Evening Standard* when Jerry tapped me on the shoulder, motioning that there was something I should come and see. I guessed it was the announcement. 'I think it's happening now, Maya,' I said. 'Take care of yourself.'

'Thanks, Steve. I'm sending you a secret handshake down the phone. I think provided I hear nothing, read nothing and manage to hide away here for a bit, I might just get through this. I'm hoping all the fuss about the bomb at that oil refinery will dilute it a bit anyway . . .'

I hung up and followed Jerry down to the foyer where a knot of people was gathering around the TV. A huge red and white BREAKING NEWS graphic appeared to be flashing out of the heads of the Sky presenters. A classic Maya headshot was in the corner of the screen. I recognised it as one of the publicity shots from *Fallen Angel*. It was clever of Sheldon to have fed them the idea of using that one as her kind of official photo. She looked strong, but also victim. Beneath the presenters ran a tickertape announcement 'Maya Lowe leaves Chivers over affair'.

The main presenter was putting on his best Queen Mother funeral voice, deep and slow, trying to hide the excitement. 'The news has just broken, so forgive me while we try to make sense of it all. But this is official, Maya Lowe and her husband Dan Chivers are separating and will divorce. Maya's agent Nick Sheldon has just issued a written statement on her behalf in which he says Miss Lowe has been made aware her husband is engaged in an extramarital affair with a senior journalist covering show business.'

'Yes, George,' said his co-presenter, 'and of course as we speak, you can be sure the tabloids will be trying to find out who this woman is.'

'To go back to the statement Sally, Maya is said to be hurt and devastated and would like to have some space to rebuild her life in private. The statement says this is a sad end to what has been in the main a very happy marriage, but Miss Lowe feels that all trust has broken down.'

'That's right, George, and if we look further down the statement, there is the sensational claim that Dan Chivers, Maya's TV-presenter husband, was briefing show-business journalists about her movements and secret details of her professional life.'

'Sally, that really is quite sensational, and I think because of the nature of that allegation, that is what will take this from being a tabloid story to something really more serious, much more clearly in the public interest.'

'Yes, anyway, we are going to stay with this now, and of course we want to hear what you say, so text and email in the usual way. You can see on the screen how to send us your views on this breaking news, the end of Maya and Dan.'

'And Sally, I'm just being told, as I know you are too, that our World Affairs report on President Mugabe's finances will now be postponed so we can stay with the Maya story. A reminder of our main headline prior to this breaking news, there has been an explosion at an oil refinery on Teesside. Police have confirmed this was a routine gas explosion, not, repeat *not*, terrorist-related, as was suspected earlier, so good news there.'

There was a large group of Globus employees around the TV now. A noticeable look of relief crossed their faces when they heard the explosion wasn't terrorist-related. Not mine, though, because I knew it meant that Sheldon's plan to limit the impact of Maya's announcement had failed. Meanwhile, the Sky presenters were chattering on.

'Now, Sally, one interesting aspect of this breaking news is that Nick Sheldon also represents Dan Chivers to the media. In a separate statement, he says releasing the statement will be his *final act* for Mr Chivers. The statement describes Mr Chivers as very contrite and ashamed. It says he loves Maya very much but he realises he has lost her trust and has to accept she is within her rights, legal and moral, to do as she is doing.'

'Now we are joined on the phone by Andy Cooke, who is a well-known PR expert in the film world, who some of you will have seen reviewing the papers here on *Sky News*. Andy, thanks for joining us. Did you have any hint of this at all?'

'No, I didn't. I don't think any of us did. It literally has come out of the blue.'

'And you know this world well, Andy, what will this mean for Maya Lowe's and Dan Chivers' careers?'

'Well Maya is a big star, she is the wronged party, she has a huge film with Matt Damon apparently in the pipeline, so she is big enough to rise above this, I guess. I think for Chivers, it's different. He is a very successful chat-show host and popular with a certain middle-aged woman type, but I think ITV are bound to have some concerns about this.'

'Just hold it there, Andy, because we are getting news in now about the identity of the woman involved, apparently being confirmed by media sources as we speak. Our Royal reporter Ella McColl is at a Variety Club reception due to be attended by Prince Charles and I understand there is breaking news to report, Ella?'

'George, yes, well a lot of senior showbiz people here for

this event and of course excitement anyway with Prince Charles due any moment. It would be interesting to hear his views on the Maya-Dan separation, given that he and Princess Diana went through a similar thing some years ago, George . . .'

'And Ella, the breaking news . . .'

'Well what all the showbiz reporters here are saying George, and one of them says he has this confirmed one hundred per cent, it will be in the last editions of some of the evening papers, is that Dan Chivers' mistress is a journalist well known in showbiz media circles, Sheila Hegarty.'

'So who is she, Ella, what is she like?'

'Well, George, she is South African or possibly Australian, that's what I'm hearing,' said Ella. 'She runs the popular new website We-know-the-stars.com and it would seem Dan Chivers is one star she got to know too well.'

'Yes indeed. Andy Cooke, you're a PR expert in the film world, how will a journalist like Sheena Hagerty react to being the story all of a sudden, if this is indeed true, and I should emphasise at this stage this is speculation based upon what we believe will be in newspapers later today. Andy?'

'Journalists like to report the news not make it, but this is clearly, I mean it's obvious from the way you are covering it, it's a massive story, and I think the media will lap up every detail, and if that means exposing journalists and digging into their lives, that's what they'll do.'

'Presumably you know this woman, Andy, Miss Hagerty.'

'Well, obviously I know the website, but I do not know her, but as Ella said she will be well known in showbiz media circles.'

'Thanks for that, stay there if you will, because we have received footage of Dan Chivers, just in, the first pictures since the news of his marriage break-up. There he is, he is leaving his house, you can see he is looking strained as you would expect of course, and there trying to fight his way through photographers from the tabloids and the magazines, and some TV cameras covering it you'll see, quite a few really, these pictures going around the world of course, and he is as I say looking strained, Dan Chivers, clearly not adding to the statement, his separation pending divorce announced today, and there he goes, getting into the car now, that'll be a driver in the front you can see, wearing a pullover so perhaps a friend not a professional driver, and Dan Chivers is not saying anything, and there he goes and the cameramen chasing now, running after the car, one or two on to their motorbikes to give chase, and there he goes. Andy Cooke, PR expert in the film world, Andy, you saw those pictures, what did they say do you think about how Dan Chivers is trying to deal with this?'

'Well no, actually George you got me on a mobile and I pulled off the motorway to take this call, so sorry, no, I haven't seen the pictures but I heard your commentary and I think obviously this is going to be a difficult time for him and for all his team.'

'Indeed and of course as you heard earlier on *Sky News*, Dan has lost not only his wife but his agent, so a very lonely man as the night draws in. Andy Cooke, thanks for talking to us. Drive safely.'

More colleagues had joined us. They knew my special interest, but most of them would have been there anyway. I imagined how this scene was being repeated in workplaces all over the country. Most days, TVs babbled away in corridors to audiences of none. But this was one of those stories, as

Nick had said it would be, that got people excited.

I could see him on the screen now, the uber-agent, coming out on to the street in front of his office. The flag of a nearby embassy – Belgian I think – was blowing gently behind him. Passers-by were stopping to see what was going on. He looked smart in a dark blue suit, white shirt and plain purple tie. He had what looked like a postcard in his hand.

'Ladies and gentlemen,' he said.

'Here we go,' said George, 'Nick Sheldon, Maya Lowe's agent and till recently Chivers' agent too, let's hear what he has to say.'

'. . . and will then take your questions. You will have seen the statements and I can confirm Maya and Dan are separating and that Maya will be seeking a divorce on the grounds of his admitted adultery. Maya was also very upset that he gave journalists stories about her. He has apologised and said he is ashamed but Maya feels what he has done means there can no longer be trust between them and their marriage is at an end. As you know, we are in the process of completing a deal for Maya to play a leading role in a new film, *The Hunter Hunted*. I can confirm that will go ahead. I have spoken to the producer and director who have expressed their solidarity at this time. We have received a message of support from her future co-star Matt Damon, for which Maya is obviously grateful and touched. As you will have noticed, Dan did not present his show today and will be taking the next week off. Both of them are now entitled in my view to some privacy.'

Sheldon now had his hands in the air, calling for order as journalists shouted out their questions. George at the Sky News Centre butted in.

'It looks like he is taking questions, so let's stay with this.'

'Where is Maya?'

'She is with friends.'

'In Britain?'

'I am not saying where she is.'

'How is she?'

'Very upset, hurt, confused, but she is a great actress and a strong woman and I'm confident she will emerge stronger.'

'When will we see her?'

'She wants a bit of space and I hope you respect that. But she will not hide away for long.'

'Do you know Miss Hegarty?'

'I do. But this has come as a total shock to me.'

'Mr Sheldon, Adrian Alexander from the *Standard*. Our crime reporter has filed a report, which is the front-page lead in our final edition tonight, and already running online, that Maya also discovered he was using cocaine despite having promised her he would give it up.'

'I cannot comment on that.'

'Does he use cocaine?'

'I have nothing to add to the statement I issued for him. I no longer represent him.'

'Mr Sheldon, I must ask you again. Are you or are you not aware that Dan Chivers and Sheila Hegarty are habitual cocaine users?'

'I have nothing to add. I am not their spokesman. I speak for Maya Lowe.'

At this point George cut in again: 'Well sensational stuff there, it really is, Nick Sheldon stonewalling a bit, but the journalists at the press briefing outside his office helping to fill in the picture, I think Ella is still here, so if Ella is still there, Ella, what do we make of the drugs allegation made by the *Standard* there, and I should make clear here at Sky News Centre we have no way of knowing that is true but Ella, if true, how damaging is this now, for Dan Chivers, that allegation from the *Standard* made just now live on *Sky News?*'

'Well first, George, Prince Charles has arrived, with Camilla, and as expected, they said nothing about the breaking news of the day, about Maya Lowe, who they have both met at Royal Variety events, so glad just to lay that to rest, no comment from Charles, though frankly he would not be human if he was not thinking about his own high-profile divorce today of all days, and yes George I think the drugs allegations which as you say are media allegations only, the *Standard* in London, that would take it to another level really. George?'

'Ella, thank you. And Sally you have the first texts and emails.'

'Your thoughts pouring in here,' Sally was saying. 'Alfie from Sidcup I think speaks for many. "Maya is the best-looking woman in Britain and he can't resist playing away. Silly fool." Meg in Bristol: "What is it about men? Any man in the world would give their eye teeth for Maya, but the one who has her can't see it."'

'I think plenty of men would say amen to that,' said George.

'And women,' said Sally. 'This story breaking around the world of course and Norwegian viewer Jens Kalvenes says simply, "His loss, her gain." Colin Caldwell in Dubai says Maya has the chance to be one of the greats and great actors always have troubled private lives. Interesting perspective from Colin, George. Pat Duff from Cheltenham says, "This is sad news. I am a great fan of Maya and I hate to think of her being hurt and lonely." Lance from York: "Maya is better off without him. His programme is rubbish which is why I don't watch it, and I am glad it is off the air today. And well done Sky for your coverage so far." That's nice. Finally – and I have to say, George, there is not one text or email coming in support of Dan Chivers – there is one I should read out, not happy with us I think: "Is this really such a big story that you drop all other news for the day?" And that is from Stanley in Accrington.'

George looked at Sally to see if she realised what she had read. 'I think that one might be a spoof,' he said. She looked nonplussed. 'Accrington Stanley,' he said. 'It's a football team.' She still looked nonplussed.

'Anyway,' said George, 'keep those texts coming and just to remind you, the explosion on Teesside, as we reported earlier, was not a bomb, repeat not a bomb. Now I am being told we have the crime reporter of the *Evening Standard* on the line. So let's get to the bottom of these allegations about drugs.'

Just at this moment, Brandon appeared, pushing his way through the now twenty-strong gaggle of his staff. He reached up to the TV and pressed the off button.

'Hey what is this, an office outing to a freak show? Kindly get back to work, all of you.'

As we filed back to our desks, he called me over. 'This anything to do with that little fracas in the corridor last week?' he asked. I nodded. 'Well, I hope it means we won't be having any more Maya-related visits.' I nodded again and shuffled, shamefaced, back to my desk.

'Well, well, well,' said Jerry, as we pretended to settle back into our work. 'Sheila bloody Hegarty.'

'You have your little place in history, my friend.'

'Well so long as I get those tickets for the premiere.'

'*The Hunter Hunted.* You'll be there.'

He looked happy, genuinely happy, like he had been touched by her. 'I can't believe that just happened,' he said. 'I felt part of it.'

Five minutes later, Vanessa called. 'Steve, have you seen the news? I can't believe it. Maya and Dan are splitting up. Did you know about this?'

I glanced at Jerry. 'She sent me a text this morning,' I said. 'I knew something was up, but she didn't say they were divorcing. I'm in shock.'

'Poor poor Maya,' Vanessa said. 'How awful. He seemed so in love with her. Anyway, I'd better go. I'm leaving early to drop by the hospital.'

'Do you think they'll have the result of the test?' I asked.

'Not sure. Try to come home as early as you can, in case they do.'

I had a four o'clock meeting with a contractor in the canteen, after which I stole ten minutes at the TV in reception. Dan was getting a hammering. There was widespread incomprehension that anyone could do this to Maya. Maya, on the other hand, was getting lots of sympathy. It was clear, though, that her ordeal was only just beginning. The tabloids would be preparing dozens of pages. The broadsheets would have their usual orgy of discussion about how the tabloids and TV were covering the story. It was obvious from the stampede of magazine editors competing to air their views on TV and radio that they would want to keep it all going for months. I wondered how you stopped being famous. It wasn't like a train, with a clear beginning to the journey and a clear and finite destination, because along the way you were collecting baggage and even if you could throw your own baggage out, if you were really famous like Maya, you had so many other people travelling with you. I felt awful for her.

Bearing in mind Vanessa's desire for me to get home early, I managed to clear my desk by 5.30. I bid a hasty farewell to Jerry and dashed downstairs, not waiting for the lift. Just as I was coming out of the main entrance there was a sudden rush of noise and movement which disoriented me, and I only recovered my balance when I heard a female voice saying 'ITV' and felt a hand on my forearm trying to slow me down.

'Mr Watkins, a quick word please. You'll have heard the news about Maya Lowe and Dan Chivers. As her first boyfriend, what's your reaction?'

Shit, I couldn't believe I was being doorstepped. This was the last thing I needed. I had just seen what happened when the media industry crashed into the illusion industry and it was not a place I wanted to be.

'I'm sorry,' I said. 'I need to get home. My wife is not well.'

Now a cameraman was just a couple of feet away, walking backwards ahead of me, shepherded by a young woman holding one of the furry microphones I had seen on the news, who was making sure he didn't bump into any of the parked cars as we walked towards mine. I felt her microphone tap the top of my head as she struggled to keep it close to me whilst also steering the cameraman. Surprise having failed, the reporter tried charm, said she really wanted to speak to me as part of a nice, positive package about Maya and why she was so loved and popular, and it was important to get the perspective of someone who had known her all her life. Even that I managed to resist. It was when she asked me direct 'Did you know this was coming?' that I found myself replying – 'Yes, I did.'

'You still talk to Maya, still see her?'

'Yes, I do. Course I do. She's my closest friend.'

'And how do you feel, for Maya?'

'I feel very sad for Maya, obviously, but I think it was

inevitable. Dan has done some terrible things to her, more maybe than you people know.'

I was at the car. She was trying to manoeuvre me into stopping, but I felt I had said enough. 'Excuse me, would you mind letting me open the door?'

'What other things? What other terrible things?'

'I really have to go.'

She stood aside, still firing questions at me. I had stopped listening.

I drove home on autopilot, barely aware of the cars or street lights or the billboards which usually caught my eye. I'd always been so critical of the fumbled responses people in the news made when caught unawares in the street, but now I knew what it felt like. God, this was the kind of thing Maya would be having to cope with for weeks to come. I suddenly admired her courage all the more. Pulling up outside the house, I sat in the car for a few minutes, taking deep breaths, trying to gear myself up to face down the fear that, when I got in, Vanessa might confront me with the results of the test. In fact she confronted me with something else entirely.

'Why on earth did you do it?' she shouted as I walked through the door. 'Why do that?'

'Do what?'

'That interview! What do you think I'm talking about?'

'How do you know about the interview?' I asked, totally bemused.

'It was on the news. It's been on twice already. No doubt they'll be showing it a few more times.'

I couldn't believe it. How could they have got it on air so fast?

'Did I look bad?' I asked.

'Why are you caring about how you looked?' she said, still shouting. 'It was more what you said. Pretending to say nothing, but in fact saying enough to hurt Dan. It made you seem conniving and shifty, Steve. You should have stayed out of it.'

'Sorry. I'm really sorry. But I didn't know what to do. The woman just came at me. I was confused.'

'Why is it,' said Vanessa, plonking herself down angrily on a kitchen chair, 'that Maya seems to be constantly intruding on our lives these days? I mean, today of all days. The day we get the result of the test.'

I sat down too. 'So you got it? . . . And?'

'You mean you actually want to know? You're not too busy giving TV interviews?'

'Vanessa, that's unfair . . .'

'It's OK. Everything's OK. There are no abnormalities.'

For a moment we were silent. Looking at each other almost as strangers. Then I went to hug her, but beneath the shared relief, I could feel her anger still there. It was like hugging a stone. An embrace that should have brought us together felt like a moment of rupture. Just to make it worse, my phone rang. It was Brandon. Livid.

'Can you explain to me why I have just seen a fucking TV interview being done in my fucking car park, with my fucking company name in lights in the background?'

'Mike, I'm sorry. I didn't intend it to happen. I was just ambushed by them.'

'I am losing my patience with you, Steve, and you had better know it. Any more of this and I might have to reconsider the terms of your employment. And Websters? What do you have on Websters? You've got until the end of the week to give me a report otherwise I'll get Jerry on to it, solo.' He slammed down the phone.

Vanessa gave me a long, hard look after the call, but at least she didn't lay into me any more. Just went up for an early night. I knew I wouldn't sleep so I sat and watched *News at Ten* which devoted the whole first half of the programme to Maya, with my little on-the-move interview just before the commercial break. When I first heard the announcer say my name, I thought I was going to be sick. Vanessa was right. I looked shifty, unsure of my ground, an amateur outsmarted by pros.

The rest of the programme was done fairly straight by another his-and-hers presenter team, in almost identical dark blue suits. They had even rushed up a quick internet poll – does the split make you like Maya more, less, or don't know? And then the same question about Dan. The presenter was professional enough to be embarrassed when he admitted it was a self-selecting poll and it was impossible to know if people took part more than once. And the results were wholly predictable. 62/9/29 for Maya. 7/81/12 for Dan. Who on earth, I wondered, would take the trouble to fill in an internet poll and say 'Don't know'?

I switched to Sky where they were now reviewing coverage from around the world. Fox News in the States said the story had more play than Paul McCartney's split from Heather Mills. Their London correspondent was pictured with Parliament in the background saying that, for today, politics took a back seat to showbiz. French TV had it as their second story behind a speech by President Sarkozy saying France needed to be more like America. Sky ran a montage of headlines from around the world before the presenter joked that they were still waiting for Iran, North Korea and Belarus. Later they did a round-up of the next day's papers. The presenter obviously relished it. "'Maya's heartbreak" there in the *Mirror*. "You Rat Dan" is the *Sun*'s take, with the story taking up several pages and a special Maya pull-out. Here's the *Express* – a picture of Maya looking at her best on the left there, Sheila Hegarty on the right, and the headline makes clear what they think: "Desperate Dan drops beauty for beast". A bit harsh. Other papers actually commenting on Hegarty's good looks. Quite a few Desperate Dan cartoons of course, and another Desperate Dan headline in the *Mail*: "Desperate Dan gets the boot from Maya". Room for one more story on their front page: "Blair failure as bomb rocks Middle East deal". *The Times* has a dramatic picture of the Teesside oil-refinery fire, a fairly short story on Maya and Dan, though they are making a bit more of the drugs angle inside. *Telegraph* front page dominated by the picture of Maya at a recent charity ball and her famous "oops moment" and the headline there: "Maya makes a clean breast of it". *Telegraph* getting quite saucy in their old age. *Guardian* and *Independent* both have it as a picture story on the front, and the *Guardian* second section has a lovely full-page picture of Maya and the headline "Do we care?" Well I think apart from the *FT* we do. Now to discuss the papers I'm joined by—'

I switched it off, sickened. I felt terrible about abandoning Maya in the midst of all this, but it had to be done. I had a wife and future child who needed me more. From now on, Maya would have to understand that I couldn't just drop everything for her.

PART TWO

Chapter Twenty

That should have been the end of the story. Events had forced me to make a choice as to who came first, and I was clear that the answer was Vanessa and our unborn child. If things had been that simple, I could put my pen down now. Then again, I wouldn't be writing this in the first place if the story had stopped there. Vanessa will deny it, but it was her fault as much as mine that it didn't. She was the one who thought I was going too far, that I had to keep up my friendship with Maya in some way. I was doing a good job of being un-involved, watching the coverage from afar, concentrating on my work, on Vanessa and the baby. I was happy. Vanessa was happy. Maya was not happy, but she was coping, largely due to the amazing support of her parents and the clever strat-egising of her agent.

You had to hand it to Nick Sheldon. Putting to one side the personal suffering Maya was enduring, in pure PR and profes-sional terms, he could not have delivered a better landing. All the heat was on Dan and Sheila Hegarty, whose reputations were being shredded.

The media were on Dan's case relentlessly for days and without Nick's guiding hand, he made terrible, near fatal errors. I caught one interview, done on the run trying to escape the media pack as he left a bar, in which he started to talk about plots and conspiracies and suggested this was all the work of rival TV channels. His eyes were bloodshot from crying, lack of sleep or drugs, maybe all three. The press said he was sleeping on a friend's floor in Battersea. I guessed it was one of the few friends he had left. Then a video appeared on YouTube, posted by someone who had been in the bar, who had filmed Dan snorting cocaine in the toilet, then charging at the intruder wildly, fists pumping, screaming 'Gimme that fucking phone, gimme that fucking phone.'

The grand TV finale came when Dan made the dreadful decision, which his bosses immediately regretted judging by the vicious 'senior ITV sources' briefing against him in the weekend press, to devote the entire hour of his show to defending himself. It was car-crash television, like watching a human being implode before your eyes. The programme started sedately enough. The opening titles were slow-motion shots of Dan fighting through a media scrum, then Maya walking elegantly down a red carpet at last year's Baftas. They had changed the jingle to something more sombre and dispensed with Dan's smiley skip down the studio stairs. Instead he was already centre stage as the title shots ended. He stood, paused to compose himself and stared into the camera lens. I really felt as if he was talking to me.

'This is going to be the toughest programme I have ever done,' he said. 'Because today . . . the big guest . . . is me.' Cue reprise of the sombre jingle. Watch Dan turn to a different camera.

'I owe it to you, my viewers, my friends and supporters, to explain how it came to this. But first we're going to show you a short film. I'm not sure I'll be able to watch it. It's the story so far: my life with Maya, and the tragic, painful end that you all now know about. And then it's going to be me in that hot seat, and this time it is you the audience who will be asking the questions. First let's see the film . . .'

It was a straight enough account of their relationship, using old footage. How they met. Clips from that first interview. When they realised they were falling in love. What they said about each other. Things they did together. But even before the film reached their wedding, I knew the live audience would be feeling manipulated, and whereas in the past they had loved to be manipulated by Dan, not even noticed it happening, or not cared when they did notice, now the lens through which he was viewed had changed. Only Dan couldn't see it. The film ended with shots of him running the gauntlet of another paparazzi scrum and as the camera cut back to him, he was clearly shaken. I noticed his hand trembling ever so slightly. There were shouts from the audience, the beginnings of a slow handclap, and panic etched on every cell of his over-made-up, orange face.

'OK, OK, I am hearing it, I am hearing what you say, but this is live TV, ladies, so let's have some decorum, let me have my say and then you can ask whatever you like,' but the ladies were having none of it. The camera panned to a large woman wearing a tight green vest who was gesticulating angrily, pointing at him, jabbing her finger, and I could lip-read her saying 'You let us down, you bastard.' Dan was continuing to try to restore order, but it was hopeless. In the front row a group of young women started to chant Maya's name and clap in time – 'My-er, My-er, My-er' – and he looked increasingly helpless as the chant spread through the audience, till they were on their feet, like an all-female football crowd, and then the women at the front changed the chant to 'Dan out, Dan out, Dan out' and the rest applauded wildly and began joining in until it got so bad that one of the production staff walked on stage, took Dan's arm and led him off. That provoked another wild cheer and then a real football chant which I had heard at Chelsea a few times on those days when Chelsea fans made some noise, sung to the fans of a losing side as the game neared its end. 'Time to go, time to go, time to go.' A man in a badly fitting suit walked on stage and announced there would be a commercial break. It was Dan's 438th afternoon show, and his last.

Maya phoned me a couple of times during those terrible days, but our conversations were short. She would fill me in on the latest press horror, I would express my sympathy, she'd say goodbye. For the first week of her stay in Taplow, the media had a fairly sizeable stake-out at her parents' home. When Sky periodically flashed over to their correspondent there, you could see all the other reporters in the lane. It was obvious, though, that they had no idea whether she was at the house or not, and after a while the numbers started to dwindle. They were reduced to shouting questions towards Mr Lowe's car whenever he left the driveway. He spoke to them only once, on his return from a trip to the supermarket, when he wound down the window and said 'You are all wasting your time. She is not at home. She is with friends.' After that they went away.

He called me a day or so later sounding very chuffed with himself. 'It was Nick's idea,' he said. 'Not a lie as such, but put them off the scent. Not at home – true, not at her own home that is. And with friends – what better friends does she have than me and Anna?' It was good to hear him laughing like the old days.

Sheldon also planned Maya's first public appearance to perfection, with words and pictures that hit front pages and bulletins around the world. Spiriting her out of the Lowes' house in a blacked-out Mini Cooper, he accompanied her to a dinner at the Victoria and Albert Museum where the entertainer Stephen Fry was hosting the launch of a new charity dedicated to helping young kids off drugs. Vanessa and I were there. Mr Lowe had asked Sheldon to send us an invitation which Vanessa had insisted we accept. She couldn't understand my reluctance. 'She's your friend, for God's sake. Don't you want to support her?' When I told her I'd rather stay at home and decorate the nursery she looked at me as if I'd gone mad. In the days since we'd received the result of the amnio test, Vanessa had been in a state of euphoria. She'd even forgiven me the debacle of my first, and she hoped last, TV interview. Once her temper had cooled, she had been really sweet about it, said, 'It's the old problem, Steve. You're just too honest, no good at telling lies.' Now she was determined to get out and about, to enjoy life to the full before the baby came. She told me that if I wouldn't go to the V&A dinner she'd go alone. It was far too glamorous to miss. So in the end, I capitulated.

Even before Maya's surprise appearance, the audience was in a state of high emotion having heard a series of little speeches by youngsters telling of their struggles with heroin and crack cocaine. There was a film about a teenager from Peckham, Bella Chadwick, who never made it through, and her parents went to the stage to issue an appeal to dig deep so other parents did not have to suffer like they did. Finally Stephen Fry, on a signal from Sheldon, called for quiet, as a freelance photographer and agency cameraman, also cued by Sheldon, moved to the base of the stage.

'We have one final speaker, ladies and gentlemen,' said Fry, 'someone you all know and love and who has her own reasons for knowing the damage drugs can do to people's lives.' I was watching the audience look around to each other as they tried to guess and I think one or two worked it out straight away because they were getting to their feet even as Stephen Fry continued the big build-up: 'She is the jewel in the crown of British film, she has had to endure some very painful things of late, but she is a wonderful actress who gives so much of her time and success to others, and she is here to give her time and support to this great cause tonight, will you please welcome . . .'

Even before he got her name out they were cheering, and as Maya walked slowly on to the stage, a smile spreading across her face, the whole audience rose. It was the first time I'd seen her since the separation. I'd expected her to look pale and gaunt, but her beauty took the breath away. She had changed her hair so that it fell down to one bare shoulder. She was wearing a strapless gold dress ('Dior,' Mrs Lowe whispered to me) cut just above the knee, with matching shoes and clutch bag. She stood, the smile widening as the applause grew; she started to laugh, and the cheering got louder. Next to me a middle-aged man was shouting at the top of his voice 'We love you.' Next to him his wife was whistling. Another woman was jumping up and down as though she was going back thirty years to her first ever rock concert. I thought her breasts were going to fall out of her low-cut ballgown. Maya had complete command. I moved closer to the front and tried to catch her eye from the side of the hall where I had been standing with her parents, but the lights were in her eyes and she couldn't make us out. The noise eventually calmed and she gave a big sigh and said 'Well, well, well, what a welcome.' That set them off again.

'Thank you so much. Thank you from the bottom of my heart. Thank you Stephen for those kind words. And thanks to everyone who has sent their lovely messages these past few days. This is a very difficult period in my life. But what tonight makes clear is that however difficult our lives may be from time to time, we have our health, we have our strength and we have food to put on the table. Tonight you have heard stories of people whose lives have been lost or ruined because of drugs. And those of us who are lucky in our lives, as I have been – most of the time' – she paused for laughter – 'owe it to others to put something back. So thank you for your support, thank you for the welcome. Thank you for giving me the strength to carry on as I look forward to leaving for the States soon to make my next film. And if you really want to thank me, listen to Mr and Mrs Chadwick, dig deep tonight, fill in those forms on the table, go the extra mile in the raffle and the auction. Let's help people less fortunate than ourselves.' As she stood back from the microphone, the audience were up on their feet again. Stephen Fry walked over to embrace her, then led her to the side of the stage.

We were taken to a VIP suite where she was surrounded by people telling her how wonderful she had been. She hugged Mr Lowe, then her mum, then Vanessa, then me. Mr and Mrs Chadwick told her that her words really made them feel some good could come of the loss of their wonderful daughter.

'I hope so,' she said, taking Mrs Chadwick's hands in her own. 'I so hope so.'

'That was quite a performance,' I said when she finally got free of all the charity people.

'The start of the rest of my life,' she said.

It was the start of the rest of mine, too. Things were good at work. According to Jerry, Brandon had come round to thinking that it wasn't such a bad thing that the Globus logo had been seen on national TV in the context of the pro-Maya reporting. And when Luke Morgan at Swift International came back with two clear examples of negligent service by Websters, one of them leading to a contract being torn up and Websters facing the threat of legal action from Jensen Logistics in Denmark, Brandon actually bought me a cup of coffee in the canteen. A few of the newspapers had picked up on my car-park interview to speculate about what other 'bad things' Dan might have done, but since he was committing plenty more faux pas in real time, the issue appeared to have been set aside, I hoped for ever. Angela Cairns, it seemed, was going to come out of this unscathed. I couldn't help wondering if Sheldon was somehow protecting her. But it didn't matter. The goal had been achieved. Dan was destroyed by the public and media outrage over his behaviour. He even seemed physically smaller, and his face was beginning to take on a shrunken look. Without Maya to keep an eye on him, he was clearly eating and sleeping less, taking drugs more. He had the appearance of a loser now. So did Hegarty. All that confidence I saw on Stafford's video as she swaggered from her house in Abercorn Close and swung her legs into a car had gone. I couldn't imagine them having the nerve to hire someone to rough me up. No, I thought, Dan was well and truly out of my life, and I would never again have to put up with his irritating, perma-tanned face except when it was staring miserably from tawdry photographs in tabloid newspapers and mid-shelf magazines.

Unfortunately, not for the first time, I got Dan all wrong.

It was a Tuesday when Maya — or rather Sheldon — announced in a short statement on her website that she would be initiating divorce proceedings, which obviously sparked another mini frenzy, even though it had been expected. The following morning, I pulled into my bay in the Globus car park only to see a menacingly familiar black Mercedes drawing up. I was debating whether to cut the engine or try to drive off again when Dan leapt out and strode towards me. He was wearing jeans and a scruffy white polo shirt, and his face looked tired and unshaven. There was a powerful, almost tearful fury in his eyes. I could feel myself beginning to panic as I tried to decide what to do. I could back up, but he was standing directly behind me, and I had visions of running over his feet, crippling him. I pictured Brandon finding him and deciding that, because I was still caught up in the mess that Maya's private life had become, it was time to fire me.

Before I could make a decision, Dan's face was looming up at the window.

'Get out of the fucking car, you,' he snarled.

'Not until you calm down a little,' I said, pathetically, not even sure he could hear. He was shouting. I was not. There was a pane of glass between us.

'I said get out of the fucking car.'

'Not until you calm down.' I said it more loudly this time. He snorted at me, then started hammering on the windscreen.

Brendan Paterson from marketing was parking up a few bays away. I was going to have to do something before this became embarrassing. The car park was overlooked by offices on three sides. It would be amazing if Dan hadn't been spotted already. There seemed only one option: try to get Dan into the car with me. At least if he hit me inside the car, there was less chance of people seeing. A strange, fatalistic calm came over me as I leant over to the passenger door, and opened it.

'Dan, let's talk, please come and sit in the car.'

He stared for a few seconds but then came round and shuffled in alongside me.

'Close the door,' I said. He did.

I said it was in neither of our interests to have a big scene at my office so we should go somewhere else. He nodded. I decided to drive to the same lay-by to which I'd taken Stafford. At least there would be witnesses there if anything happened. And maybe it wouldn't. Now that he was in the car, Dan seemed less aggressive. As I manoeuvred my way past his Mercedes and out of the car park, he sat slumped in the passenger seat, breathing heavily. It was as I was turning on to the main road that he punched me in the side of the face. It was a jab, flashed out without warning. It cannot have been easy punching, side on, from a sedentary position. I instinctively pulled away and the steering wheel came with me, towards the right, so that I almost mounted the grass verge separating the two sides of the road. I managed to steer back on course as the car behind me braked and the driver blasted on his horn. The punch hurt, but not as much as I feared when it first landed.

'Dan, you'll kill both of us,' I shouted.

'You've already killed me, you bastard,' he said, and he punched me again, harder. I managed to pull into the left-hand lane. 'Don't do that Dan, please. What if someone recognises you, they could call the police, call the press—'

'Oh yeah? And make my life worse than it is now?'

Then he hit me a third time, again calling me a bastard. Somehow I managed to make it to the lay-by. I pulled over and switched off the engine, then realised I should have driven on a little further so that I was closer to the tea van and the old couple who ran it. I thought about moving forward but now the pain in my head was becoming severe. I put my hand to my cheek. No blood. But searing pain in my temple and across my left jaw. I had managed to get through the whole of my life so far without ever being hit like that. I caught sight of myself in the mirror. All colour had drained from my face.

'So, what do you have to say for yourself, you two-faced, manipulative, low-life, lying bastard?' he asked, grabbing the collar of my shirt so that my tie was strangling me.

I looked at him. I thought about asking whether he thought the same words applied to a drug-taking adulterer who betrayed a wife's secrets, all in the furtherance of his career, but I did not want to draw further blows upon my head.

'About what?' I asked.

'About what you did to destroy my marriage.'

'I didn't destroy your marriage, Dan. You did.' He punched me, on the bridge of my nose. This time he drew blood, and I wiped it with my tie. I was incapable, physically and morally, of fighting back. The thought crossed my mind that if he kept hitting me, I might die. Or that this was merely the warm-up act before he took out a gun and shot me. He had nothing to lose. He looked like a man whose life was over.

'Please don't hit me any more, Dan,' I pleaded. 'You've made your point. Couldn't we just discuss this like rational human beings?'

He rubbed his right fist which was clearly hurting.

'OK,' he said. 'I'm listening.'

I stared ahead, hoping that if I looked out of the window, not at him, he would be less tempted to keep hitting me.

'I won't pretend I have ever liked you,' I said. 'I never have. But I had nothing to do with any of this. How could I have known about your other life? Do you really think it was me who told Maya all that stuff? It's just not my world, Dan.'

He was staring intently at me, concentrating on a trickle of blood that I could feel curving from my nose to the corner of my lip.

'Don't play Mr fucking Innocent with me. I can smell a rat a long way off. And you, Watkins, are a rat.'

He raised his hand to hit me again. I put my hands to my head and felt his fist land on my wrist.

'Please, Dan. Hit me once more and I get out of the car, I go to those people at the café and I tell them "If you want to make some money take your mobile and go get some pictures of Dan Chivers over there and tell the press he's beating up the man they call "Maya's first love" in a lay-by.'

'My, what a lot we've learned at the feet of the great Nick Sheldon,' he said. 'Quite the little media manager aren't we?'

'Sheldon did what was best for Maya.'

'Oh you all did what was best for Maya, didn't you? Well you may not believe it, sonny boy, but I was doing my best for Maya too.'

'Screwing another woman?'

'OK, I admit it – that was wrong. But the woman I was screwing was helping Maya.'

'I can't believe you said that.'

'Well it's true. It wasn't just about getting *me* the right profile, it was about Maya too. She's great at what she does, OK, but I helped. I worked on that image too. Wrong to screw, right to get good press for Maya.'

'But Maya hated having people turn up in restaurants, or

writing about her private life, or all the speculation about what she would or would not do, may or may not think, the stuff you fed out.'

'*Said* she did. She didn't mind the end product though. That book she complained about – it was fucking brilliant for her.'

'And the drugs?'

'Wrong, but I never did it near Maya. She needn't have known. I know you think I just loved the whole "Maya and Dan" thing, the fame, the bollocks, and I did love all that, course I did. But she was what came first for me. I loved her and she loved me and it was all going fine till you wheedled your way in and destroyed it. Because you're the one who's never had anything, never done anything, you're the one who's nothing without her, and you can't fucking live with it.'

'You destroyed it Dan, when you punched her.'

He went quiet.

'So she told you about that, did she?'

'She didn't need to tell me. It was written all over her face.'

'Yeah, well, it was an accident. And don't you think I've regretted it every minute of every hour of every day since? Do you think I don't want kids too – of course I do, just not yet, and you were wheedling away there too, weren't you, wheedle, wheedle, and I took everything out on her. What's the song – "you always hurt the one you love"? Well that was me. There was no justification but that doesn't mean I don't love her.'

He was looking at me now, desperate. I noticed a film forming on both eyes and a tear started to fall from the corner of his left eye. Seconds later, he slumped forward, his head in his hands, sobbing. There was no way my years of hatred were going to be washed away by a few tears, but he was suffering, and I took little pleasure in it.

After a while, he sat up, sniffed loudly, wiped his eyes with the collar of his shirt. He let out several large, loud breaths. He was calmer.

'I know what you think,' he said. 'You think I'm crying because I'm all washed up, off the telly, yesterday's man, no hope of getting back in the big time. And maybe, a little bit, I am. But I'm also crying because I love Maya. And I've lost her.'

We sat there for a few moments. I asked if he wanted me to fetch him a cup of tea from the van. He shook his head.

'I'll take you back to your car,' I said. We drove in silence. I parked alongside his Mercedes.

'I'm sorry, Dan,' I said. 'Sorry it's worked out like this.'

He gave me a look of pure hatred.

'Sure you're sorry. It's exactly how you fucking planned it.'

The next time I saw Dan, he was on the TV. He was filmed being driven into a drug rehab clinic in Oxfordshire that had become something of a magnet for celebrities. Vanessa was watching with me. We were both relieved to see those pictures. Although I'd told Brandon that my black eye was due to a mugging, I hadn't hidden the truth from Vanessa.

'He'll be out of harm's way there,' I said. 'And get the help he needs hopefully.'

'It was because of what you said at that dinner party, wasn't it?' she said anxiously. 'I told you to be careful about getting involved in other people's marital problems.'

'I guess he assumes that I somehow managed to turn Maya against him . . .'

'And all the time you were singing his praises!' said Vanessa with a curt laugh. 'Still, I can't help feeling a bit sorry for him,' she went on. 'Maybe he did love her. He found a way in his mind of boxing off the affair, but he still loved her. And maybe in that world they live in, that's every bit as much the done thing as not doing it is the done thing in our world.'

'Maybe.'

'Will you tell Maya what he did to you?'

'I doubt it, unless she asks.'

'I think that's right,' said Vanessa. 'It would only worry her. Probably safer to keep well out of her affairs from now on, eh?'

'That's exactly what I plan to do,' I said, kissing her.

Chapter Twenty-One

Three months passed. London finally threw off its drab clothes and started to look pretty again in the sun of early summer. Vanessa bloomed. Pregnancy was suiting her. She wore her bump with pride, and people began standing up for her in the Tube.

Meanwhile, in New York, Maya was adjusting to life as a single woman. She'd moved over there slightly earlier than *The Hunter Hunted* team needed her because she figured that the story of her separation would die more quickly in America than England. After all, Dan's name meant a lot less over there. Also she needed to get away from Blomfield Road. She had decided to sell the house, partly to banish the memories, but also because she had instructed her lawyer that whatever her rights, she did not want to leave Dan empty-handed from the divorce, and had agreed to him getting a quarter of the proceeds from the sale.

'Time to move on, Steve,' she said in one of our rare phone conversations. 'I'm thinking maybe Hampstead or Chelsea, or even move right out of London.'

On Sheldon's advice, she had upped the money she was putting into *The Hunter Hunted* and her co-producer role meant she was in on all the pre-production discussions. She was really enjoying it, and I was happy for her. She had a new cast of characters around her now, and I was hopeful she could draw fresh energy and focus from them. The only problem was the continued media obsession with her every move. They might not be interested in Dan in the States, but there was nothing about Maya that was not deemed newsworthy by someone. The *New York Post* ran a whole page on which flavours mixed well after Maya's driver was spotted by a photographer parking up, getting out at an ice-cream stall and taking a triple cornet with pistachio, blackcurrant and rum-raisin to Maya in the back seat.

I wondered whether, once the film was finished, Maya would feel an even stronger desire for a normal life. 'I'm so jealous of Vanessa,' she said in one of our phone calls. 'Can you imagine if I ever got pregnant? They'd be naming my child before I even knew what sex it was.' 'If I ever got pregnant'? She had clearly forgotten she once was. Or forgotten I knew.

A young guy called Martin Sampson was looking after her PR in the States. Nick had gone out to oversee her arrival but once things had cooled off, he came back home, leaving Sampson, who worked out of his New York office, in charge. Maya described Sampson to me as a very professional, highly motivated thirty-something Bostonian who wore short-sleeved shirts and bright stripey ties and who had looked after some of the biggest names in the States. Nick had been using him to try to diversify into US baseball and basketball. He had assured Maya Sampson was his 'brightest and best' but I got the feeling the young man's boundless enthusiasm was clashing horribly with a mood still dominated by mourning for her marriage and lack of certainty about how she wanted to spend the rest of her life.

Vanessa and I had very different views about Maya and her intentions for the future. Vanessa was more convinced than ever that whatever Maya said in her low moments about fame, she would no more give it up than a baby would turn down its mother's breast. 'It's what she is – she's a performer, she's a star. Look at how she worked that crowd at the V&A. Or how she let her agent destroy Dan's reputation.'

'Dan destroyed his reputation himself,' I shot back. 'And all she was doing at the V&A was trying to get something good for others out of something bad for herself.'

'Oh come on, Steve, it was as cynical a piece of Nick Sheldon mega-manipulation as you can imagine.'

'I don't buy that,' I said, though even as I said it I felt she had a point, or a bit of one. It had certainly led to a glut, global, of great headlines and pictures for Maya, all generated by Sheldon's two hand-picked cameramen. Perhaps I was arguing for the sake of it or because I didn't like it when Vanessa criticised Maya. 'She had to face the world at some time and Sheldon rightly found an event where she would be warmly received.'

'The way he had set up the media she'd have been warmly received in a fridge.'

'It was brilliant. Good for her, good for the event and the charity, why are you complaining?'

'I'm not complaining. I'm just not buying the line that it was all so sweet and innocent. And I'm certainly not buying the line that she's going to throw it all in. No way.'

I wasn't so sure. When Maya and I spoke in June, I could sense the tension with this guy Sampson was growing. Maya had invited her parents to come over and stay with her for a few weeks, before the filming itself began, and Sampson had come up with a barking plan for a big set-piece press conference with the whole family on the theme of 'how they overcame betrayal'.

'Can you imagine Dad agreeing to that?' she said, half laughing. 'Martin is a lovely boy in lots of ways, and I can see why Nick thinks he is the business,' she complained, 'but he is constantly fizzing with ideas and thinking up ways of keeping this wave of good publicity going, and I want it to stop. His job is to get coverage, but I've had more than enough of it. I honestly could not care if I was never in a newspaper again in my entire life.'

'Have you said anything to him?'

'Kind of, but he is very American. Has his ideas, not great at adapting as quickly as Nick and the people I use at home.'

'What does Nick say?'

'The thing is I don't want to drop Martin in it because he is very good and it's not fair. But maybe if it carries on I'll say something.'

I was following her US coverage via the web and fair to say she was making an impressive impact. The drugs speech had also woken the serious press in the States to the social-conscience side of her profile, so there was a new surge of interest in anything she had to say on Aids, breast cancer, education, Africa. Bono and Bob Geldof had made a short film as part of their latest campaign on preventable diseases, and they'd asked Maya to do the voiceover and a really powerful piece to camera at the end. She told me how the PR director for *The Hunter Hunted* had asked her to slow down a bit so they could use some of her publicity hits nearer the time.

'I told him to speak to Sheldon's office,' she said. 'I'm not even hitting.'

Still, she didn't sound too miserable. It was a bit like the old days and the calls we made when she was first out on the road doing parts in regional theatres around Britain. She babbled on excitedly about how much she was looking forward to seeing her parents, and about her developing social life. She was enjoying getting out and about, despite the media still bothering her, and I noticed that one name kept cropping up.

'Bernard, but pronounced the French way, Bare-narde.'

'Does he have a surname?'

'Dufay.'

'So is this a post-Dan moment?' I asked when she called me again a week later to talk about how much she loved the French accent.

'Do you mean is he catching me on the rebound?'

'I just wondered if it was going down a romantic track at all.'

'We've seen each other most days because of work, and we've been out together twice. We went to nice restaurants. We had nice conversations. And if he said do you fancy doing it again, I would say yes.'

In fact he did ask her out again, and this time, because the press had staked her out at the restaurant last time, he invited her to his rented apartment in Brooklyn.

'This sounds like it is going somewhere,' I said when she told me that.

'Well let's see,' she said, which I took as a yes. 'And Steve, I know you turned out to be right about Dan, but do not assume every man I meet is going to treat me badly.'

'What's he like?' I asked.

'Really nice guy. Bit older, 40s maybe, I don't know. Very

French, apart from his hair, which is bright blond, wears chi-chi clothes, keeps himself in shape, a teeny bit camp when he's ordering people around, but very clever. You'd like him.'

It turned out to be a really common name, so it took me a while to work out which of the many Bernard Dufays on Google was likeliest to be him. Finally I found an 'ency-clopaedia of French cinema' and there he was, award-winning location director. Maya had mentioned that he had been to 'places even most Americans didn't know existed'. It must be him. Then I noticed one of his awards was for *An English Rose Abroad* which had been filmed mainly in Spain. That must have been how she knew him. There weren't any photographs that I could find, but there were plenty of accolades from people who had worked with him, saying he was the best in the busi-ness. I have to confess that I felt the tiniest stab of jealousy.

What were Dan's words again? 'It's exactly how you fucking planned it.' Wrong, Dan, so wrong. Looking back over the train of events that has led me to where I am, I'm not sure I ever planned anything. Sheldon planned things. Dan planned things. They were the manipulative ones. I just reacted to the circumstances I found myself in, and did what I thought was right. For example, the day Maya called to tell me she'd slept with Bernard – I had already guessed to be honest – was the day I got a big red letter from Swift International, reminding me (as if I needed it) that their invoice remained unpaid.

'You're the only person I can tell this to, Steve,' said Maya breathlessly, 'but I think I'm falling in love.'

'Wow,' I said, taken aback. 'That was quick.'

Fortunately Jerry wasn't in the room. It was the first week of the school holidays and he'd taken his family to Spain. The final Qatar presentation was taking place mid-August and he'd decided to fit his holiday in now so that he would be in the office while Brandon was in Qatar, on call if he was needed.

'I've known Bernard for a while,' said Maya. 'It's just that we never thought about each other that way. I was married. He was married . . .'

'Married? So he isn't any longer?'

'Well, technically he is, but he and his wife are separating.'

'How do you know?'

'For God's sake, Steve, he *told* me.'

The phone call lasted a good hour. She described in some detail the evening leading up to the moment when she went back to Bernard's apartment with him, stopping when she realised her story was getting a bit steamy. 'Slept with' wasn't quite the right way to denote what Maya and Bernard had got up to, since no sleeping took place. Mr and Mrs Lowe were staying in Maya's apartment so she had to be home, and tucked up in bed, at a reasonable time. She laughed as she talked about a speedy taxi ride home from Queens in the middle of the night.

I put the phone down feeling slightly sick, but then I told myself not to be ridiculous. This wasn't like when she told me about sleeping with Dan. I'd known who Dan was, then. I already knew he was a jerk. I didn't know anything about this Bernard. He could be perfect for her. So why did I have a feeling that all was not well? Was it more than a stab of jealousy? Was I in some way an extension of her, that missing ingredient lacking among all the other qualities she had – good judgement about herself and her relationships?

I stared down at my desk and at the red reminder from Swift. It was Maya's lack of judgement that had got me into all this. Now, just when I was trying to get out of it, I was confronted by a bill I couldn't pay. I'd been toying with various options for dealing with the invoice. Ring Stafford and ask him to give me until September, when I'd have received the Qatar bonus. Pay the money now out of Globus funds, hope Brandon wouldn't notice, and then ask Stafford to do a recharge when I could afford to write him a cheque myself. Now I had another idea. What better way to keep Stafford waiting than to give him some more work?

If Bernard Dufay's situation was as he recounted it to Maya, then he had nothing to fear from a few gentle enquiries by Stafford. If he was lying to her – and given her track record with men there had to be a chance of that – then surely this was the right thing to do. For her. It was incidental that it helped me buy a little time with Swift.

'Well hi there, Mr Watkins,' said Stafford, when I finally got through to him. 'I've been wondering when I'd get the opportunity to discuss the aftermath of that little job we did for you. Not surprised it went that way. I got the impression she's a real family-values person, and Desperate Dan is a bit of a slimeball.'

'Right on both counts,' I said.

'One bird on the side, I might not approve, but I suppose I can understand. But two? And all that feeding them stories about his missus. It's kind of revolting.'

'So you weren't sad to see how things turned out?'

'When it comes to work, I don't do sad or happy. Let's just say you really get to know people when you've got them under surveillance, and I have to say I quite liked her and I didn't really take to him. Mind you, I will say this for him – ten per cent of all his earnings go to his dad, which is a tidy sum. And he has standing orders to three charities, one of them pretty big. Anyway, talking of money – you'll have received the bill I hope . . . again . . .'

'That's why I was calling,' I said hastily. 'I've realised that this job isn't quite as finished as I'd thought. Maya may be in need of your services again . . .'

'That sounds intriguing,' said Stafford. 'Tell me more.'

'Do you work overseas?'

'We do yes. We have mutual arrangements in most countries and we do some stuff overseas ourselves. Depends. What is it you need?'

'Nothing as big as before but I would like a very basic check on a French guy.'

'You want him followed?'

'Not yet, I don't think so.'

'Any clues as to why we're looking at him?'

'We've got a feeling he is trying to move in on Maya's finances.'

'We?'

'I'm not alone in this you know.'

'I wasn't implying you were. And I'm sure you're right to check him out. It does happen after a woman splits from her husband so you're probably wise to be vigilant. Do you have a name?'

'Bernard Dufay, fairly well known in the film world, does sets and locations and shit like that.'

'OK, I can get you a basic picture pretty quickly.'

'And the bill . . . ?'

'We'll add this on and send a revised invoice. After all, Globus aren't going to default on payment, are they? Wouldn't do their reputation much good.'

He hung up with a wicked chuckle.

It had felt like a great idea when I called him. Now I was less sure. I felt anxious suddenly, uncertain whether he was my pawn or I was his. He seemed to enjoy the game more than I did.

'Pretty quickly' meant forty-eight hours. At the end of a scorching day, I drove from Heathrow to Kensington to meet Stafford behind the Hilton, two bays down from where we met last time. He had used a French firm to do basic checks and had come up with the following summary of Dufay:

- Successful and affluent.
- First marriage dissolved after two years on grounds of wife's admitted adultery.
- Seemingly happy second marriage. Three children aged 5 to 11.
- Extensive property interests — sizeable apartment in Paris, country home in Sainte-Preuve (Aisne départe-ment), also original purchaser of home of former wife near Rheims, and has apartments in Rome and Los Angeles.
- Income legitimate.
- No criminal record. (One motoring offence.)
- Currently based in New York.
- No evidence of behaviour likely to interest blackmailer or concerned partner.

I asked Stafford why the reference to blackmail. He said it was how the French tended to look at things. Because of French privacy laws, and the closeness of the press barons to political and business leaders, the tradition in France was that sexual affairs were not such a big deal in the media. Instead

of being plastered all over the papers, extramarital relationships are more likely to be used for blackmail. 'It's my French
colleague's way of saying this guy is not your typical French
serial shagger.'

'I see.'

The information confused me. Here was a guy who was
happily married with three kids and yet was prepared to risk
it all for an affair with Maya. Did his wife allow him to play
away from home, given that he worked abroad so often? I
knew the French were different to us, but were they really
that different? . . . And then, he'd lied to Maya. He'd told her
he was in the process of separating from his wife. It was half
true. He had gone through that process with one wife a number
of years ago. But it seemed he had another with whom he
lived happily. What was certain to me was that he was raising
expectations in Maya that he wouldn't be able to fulfil. She'd
sounded so happy on the phone, and this Frenchman was jeop-
ardising the fragile stability she'd worked so hard to put back
into her life. I wanted to warn her, tell her not to invest too
much of herself in this relationship, but I knew I couldn't. To
do so, I'd have to admit what I knew about Bernard, and how
I knew it. It was impossible.

Vanessa could see I was low when I got home. She put it
down to work fatigue. We hadn't been away all year and had
been discussing taking a long holiday in August – perhaps three
weeks. 'After all,' Vanessa had said, 'it's your birthday. And
soon they won't be letting me on aeroplanes!'

She brought up the subject of holiday destinations again that
evening. 'What about New England? You know, I've always
wanted to go there since I saw *On Golden Pond*.'

'What are you saying? Now we're pregnant, we might as

well be as old as Henry Fonda and Katharine Hepburn?'

'No! Just that the countryside looked so beautiful in the film. And it will be our last chance to have a peaceful, romantic holiday in a distant location for a few years to come.'

I wasn't sure. I had been thinking more of Europe. Not France, certainly not now. But Italy, perhaps, or Spain, even Greece if Vanessa could bear the heat. However, New England suddenly seemed more of a possibility when I opened my email later that night and found a message from Maya:

Been thinking since we spoke. Having Mum and Dad in the flat is making it rather tricky with a certain Frenchman I mentioned. Do you and V fancy a holiday in New York? It would be great to see you, and if you were coming, I could persuade Mum and Dad to move into a posh hotel nearby, give you their room. I know they'd go for it – Mum loves posh hotels. That way Bernard and I could have some time at my place. Plus you could help me entertain Pa and Ma – I'm having difficulty keeping them occupied!

XXXX

I wasn't sure how to read the invitation. On the one hand it looked like a rather blatant request for a favour and to stitch up her parents. Nor did it help with the vow I'd made to be less involved in Maya's life, and I certainly didn't want to do anything that might help Bernard get access to her bedroom. On the other hand, it provided the perfect excuse to go and check out Dufay myself – and to have a cheap luxury holiday before the baby came along.

To my surprise, Vanessa jumped at the idea. A week of city

life in New York followed by a rural idyll in New England was her idea of the perfect holiday. She didn't even mind when I mentioned that we might be required to shepherd Mr and Mrs Lowe around.

'They're lovely people,' she said, 'and what a way to see the city! From a chic apartment overlooking Central Park!'

'From *Maya's* apartment,' I reminded her. 'And you told me I shouldn't get involved in her life.'

'This is different. This isn't getting involved. This is making the most of knowing a movie star.'

I thought about mentioning Bernard but decided against it. She'd find out soon enough.

The next week was a whirlwind of activity. Vanessa was frantically shopping for suitable maternity wear (Maya had suggested we imagine being hot and then imagine walking into a sauna being *that* hot already) while I was putting the finishing touches to Brandon's Qatar presentation. Luke Morgan had come up trumps. We had now had five examples of cock-ups by Websters, two serious, with all the details. I was confident the contract was effectively ours.

Then, three days before we were due to leave, something happened to put a massive dampener on my enthusiasm about the trip. I had just got home from work when Maya called to say that she had spoken earlier to Dan, who had come out of rehab. I had taken to heart her strictures about my needing to grow up about Dan, so I held in my immediate reaction, counted to three before asking 'How was he?' with as much nonchalance as I could manage. I'd been true to my word and hadn't told Maya about the battering her ex-husband had given me.

'Well, he's not great. He's pretty cut up. Shell-shocked at

the way everyone has dumped him. Full of hate, anger, remorse. Seems he did a lot of thinking while he was in rehab. Asked me to forgive him.'

I almost choked.

'Get back together with him, you mean?'

'No, forgive him. Like in a religious kind of way, I think . . .'

'And will you?'

'I don't know. It's not easy to go from loving someone so much to feeling so hurt by them. Some of the love still lingers, along with the hurt. I don't want him to be desperate, Steve.'

It was frightening how quickly I had moved from the warm glow I felt on hearing her voice at the other end of the line to the feeling of deep unease I had now. But I was determined to hide it.

'I understand that, of course I do.'

I could hear a siren in the background.

'He was vile about you. Vile.'

'Like what?'

'Just horrible. Blames you. Thinks you got at me in some way.'

'Sometimes it's hard for people to face up to their own mistakes.'

'I know. I said that to him. I said, "You may not want to hear it, but I was really grateful that Steve was around when it was all falling apart."'

'That's kind.'

'Well it's true. And I told him how you would always be my friend, and in fact you and Vanessa were coming out to see me next week. How wonderful you were with my parents.'

'Thanks,' I said, though I hated the idea of Dan knowing I

would be in New York. 'How did he get to you? I mean, why did you take the call?'

'I called him, actually. I got a message through the lawyers that he would welcome a conversation with me. My lawyer was opposed, thought there was something a bit iffy about it, but I felt I should. The last thing I want is for the divorce to be nasty. It's what his team wants of course, because it means more money and publicity for them. Apparently his lawyer's been profiled in the *Lawyer* magazine twice already.'

After the phone call ended, I went into the bathroom and felt a sudden wave of nausea so strong that I gagged into the sink. Nothing came but choke upon choke of anxiety, then a tiny trickle of vomit. It was as if all my fear of Dan had suddenly welled up inside me and needed some kind of release. I'd calmed down a bit by the time Vanessa came home from work. After all, there was no reason to believe that just because Dan knew I was going to visit Maya, he would do anything about it. His rehab must have cost a fortune and he was never a saver. If the papers were to be believed, he was virtually penniless and the divorce settlement was far from complete. He was hardly going to be able to afford a visit to New York. No, I should stop fretting and enjoy the holiday, I told myself. It was all going to be fine. It was not Dan I should be worrying about, but Bernard.

Chapter Twenty-Two

There's something about a pregnant woman that makes even the most brazen queue-jumper stand back. I noticed it immediately as Vanessa and I made our way to the check-in desk at Heathrow. Fellow passengers ushered us forward, grumpy old men beamed at her. 'I realise now that, all these years, I should have been travelling with a cushion under my jumper,' she joked as she returned the smile of an old lady who, moments before, had been haranguing a child who banged his trolley on her shin. Vanessa put her hand on her stomach as if to protect the baby from the noise of the airport. She seemed serene and confident. I on the other hand was a nervous wreck. Despite my determination not to worry about Dan, I'd had trouble sleeping for the past two nights and the effects were beginning to show. I had bags under my eyes and, that morning, I had detected a scattering of grey hairs above my left ear. There was no getting round it: I looked like shit. How would Maya feel about having such an indecorous person around the place, I wondered? It would be awkward to be in her apartment with lots of beautiful things and beautiful people. And Bernard, of course. I figured being pregnant would protect Vanessa from feeling any sense of inadequacy: every time she looked at Maya's perfect figure, honed through daily workouts with a personal trainer in the bedroom she'd had converted to a gym, she could comfort herself with the thought of the baby. But me? How would I feel around Bare-narde with his French chic and adorable accent? Pretty rubbish was my guess.

'I hope this is going to be OK,' I said to Vanessa as we sat waiting for our gate to be called.

'What, flying when I'm pregnant?'

'No, going to stay with Maya.'

Vanessa was full of energy, buoyed up by the adventure of such an unusual holiday.

'Don't worry so much, Steve,' she said taking my hand. 'She invited us, didn't she? Let's just relax and enjoy our last bit of freedom before we're surrounded by nappies and soggy biscuits. You've got to remember, Maya stays friends with you precisely because you're *not* like all the people around her. Be yourself and it'll all be fine.'

I kissed her, and stroked the bump, but I didn't feel any better. Vanessa's reassurance was usually an immediate cure for any anxiety I was experiencing, but it was as if I had become immune to its effects.

Once the cabin crew noticed the bump, she became passenger priority number one; they could not have been nicer, fussing around her, helping her adjust the seat to the most comfortable position, making sure she had enough water to drink. When I dropped in that we were staying with Maya, they became even more solicitous.

'I feel like royalty,' she said.

While Vanessa spent the five-hour flight poring over the guidebooks, I looked out of the window at the clouds, revolving my anxieties around my head.

I felt slightly better, though, when we got off the plane.

Whatever was going on with Bernard, at least I would be there to keep an eye on it. Far better to be on the spot to see things for myself than to listen to Maya raving about him on the phone and be powerless. And what a bonus that I was finally going to see New York, a city I'd dreamt of visiting ever since seeing Eddie Murphy and Richard Pryor in *Harlem Nights* at the Ealing Odeon. My mood improved even more when I saw Maya's driver, Nelson – named after Mandela, she'd told me – waiting for us at arrivals with my name on a card. Despite my protests that we could get a taxi, Maya had insisted that she could do without her personal driver for the morning, and I had to confess it felt great to be ushered towards a waiting car as if we, too, were celebrities. At least, it felt great until I spotted something that stopped me in my tracks.

'What's the matter, Steve?' said Vanessa. 'I almost tripped over you. Have you forgotten something?'

'It's Dan,' I muttered. 'I can't believe it. It's Dan fucking Chivers.'

She followed my gaze and we both stood stock still as we tried to take in the spectacle of Dan being berated by two security guards while a guy in black jeans and a ripped T-shirt danced around them filming the argument with a video camera. It was impossible to hear what was being said except when they raised their voices and phrases like 'can't film here' and 'accompany us to immigration' made themselves heard above the hubbub of the arrivals hall.

'Oh my,' said Nelson. 'Maya ain't gonna like that.'

'What do you think they're doing?' asked Vanessa.

'I don't know, ma'am, but what I do know is that it won't be long before Mr Chivers turns up at the apartment and causes chaos. Me and the doorman been waitin' for it to happen. The locks and everything are changed, but still . . .'

Eager for Dan not to notice me I grabbed hold of Vanessa's arm and started running for the exit.

'Quick, let's go before he sees us.'

It was too late. I suddenly heard a shout of 'There he is!', followed by 'Steve! Steve! I've got a few questions for you!' and Dan and his cameraman came rushing towards us, giving the security guards the slip.

'This way!' said Nelson, gesturing towards a black Lexus parked directly in front of the terminal doors. We threw ourselves into the car and Nelson immediately pulled off.

'What was all that about?' said Vanessa, panting hard from the exertion of having to run.

I sat back, grabbed the bottle of water in the side of the door, leaned over to take Vanessa's hand. I couldn't answer her. All sorts of mad thoughts were running through my mind. That Dan had come to kill me. That he had found out about Stafford. That the cameraman was there to film my dying confession.

'Jesus. Now what?' said Nelson, looking anxiously into his rear-view mirror. I turned round. A yellow taxi was following us with Dan and the cameraman (video camera in hand) leaning dangerously out of the side windows. Nelson speeded up, so did the cab. Eventually, when Nelson was forced to brake because of a car in front, the taxi drew up alongside us, close enough for me to notice a fake diamond stud in the cameraman's ear. Dan, who was sitting in the front passenger seat, was waving and laughing manically.

I lowered the window. 'Dan,' I shouted, 'this is fucking dangerous.'

'Don't worry,' he said. 'We'll bleep out all the f-words.'

'What are you doing?'

'I'm making a film about my fightback, Steve, my side of the story. And you're in it.'

'What do you mean?'

'Exactly what I say. You wanted a starring role, you just got one.'

Then he drew his head back inside the taxi and told the driver to overtake us so they could film from a different angle. Vanessa, Nelson and I watched in disbelief as the yellow cab shot in front of us. It enabled Nelson to tail them to the next junction, where he pulled off at speed and finally managed to get away from them.

'Steve, do you know anything about this?' asked Vanessa, her face white. I shook my head, dumbfounded.

Nelson saved the day. As soon as he could, he pulled up at a drive-in diner and bought us both a cold Coke. Then he talked us through how we should break the news to Maya that her ex-husband was hell-raising in town.

'Don't tell her in front of her folks,' was his advice. 'Wait till I drive Mr and Mrs Lowe to their hotel . . . And try not to get worked up about it. I know Maya. She'll bring him to heel in no time. This ain't gonna ruin your vacation.'

I wished I was as confident. It was hard, though, to dwell too much on the problem of Dan while the familiar yet unfamiliar scenery of New York was unfurling before our eyes. Nelson kept up a running commentary, perhaps in order to distract us. 'That's where the Twin Towers used to stand', 'This is Brooklyn Bridge', 'Down there is Theatreland' . . .

I used to argue with Maya that cinema could never truly capture mood and place, and the drive towards Manhattan confirmed me in my opinion. I had seen that vista so many times, in countless films, but this was a virgin journey. It all seemed totally new. As we crossed Brooklyn Bridge Vanessa wound down the window, despite Nelson's warning that it would mess up the air conditioning. She wanted to feel the warm air on her face and breathe in the view, make it one of those memories she could force to stay with us for ever. When we drew up in front of a sandstone apartment block with a red carpet running from the ornate brass doors across the pavement to the kerb, I could tell she was trying to make another memory.

Having checked that there was no sign of Dan and his companion, Nelson called up to Maya that we had arrived. Within two minutes she was down in the lobby to greet us, barefoot and dressed in shorts and a flowery top. There were plenty of hugs and kisses and excited chatter, before she took us in the lift to the ninth floor and her apartment. It was a little bit like walking into the white-sofa sitting room at Blomfield Road, only higher up, and with an even better outlook. The flat was done up with very light colours, mainly whites and yellows, most of the furniture comfortable as well as stylish, nice artefacts, classy lighting. Maya took us into the kitchen where Mr and Mrs Lowe were waiting with iced tea and a warm welcome.

'Steve, old friend!' said Mr Lowe, clasping my hand. 'So good to see you. So good.'

Mrs Lowe fussed over Vanessa's bump and launched into stories about how she'd deliberately tried to time her pregnancy with Maya so that she wasn't big during the summer.

'Mum!' said Maya, laughing. 'I'm not sure I should be hearing about this stuff.'

We chatted for an hour until Vanessa and I started to wilt with fatigue. It was Mrs Lowe who noticed.

'We'll go now,' she said, nudging her husband. 'Maya darling, will you ask that nice driver of yours to take us over to the hotel.'

When they'd gone, Maya showed us to our bedroom. The double bed was slightly raised on a platform. Intriguingly, there was a painted portrait of Maya between the main windows, which meant it would be the first thing I saw each morning. I asked if that was why she put it there, and she laughed.

'Dan commissioned it as a thirtieth birthday present but I can't stand it. I look mean in it. So it's in the room in the apartment I least use.'

'Don't take it personally, Steve,' Vanessa chipped in.

We had our own bathroom and jacuzzi. A little dressing room for Vanessa. Maya told us she had an in-house laundry service. 'Just throw any dirty washing in the basket between your sinks,' she said. 'It'll be back same day or first thing next morning.' Her own room was just across from ours. It was all very Maya. White walls. One large painting, of a tiny sliver of blue sea and enormous yellow skies. King-size bed, immaculately made but with one corner turned down as they do in hotels. Dresses hung on an overspill clothes rail by the window. Books piled up on her bedside table, with an old biography of Vivien Leigh on the top.

When she'd finished the tour, Maya suggested we had a rest in our room but warned us not to sleep. 'It's best just to keep going till New York bedtime,' she said. 'That way you beat the jet lag. Can you cope with that Vanessa?'

'Oh sure,' said Vanessa, not terribly convincingly. She was giving me significant looks and I realised that I could no longer hold back the news about what had happened at the airport.

'Maya, there's something we need to tell you,' I said. 'About Dan.'

Maya looked pained just at the mention of his name.

'He was at JFK when we arrived.'

'What?'

'And he had a film crew with him.'

'You're kidding me!'

'I'm afraid not.'

'Did he speak to you?'

Vanessa and I looked at each other.

'Yes,' I said.

'And? What did he say?'

'That he was making a film about his fightback – his side of the story.'

'Oh my God,' said Maya. 'That's just the idiotic sort of thing Nick said he might go and do. I'd heard he'd hooked up with a new agent. Some D-league, money-grubbing TV producer must have persuaded them it was a good idea. Now I understand what that phone call was all about . . .'

'What do you mean?' I asked.

'You know, the one I mentioned to you? Where he asked for my forgiveness? I thought at the time it sounded weird. Well, he would have been recording it, wouldn't he? To use in his film . . .'

Maya put her head in her hands for a moment, and then seemed to rally, as if she were instructing herself to pull herself together.

'Look,' she said, 'we can't let this spoil your holiday. I'm sure Nick and the lawyers can sort it out. We'll forget all about it and enjoy ourselves. Mum and Dad are going to spend this evening settling into their hotel, so I've booked a table at Robert De Niro's restaurant in Greenwich Street. A few people from the film are going to come along.'

'Oh who?' said Vanessa, excitedly. 'Not Matt Damon surely?'

'No, but I've met him now and he's really nice. I'm sure it's going to be great working with him. There's another actor, Curtis Stadler, who's gay and coming with his partner, and a French guy I've mentioned to Steve.'

'Bare-narde,' I said.

'You'll really like him, I promise.'

Perhaps I should have told her, there and then, that just as I had been right about Dan, it looked like I was right about Bernard too. He was married. Still. Happily married. Maya was a fling for him. He knew she would be as keen as he was to keep it quiet. They had different but shared vested interests in that. I wanted to say it, but I couldn't. It raised too many questions, not about Maya, or Bernard, but about me, and how I knew.

She left us to go and get changed. Vanessa and I stood at the window and looked out over Central Park. It didn't feel real being there.

'That was so weird with Dan,' said Vanessa. 'I hope he's going to leave us alone. What did he mean about you wanting a starring role?'

'God knows,' I said, and hugged her hard.

Chapter Twenty-Three

Robert De Niro's restaurant was full to overflowing, and noisier than I had expected. I had been anticipating something like the more upmarket places Maya and I went to in the West London rectangle, but this felt less stuffy: women decked out in haute couture alongside men in jeans and brightly coloured shirts. There was a gaggle of people by the entrance waiting for early diners to leave, but as we arrived the manager greeted us at the door and led us straight to a corner table. A waiter was weaving between the tables, giving a loud running commentary as he went, 'Move to the left ladies, grilled chicken for table seven, coming through, vegetables to follow, sea bass for the boy, why there's a face I know, welcome Miss Lowe . . .'

I was keen to see whether Maya provoked the same kind of response in New York restaurants as she did in London. It was not far off. I would say that, whereas in London she got heads turning on ninety per cent of the tables, here it was about seventy per cent, perhaps a little less. Curtis and his boyfriend, Doug, were already there, and so was Bernard, who stood to watch her walk through the restaurant, then welcomed her with a kiss on both cheeks. He was not what I expected at all. Maya's depiction had led me to imagine a pink-shirted, tight-trousered, suede-shoes-without-socks Parisian, short, as many Frenchmen are. In fact he stood at least two or three inches above me and had the physique of someone who spent a good part of every day in the gym. He had piercing light blue eyes surrounded by whites without a speck of red or any other blemish. His hair was more sandy than blond. He was wearing a linen jacket and a stripey blue and white shirt. He wore a watch on his right hand, so I assumed he was left-handed, like Maya. Creative people often are. It was one of Maya's little truisms.

I was of course keen to see the interplay between them. The kiss as we arrived was no more intimate than the kiss from Curtis or his partner. Bernard made no apparent effort to sit next to her although as things turned out, because Vanessa sat next to Curtis and motioned to me to sit down on the other side of her, Maya and Bernard ended up together. But the body language between them was of professional colleagues more than lovers. Maya was clearly the hostess and Bernard was behaving like a polite guest. It was when it came to ordering food and drink that I noticed a change in Bernard's behaviour. Perhaps it was because he was French, and assumed mere Brits and Americans wouldn't dare to challenge his judgement on wine and cuisine. But it looked to me like he was suddenly making a move to be head of the table which, given the dinner was supposed to be Maya's welcome for me and Vanessa, struck me as presumptuous. When the wine waiter brought over the menu, he signalled he did not need to see it. He asked for a Bâtard-Montrachet 2001 and a Château Pavie Decesse 2003 and I could tell that the wine waiter was impressed.

'We usually like to see a credit card before purchase on

those wines, sir,' he said, bowing a little towards Bernard, 'but seeing the company you keep . . .' and he shifted the bow to Maya, while Bernard opined sagely to the table 'You won't be disappointed.'

'Bernard studied wines at university,' said Maya.

'Wow,' said Curtis. 'Beats drama school.'

When we were discussing what to eat, Bernard kept offering suggestions and judgements, especially to Maya, in a way that really irked me. He did that irritating French thing of puckering up his lips, putting thumb and three fingers against them and giving his fingertips a little kiss to signal his approval of the anticipated taste. Maya was lapping it up though. I noticed Vanessa was directing most of her conversation to him too. She clearly found him the most interesting of the three of them, though she might have been troubled by the very open displays of affection between Curtis and Doug. Maya had warned us in the cab that Curtis was 'even more actorish off set than on it', while Doug, a costume designer, was constantly reaching out to touch his partner's hands, hair and face.

'Will you two calm down?' Maya said with a laugh at one point.

'Oh we're just so happy to be here on such a happy night when your old friends are over from London,' said Doug. 'We're having a ball.'

'Oh, Maya, stop being so *Eengleesh*,' said Bernard, tapping her hand lightly in mock reprimand. 'If it was a man and a woman kissing and touching and all this, you would not say calm down I don't think.'

I don't know what came over me but I suddenly blurted out the question 'Are you gay, Bernard?'

Maya stared at me as if I'd taken leave of my senses. Vanessa blushed. Curtis burst out laughing.

'You'd have to ask my wife that question, Steve,' Bernard said with a wink.

'So you're married, Bernard?' said Vanessa, trying to divert attention away from my comment.

Bernard made a very French little gesture, said 'Bof' with an upward curl of the top lip and a shrug of the left shoulder, then started chatting away about some of the fantastic locations in *The Hunter Hunted*. Vanessa gave me a bemused look. Maya's face was a mask. For the rest of the meal, everyone studiously avoided the subject of relationships.

I was interested to know if Bernard would come back to the apartment, so I became a little irritable at how long we took over coffee, especially since Vanessa was falling asleep against my shoulder. But eventually it was time to leave. Bernard paid for dinner despite Maya's half-hearted effort to grab the bill and then, with the same chaste kisses with which he'd greeted her, he left for Brooklyn, with Curtis and Doug, in a pre-ordered cab.

When they had gone, leaving us sitting at the table, Maya did not exactly explode, but she wasn't happy.

'What on earth was that about, Steve?'

'What?'

'Asking Bernard if he was gay?'

'I was just making conversation and I guess the other two carrying on like they were made me think of it.'

'I could not believe my ears.'

'I agree it was a bit odd,' said Vanessa, 'but I don't think he meant any harm, did you, Steve?'

'No, of course not. It was just unfortunate. He didn't seem to take offence.'

'It was like you were trying to insult him.'

'Rubbish. It's not an insult to ask someone if they're gay.'

'But you know he's not.'

'Why didn't he want to talk about his marriage?' Vanessa asked, trying to cool the exchange between Maya and me.

'He's in the middle of a difficult separation, that's probably why,' Maya replied.

'Or so he's saying,' I said.

'And I believe him,' Maya said. There was a steel in her eyes, but they softened as she turned to Vanessa.

'You guys must be really tired after your travelling and the time difference and everything. I think we should head for home.'

She painted back on the 'star look' as we headed out through the tables. Two or three people sought to stop her. One managed it, and, pen in hand, got her to sign a theatre programme. I worried there would be a sudden crush of autograph hunters, so stepped forward to put my hand on her back and shepherded her towards the exit. Nelson was waiting with the engine running. When he saw us coming, he got out to open the passenger door. I was guiding Maya gently towards it when a familiar voice cut across the hubbub of traffic and talk.

'Maya, stop! I have to talk to you.'

Maya froze on the curb, went pale in an instant and turned to see Dan, ear-studded cameraman alongside him, striding towards her. She put out a hand as if to stop him, but he seized hold of it and pulled her towards him.

She snatched her hand back. 'Not like this, Dan. No, I won't talk to you.'

'It's because he's here, isn't it?' said Dan, almost spitting in my direction.

'No, it's because we're in a public place and there's someone filming us.'

'Tomorrow, then? At the Carlyle. Think of all the times we had there before we got the apartment. The best breakfast in the world, you used to say. Remember?'

'I'll think about it, Dan,' said Maya, getting into the car, 'but only if you and this ape with his camera now kindly leave me alone.'

Nelson, who had been poised, ready to intervene if Dan had grabbed her again, gave him a scathing glance, ushered Vanessa and me into the car, and slammed the passenger door. As we pulled away, I saw Dan mouthing the word 'Sorry' towards Maya. I thought I saw a tear falling from his left eye.

Maya was stunned. She said nothing, for several blocks.

Vanessa broke the silence. 'Are you OK?'

She breathed heavily, mumbled 'Yeah' then stared out of the window.

'Do you plan to meet him?' I asked.

'I don't know, Steve,' she said, I thought slightly sharply. 'It's not a decision I can make on my own. I need to call Nick.' She reached into her bag for her phone.

'You can't call Nick now,' I said. 'It's quarter to five in the morning!'

'It's always the wrong fucking time in England when I'm in America,' she said, punching the headrest on Nelson's seat.

Vanessa reached over to stroke her arm.

'Well, I'll call him in the morning,' said Maya. 'I don't want to hear another word about it till then.'

We were silent the rest of the drive back, and I began to notice that Nelson sniffed quietly every few seconds. He had seemed the perfect driver, but the sniff – I don't think he was even aware he was doing it – quickly became irritating. I was still in shock after Dan's sudden appearance. What, I wondered, might have happened if Bernard had still been around, and Dan had sensed that he and Maya were a couple? Things could have got even more out of hand.

Vanessa fell asleep in the car, and when we got back to the apartment I helped her straight into bed and then went to find Maya to say goodnight. She was sitting on the sofa, a glass of bourbon in her hand.

'Hi Steve,' she said, seeing me come into the room. 'Sorry I lost it in the car.'

'That's OK. I think Nelson was a bit shocked.'

'Nah. He's seen worse, believe me. I don't know, Steve, I just think . . . why can't my relationships be as straight-forward as yours? You and Vanessa seem so strong together. It's lovely to watch.'

I didn't know what to say. 'Because you didn't choose me' came to mind, but of course I couldn't say it. Instead I went to give her a kiss on the cheek, suggested she get some sleep, then left to join Vanessa in bed. I barely slept though. Every time I tried to banish Dan from my mind, Bernard intruded. Smooth, handsome, cool, sophisticated Bernard. Married Bernard. Lying Bernard. Having one jerk to deal with was bad enough. Having two on the reservation was a nightmare.

Chapter Twenty-Four

How often I've wished I could sleep like Vanessa does. If the alarm clock had never been invented, she'd be late for work every day of her life. She is blessed too in that she never gets jet lag. On our honeymoon she got straight into a new sleeping pattern, whereas for the first three days in Florida I woke up at 4.30 a.m., feeling exhausted but wired and unable to get back to sleep. It was just the same on my first morning in Maya's apartment. It was almost six o'clock when I gave up trying to get back to sleep, washed as quietly as I could, put on the white dressing gown hanging behind the bathroom door, kissed Vanessa on the side of her head, then went through to make myself some coffee. As I walked across the hallway, I could hear Maya's voice coming from her study. The door was open a few inches, and I looked through the gap.

'I know, Nick,' Maya was saying, 'but it's just not good enough. I need you here now . . . How long then? . . . And what should I say about meeting up with him?'

She was on her feet, pacing around angrily, dressed only in a sleeveless pink T-shirt and what looked like a pair of men's boxer shorts. I could see she was braless and felt a surge of lust so strong it gripped me by the throat, and I had to take two deep breaths and tell myself to be calm. I had known her for so long, yet still, even though she had been starved of sleep, her hair was wild and unkempt, and she was without an ounce of make-up, her beauty had the capacity to move me as though I was seeing her for the first time all over again.

The phone call went on in the same manner for some time, with Nick clearly not giving Maya the answers she wanted. As she turned from the window by the corner bookshelf, she saw me standing in the doorway, walked towards me, fast, and abruptly handed me the phone.

'Christ, Steve, will you speak to him. Just tell him how bad it is.'

I took the phone with reluctance. It seemed wrong, somehow, to be talking to Sheldon in my dressing gown.

'Steve, my man,' said Sheldon jovially. I could see why she had found his manner irritating this morning. 'Fancy you being in New York. You always seem to be around when it's useful, don't you?'

I wasn't sure whether or not he was being facetious, but I didn't have time to mull it over because he was in full swing: showering me with his own confidence in the hope that somehow it would make everything all right.

'Thing is, Steve, I'm in Madrid, I can't say who, but I'm tying up a major transfer . . .'

'Van Nistelrooy to Milan, I read about it.'

'That's fucking horseshit Steve. Paper talk. No, I'm bringing in, not taking out. Anyway, there is no way I can leave here till it's done, we're talking a 30-million euro deal, so you're going to have to keep her calm till I can get there, OK?'

'I guess, yeah. But she matters more than some footballer, Nick.'

'Maybe, OK, but listen to me . . . For some reason, Maya

thinks you're the fount of all wisdom, so she'll take your advice. Tell her not to worry. This Dan thing will be freaking her out and from what I can gather he's been paid a fair whack by this cowboy TV firm so they will be getting him to do all sorts of crazy stuff.'

'I think that's right,' I said. I told him about the scene at the airport.

'Must have been tough for you, Steve. I hope your missus is OK? Not feeling her holiday's been ruined?'

'Vanessa can deal with these things.'

'I'm sure she can. Seems like a woman with a good head on her shoulders to me. Anyway, I'm not too worried about Dan's escapade. When his programme comes out, it will be a pain in the ass, and there might be a bit of media blah but at the end of the day' – he was even beginning to talk football-speak – 'if she stays dignified and above it, there is no harm to Maya, and that is all I care about. Now I will get there when I can. But you and Sampson need to look after her for now. You got that?'

'Sure.'

'Good man. Now pass her back to me will you . . .'

I was surprised, even a little touched, that Sheldon had confided in me, entrusted me with this task of trying to keep Maya calm which, in my own way, I had taken on anyway. I found it hard to admit, but Sheldon's approval mattered to me, and until now, I had never really believed I had it. I returned the phone to Maya feeling gratified that he recognised the strength of my relationship with her, but a bit affronted by the way he spoke to me. I was also concerned that he didn't know about Bernard, and I hadn't wanted to mention him with Maya there. But one of the worries that had been running around my mind as I lay in bed failing to sleep was how much more complicated the whole Dan thing was with Bernard on the scene. If somehow Maya and Bernard had got filmed in a way that showed they were an item, and then it came out that Bernard was married, Sheldon might have to revise his prediction that there would be 'no harm to Maya'.

She, however, appeared somewhat comforted by the time she put the phone down. She said Sheldon seemed to think a combination of me and Sampson could keep things under control until he got here, and he wanted her to go and have a meeting with Sampson about it all that morning. She was anxious that her parents should know nothing about what was going on and asked that Vanessa and I spend the day with them, as agreed, and make sure that Dan got nowhere near them. She said she would send Nelson along to help.

To my surprise, it turned out to be a lovely day. Nelson dropped Maya at Sampson's office and then drove us to the Essex House hotel to pick up Mr and Mrs Lowe. They too were raving about breakfast.

'You've never tasted scrambled eggs like it,' said Mr Lowe.

It was great having Nelson to show us around. Short drives, short little looks around some of the sights, till the heat became too much, then back in the car. Even with the heat, though, there was an energy to New York and the people that made me wish I had discovered the place earlier in my life. I worked at the world's busiest airport, yet had travelled so little.

We had lunch in Little Italy, then did the ferry ride out to see the Statue of Liberty and got back to squeeze in an hour at the Museum of Modern Art, although Vanessa and Mr Lowe spent most of the time in the café, Vanessa because she was overcome by the heat and needed to take the weight of her feet, Mr Lowe because, by his own admittance, he couldn't stand paintings when he didn't know what they were of.

There was no sign of Dan, but it was reassuring to know that Nelson was always waiting no more than a block away. As the day went on, I stopped worrying that Dan was about to jump out from behind a hotdog-vendor's stall, and started having fun. Mr and Mrs Lowe were good company – funny and warm. It felt almost as if they were my own parents, and we were enjoying a very old-fashioned kind of holiday together.

'I think we should do the open-topped bus tour tomorrow,' said Mr Lowe, looking at a leaflet we'd been given on the ferry. 'Harlem, Brooklyn, Queens, goes right round the place,' he said. 'You can hop on and off, stop in different places, wait for the next one.'

'We could make a day of that, love,' said Mrs Lowe. 'Fancy it, Steve?'

'Sure,' I said, '. . . unless Maya needs us for anything.'

Maya called to ask us to meet her for an aperitif in a place midtown on 32nd Street called the Me Bar, on the roof of La Quinta hotel. It was quite a shock after a day of diners and cans of 7UP bought from a guy on the street corner. It was plush, full of exec types who were as excited to see Maya as her mother was to enjoy the view out on to the Empire State Building.

'What a wonderful, wonderful day we've had,' said Mrs Lowe when we dropped them back at their hotel where they planned to have a light supper and an early night.

On the way back to the apartment, Vanessa said that she wasn't sure she was up to going out again.

'That's OK,' said Maya. 'Bernard has offered to cook for us tonight.'

I felt a groan welling up inside, but I forced myself to try to react positively.

'It was clear last night that he really knows his food and wine,' I said, and I could see how touched she was that I had been warm about him.

'I checked out those wines on the internet this morning,' I said. 'With the usual markup, I doubt he got much change out of a grand.'

'The French,' said Vanessa. 'We eat to live. They live to eat. Isn't that what they say?'

'I've had some terrible meals in Paris,' said Maya. 'But Bernard's cooking is terrific.'

'Forgive me for asking,' said Vanessa, in that wonderful direct way of hers, 'but we're not going to be intruding on a romantic dinner, are we?'

'Romantic, yes,' said Maya laughing, 'but not intruding. Bernard is the most hospitable person I've ever met.'

'You really like him, don't you?' said Vanessa. Maya was almost purring as she absorbed the warmth of the question.

'I do, yes. I really do. It's completely hush hush with the rest of the team, which is why he went home last night. Curtis is basically the film gossip. But yes, I'm happy for the first time since I lost Dan. He makes me feel like I'm a real person again.'

'That's great Maya, it really is,' Vanessa said, throwing me a questioning glance.

'It's why it was so upsetting to see Dan like he was. Not getting over it, just as I'm beginning to.'

'So how was your meeting with Sampson?' I asked, eager

to find out whether she intended to agree to Dan's request to a meeting.

'He thinks we should stall,' said Maya. 'Not say no, which would get him all het up, just keep him involved in negotiations about it so he stays out of our hair, and wait till Nick gets here and he can hopefully get him to see sense.'

'Sounds a good plan,' I said. 'Perhaps Sampson has his uses after all.'

Maya didn't answer that. I felt like I had touched a nerve. She was fickle when it came to her agency, half the time saying she didn't need them, half the time not being able to move without their say-so. And just as I resented it when Vanessa made the same criticisms of Maya as I sometimes made, Maya didn't like me having a go at people she viewed as being hers.

When we got back, Bernard was already there, busy in the kitchen. He had prepared a fabulous coq au vin preceded by an asparagus dish and followed by a rich chocolate mousse.

He was also there to make us breakfast.

The next day followed the same pattern. Mr and Mrs Lowe were flying home in a few days' time, and were eager to make the most of every minute. I couldn't believe how energetic they both were. Mr Lowe had been out before breakfast and bought the tickets for the hop-on, hop-off bus tour and they just did not flag. First we did the downtown tour, sitting in the front row of the top deck. Times Square, Macy's, Empire State Building, hop off at Soho, back on to Chinatown where we hopped off for a coffee, Wall Street, United Nations, hop off on Broadway for lunch in a deli, where Mr Lowe had a pastrami sandwich so large he could not get it into his mouth, and we ended up in fits of giggles as Mrs Lowe took dozens of photos of him trying to get his teeth around it. The uptown tour took us to the Lincoln Center, the Time Warner Center, then right by Maya's apartment, hop off for the Apollo theatre, hop back on for Harlem Market and a cup of tea for me and Mr Lowe while Vanessa and Mrs Lowe bought a few knick-knacks.

'Now I know where you get your energy from,' Vanessa told Maya when we all met up for dinner at the hotel. 'Your mum and dad are like dynamos.'

By the time the main course arrived, though, Mrs Lowe was finally getting tired, and they went up to bed by half past nine. As we walked through the foyer to Nelson's waiting car, Maya mentioned that Bernard would be at the apartment. Vanessa and I gave each other a look.

'We'll walk back, Maya,' I said. 'Perhaps take a turn around the park, maybe have a nightcap. Give you two some space.'

She grinned at me, then waved goodbye.

It was a beautiful night. Hot, but the kind of hot that makes you want to walk the streets rather than seek out shelter in some cold, air-conditioned room. The New York hum was quieter but somehow more intense once darkness fell. As we started our walk, I worried Dan might suddenly appear, but once a few minutes had passed, the anxiety went, and we were able to enjoy finding ourselves on our own, just walking, talking, pointing out people and places – people mainly – losing ourselves in the swirl of noise and humanity, as though we were our own tiny world and this other world was spinning unthreateningly around us. It was when we stopped at a little bar two blocks from Maya's apartment, and Vanessa mentioned Bernard, that the real world came back with all its worries and niggles.

'It was lovely of you to find a tactful way to give them some time,' she said.

'I don't know about lovely,' I replied. 'More like foolish.'

'Because he's married, you mean?'

'Of course because he's married.'

'But Maya said he was separating from his wife.'

'That's what he's told her,' I scoffed. 'But how does she know he's not lying? I don't want to see her heartbroken again, that's all.'

'It is a bit odd for you to worry about it if she doesn't.'

'Sometimes that's what friends are for – to take over the burden of worry, and to help heal past pain.'

'Maybe a new man in her life is the best way to heal that pain?'

'Oh really, do you think so?'

'You're not her father, Steve.'

'Meaning?'

'Meaning she can make her own choices and it is not for you to approve or disapprove. She is a grown woman. She is single again. She has met a nice guy. They are having a bit of fun.'

'I cannot believe how you are looking at this Vanessa. She is not some secretary in a bank. She is a major-league film star whose private life is major-league news. Bernard is the first man post-Dan. That's big news.'

'They both know that so I guess they'll be careful.'

'And you think his spending the night at her apartment is being careful?' I said.

She was now looking, by her normally even-tempered standards, a bit cross.

'Anyone would think you were jealous.'

'That is ridiculous.'

'Hmm . . .' said Vanessa, taking a sip of her iced tea. 'Anyway, let's not have yet another discussion about whether or not you should be trying to orchestrate Maya's love life. Let's just enjoy the moment. We're in New York, in a nice bar, at the end of a nice day, we're having a great holiday, and we're going to have a baby. What shall we call it?'

'Brooklyn,' I joked.

'Didn't they call him that because that's where he was conceived?'

'Better call ours Hammersmith then,' I said.

She laughed. 'Actually I'm thinking Nathan,' she said, 'after my dad.' I shuddered. I knew another Nathan. The one who had made my seventeenth year a misery by depriving Maya of her virginity. I didn't say it to Vanessa there and then, but I was determined to find a way to veto Nathan. Thinking about him brought me back to the Bernard problem. I knew that I had to act fast. It was only a matter of time before Dan and he collided at the entrance to the apartment block, and Maya's world came tumbling down again.

Chapter Twenty-Five

'Yes Martin . . . No, Martin . . . Sure, Martin. OK. Well you speak to Nick and one of you call me back.'

Vanessa was sleeping in again, Bernard had left at dawn and Maya was on the phone to Sampson when I went to the kitchen to make myself a cup of coffee the next morning. She had a tortured look on her face and was running her hand nervously through her hair.

'What was all that about?' I asked, when she got off the phone.

'Dan,' she said. 'Martin isn't sure how long he can keep up the negotiations over this meeting. He thinks Dan's producer has twigged we're just stringing them along, and he'll go back to terrorising us if we don't give them an answer.'

'Which will be?'

'I don't know. Martin's calling Nick. Either we say no, and he comes at us anyway and just makes life a screaming pain in the ass, or I agree to a meeting so long as it isn't recorded. But that's dodgy. If these guys are paying him, they're going to push him to get it on camera. They can hide cameras anywhere these days.'

Now was the moment, I thought, to raise my fears about her relationship with Bernard becoming public. But, as I suspected, she was very touchy about it.

'I don't see what the problem is,' she said. 'There are only four people who know: me, him, you and Vanessa.'

'Well I'm glad you tell me it's a secret now. What if Nick had called when you were out and I'd happened to mention it to him?'

'I'll tell Nick when I'm ready.'

'That's not the point Maya. The point is not whether it's Nick. I or Vanessa could have mentioned it to anyone.'

'I trust you both not to. That goes without saying.'

'But you're not thinking it through. Whether you like it or not, your love life is a big story, especially after what happened with Dan.'

'I know that. It's why I keep telling you I hate this shit. But I am not going to stop having a life because of the fucking media, Steve. No way.'

'That's not what I am suggesting. I am suggesting that because of the profile, you do have to think about implications, or other people have to think about them for you.'

She seemed irritated by what I was saying, but I said I was sure Nick would agree with me.

'And also, Maya, I hear what you say about his marriage, but I don't want you to get hurt again.'

'I know, Steve, I know that. But Bernard and I know what we're doing. My eyes are wide open and so are his.'

'I hope you're right.'

She stood up and went to get her itinerary for the day from the printer. 'Now,' she said, looking over it . . . and with that one word, she made it very clear that she considered the conversation over, and I had to give up.

I had a bit of time to myself that morning. Maya was having a script meeting at the offices behind Times Square where *The*

Hunter Hunted team was based, Vanessa and Mrs Lowe had planned to go clothes shopping and Mr Lowe had said he fancied a few hours in the hotel lounge people-watching and flicking through the papers.

As soon as Maya and Vanessa had left I called Stafford. He was in a meeting. I asked his PA if she minded going in to say that Steve was calling from the States about the Frenchman. Half a minute later he came on the line.

'Sorry to disturb your meeting but I was worried I wouldn't get you later. I will be very brief. We need to know a little more about the Dufay marriage. The report said it was happy. Dufay seems not to share that view and he should know. Is there any way you can find out in detail what Mrs Dufay thinks and also how often he and she speak by phone when he is here and what they talk about?'

'Here?' Stafford asked. I detected a note of amusement in his voice. As if he found something funny about the way I'd tried to be as professional as I could in my briefing of him.

'I'm in New York. Staying with Maya.'

'Ah. Her constant companion.'

'Something like that. So, can you do it?'

'No problem, but we're starting to talk rather bigger bills than a quick and dirty one-day probe like you got from my French guy.'

It was the last thing I wanted to hear, but I tried to swallow my anxiety. 'That's fine,' I said. 'Do what you need to do.'

'OK, leave it with me.'

I found him irresistible, and cheapening, every time we spoke.

Maya seemed to have taken our chat to heart because though Bernard came round for a drink before we left for the theatre that evening, he did not accompany us to the show, saying he had work to do briefing the direction team on the more remote locations in which the filming would take place.

The day we'd arrived in New York, Maya had told us that she had booked tickets for all of us, the Lowes included, to see a play that had been getting great reviews, called *Blackbird*. It was starring Jeff Daniels and Alison Pill, and was a pretty harrowing drama about the reunion between a man and a young woman he had molested when she was a girl. When Maya had explained what it was about to her parents, Mr Lowe said 'Can't we go to *Grease* instead?' but she had read in one of the reviews that Alison Pill 'shared Maya Lowe's ability to say much in few words' and wanted to check out whether the young Canadian was as good as everyone was saying. Added to which, Maya had always kept in touch with theatre, and had mentioned once or twice that she might try to fit in an occasional stage play if she could get a big enough gap between films.

Once word reached the management of the Booth theatre that we were there, they came to ask if Maya would like to visit backstage afterwards. It turned out that a former colleague of hers from drama school in England was Pill's understudy, and she and Maya went into ecstasies over each other, as if they were long-lost sisters. Maya wanted me to take a photograph of the two of them together. Later, she asked if I could email it to Sampson so that he could place it somewhere. She said it was to help her friend, but I could see it wouldn't be a bad thing for Maya either, reminding people that her acting went back a long way, and she didn't forget her roots.

It was as we were leaving that the thing I had been dreading happened. Word had got out to the media that Maya was at the theatre and there amid the gaggle of photographers now gathered at the steps were Dan and his ever-present cameraman leaning against a car. Luckily I was leading the way out of the front entrance, because Maya had been surrounded by autograph hunters thrusting their programmes and scraps of paper towards her, while the Lowes hung back, chatting excitedly with Vanessa both about the play and Maya's chance encounter with her old friend. It meant I was able to go back in and divert them. I told the Lowes that Sampson had stupidly fixed for Maya to do a short TV spot at a nearby studio, and that Nelson would come back for us later. Then I steered them towards the bar. As the crowd around Maya subsided, I took her to one side.

'Now don't panic, and don't react when I say this, as there are people still watching you, but there are photographers outside.'

'That's OK,' she said. 'Always happens when I go to the theatre. Just make sure Nelson's at the kerb.'

'He is.'

'Fine, let's go. Where are Mum and Dad?'

'Dan's out there with the pack.'

'Oh for fuck's sake.'

'So just wait there while I warn Nelson you're coming. I'll have the door open for you. When you see me walk back in, you walk out, and send Nelson to collect us once you're home.'

Moments later, she strode out through a sudden blitz of light, which was over in seconds, and she was gone. As I arrived at the bar, my phone rang.

'It was pathetic, Steve. He actually went down on his knees on the pavement, in front of all those cameras, to beg my forgiveness.'

'How noble. I presume the photographers liked that.'

'The bastards went mad.'

'And what if you'd been with Bernard?'

'That's precisely why I wasn't.'

'What do I tell your mum and dad?'

'Nothing.'

'What if they see the pictures?'

'Chances are they won't. They try to avoid that crap. We'll just have to be careful I guess.'

'Well, it's lucky they're going home on Monday. Less of an opportunity for Dan to catch them on camera. He'd love that. What are you going to do about the meeting?'

'Nick will sort it.'

'So he's coming?'

'He will be when he hears about what happened tonight. Otherwise I'll tell him I'm looking for a new agent. It's ridiculous he's with some poxy fucking footballer when I'm having to deal with this madness.'

Sheldon's arrival was a major event, and a calming one. His transfer deal had gone through and assuming the figures in the papers were accurate, and he was on ten per cent, he was now 15,000 euros a week better off, plus whatever cut he took on the transfer fee itself. It was no wonder he was in a good mood despite all he was flying into. He hired one of the smaller function rooms at the Essex House hotel and held a little drinks do for the Lowes (being very careful not to mention what was going on with Dan, of course) and held forth to Vanessa about the glories of Madrid while Sampson sycophantically lapped up his every word. Vanessa wasn't fooled though. She saw him for what he was. In fact she was beginning to tire of living in Maya's media circus, realising that a fortnight in a beautiful apartment wasn't quite the luxury she had expected if it entailed sharing it with an A-list actress who had just had a very messy and public marriage break-up. Picking up on her mood, I whispered to her as Sheldon topped up Mr Lowe's champagne glass, 'Don't worry, there'll be none of this in New England.'

There was another little bonus from his arrival. 'I want to propose a toast,' he said. 'No, not to you Maya, but to four very special people. Your parents, who brought you into a world you have lit up for us so many times. And your friends Steve and Vanessa who have given you so much support over so many years. As a thank you from me to all of you, while I stay in New York and do some work this weekend, I want the five of you to go to my house in the Hamptons, and just treat it like your own.'

'Aw, Nick,' cried Mrs Lowe, moving towards him to kiss him on the cheek. 'That is so kind.'

Mr Lowe said he was craving the sea, and it would be the perfect way to end their stay. Maya was less obviously enthusiastic. I could tell she was down. Bernard had just told her he was going back to France for the weekend 'to sort some things out' and then, when he came back he was only going to be in New York for one day before he had to travel to a remote part of Missouri where a key scene in the film was set.

'Why did the silly French fuckwit have to choose this weekend?' she moaned to me as we were leaving the hotel. 'Just when I'm going through this shit and need him around. Doesn't he realise the lengths I went to in order to get time with him while my parents were around?'

Those lengths, I presumed, entailed hosting Vanessa and me

for a couple of weeks, but I didn't say anything. I, for my part, was glad about Bernard's weekend away. Not only would it relieve me of my worry that he and Maya were going to be spotted together, it would help with Stafford's enquiries. When I managed to find a moment alone, I gave Stafford a quick call, simply to alert him to the fact that if Madame Dufay appeared with a man on her arm at the weekend, it was likely to be Bernard.

'Don't worry,' he said. 'I've got one of my own guys out there overseeing it.'

'So I'm paying Eurostar fares too now am I?'

'He went standard class, you can afford it,' he said, 'and he is staying on for a holiday when your man comes back, touring war cemeteries in northern France. It's his hobby. So we'll only charge you one-way.' I was impressed by that. There was no way I would ever have known, yet he chose to volunteer information that would save me a little bit of money.

When Vanessa and I went to the film's office to meet up with Maya — she and Vanessa were going on a shopping trip, and Maya had said I could use one of the office computers to catch up with emails from work, and try to get news from Brandon and Jerry — I noticed a huge whiteboard covering half a wall, on which were written the various movements of key production figures in the film. Under Bernard's name it was noted that a driver was meeting him in Paris. Air France flight 011. I texted Stafford to give him the flight number.

'*Merci*' came back the answer. I was warming to him.

When I was back at the apartment, and Maya and Vanessa arrived carrying four armfuls of brightly coloured bags, I asked Maya what French for "my pleasure" was.

'My God, you sound just like you did when we used to do

our homework together – always asking me for the answers.'

'All right, Miss Cleverclogs, just answer the question.'

'It depends on the context.'

'Oh yeah, I remember that one. It's why I could never do languages. It always depended on the context.'

'OK, so what's the context? If you literally mean "my pleasure", just those two words, it is "*mon plaisir*", like the restaurant.'

'No, it's not that. If you do something for someone, and they say thank you, how do you say "my pleasure"?'

'*De rien,*' she said and she spelled it out.

'That means "of nothing".' I said.

'I know. It's like "you have nothing to thank me for" I guess.'

'OK.' I removed the predictive text facility on the phone and texted '*De rien*' to Stafford. His reply '????' suggested he was as poor at French as I was, or he had forgotten the earlier message he sent.

'Glad to see you're brushing up your French,' she said. 'Is that so you can be nicer to Bernard when he gets back?'

'Yes,' I said.

Only Bernard didn't come back on Monday as planned. The former paratrooper from Newcastle who was leading Warren Stafford's French brigade saw to that.

Chapter Twenty-Six

The whole, complicated story started with a call from Stafford first thing on Saturday morning, early afternoon London/Paris time. We'd all arrived at Sheldon's beautiful six-bedroomed house in Hampton Bays the night before, and no one had yet emerged from their bedroom except for Mrs Lowe who was chatting away in Spanish to the maid in the kitchen. Vanessa groaned when my mobile rang, but I told her the call was from Jerry and left her to go back to sleep while I went out on to the front deck and listened to Stafford while staring out to sea.

He was precise and to the point. Dufay's plane had touched down a few minutes ahead of schedule on Friday morning, he said, and as he only had hand baggage, he was out of the airport in less than a quarter of an hour. Stafford's team followed him to a house on the outskirts of Reims. The traffic was light, and they were there in under ninety minutes. He had been met at the house by a beautiful woman in a fluffy light blue dressing gown. They quickly established via photochecks with neighbours that she was Cécile Dufay, his former wife. Previous checks had established that Cécile and Bernard had married very young and divorced not long afterwards because Cécile had taken a lover while Bernard was in

South America working as a junior set designer on a Spanish film about the life of a Colombian prostitute. He had come home early – without warning because he had wanted to surprise her – to find her in bed with a local hotelier. Devastated, he left her, but almost immediately met Emilie. As soon as the divorce came through, he and Emilie married. But after the birth of their second child, he got back in touch with Cécile. Neighbours said he was a fairly regular visitor.

'So wait a minute,' I said. 'He left his wife for another woman because the wife had another man, he married the other woman, and now he's back with the first wife? Is that what you're telling me?'

'"Back with" isn't quite the right way of putting it,' Stafford said. 'It's more of a sex thing. I've just spoken to our man there, the Geordie. He says our Target spent a couple of hours inside the house with his ex, and when they came out – to sit by the pool – it was very much a post-coital, lovey-dovey situation. Lots of kissing and touching, all very French.'

'Did he get pictures?'

'Video and stills, including one shot of her hand right down his trunks and then he goes back into the house with a stonking great hard-on. But wait. Let me finish. He leaves there an hour later, gets back in the car, and he goes to his own place in a little village maybe half an hour away, Sainte-Preuve. Not a particularly fancy village apparently, but he has a house to die for there. No pool but a big garden, only this time it's all one big happy family, not just a shagerama situation, but kids too, and lots of friends, quite a big do, all eating out on a terrace.'

'And how was he with the wife?'

'Pretty much the same as with the other wife, according to

Geordie boy. Not as sexual but intimate. Big hugs when he arrived, presents, that kind of thing. Clearly man and wife. No doubt about that. They ate outside in the garden, there was enough to suggest he was happy to be there, the kids clearly loved having him around, and that's where he stayed the night.'

'Is he still there now?' I asked.

'Yeah.'

'Amazing.'

'So do you have enough? Can I tell my guy to start his holiday?'

'Yeah, OK.'

But the moment the call ended, I had a thought which required me to speak to him again. I quickly phoned him back.

'How good an actor is your Geordie guy?'

'Never tried him, but my suspicion is, not bad. Bit of an extrovert down the pub, anyway.'

'Can I tell you something in total confidence?'

'Mr Watkins, haven't I proved myself to you? We could have gone to the press with that Chivers stuff, couldn't we? We didn't because we have a reputation to protect. We want our clients to come back to us.'

'OK, well here's the situation. The reason I'm worried about this bloke is that he has targeted Maya and he has got her. They are an item. Of course Frenchie boy has told her his marriage is on the rocks and so it's all above board as it were, and she's not going to get caught up in a big sex scandal again.'

'But now you know what you know, you're not so sure.'

'Exactly. I was wondering if your man could put the wind up him, perhaps by pretending to be a reporter.'

'A reporter doing what?'

'Well . . . he could approach Dufay, say he is a journalist, ask him to confirm he is the new man in Maya's life, say that he has been spotted leaving her apartment after staying the night with her, and how does that square with his happy family life? And then weave in that he knows about his trip to the former wife.'

'Hmm . . . possible. Do we show him we have proof?'

'The pictures with the other wife? Yeah, maybe. Your guy is going to have to play it by ear a bit.'

'I will brief him now and get back to you when it's done. I suppose there is a risk the guy takes pre-emptive action, goes to a court to try to suppress it, and it would then come out that way, so maybe I should get my man to play down the Maya thing, play up the two wives instead.'

'He may be less worried about that. Maya is the bit that makes this news, not his former wife. I think your man has to lay it on the line.'

I was impressed with myself. That was quick thinking. It was streetwise, sassy. Dufay was going to find out what it was like to feel scared. He deserved it. He shouldn't have lied. He shouldn't have tried to wheedle his way into Maya's life on such a false prospectus.

I watched a group of four joggers running barefoot on the beach, one of them a beautiful girl, maybe 18 or 20, wearing a red bikini. As they passed from view, I saw Maya emerging from the distance into which they were disappearing. She was wearing a purple bikini top and a silver sarong which was billowing behind her as a gentle breeze cooled the shoreline. She looked so vulnerable – a small speck against a vast ocean – and I wanted to reach out and take her in my hand. Hold her safe for ever. It was bad enough, as when Dan hit her, sharing her secrets. It was even harder when only I knew things that could tear her apart. Perhaps I should have just let events take their course. Maybe I had been wrong to force the pace.

I waved towards her, but she couldn't see me and now, she too started to jog. When I could no longer see her, I went in to join Vanessa and the Lowes for breakfast. We sat around chatting and working our way through the *New York Times* and its mass of sections.

It said something about the kind of money Sheldon had that he owned a house like this, with a full-time housekeeper and gardener, and spent two out of fifty-two weeks a year here. The gardener fancied himself as a bit of a builder too and had tagged on all manner of little decks and terraces so that there was always somewhere, shady or sunny, to lounge around. I got the sense that Mr Lowe was a bit bored, and he didn't like the way they'd organised the garden, but Mrs Lowe was in her element. She was a sun-and-sand person and she spent the whole morning on the beach, reading, walking, people-watching and picking up shells. It was great to see her so happy. I wished her daughter could have the same easy relationship to life.

When Maya got back from her run, she and Vanessa camped out on the main deck overlooking the beach, each with a book they never opened. There was lots of giggling, so I guessed they were content. I couldn't settle. I snooped around the house looking at Sheldon's collection of autographed photographs and waiting for Stafford to ring.

I had left my mobile in the dining room so that when Stafford called I would have to go through there, away from Maya and Vanessa. It was a long wait. We were eating lunch around the huge marble kitchen table, just before 2 p.m., 7 p.m. UK time, 8 p.m. France, when I heard its ringtone, and raced through to answer.

'Bingo,' he said.

'Go on.'

'Plan went like a dream. And all on tape. Every word, every worry, every little wriggle.'

'Can I hear it?'

'What – you don't believe me?'

'Of course I do, but I want to hear for myself.'

'Can't say I like doing stuff over the phone, but you're paying I guess . . .'

He said it would take a couple of minutes to set up the tape to play down the phone. I went through to the downstairs bathroom, took a drink from the tap, then looked in the mirror, clenched my fist, punched it against my chest and said 'Yes' loudly to myself.

It was stupid, because Vanessa heard and came through to ask what was happening.

'Nothing. It's a business thing.'

'Has Brandon got the Qatar job?'

'Not yet. Got to take one more call and I'll be back with you.'

'We're on holiday, Steve.'

'Yeah I know. I won't be long.'

I went back to the mirror and chastised myself. 'Idiot.' I was thrilled that Dufay had been caught out, and he was clearly scared; but I had been stupid to react that way, even to my own reflection in the bathroom. I was growing impatient for the phone to ring. When it did, I felt a sweat forming on my neck, front and back.

'Just wait there,' said Stafford. 'It will sound like the line's gone dead, but that's me transferring the phone, then you'll hear the tape as live. My man has just played it through to me. Here we go. Are you there?'

'Yes.'

The line went dead as he had warned. Then a youngish but authoritative Geordie voice said 'Home of Bernard Dufay, Sainte-Preuve, France, tape 102s-1.' I heard steps on stones or shale. I could hear birds and an occasional passing car. This was an outside scene. I could hear people talking French, and the clinking of cutlery on plates.

'Mr Dufay, could I have a word in private please?' said the Geordie.

Then came Bernard's voice, saying something in French.

The Geordie again: 'Sorry sir, I understand you speak English. Could I have a word in private please?'

'Who are you?' Bernard sounded rattled.

'I would rather we spoke away from your family, sir. It's better that way.'

A woman's voice shouted something. Bernard replied, as if he was trying to reassure her. Then there was the sound of two sets of feet on the shale or stones. I heard what seemed like a fountain followed by the noise of a door or gate and shuffling feet as they came to a halt.

'Who are you?' said Dufay. 'Why are you disturbing my precious time with my family?'

'I am a journalist. And I have three very simple questions for you. Is this your home and was that your wife? Did you see your former wife this morning at your house in Puillon, and did you have sex with her? By the way, I know the answer to that one because I have pictures of you by the pool before

332

you went back inside for seconds. Third, did you sleep with Maya Lowe in New York on Tuesday night?'

There followed a silence of maybe ten seconds. But for Dufay it must have felt like a lifetime. I thought to myself, I wouldn't know how to deal with something like that. I would collapse.

Eventually, he spoke. 'What is your name?'

'Chris.'

'Chris what?'

'That'll do. Chris Watt. Now, will you answer the questions?'

'Who do you work for?'

'Me. And the truth.'

'Are you aware this is French soil, and there is a privacy law here. You cannot write about this.'

'I'll go to America and do it from Maya's point of view then. She's the one who matters in this. No privacy law in America, or Britain.'

'Maya Lowe is a friend and a colleague. We work together. No more than that.'

'So why did you stay the night?'

'There were other people there too.'

'What? An orgy?'

'You are disgusting.'

'At least I've only got one wife, sir, and she is waiting for me in the car. We're going on to visit the British military cemetery at La Ville-aux-Bois because my great-grandfather, who served in the Northumberland Regiment, is buried there.'

'It doesn't make you a better person,' said Dufay. 'You are still disgusting.'

'Is that so, sir? Well just remember that if it wasn't for him and his mates, and his kids and their mates, you and all your posh friends would be sitting around eating bratwurst and sauerkraut in fucking lederhosen.'

'Get out of here,' snapped Dufay. 'I have a wife too, sir, and I have a family, and I would like to rejoin them.'

'Answer my questions then, and I'll let you go.'

'Who are you writing for?'

'Haven't decided. Depends how good the story is.'

'Well may I suggest to you that a location director not very well known outside his own little world who stays in contact with his ex-wife – I don't think even your English yellow press will go for that. And as I do not have the relationship with Maya Lowe you suggest, and never will, you have no story.'

I was chuckling at that when Vanessa appeared at the door, looking anxious, clearly thinking a long call received in silence meant bad news. You can communicate a lot by a quick facial gesture and a hand movement when holding a phone. She got the message that there was nothing to worry about, I would not be long, but I would prefer to be alone. She nodded and left.

'Mmmm. I am probably the better judge of a story for the British press,' the Geordie voice was saying. 'But I hear what you say.'

'Do you have a card?'

'I don't, I'm afraid.'

'Now please leave.'

'Thanks for your time. *Bon appetit*.'

Then more feet on various hard surfaces before the Geordie said 'Tape 102s-1 ends.'

Stafford came on the line.

'Did you get all that?'

'I did. Amazing quality.'

'We have these new hidden recorders now, size of a shirt button, but they're broadcast quality. He's got film too, off his lapel.'

'Wow, he was cool wasn't he?'

'French sangfroid.'

'I meant your guy. Took a bit of nerve to do that. The silence after he asked the three questions. Dramatic or what! And that jibe about sauerkraut and lederhosen! Fucking brilliant. Still, I wonder if it worked. Dufay sounded pretty calm about it all.'

'Don't worry. It should do the trick. I agree he sounded calm, but my man said he had panic in his eyes. Constantly looking over his shoulder to see where his wife was, bit of a facial tic, so he's got the message.'

'Thanks a lot for that.'

'Are you sure I'm not dealing with a love-rival situation this time?' asked Stafford.

'No,' I said. 'It's about protecting the reputation of someone I care for.'

'If you say so. Anyway, always happy to be of service. If there is ever anyone else whose weekend you want me to ruin in the service of protecting people you care for, you know where to find me. The bill's in the post.'

When the call was finished, I tiptoed quietly up to our room and lay down on the bed. I could not have felt more exhausted if I had run the length of the beach outside. I knew now that my instinct about Bernard had been right. He was a barefaced liar. A dirty, double-crossing, two-faced, supersmooth, lying French bastard. I also had learned enough about the way the media worked to see that Maya would not come out well from this if it should leak. The break-up with Dan was different. She was the victim, the wronged party, and she handled it with such style and elegance while he crashed around like a wounded elephant. If the relationship with Bernard came out there was a danger of her being cast as the marriage-wrecker. I had visions of poor Madame Dufay, children gathered to her sides, family dog skulking in the background, addressing a sympathetic media pack at the gates of her beautiful garden. 'I thought we had the perfect life. Maya Lowe has ruined it.' It was a frightening prospect.

While I was lying there, Vanessa poked her head round the door.

'Steve, this is getting ridiculous. We've all finished lunch now. Are you coming back to join us or not?'

'Sure. Yes. Sorry. That was Brandon. Things are a bit hairy in Qatar. We had to talk a few things through.'

'I thought you said this deal was a dead cert. Bloody hell, you've put enough time into it!'

'Yeah, well. It is. Brandon just wanted to let off steam.'

We went back to the kitchen but I found it difficult to swallow my food: I was so tense, wondering whether Bernard would call Maya. As it happened, I didn't have long to wait.

Her phone rang about an hour later as we were getting ready to go out. Sheldon knew that Mrs Lowe and Vanessa liked museums and had recommended the Hamptons Museum in Southampton. Apparently there was a nice ice-cream parlour nearby to visit afterwards. From the look of sheer joy on Maya's face as she answered the phone, I knew it must be Dufay. Vanessa and the Lowes had gone to change their clothes so it was just me and Maya in the living room. I didn't know whether to go to my room and leave her to it, or sit and listen and have to go through another piece of acting. She made up my mind for me. I was getting up to go when Maya raised her hand and looked at me with an expression I knew well. It said she was receiving bad news and she was going to need my support.

'You're not being clear Bernard. I don't understand . . . Where was he from? . . . No, no, I don't mean what country, I mean which paper . . . So you don't know for sure he will do anything . . . Yes, I suppose so . . . But I don't understand, why did you deny it? . . . First rule, say nothing or tell the truth . . . It would not have been the end of the world if people knew . . . I wouldn't mind. It would be a pain in the ass, but not the end of the world . . . Nick could have dealt with that . . .' And then, after these short staccato bursts, she was silent for a while and I could see from her eyes, suddenly staring at her knees, and draining of life and energy, that he was telling her at least some of the truth. 'But I thought . . . Bernard, I thought you weren't really together . . . you said you were going back to see your children, not your wife . . . So you lied . . . That's not the point, you lied to me . . .' She listened to him pour out his heart, but tired of it as he was still speaking, hung up, and I could see she was about to cry.

'What is it?' I asked. 'What's happening?'

She stood quickly, forced the tears to halt behind her eyes, and instead turned her shock into a rage against Bernard.

'The bastard. The fucking French bastard.' She threw her phone on to the floor.

'Maya, what is it? What's happened?'

'Bernard. Some scumbag journalist doorstepped him and asked if he had slept with me.'

'Christ!'

'Yeah. He denied it, silly fool.'

'Did they have any proof?'

'I don't know, and it doesn't matter. The reason he denied it was because he was with his family, and he has basically just told me that when he is with me, it feels right to be with me, but now he's home he realises his family is his life, and he must not put it at risk. Apparently he's suddenly getting on better with his wife and he wants to try to make a go of it. He thinks it's best if we don't see each other socially. He made it sound like it was all my fault too. You know what he told me? "Having journalists at your house asking horrible questions when you're trying to spend time with your family is not a nice feeling and it's because you are too hot." Can you believe he said that?' She began to mimic him. '"Eet es becuz yar too ot." Bastard. It is perfectly obvious now his marriage was fine all along. I was just someone to pass the time with.'

'Well, at least it's ending before you are too deep in,' I said.

Maya wasn't listening. 'Why do they lie to me?' she muttered. 'Why do I attract the ones that just want to use me for something? What the hell is it with me and men? I'm not a bad person, Steve, you know that. I'm a good person. I didn't ask for all that I have. I'm the same person I've always been. But why, why did he think he could have me on his terms, without any regard to mine?'

'Some men are just like that,' I said. 'The problem is you're too genuine a person to spot the signs.'

'And what is it with journalists, always in there fucking things up for me? I'm too hot! All that means is he gets scared when he has journalists close in. He should try living like that 24 fucking 7, shouldn't he?'

By now she was almost shouting and I was worried her parents would hear. I tried to be soothing.

'We have to wait and see now where the story appears. It may not happen. If they have no proof, all they have is an allegation and a denial. And at some point they will have to come to you for a comment. They cannot accuse you of sleeping with someone without putting the allegation to you when the man in question has categorically denied it. I have a feeling it won't come to anything.'

Of course I was right, but obviously couldn't tell her why I was so certain. My words seemed to calm her down a bit, though, and she took to pacing the room rather than ranting. I was just thinking we might get away with hiding the whole thing from her parents when Mrs Lowe walked into the room. With motherly instinct she stopped in her tracks the moment she saw Maya's hunched shoulders.

'Darling, what's wrong? Something terrible has happened, I can see.'

Maya threw herself into her mother's arms and burst into floods of tears.

Sunday morning felt like the hours before a funeral. Even in the privacy of our bedroom, the sound of church bells tolling nearby, as Vanessa and I rose and dressed in silence, added to our feeling that we too were weighed down by the sense of loss and grief coming from Maya's bedroom. She didn't leave her room all day. She lay in bed, sometimes crying, mostly just staring at the ceiling or the window. Her mother was in and out with cups of tea, but as Mrs Lowe wasn't able to hold back her own tears, she didn't seem to be doing a very good job of comforting her daughter. At various points in the day

I knocked on Maya's door and tried to console her, tried to persuade her that things would work out OK, but she was having none of it.

'I really want out of this life,' she said. 'I've had it with the industry. I've had it with fame. I've had it with relationships. I just want out.'

Vanessa, in her own more understated way, was also getting agitated.

'Let's just go back to Manhattan now, pack our bags and leave early for New England,' she muttered to me when it became clear that the weekend was a total disaster. We were standing on one of the little side decks halfway up the shady side of the house. The sun was fainter than yesterday. It was one of those hot, close days with low cloud, where everything looks grey and flat.

'We can't do that, Vanessa. Maya needs us.'

'Needs *you*, you mean.'

'No, *us*. It's clear she really enjoys your company.'

We continued to argue about the pros and cons of leaving when Mr and Mrs Lowe came out to join us.

'Can we ask your advice, Steve?' said Mr Lowe. 'Anna thinks we should change our flight tomorrow so we can stay on and look after Maya. I'm not sure that's a good idea. What's your view?'

There was real anger in Vanessa's eyes, but I tried to pretend I hadn't seen. I was picturing the kind of emotional chaos that might arise if Sheldon, Bernard, Dan *and* her parents all found themselves trying to influence Maya's behaviour.

'Can I give you my honest opinion?' I said. 'I think it would be better if you went. Vanessa and I will be here until Friday. We can look after her. And we can keep you updated about how she is, so you don't need to worry.'

'Steve . . .' Vanessa tried to interrupt, but Mr Lowe was already wringing my hand in gratitude.

'I think that's the right advice, Steve. Thank you so much. You're always a rock in a crisis. You're like my own son to me, you know that, don't you?'

Then he gave me a big bear hug. I think it was the first hug a man had ever given me. Out of the corner of my eye, I saw Vanessa stroke her bump, and heave a big sigh.

'I'm not sure I can forgive you for that,' she said to me when Mr Lowe had left the room.

'I'm sorry,' I said. And I was. So sorry.

Things moved quickly after that. Nelson drove Maya and the Lowes back to Manhattan so that the Lowes could begin their packing. Vanessa and I waited for another car to take us to the apartment. We weren't going to see Frank and Anna again before they left, so there were emotional farewells. Mrs Lowe brought out a gift she had found for Vanessa – a foot rub to soothe her aching feet after all the walking they'd been doing – and Vanessa couldn't help but love her for it, despite being peeved with her daughter.

After Nelson's car had left the driveway, Vanessa and I surveyed Sheldon's empty house and felt a pang of regret that we were leaving it without having had the dream weekend we envisaged.

'They pay a price for all this, don't they?' said Vanessa. 'A real price.'

Chapter Twenty-Seven

The next few days were so nightmarish I worried Vanessa was just going to walk out on us and head home without me. As soon as Maya got back to the apartment, she went into her room and refused to come out, no matter who was asking for her. She wouldn't eat, she wouldn't take calls. She missed every appointment in her diary, including a dinner with the three men providing most of the funding for the film. They were only a couple of weeks from shooting and she was supposed to be in rehearsal. The phone didn't stop ringing. Then the production company started sending people round with messages. First it was the runners, but as the days passed, the messengers became increasingly senior. On Wednesday, it was the director himself. When *he* got turned away, Sheldon came over and spent over an hour closeted with Maya in her bedroom. Eventually he emerged, holding a wan Maya by the hand.

'Steve,' he said, 'you've got to make your friend see sense. She wants to pull out of the film unless this Bernard character is sacked.'

I was glad Vanessa wasn't around. She'd spent the past few days going to museums on her own, leaving me to answer the door to a succession of disgruntled film-makers and their minions. I felt easier being Maya's negotiator without Vanessa's penetrating, disapproving gaze upon me. And in this case I felt particularly torn. I too thought it might be best if Bernard wasn't around. Also I felt my role was to protect Maya when I considered her agent was giving her the wrong advice.

Maya was crying again.

'How do you expect me to work with him, Nick? After what he has done to me?'

'Well, maybe if you hadn't hooked up with him in the first place without thinking it through . . .'

'Hey, steady on,' I said.

'Who I hook up with is my fucking business, Mr Sheldon,' she said.

'He's a fucking location director,' said Sheldon. 'You barely have to come into contact with him.'

'It's the principle,' she said.

'There's a bigger one at stake. You committed to this movie. You're getting paid shedloads of money to make it and you've gotta see it through.'

'Stop bullying her,' I said.

'Butt out, Steve. And Maya, you listen to me – from the silence in the press, looks like that journo has decided not to pursue his story, but if Bernard gets kicked off the film, people will start asking questions and the answers aren't going to look good. This time it's you breaking up the marriage. No good press out of that, honey. No nice victim charity events with Stephen Fry. No phone-ins saying poor poor Maya. Oh no, it's how could she do that to that lovely French family?'

It was my analysis exactly, but I hated the brutal way he said it to her.

No one spoke for a while. Nick moved to sit by her.

'Come on,' he said, 'you've been burnt on the rebound. It happens. The difference with you is you feel things deeper than most. That's what makes you a great actress. And you're news, so the media are on your case the whole time. But we'll get over it, we'll get over it.'

She nodded, but said nothing.

'What's happening with Dan?' I asked.

The look Sheldon gave me, you'd have thought I'd vomited on the carpet. 'Not sure it's the moment, Steve . . .'

'I think Maya needs to know.'

'Let's just say, I saw him at the weekend and we're working something out. We may well need your involvement, Steve, but just not at this precise moment. In fact, could you give Maya and me a little space? There's something else I want to talk to her about.'

'I want Steve here,' said Maya, suddenly seeming to pull herself together. 'He has been incredible through this whole thing. Right now, I'm feeling like he's the only man I can trust.'

I glowed with pride. Sheldon shook his head in disbelief.

'OK, honey, if that's what you want, Steve stays. But this is all highly confidential. I don't want a word said outside this room.'

'What is it?'

'I took a call this morning about something big – something that's gonna take you into a whole new league.'

'What?'

He smiled, trying to nudge her into a better frame of mind. She wasn't warming though. She looked stern.

'OK, the call was from Bono. He says he and Bob Geldof are going to a meeting at the White House on Friday and then there's a reception or something because the president is hosting a group of African leaders on their way to a Commonwealth summit in Vancouver. He says the president is sick of the sound of him and Geldof so why don't you join them and put a smile on the president's face. Tell the president what you guys think he should be doing in Africa, all the stuff from that little film we did for them.'

Even I thought Maya would be impressed by an invitation like that. But the stern look remained fixed.

'Make your mind up, Nick,' she said crossly. 'One minute you want me working flat out in New York, the next I'm supposed to be off to Washington. Well, I'm not doing either.'

'For Christ's sake Maya, two of the most influential campaigners on the planet have asked you to join them on a trip to meet the president of the United States. Can you tell me on what possible fucking basis you say no to that?'

'Do you need to swear at her the whole time?' I asked.

'Steve, can you shut the fuck up or fuck off outside?'

'On the basis that I am fucked off,' said Maya. 'Fucked off with men, fucked off with making films, fucked off with fame, fucked off with you and your fucking wheeler-dealing, fucked off with the whole fucking shooting match.' She stood up, picked up a bowl from the glass table beside her and threw it against the curtain where it smashed. Then she stormed out to her bedroom.

There was a long silence. Nick went to a drinks tray and poured himself a Scotch.

'Can't you see she is fragile?' I said.

'I can,' he said. 'Yes indeed, Stevie boy, I really can.'

'Well could you maybe stop making it worse? You're meant to be here to smooth things out.'

'Am I, Steve? Is that why I'm here? And why exactly are you here?' He looked harsh, threatening.

'Because I'm Maya's friend.'

He nodded, smiled, then said slowly, each word individually laced with rising sarcasm, 'Maya's friend. Maya's friend. Of course you are. It's a shame, dear friend, that you didn't think to warn me about what was going on with this Bernard guy.'

'I was going to! I was just waiting for the right moment. I thought perhaps Maya would tire of him before it got serious. But actually that Geordie journalist has served us well . . .'

As soon as the words came out of my mouth, I knew I'd screwed up.

'Geordie?'

'Yeah. That's what Bernard told Maya.'

'Interesting. I wouldn't imagine a Frenchman to be so up on English accents.'

'Well, he is a locations director . . .'

'Fair point.'

He stared at me for what felt like a whole minute, and then said, 'Listen, Steve, I think it's time you and I started talking straight to each other.'

He took an envelope from his pocket and handed it to me.

'Open it,' he said. 'Read it. Won't take you long.'

I took out a single sheet of white paper. As soon as I saw the heading, I felt as though a slab of stone inside my guts was sinking towards my ankles. 'Main points' it said. In bold. Underlined.

- Call to Sheila Hegarty made from phone of Jerry Coleman, colleague of Watkins.
- Envelope of first report contained compliment slip from

the bank that employs Vanessa Watkins — seemingly left there by mistake.

- Fingerprints from teacup used by Watkins in Blomfield Road match prints on pot plants and lawnmower in ML's father's greenhouse, Taplow.
- Watkins' sole fingerprints on label of second anonymous report on activities of DC.
- Watkins seeking to use company funds to fund investigation into client's former client DC. Increasingly concerned re debt.
- Watkins most recently hired Swift to investigate private life of French location director Bernard Dufay.

I couldn't bring myself to look up from the single sheet of paper. I read it twice, then stared at the white space at the bottom of the page, cursing my stupidity in taking one of Vanessa's envelopes without looking inside, and in not thinking to wear gloves.

'You're not the only one who knows how to dig the dirt, Steve.'

I felt his stare ripping through my skin. Then he walked towards me, put his arm on my shoulder.

'Here you are,' he said, 'I think this is yours. Don't lose it again eh?'

I immediately recognised the little blue-felt elephant dangling from the ring with 'Don't forget' embroidered on it. It was the key to Maya's front door in Little Venice. The last time I'd seen it had been in Stafford's car when he'd given it back to me, and I'd put it in my pocket. I realised I'd never checked for it again. How had Sheldon got hold of it?

'Now,' he said, 'you and I are going for a little walk.'

For one irrational moment I worried he was going to take me out and kill me. We went down in the lift, in silence. I stood head bowed, trying to avoid his gaze, but I could feel his reflected stare in the darkened mirror on the back wall.

Once we were out of the apartment block, he steered me into Central Park.

'I've never been able to work you out, Steve. But one thing I know is that Maya likes you. It's real. It goes back a long way. Deep stuff, boy. Madwoman that she is, she trusts you. Now, that little document you just read gives me the ammunition to destroy her trust, doesn't it? To flush you out of her life like the dirty little microbe you are. But I'm not going to do that, Steve. I'm going to give you one more chance.

'I once told you I'm in the illusion business. Remember? I'm also in the keep-Maya-happy business. And from now on, you work for me, sunshine. You help me keep her happy. You do what I tell you. Do you understand? And maybe, who knows, if you're a good boy and you do as I say, I might be able to see my way to helping pay off your big bad private detective without your lovely wife, your best friend Maya or your boss finding out what you've been up to. That fair?'

I said nothing, looked at my feet as we walked. He now had his hand on my lower back.

'So because she listens to you, tonight you are going to persuade her to get back on the movie. And because she listens to you, you are also going to convince her she cannot give up the chance to meet the president. And because I'm going to stay in New York and take care of Dan so that he and that lunatic cameraman of his don't try and do anything rash in front of Mr President, you're going to Washington with her and Sampson, to hold her hand. You got that?'

I was boiling with fury inside, but I nodded. I needed to play for time. Work out where I stood. I couldn't help admiring Sheldon. He was killing two birds with one stone. Sorting me out, and solving the problem of Dan for Maya. By packing her off to Washington on this high-profile assignment, he would distract media attention from the more messy story about her ex-husband making a film about his attempt to win her back. The pictures of Dan on his knees in front of the Booth theatre had gone everywhere. It was a pathetic piece of melodrama but Dan's production company was milking the publicity opportunity for all it was worth.

'You can also be the first to know my long-term plan on this,' Sheldon said with mock confidentiality, squeezing my biceps, 'and who knows, perhaps you can help in this too.'

He stopped, and stood in front of me, as if he was about to make a statement to the press.

'Maya and Dan back together again one day. Reunited after their divorce. What do you think?'

I looked at him in disbelief.

He grinned. 'Wouldn't that be great? What a story. You can see the headlines now, can't you? All the mags will be falling over themselves with their tongues and their chequebooks hanging out. Let's face it. Maya's getting a bit old to be the girl next door. She needs a new image. Young but mature woman of wisdom who has put her mistakes behind her. That's how I'm seeing it. The offers will come rolling in. There's a book in it. Maybe a documentary. DVD for Christmas. Maybe even a movie, Maya plays Maya. Oh it's a beautiful beautiful thing, Steve, and you're going to help make it happen. It will open the door to a whole new range of roles for her . . . the grieving widow, the lawyer fighting for justice, the mother on the run to save her children . . . she's been Kate and Keira, done all that stuff. Now we move into a new phase, more Julia Roberts, maybe even Meryl Streep. You see what I mean, Steve? You get my drift? Are you learning about how it works?'

Sheldon looked up at the sky as if he could see the trailers for all these future films projected on to the clouds.

'They are stronger as a joint brand, you see, Steve,' he continued. 'Maya's got to understand that. I mean, as a singleton she's cute but threatening; as part of a happy couple who have sorted their differences she's every woman's role model and every man's fantasy.'

He heaved a great, satisfied sigh, and then slapped me on the back.

'OK then. We understand each other. Enjoy Washington. Sampson will organise everything. Ciao for now. Don't fuck up.'

After he'd gone, I stood for a moment beneath the trees trying to take in what had just happened to me. I was being blackmailed. It was a horrible feeling. But was Sheldon's ground as solid as he thought it was? Yes, he knew about my debt. But he didn't seem to know about the Qatar project with the big bonus to come. And how could he be so sure that Maya would lose all trust in me if she found out what I'd done? She more than anyone would see that everything I had done was aimed at helping her. Especially if she realised that her agent was a devious, double-dealing shark whose goal was to turn her and her wife-beating ex-husband into a new brand that would become his own personal multimillion-pound pension plan.

'Fuck you, Nick Sheldon,' I said under my breath. 'Yes, I'll persuade Maya to go to Washington. Yes, I'll go too. But I'm going to play you at your own game. By the time I get back, it's you she'll have lost all trust in, not me.'

Chapter Twenty-Eight

Vanessa had a rare temper-loss when I told her I had to go to Washington.

'You've got to do what?' she shouted.

She was standing in our bedroom, her arms suddenly folded, a sea of clothes from her abandoned packing spread around her. 'Over my dead body.'

'It's only for one night, Vanessa. I'll be back on Saturday morning.'

'But we were supposed to leave for New England *tomorrow*!'

'I know, but come on, surely you realise how important this is? I mean, Maya has been invited to meet the president for God's sake.'

'I couldn't care less if she'd been invited to meet God for the president's sake. This is supposed to be a special holiday for us, Steve. Our last before the baby!'

'I know . . .' I said. I just didn't know what to say. I sat down on the bed and put my head in my hands. This seemed to make Vanessa relent a bit because she came and sat next to me.

'So she's up for going to Washington, is she?' she asked. 'No more tears, no more tantrums?'

'She's an actress.'

'Oh, sorry, I forgot.'

In fact I hadn't yet talked to Maya about it. When I got back to the apartment I had found Vanessa in the midst of packing. Maya seemed still to be in her room. Getting Vanessa's approval was just the first step in the long haul to the White House. Next I had to convince Maya.

I put my hand on Vanessa's. 'Please let's not argue about this,' I said. 'Let me do just this one last thing for Maya and then I'm all yours. New Steve, New England here we come.'

Vanessa gave me a look that seemed both sympathetic and dubious at the same time.

'Can't Sampson go with her?'

'Sheldon thinks she needs both of us.'

'What about him?'

'He's got to stay here and sort out Dan.'

She looked fierce.

'OK, Steve. You go. But listen to me now – if, when this baby's born, you ever put Maya before me, I will never, ever forgive you.'

'You don't even have to say that,' I said.

I found Maya lying on top of her bed wearing jeans and a pink T-shirt, a discarded iPod at her side.

'Have you eaten anything today?' I asked.

'I made a sandwich,' she said. 'While you were out.'

'Good.'

I sat on the bed, and took her hand, stroked it gently. On the bedside table was an alarm clock and a book. The book, I noticed, was in French – by an author called Yasmina Reza. Maya had done GCSE French, but I doubted she was capable of reading French novels. It was pretty clear who it belonged to. I was surprised she hadn't lit a fire and burnt it.

'How you feeling?' I asked.

'How d'you think?'

'Sorry,' I said. 'Stupid question.'

She smiled half-heartedly. 'That's OK. I know you're trying to be kind. If only all men were like you. I mean, I just don't get why Bernard would deceive me like that.'

'People like him think they are invincible,' I said. 'They believe their own reality. When he is at home, he believes his home reality, the happily married man with a lovely family. When he's away working, he's the cool, free, man about town. He probably arrived here with loads of fantasies about you. But then realised he could make those fantasies real – his New York Maya reality. And it was so good, amazing, he was out on the town with Maya Lowe, then he was sleeping with Maya Lowe, with his own side of the bed where he could put his book, and a luxury kitchen where he could show off his cooking. And so he parked the home reality in a separate little corner and hoped that with good luck and planning, nobody would get hurt.'

Maya was fiddling with a purple hairband, wrapping it again and again round her little finger.

'Is that what I am Steve, a fantasy?'

'Not to me, no, but to a lot of people, yes. So if a man has the fantasy and then one day he can have some of it, he's going to find it very hard to resist.'

'And what about me the person? Where do I fit in that? What happens when my feelings come into play?'

'It's a hard thing to face, Maya, but I doubt if Bernard ever gave that a thought.'

She looked as if I'd slapped her in the face, but I felt there was a clear truth here that had to be told, and it was best told when she was in this state, raw from the rejection, churning inside at her own naivety and her own failure to understand why men reacted to her as they did. She had never got it, despite years of my telling her, and I felt I had to say what I thought.

'Once you get to the kind of fame you have, it is hard to see how you can make new, genuine friends. It's not you the person they're interested in. It's you the phenomenon. What else are they to know? Anyone you meet now, they all have some kind of preconception in their minds. You touch people. You change people. I saw it when we arrived at that restaurant the first night we were here. Bernard was not Bernard Dufay set designer and location supremo. He was feeling part of your stardom too. I could see it in his every move, he was like "Look at me! I'm standing up to make sure everyone knows I'm the one Maya Lowe is coming towards." He was wanting to be bathed in your glow. I go so far back with you, you will always be the old Maya I grew up with. But Bernard and all your film people can't see that part of you. They only know Maya the superstar, Maya with the glow. They feel the glow. They love the glow. Because it says they're special too, that you chose to be with them.'

She shook her head lightly from side to side.

'Do you get what I am saying Maya? Do you really get it?'

She took my hand. 'You're saying I might never find someone I could share a life with. You're saying I am just an object of desire who will occasionally have moments of excitement if the desire is mutual, but have no chance of finding a real partner again. Is that what you're saying?'

I looked at her sadly. 'Never is a strong word,' I said. 'But you know, it's hard to have everything. Vanessa and I have love, but we don't have your success, your status, your reputation, your ability to move and inspire. That is a lot to put down on the positive side. We don't have your money either. I know money is not the be-all and end-all, but it must be nice to have it.'

'Is it? Right now, I would swap every penny for being happy and loved.'

'But you are loved. It's just a different sort of love to the one you grew up thinking you were going to have.'

We were silent for a moment, both contemplating the impossibility of her situation. Then she turned to me, her face lit up with the determination I'd seen so often in the past. The determination to get over difficulties, to succeed, to shine.

'So how do I get a life back?' she asked. 'Help me, Steve. You're the one person who can.'

'I don't know!' I said. 'I think you have to decide, once and for all, whether you could live without being this famous. I think a big part of you wants to give it up. But there's another part that can't let go.'

She nodded. 'You're right. And I'm worried that even if I *do* give it up, I'll never escape it. I'll become famous for trying to walk away from fame. Sheldon and his like will just crank that story up, and it will go on for ever.'

'But there are levels of fame, aren't there?' I suggested. 'Maybe if you go back to the theatre, to the stage acting you love, you won't be such an icon of popular culture any more. You'll get back in the serious reviews, out of all that We-know-the-stars.com stuff. And it won't be so 24/7.'

'Nick always says theatre work would be a bad idea.'

'Well then, maybe he's not the right agent for you.'

I'd seized my chance to get one up on Sheldon, and it appeared to be working. She was clearly thinking the idea over. I was suddenly worried that she might decide to fire him then and there. That would be a disaster. Sheldon would carry out his threat and tell Maya about Stafford, and she'd turn against me. No, I needed to buy time – get her to Washington.

'But I do think he's right about the White House,' I said. 'You can't say no to that.'

'You think so?'

'Certain. After all, if you do decide that you want out of the fame game, what a great thing to do before retirement.'

She smiled.

'Just understand why they're asking, Maya. Because you're the best. The very best. There's nobody who can touch you.'

She squeezed my hand and, for a few moments, ran her thumb up and down my forefinger.

'So get some sleep,' I said. 'Tomorrow's a big day. I'll go with you. I'll see you through it. Then when we come back, you can get back to work on the movie, and we can take stock. That OK?'

'I'll think about it,' she said. But I could tell she'd decided to go.

Chapter Twenty-Nine

The plane to Washington the next morning was almost full. We had the front row but the seats were rather small and uncomfortable. Maya had slept OK and she seemed up for it now. Added to which Martin Sampson's gushing enthusiasm was helping to build a sense of how important this was. Maya sat by the window, Martin in the aisle seat. I was in the middle. They were talking across me the whole time.

'What do I call the president when I'm addressing him?' Maya asked Sampson as we took off.

'Well, I've never talked to him, Maya, but basically Mr President.'

She whispered to me. 'You don't have to curtsey, do you?'

'I think that's the Queen,' I whispered back.

Then she was talking across me again, leaning forward so that her silk top fell forward, and I couldn't help staring at her breasts and a purple bra that held them. I stole a look at Martin to see if he was similarly challenged but he had his eyes fixed firmly on her lips, trying to hear her properly above the noise of the engines and the repetitive announcements from the pilot and chief steward.

'What about all these African leaders we're seeing at the drinks reception, are they Mr President too?'

'Well, some will be and some won't. Some will be prime minister. I think when in doubt just say "sir".'

'Good idea, Martin.'

'Unless they're women, obviously,' he added, without any detectable sense of irony, and he seemed a little hurt when Maya laughed.

She turned back to me. 'I sort of feel I shouldn't be as excited as this. I mean presidents are only flesh and blood like all of us, aren't they? But when you think of the historical figures that get remembered, the really big ones, so many of them seem to be political leaders. And lots of them are American . . .'

Maya's addition to the president's guest list had been so last-minute that Sampson wasn't sure whether the press would be waiting for us when we landed. He needn't have worried. He switched on his mobile as we taxied to the terminal building and it pinged for about fifteen seconds as a flood of messages came in, mainly from British media but some US too. Word had got out. When I turned on my phone to call Vanessa, there was a text from Jerry saying 'Call me asap'. I was intending to do it as soon as I found a quiet moment, but from the second we walked out of the aeroplane, it was as if I had entered an alternative reality.

A gaggle of cameramen was just inside the arrivals hall to greet us. I was impressed by the way Martin organised them so that they got a nice clean shot of Maya arriving and walking to the car, though at one point he had to motion to me to step back and avoid being in the picture. He also took a call from Bono's press officer to say that the White House would be releasing an official photo of the moment she met the president, if we wanted to alert the UK media. Martin took it as an instruction and spent the first part of the car ride to the

Hay-Adams hotel on Lafayette Square calling picture desks in London. His non-stop chatter obviously irritated Maya.

'Do you have to do that, Martin?' she said. 'Surely if they want the photo, they will get it. It's hardly going to be a state secret, is it?' He looked hurt, but she carried on. 'And do we really have to try to generate more interest, when what I'm wanting is to stay more out of the limelight?'

'I'm only doing what Nick said I should,' Sampson mumbled, and then shut up. His enthusiasm crushed, he had a hurt, hangdog expression for the rest of the drive, but couldn't resist tapping out messages on his BlackBerry. Maya looked over to me and shook her head as if to say 'See! This is what I have to put up with.'

The Hay-Adams was across from the White House and just as splendid. We were met by the manager and led through a wood-panelled foyer to our rooms on the third floor. I felt my feet sinking into the lemon-coloured carpet. Maya and I had rooms on the same corridor, at her request. Martin was on the floor above. The meeting with the president was at two, so Maya had less than an hour to get ready. She had brought half a dozen outfits with her, and we were ten minutes from leaving when she called me up to her room to take a look at the one, finally, she had chosen.

'What do you think?' she asked.

'I'm kind of biased,' I said, 'but I'd say you look fantastic.'

'But do you think it works? I mean, is it appropriate?'

'I don't know what to say. You look fabulous.'

'Do you think pencil skirt is OK? Not too tight?'

'No, looks great.'

'Yves Saint-Laurent . . . thought that was suitable. I thought navy blue was better than anything bright, don't you think, because it's so serious what we're talking about, but the jacket and the shirt are a bit sassier, that's my thinking anyway.' I don't know how to describe the top. It looked a little bit like a corset with sleeves. Strapless. Same colour as the skirt but with gold buttons millimetres apart running its whole length. She really did look good.

'What about the shoes?' she asked. 'Heels not too high?'

'They're fine. Really fine.'

'I was going to wear Jimmy Choo but I think Kurt Geiger is more, I don't know . . .'

'Presidential.'

'Yeah, maybe.'

'Well you look a million dollars, so let's get going.'

As we went to the private lounge downstairs, I noticed her make-up was perfect (which made me wonder why she usually felt the need to travel with her own stylist) and her hair bounced and shone like something out of a shampoo commercial. Bono and Geldof arrived shortly afterwards, shown in by the manager.

'Hey Maya,' they echoed, and they were all over her, kissing and fussing and generally telling her how great she was and how she was going to knock the president dead. I couldn't quite believe I was in the same room as them. I'd once seen Bono in concert, and I'd seen Geldof in an airport lounge, chewing nuts and reading a paper, but this was different. This was them, not the performing characters. They were right there, flesh and blood before me. Maya seemed suddenly transformed by their presence.

'I am so so grateful for this,' she said. 'I mean, you guys have been campaigning for years, but for me to meet the president of the United States, I mean, that's major.'

'Hey, babe, presidents shit and fart the same as all of us,' said Geldof.

'God, listen to you,' said Bono, 'can you not say it a bit nicer?'

'Just putting her at ease, that's all.'

Maya laughed and, finally, introduced me. I went to shake Bono's hand. I almost said 'I've heard a lot about you' but just managed to stop myself and instead muttered hello.

If Maya had looked gorgeous before, now that she was chatting away animatedly about what she should say, and how, she was absolutely radiant. Martin was rendered speechless, and even more so when we discovered there was to be White House access for only one support person for the whole group. Bono's assistant, an expert on Africa, pulled rank on me and Martin, but it was not a big enough issue for Maya to fight over.

'I cannot do my job properly if I am not there,' Martin protested.

'Don't worry about a fockin' thing,' said Geldof. 'We'll take care of her.'

Maya came over and kissed me on the way out.

'You look great,' I said.

'You OK about not coming?' she asked.

'If you mean do I wish I was, of course I do. But I'll try to catch some of it in my room.'

'Will you call my mum and dad and tell them to watch the news?'

'That's a first! You normally tell them not to watch it.'

'This is different. It's not every day their little Acton princess gets to go to the Oval Office.'

'Too true,' I said.

'Hey Maya, can we get a fockin' move on here,' Geldof shouted over at her. He had not taken quite the care over his appearance that she had. I couldn't believe he was going to the White House in jeans, a pink sweater and cream-coloured jacket. At least Bono had a kind of suit on, albeit a very rock-star kind of suit: shimmering black jacket almost down to the backs of his knees.

After they'd gone, I left Martin sitting disconsolately in the lounge and went up to my room. I picked at the red grapes that sat atop a huge fruit bowl next to a complimentary bottle of champagne on ice. First I called the Lowes, as I had promised. Then I turned on the TV. I was delighted to discover that I had access not only to the US channels, but to Sky and the BBC as well. I channel-hopped for any trailers of live coverage. Fox News said the president was due to make a speech at the reception, but there was no mention of the meeting. CNN also trailed the speech and said he would be announcing a new fund for Africa, but again no mention of Maya. I switched to the BBC and watched the tickertape at the bottom of the screen. That was where I saw her name for the first time. 'Maya Lowe to plead for African children in White House meeting. US to announce new fund for Aids and education.' Over to Sky, where a picture of Maya came up in the corner, with a 'White House visit' caption. I quickly turned up the volume and sat on the end of my bed to watch.

'Now . . .' said the overweight, over-made-up anchorman, 'She has endured a painful split from her husband, she's landed a big film deal alongside Matt Damon and today Maya Lowe will be meeting the president of the United States. So quite a time for one of Britain's biggest exports. Our Washington correspondent Max Freeman is at the White House. Max?'

'Greg, yes, I'm here at the White House, and so is Maya Lowe. She arrived a short while ago, with Bono and Bob Geldof, and was led through the door behind me into the room where people wait before seeing the president, a kind of waiting room really, with portraits of former presidents on the walls, so she may well have been looking at those while she waits. A little bit later, she will be taken to the Oval Office and we have been told, Greg, that there will be video footage made available by the White House, which is an important development as until very recently we had been expecting only to see photographs. So good news there, Greg, even before the meeting has begun.'

'And just for the benefit of viewers who don't understand the niceties of American media diplomacy as you do Max, what is the significance of the White House giving us video?'

'Well, Greg, the president's presence is an important commodity if you like. Everyone who meets the president has their photo taken to record the event. But the video development suggests in status terms this is a meeting being taken very seriously at the highest levels.'

'Is that something the president would actually have decided, Max, rather than officials down the food chain?'

'Greg, a president has a lot of decisions to make as you know, but it is perfectly possible that he made this one, because of course it changes the nature of the meeting if in advance we are being told it is more important than we thought.'

'And, Max, what do we know about the substance here, about what Maya Lowe will be saying?'

'Well, we don't know her exact words yet, Greg, but we can expect her to be discussing Africa's ongoing problems, its famines and wars, and Maya's message to the president, like Bono's and Bob Geldof's, will be simple – "Do something." So quite a powerful message from a very powerful delegation of celebrities.'

'Max, I don't know if you can see these pictures but we are now looking at her arrival in the Oval Office, pictures just in here at the Sky News Centre, and there she is. Well what a moment that must be for her, Maya Lowe, the "girl next door" as she is so often called, a working-class girl from West London, and now in the West Wing as it were.' He chuckled at his own joke. 'There she is being shown to a sofa and she is sitting down as you can see, her clothes somehow managing to combine a movie-star look with the seriousness of the venue, and of the occasion. Smart, but also special, many people watching might feel. And there's Bono sitting next to her in a long coat and black vest, and the president is sitting too now, all sitting, and let's see if we can hear anything of what is being said . . . No, it appears they are just smiling for the cameras, a bit of small talk maybe and the cameramen are now being asked to leave, you can see there the woman in the dark suit, trying to shepherd them out, and there they go trying to get one last shot . . . this room of course where so many important decisions have been made to change the course of history. Kennedy was once there, before his tragic assassination, Nixon of course who had to resign over Watergate and don't forget this is the room where President Bill Clinton and Monica Lewinsky had the sexual relations subsequently denied by the president but which turned out to be true and Max, as we lose the feed there and come back to you, surely some of that history must be very much to the forefront of Maya's mind.'

'Greg, it is easy to be cynical about celebrities getting involved in these causes. But I have heard Bono and Bob Geldof talk about these issues and frankly, Greg, they know their mustard they really do and I don't believe Maya Lowe would be there if they did not think she could hold her own in a discussion like this. And let's not forget, you talk about history, this is someone with an A level in history who could easily have gone to university but chose to go to drama school instead and the rest, as they say, *is* history.'

'Max we will be back to you shortly and those pictures will be played all around the world tonight. Maya Lowe, dressed very simply in bright colours, certainly her skirt and shoes, but a classical smart look, in keeping with the occasion and we will go back to Max as soon as we have more.'

I flicked back to the BBC where another man, with the White House in the background, was also talking.

'So Michelle, you've seen there in those pictures of her arrival a really fascinating look at a group of people interacting with the most powerful leader on earth and as you say, what a moment for Maya Lowe, really the icing on the cake after a difficult year for her.'

'Matt, what will this visit mean to the people of Africa do you think?'

'Michelle, it's hard to know, standing outside the White House, exactly what they will all be feeling and thinking, the people of Africa, in Africa itself. Many of course won't know because they do not have access to TV and our live coverage. But as for those who do know, I think it must help to see that a delegation of people as high profile and powerful as this one is saying to the president "We are on your case, and we have many fans who watch our films and buy our music and they are going to be on your case too." So I think if you are the people of Africa, you're thinking "I am glad we have this kind of support," and if you are the president, particularly after the difficulties in Iraq and Afghanistan, you're thinking "I don't want these people on my case, because they can mobilise a lot of public and media support behind them, so I will do something."'

'Matt, fascinating as ever. And we'll be back to you when there's more. Matt Eagles there in Washington.'

I switched back to Sky, where half an hour later Max Freeman struck lucky while doing a live report from outside the White House. The celebrity delegation came out as he was on air, and he was able to keep talking until Maya, Bono and Geldof had taken their places in front of a bank of microphones and a semicircular arc of reporters from around the world. Bono spoke first, silencing Freeman. 'It was a good meeting. As you know, we applaud the progress there has been, but we believe there has to be more, and the president is uniquely placed to make that happen. He briefed us on the detail of the fund he is announcing later today and while we welcome this as a step in the right direction, we believe he should go further and encourage the other rich nations of the world to go further.'

'A hell of a lot further,' Geldof echoed.

'Maya, Maya, Maya, Maya . . .' a cacophony of voices was now directed at her. She looked nervous. The other two were used to this sort of thing, but she was outside her comfort zone. 'Maya, Max Freeman, *Sky News*, what was it like for you to be there in the Oval Office and do you feel that you have finally got over Dan's demise?'

'He's not dead, you eejit,' said Geldof.

Maya was a little more polite.

'This is not about Dan. It is not about me. It is about the poor of the world and the responsibility of those of us lucky enough to have better lives to make a difference. Some of the statistics we set out for the president are frankly shocking and the world has to do something.'

'Maya, Maya, Maya . . .'

'One at a time for Christ's sake,' said Bono.

'Maya, Steven Rodriguez, CBS. Could you describe to us how it felt to be in that building with all its history alongside the person routinely described as the most powerful on earth?'

'Like a dream in many ways. It was very beautiful and historic as you say. But we had a purpose and that was to lobby for the poor of the world and we will be doing that again at the drinks reception this evening. I am of course happy to be here but it is not about me, it is about children less fortunate than me, and our belief that a world as rich in talent and materials as ours should be able to help them.'

'Last question,' shouted Bono's assistant above the next wave of 'Maya, Maya, Maya' noise.

'Andrew Gudjohnsson, *New York Post*. Maya, we get the impression you like it here in the States. Do you think you might make your future in New York, settle there permanently? And if I can be so bold, we have seen you out and about on the town from time to time. Are you dating anyone yet, or are things still too raw?'

Geldof stepped in. 'She is dating destiny, you trivial little shite.' Maya smiled, and allowed Bono to steer her away, towards the building.

The camera followed them back inside and then turned to Max Freeman.

'Well quite a dramatic end to that little stake-out,' said Max. 'Bob Geldof there stepping in to stop Maya Lowe from answering questions about her love life . . . and I'm left wondering there whether the man from the *New York Post* knows something we don't . . . Greg?'

'Food for thought, Max, but what do we make of the substance of what she said there? About Africa I mean?'

'Well, Greg, it was an impassioned performance, wasn't it, and she clearly knows the detail, talking about statistics and suchlike. Obviously they had been pressing for more than the president was prepared to give. But you know, Greg, having just been standing very close to her, just for a few minutes here at the White House, I have to say I think the president will have been impressed. I have seen her films but frankly, Greg, that does not prepare you for the force of her charisma, beauty and physical presence. There was a quite extraordinary combination of very human charm and power of character that was irresistible, and if you can hear some of the other reporters beside me in this rather crowded media set-up we have here at the White House, they are saying much the same thing. So, Greg, if Maya made the same impression on the president as she seems to have made on the White House press corps, this really could be a great day for Africa I think.'

'Max, we will come back to you for coverage of the reception Maya mentioned. In the meantime, many thanks. Superb. Max Freeman there on what, as he says, could be a historic day. And of course we want to hear what you think, so text, call, email . . .'

At that moment, my phone beeped. It was Sheldon.

'Not bad, Steve my man, not bad. Now, remember the next step. I'm setting up a private meeting between Maya and Dan for early next week. I'm counting on you to make sure she agrees to it.'

'Count on me for nothing, arsehole,' I said, after I'd put the phone down. I was pacing the room looking for something to punch when I got a much more welcome call. It was Mr Lowe, his voice choked with emotion.

'My God, Steve, was that not incredible? I am sitting here with a wife crying tears of joy. That was one of the proudest moments of our lives, Steve, and I want to thank you for delaying your own holiday to help her get there. It must have been difficult for her to find the courage, what with all the upset over that French creep.'

'Oh, you don't need to worry about your daughter's courage,' I said. 'She's the bravest person I know. And I'm glad Mrs Lowe is crying tears of joy this time. It was awful to see her so upset last weekend.'

'Well, you know how mothers are, Steve, always worrying about their children, even when they are grown-up and can take care of themselves.'

I thought of my own mother, who I hadn't heard from since Christmas, not even after I'd been interviewed on national news, and refrained from answering.

'One thing concerned us though,' Mr Lowe continued. 'What was that about settling in the States? She never mentioned that to us.'

'They make it up, Mr Lowe.'

'Well, that's a relief,' he said. 'When they talked about how that New York man might know something we didn't, I got shivers down my spine.'

'It's all ridiculous media talk, Mr Lowe,' I said. 'Don't you think that, if anything important was going on in Maya's life, you'd know before the *New York Post*?'

'I hope so. Anyway get her to call us when she's through.'

I put the phone down feeling huge relief that none of the reporters had mentioned the fact that Dan was in New York. The Lowes still seemed to have heard nothing about the Booth theatre episode and I hoped it was going to stay that way.

By the time Maya returned to the Hay-Adams that evening she was way too high to be calling her parents. I was disappointed that Bono and Geldof didn't come back to the hotel, as I was hoping to get autographs for Vanessa, but they were already on a private jet to Vancouver to do a press conference before the leaders arrived for the Commonwealth summit. Maya returned to the private room where we'd been earlier and kicked off her shoes. Martin kept trying to fill her in on the coverage – but she was completely uninterested. Her eyes were focussed on the middle distance where she was clearly reliving moment upon moment of excited fulfilment. She had so much she wanted to tell us. I urged her to write it down so that she didn't forget anything.

'I will, I will, that's a great idea, Steve.' She was telling us every little detail, about the pictures in the waiting room – not of former presidents as the Sky reporter had suggested but of great scenes from American history – the black man in a dinner suit who led them to the door of the Oval Office, the tall woman who ushered them in. 'Oh, you would not believe the rug in there,' said Maya, 'so thick and the same shape as the room, just a little gap to the wall, with this enormous crest on it. And then there was this wonderful little statue of Churchill. The president said some fabulous things about him and about Britain and I felt so proud to be British, Steve, and then when we got on to talking about Africa and he was telling us about this fund he was setting up, I was thinking this is so much more important than anything else I do and I was just so in awe of Bob and Bono because they know everything there is to know, and I want to get like them, Steve, have that sense of purpose and mission, because surely that is what the power of celebrity ought to be, isn't it, something you can use to change the world, really change people's lives for the better? Remember what you said about how I could have a different kind of fame? Well, I've been thinking: this is the kind of fame I want. A doing-good fame, like Bono and Bob. I was so impressed by them. It was like they were talking as equals to the president of America and maybe I will never get to that, but did you see, did you notice at the press conference how all the questions were for me, and Bono said when we went inside again he wanted to harness that, make it part of the next stage of the campaign? I think I could believe in this, Steve, really believe in it.'

It was clear she was going to take a while to come down to earth. When I had talked about a different 'level' of fame, it hadn't been Mother Teresa I'd been thinking of, but it didn't seem the right time to discuss this. She was on a roll. She was happy. And best of all, it was me she wanted to share her happiness with. No one else. Not her parents, not Sheldon, even though Sampson was desperate for her to ring him.

'I can talk to him tomorrow,' she said firmly. 'Tonight's too special to talk business. Steve and I are going out to dinner to celebrate.'

Sampson looked at me, the hurt of her earlier put-downs now reinforced by anger. 'But I booked a table for us all at 15 ria!' he said.

'Well done,' said Maya dryly. 'Steve and I can take the reservation while you keep tabs on all the coverage. That is why you're here after all,' she added, I thought slightly cattily. Then she turned to me with a big smile.

'Knock on my door in half an hour,' she said. 'And don't be late!'

I may have been mistaken but there was something of a Come On signal in the way she lowered her eyes, then raised them again, her smile widening as she did so. She really was flying.

Chapter Thirty

I felt almost as though life was unfolding around me in slow motion as I returned to my room. Maya was so used to this kind of luxury, whereas whenever I travelled for Globus, we could not go higher than three stars, and in the UK we had a deal with Premier Inns. I sat on an orange chair, put my feet on the table in front of me, kicking to one side a neatly laid pile of magazines, and stared at the chandelier. Maya was just down the corridor. In the course of our friendship, I'd attended a lot of glamorous events with Maya, but nothing had been quite like this: just her and me, Sampson despatched to a different floor, as if I really was part of it, the entourage. I laid my head on the back of the chair, and told myself that whatever the pressures of work, of marriage to Vanessa, of Maya's demands and tantrums, I was a lucky man to be where I was, so close to her. Worried I might fall asleep, I undressed and took a shower. Though the air had been cooler today, I felt a coat of sweat all over my body. I let the cold water fall on my head and stood there until it became a little warmer. I washed my hair, turned the water back to cold to rinse it out, back to warm to soap my body, back to cold for a final rinse. I let out a little shudder, just short of a shiver, as I stepped out on to the towel I had thrown on the floor. I looked in the mirror. It was not Dan Chivers' dream body. It was not even Dan Chivers' actual body. But it wasn't bad. I brushed my teeth long and hard, then probably overdid the deodorant and the cologne.

From the window, I could just make out the black railings of the White House gardens. I thought about that thing Vanessa was always saying, how there were only six degrees of separation between everyone in the world. Well right now, I was only a step away from knowing the president of the United States.

I picked up the remote and zapped the TV back into life. Same pictures. Same verbiage from different correspondents and anchors. The president had trumped Maya on the bulletins now, however, having mistaken the president of Nigeria for the president of Kenya in full view of the cameras. 'Gaffe' was the BBC headline. But Maya was still in there fighting, story number two, and according to one reporter, she was going to be all over the British front pages tomorrow, including the *FT* this time.

I rang Vanessa.

'Did you see it?' I said.

She sounded weary. 'It was hard not to. It's everywhere. Like the whole country has come out in a Maya rash.'

'How you feeling?'

'Tired. I'll get an early night so that I'm fresh for the drive tomorrow. I called the restaurant I'd booked for this evening. They've carried our reservation over to tomorrow. The food sounds incredible. Just a shame I can't eat shellfish . . .'

'Well, I can.'

'How about you? What are you doing?'

I'd been planning on telling her that Maya, Sampson and I were going out to dinner. Now, reminded of our postponed trip to New England, I thought it best not to.

'Oh, I'm getting an early night too. Room-service beer and a burger I think. Maya and Martin have gone off to some posh joint to debrief.'

'That's a bit much. Weren't you invited?'

'Course I was, but I couldn't face it.'

'Probably best. Just think, though. Tomorrow night, we'll be beside Lake Megunticook.'

'Great name.'

'Great lake apparently.'

I tried not to dwell on my deception when I put the phone down. I just got on with dressing.

I had a shave, put on the light suit Vanessa had bought for me on her big shopping binge with Maya, with a bright green shirt, walked down the corridor and tapped on Maya's door.

'Wow!' she said when she opened it. 'You look amazing!'

'Not bad yourself,' I said, not sure if I was blushing. Usually it was me paying her the compliments. It felt odd the other way round.

By strange coincidence, she was wearing green too: a satin-silk shift dress that hung in pleats from a low neckline so that the material billowed when she walked; green leather sling-back shoes with cute heels. It looked as if we'd deliberately dressed to match each other.

I loved the car ride to the restaurant, Maya sitting close to me in the back seat, the streets of Washington zipping by, much faster than they did in New York. It was late evening and there was that pink, dusty light you get in summer, just before night falls. When we arrived at the restaurant, the doorman signalled to the manager waiting just inside. He came out to the pavement, then led us to our table, which was tucked into an alcove in the corner of the room.

I could tell that the events of the afternoon had had an impact on people. As I followed Maya through the restaurant, I reckoned the head-turn count was closer to Britain's ninety per cent, certainly in the eighties. At the table right next to ours was a well-known TV anchor. Neither of us knew him, but one of the waiters whispered his name to me as we sat down. I relayed it to Maya and she was able to return the man's nod in a kind of mutual silent respect.

When we were in New York I had noted that the restaurant celebrity-glow tended to fade more quickly than in London. It was the same here. Once drink and food orders were taken we were able to forget about the people around us and talk intimately. We were sitting side by side on a curved soft-backed bench seat, our knees almost touching.

'I can't thank you enough for everything you've done, Steve,' Maya said, leaning towards me. She was wearing a gold necklace with a single diamond which was bouncing gently from breast to breast as she spoke.

'It's what friends are for.'

'Yes, but you've really gone beyond the call this time. First taking such good care of my parents, then dealing with me losing it over Bernard, and now this. Getting me to come here, to Washington. It has been the most incredible day of my life. I think I can finally see what it is I want from life.'

'Which is?'

'To influence the powerful. To make a difference to ordinary people's lives.'

'To do that, you'll need to stay in the public eye.'

'Perhaps. When I get home I need to have a big think about how I can get more privacy for myself.'

'But is privacy what you really want?' I asked, determined to make her confront the contradictions of what she was saying. 'I mean, think about it. How would you feel if you walked in somewhere, and nobody had a clue who you were?'

She grinned. 'I don't think that's ever going to happen, do you?'

'And how do you feel about that?' I asked. 'I mean when you are walking down a street and you know that every single person who sees you turns to the person they're with, and says "There's Maya Lowe", or if they're alone they call or text their friends to say they've just seen Maya Lowe. Don't just tell me you hate it. I know that. And don't give me a pat answer like you'd give in a telly interview with some Dan Chivers type, I really want to know what you think about it.'

She scanned the restaurant, her eyes moving slowly from right to left. People at maybe half a dozen tables were looking over. She smiled at nobody in particular.

'I think it's my burden,' she said. 'But it is also my right.'

Her answer took me aback a little. It sounded arrogant. It was her saying, rarely for her, that she was special and deserved special attention. Yet it was true, so perhaps it wasn't arrogant at all.

'I think you could live without the burden,' I said, 'but not the right.'

She took my hand.

'You know, sometimes I think you're incredibly wise, Steve. As I get older I realise more and more that what counts is having the right advisors: people who keep themselves anchored to the real world. Like J. K. Rowling. You know, she has a great idea, writes a book, becomes a multi-multi-multi-millionaire but the husband keeps on being a doctor, the kids have ordinary lives, they probably keep her sane from all the mania around her. I want my children to grow up like that, with a father like that. Someone who doesn't fill their heads with vapid nonsense. I want the people I'm involved with to have integrity.'

This was it, I thought. The moment to oust Sheldon.

'What about your agent?' I asked. 'Does he have integrity?'

Maya looked into her wine glass as if somehow she was going to find the future in there. 'I think he did in the beginning. But he's changed. Since he started branching out into sport and jetting off around the big European clubs with his footballers, something has changed. Even the way he talks is different. And he has made some really bad calls on my career recently. That skincare ad, for example. That wasn't me. He's obsessed by big one-off pay days for advertising and sponsorship . . . It's as if the acting is the least important thing.'

'So you're thinking of changing your agent?'

She laughed. 'I think it's about time I changed all the men in my life, don't you?'

'Including me?' I said.

'No, not you, Steve. I'm keeping you.'

She raised her glass.

'To the best friend I ever had,' she said.

'And to the most beautiful woman I have ever known,' I replied.

She flashed me her trademark quizzical look, one eyebrow raised.

'Not sure Vanessa would like to hear that.'

'Let's not talk about Vanessa tonight,' I said quickly. 'Tonight is about you, your success and your happiness.'

'Seriously though, Steve, you and Vanessa have got

something wonderful. Your relationship seems so harmonious. I envy it . . .'

There was a silence as we both thought about Vanessa, and I was relieved when the waiter brought our first course.

'You see those people looking at you from that table to our right?' I said. She looked, smiled, and they smiled back, then looked away, embarrassed to be caught staring. 'They know who you are in that they know your name, they know what you look like, they know some or all of the facts from your career. But I know you the person, the spirit, the soul. I see the beauty outside, as everyone does. But I see the beauty inside too. It's why I cared so much, Maya, when you fell in love with Dan. I felt he was wrong for you, dangerous. I saw ahead, I suppose, to the hurt he would cause you, and I hate to see you hurt. I hated him because I knew he would hurt you and I hate him more now because he did.'

'He is history, Steve, water passed under the bridge.'

'What about the meeting he wants?'

'I've decided not to go.'

'Even if Sheldon thinks that's what you should do?'

'Even if Sheldon begs.'

After that, the conversation returned to less personal matters. Maya chattered on about who she'd met at the drinks reception; I entertained her by sending up Sampson at his most manic. There was still an electricity between us though. Occasionally our knees would touch and Maya would keep hers next to mine for a few seconds before moving it. At one point, when I stretched my arm along the top of the banquette behind us, she shook her hair when speaking and it brushed my hand. Neither of us moved.

I wanted the meal to go on for ever, but all too soon the waiter was bringing me a coffee and Maya a mint tea. As she pulled the saucer towards her, the strap of her silk dress slipped down from her shoulder, and I was catapulted back to that summer day after our GCSEs when we sat side by side on a rusting bench in Acton Park and I decided not to kiss her.

'Do you remember that time,' I said, 'when you asked me whether I thought it was strange your best friend being a boy?'

She didn't remember. I described the scene to her. Our post-exam euphoria, her white cotton sundress.

'Oh, I remember that dress! The shoulder straps kept falling down! I was so embarrassed.' She giggled as she pulled up the strap on her green dress.

'And I wanted to kiss your shoulder,' I said. 'But I was too frightened of losing you.'

She stopped laughing. 'And I was desperately praying you wouldn't,' she said, 'because I was infatuated with Nathan Kennedy and wanted to keep you as a friend.' She stared down at the table, and then raised her eyes to look directly at me. 'Perhaps I was wrong,' she said.

We had a car waiting to take us back to the hotel. Maya suggested we walk. It was only a few blocks, and there didn't seem to be any press hanging around outside. There had been a concert in a nearby church and people were pouring out on to the pavement. There was something almost festive about the mood. The hard edge had been taken out of the day's heat and the gentlest of breezes was ruffling Maya's hair and her billowing dress.

After a couple of hundred yards, she took my arm. I leaned my head towards hers and left it there, just long enough for her to know it was a move, but not so long that it would require her to respond or, worse, to worry. Another young couple were walking towards us in the weak light thrown on to the trees and the pathway by the street lamps and the buildings to our left. They too were arm in arm. They had eyes only for each other. They did not give us so much as a glance.

'That could have been us,' I said. 'Man, woman, couple, not famous, we've never seen them before, we'll never see them again. And they seemed so happy.'

'Life takes many strange turns,' she said.

'What was the strangest for you?' I asked.

'Oh, I don't know. I've had so much luck. All of my big breaks had an element of luck to them. Getting the lead in *Picture Frame* only happened because the director was in bed with flu and watched my episode of *The Bill*, even though he couldn't stand the programme. And I was paid so badly to start off with I had to borrow £100 off you to get some Christmas presents, do you remember? Six months later I got my first six-figure cheque. It was the same for *Please Miss*. They were going to cast Kate Winslet and then the casting director read an interview I'd done talking about my school days and she called me.'

'I remember that interview.'

'Really?'

'*Sunday Telegraph* magazine. The headline was "The Girl Next Door".'

'What a memory.'

'You mentioned me in that one.'

'Did I?'

'Not by name. You said you kept in contact with friends from school, especially one. I assume that was me. And you said it was important not to lose sight of where you came from, no matter how far you went.'

'It's what I still believe.'

A rollerblader sped by, just inches away, startling both of us. I felt Maya squeeze my arm.

'Well, we're a long way from home here,' she said. 'But it is a nice place to be.'

Maya let go of me as we walked into the more public space where cars were pulling up outside the hotel. But there was a kind of unspoken agreement between us that, in the course of the evening, our relationship had changed.

I felt like an adolescent boyfriend being taken back to a new girlfriend's house as we went up in the lift. I didn't want to stand too close to her as it carried us to our floor, even after the intimacy of our walk. She was clearly feeling the same sense of excitement tinged with unease. She even said 'Here we are then' as she fished her swipe card from her bag.

'Is this the moment when I ask if you want to come in for a coffee?' she said, smiling.

She was standing about four feet away from me. I looked long and hard, trying to read those eyes. Was she still pulling me in, or pushing me away? Then, before I knew it, I was kissing her.

'Are you crazy!' she said, drawing away. 'Not here!' She unlocked the door to her room and pulled me in.

It was dark inside. The change of atmosphere froze us momentarily, as if we suddenly realised the enormity of what we were doing. Maya walked across the room to turn on a lamp. Then she sat down on the side of the bed and kicked off her shoes.

I walked over and stood by her. I held my hand towards her. She took it, and I sat down beside her. Then I bent my head towards her ear.

'You said I was the best friend you've ever had,' I whispered. 'Can I be the best lover too?'

I felt so much better now the words were out. My heart slowed, I let out a big sigh, and felt the dryness leave my mouth.

She didn't say anything, so I reached out to touch her hair. She closed her eyes. It wasn't an answer to my question but I took it as permission to go further.

I kept my fingers in her hair and with my other hand caressed her closed eyelids and then her cheek. Maya shot her hand across to hold my lower arm and for a moment I worried she was angry, felt I had gone too far, and she was going to move my hand away, but then I realised the firmness of her grasp was to encourage me. She wanted more. Her eyes remained closed, as she fell backwards on to the bed.

'Look at me,' I said.

She opened her eyes slowly.

'I love you,' I said.

'I know,' she said. 'I wish I'd seen it before, just how much.'

I moved my hand to her shoulder, then the back of her neck. I had touched her arm many times, but never her neck or her bare shoulders. The skin was softer than I could have imagined. I ran my forefinger round to her throat, then traced a line down to the place where her skin met the neckline of her satin dress. Then I allowed my hand to slide underneath the fabric. She wasn't wearing a bra. I reached down to cup her breast. She breathed in sharply, leaning towards me. I felt dizzy. I took a deep breath, my hand immobile for a few seconds, just holding a breast that had fed so many fantasies, so much frustration. It felt better than the best of any fantasy. Then I indulged another fantasy. I gripped the expensive fabric of her green dress in my two hands and I tore it. With a shimmer, the silk fell away to her waist. It was the first time

I had seen her breasts. Though there were several highly erotic scenes in *An English Rose Abroad*, Maya had never been filmed naked from the front. Now there they were, perfect objects of desire, my hands touching them and my lips moving down to kiss them. I ran my tongue around her nipples and then into the valley of her throat and up to her lips.

'Kiss me,' I said, and as she did I felt both her hands on my shoulders, then running down my back, up to my shoulders again, as our tongues ended a two-decade courtship, circled each other again and again, till I sucked her hard into my mouth, and she me into hers. She grabbed at my belt, helped me open my trousers, then force them to the floor as she pulled me on top of her. My hands fell away from her breasts but I wanted them back there, to make that moment of first contact endure. I raised myself up so that I could keep my mouth on hers but also touch her nipples once more, then I moved down to kiss them, and as I kissed and nipped and bit, she grabbed my hair, tugged it hard and began to emit little gasps, momentary bursts of sound that said to me I was giving her pleasure. Her pleasure was now my sole ambition. She brought her mouth back to mine, then tugged on my shoulder, and I was lying on top of her, the outside of my thighs touching the inside of hers. I felt her calves on mine as she locked her legs around me, our tongues danced around each other once more, and she was wriggling beneath me, her hands on my hips, then she was pulling me towards her, directing me to everything I had ever hoped for. I thought the walls were going to fall down as we stroked and screamed our way through hours of pleasure to the union for which my whole life had been a preparation.

Chapter Thirty-One

When I woke the next morning I was convinced I was at the Hamptons, lying in the surf with Maya as the sun bathed our naked bodies and the salt stung our skin, raw from a long night of lovemaking. A large wave broke over us. I moaned, reaching out for her in fear it would wash her away. My hand knocked against a cold, hard object. I opened my eyes. I was not at the Hamptons, I was in a hotel room. My flailing arm was hitting against the bedside table.

It wasn't often that I woke from a wonderful dream to find an even more wonderful reality alongside me, but there was Maya Lowe's warm body, pure white sheets tangled around her, looking utterly beautiful. I felt blessed, able to lie there and watch her sleep. She was at peace, a tiny smile playing at the corners of her mouth. A picture of Vanessa, another gentle, beautiful sleeper, came into my mind. I shocked myself at how guiltless I felt. As I gazed at Maya and stroked her hair, I realised it was possible to love two women. I didn't love Vanessa any less for having slept, finally, with Maya. It was just that right now, I loved Maya more, or differently at any rate, more intensely.

The sound of waves continued, even though I had woken from my dream. It was my phone, ringing in the pocket of my jacket which was still lying in the place where it had been flung hours earlier as we tore at each other's clothes. Ringing wasn't the word though. When we were in the Hamptons I'd changed the ringtone to the sound of breaking waves because I knew how much Maya hated loud phones. I'd never imagined that I might be worrying about disturbing her in such intimate circumstances.

Quietly I slipped out of bed and padded over to where my jacket lay in a heap on the floor. I extracted my phone from the inside pocket and answered the call.

'Steve! Christ, Steve, thank God you've answered. Where the fuck have you been?'

I was so far away from my old life it took a while for me to realise the voice was Jerry's. He was practically shouting.

'Where were you yesterday? I've been desperate to talk to you.'

'What's wrong?' I whispered.

'Brandon called from Doha on Friday morning. It's a fucking disaster. We lost the contract to K&L.'

'What?' I was having difficulty focussing. I thought I'd misheard.

'K and fucking L. All that time we were working on doing in Websters, it was actually K&L we should have been looking at. Brandon's gone mental. I think both our jobs are on the line, Steve. You'd better be back here when he gets in on Monday or the shit's really going to hit the fan.'

I sat down on the armchair closest to the window. 'But Jerry, that's impossible,' I said. 'They just don't have the capacity for a job this big. There must be a mistake.'

I was speaking as quietly as I could to avoid waking Maya, whilst Jerry was getting louder and louder.

'There is no fucking mistake, Steve. We're fucked. You're fucked. I'm fucked. We're all fucked.'

'I cannot believe we lost to K&L. It's a joke.'

'Well, I'm not laughing,' he said coldly. 'And nor is Brandon. What is it that he always says? "Don't rule out the opposition until you see them turn up at the bankruptcy court." We screwed up, Steve. You screwed up, Steve.'

Then he let out an even louder 'Shaddup' at one of his children bawling in the background.

'Steve, I'm going to have to go. Kids driving me crazy. I'll see you Sunday.'

'But Jerry . . .' It was too late. He had hung up.

I slumped down into the armchair, swearing under my breath. I must have been muttering more loudly than I thought because Maya stirred and opened her eyes.

'Well hello, Mr Watkins,' she said, leaning up on one elbow and smiling at me. 'What are you doing over there? I order you to come back to bed this instant.'

I went over and sat on the edge of the bed. Even though we had spent the night exploring each other's bodies, I suddenly felt self-conscious about my nakedness. I pulled a sheet over me.

'What's wrong?' said Maya. 'Something's wrong. What is it?'

'No, nothing,' I said hastily, leaning down to kiss her, hoping that would quieten her. My head was buzzing. I needed time, space to work out what was going on, and how to deal with it.

'Something's up, I can tell,' she said. 'It's Vanessa, isn't it? You're thinking about Vanessa. You're feeling guilty.'

'No, it's not Vanessa,' I said, although of course she was part of the whole big mess. I felt sick with worry about how I was going to tell her that we couldn't go to New England after all – that I had to be at my desk by 7.30 on Monday morning, or the baby could be entering the world with an unemployed father.

'What is it, Steve? I can tell something's wrong. Why were you sitting over there?'

'I was on the phone.'

'Who to?'

'Work. We lost a deal I was working on. I fucked up.'

'Hey, come on, it's just work . . . nobody died. Come over here.'

I did as she said. She ran her hand down the side of my chest, then across my waist, with a force and intent that said she wanted to make love again.

Then it struck me that, actually, the Qatar debacle might be a convenient excuse for calling off the trip to New England. The idea of spending a romantic week with Vanessa after what had just happened in this bed, and what was about to happen again, seemed impossible. The way she was making me feel, it was like I was Maya's now. She was running her other hand through my hair, and kissing my neck and shoulders. I found myself whispering, so softly I'm not sure she even heard, 'I'd do anything you ask of me,' then found I was asking myself the question – what, even end your marriage, and let down a woman who was carrying your child? And I was shocked by the answer: yes, I think I would, much as I still loved Vanessa. When was the last time Vanessa and I made love like last night? We must have done. But right now, I just couldn't remember.

As for my job, I wouldn't need it if I was with Maya. She was generous, I knew that. If the worst came to the worst, I was sure she would look after me. She was stroking my thighs now, and I was trying to still my mind, banish thoughts of Vanessa and of work, just trying to live in this moment, but I couldn't, I found myself powerless to put Jerry's call to one side, and was wondering whether I could plead my case with Brandon, imagining the conversation I would have. After all, his eye hadn't exactly been on the ball when it came to K&L. He had to take some of the responsibility. It could all have been down to his dreadful presentation for all we knew. He might want scapegoats, but surely he would recognise that Jerry and I were trusty foot soldiers. He wouldn't want to have to employ and train a whole new team. If it wasn't for Stafford's massive bill, I'd be OK at Globus.

Maya could tell I was distracted.

'What's wrong?' she said.

'Nothing, honestly.'

'Don't you feel like it?'

'Of course I do.'

'You're worried, I can tell.'

She suddenly knelt up on the bed, put her arms around me and ran her hand across my chest. 'I know why you're worried — everything you've thought all your life tells you this is wrong, because you've been unfaithful to Vanessa, but it all feels so right.'

I nodded, though in fact it was a lot more complicated than that.

'I know this is a really difficult situation, but we can work it out,' she said. 'I know we can. You know we can too, don't you?'

'Yeah sure.'

'I'm not a marriage-wrecker, Steve. It's not my style, you

know that. But it felt right last night, didn't it? And it feels right now, doesn't it?'

'Yeah, it feels right.'

'You don't sound sure to me. We just need a bit of time. We've gone into a new place, Steve, and we need time to adapt to that. Perhaps you could tell Vanessa that I need to stay on in Washington for a few days, to have extra meetings, and that you'll be back on Monday. That way we could have the weekend to talk, think it all through, make any plans we need to make. There is only one rule here . . .'

'What's that?'

'If either of us is not happy with the plan, we don't do it. We have time, Steve. God knows we took long enough to get here.'

Then she laughed, and the joy in that sound, the sensation of her skin against mine, her breath on the nape of my neck combined to make all my other worries suddenly melt away. Screw Brandon, he was thousands of miles away. Who cared about K&L? I would work it out with Vanessa, I assured myself. I should stop worrying. 'This is the most beautiful woman in the world here, Steve,' I thought to myself. 'Nothing else is important but the love you are feeling for her, the love she is feeling for you, and the barriers that are tumbling down between the two of you. She'll understand. There must be no secrets.'

I looked into her eyes.

'Maya, I want nothing more than to make love with you again,' I said. 'I really do, and we will, soon, but first there is something I have to tell you.'

'I knew there was something,' she said. 'Come on then, tell tell.'

'I don't know where to start.'

'At the beginning.'

'It kind of doesn't work like that. It's so fucking compli-cated.'

'OK, try the end.'

I really didn't know how to tell her everything. I just knew that I had to.

'Right,' she said, clicking her fingers. 'What was the last word you thought of, right now?'

'Park.'

'Why park?'

'Because I was thinking of Sheldon.'

'And Sheldon makes you think of parks?'

'He took me for a walk in one.'

'OK . . . and is that what you want to tell me about?'

'I want to tell you about everything. I'm just worried you won't understand.'

'Well try me. What happened in the park?'

She was smiling gently, and looked warm, trusting.

'Come on,' she said. 'You're carrying a weight. Let me lift it from you.'

'OK,' I said. 'Before we came here, Sheldon gave me a job.'

'A job? What do you mean a job?'

'Well, perhaps not a job exactly, more of a task. He wants me to convince you that it would be a good idea to get back together with Dan.'

She looked momentarily stunned, and sat up straight. 'Why the hell does he think that's a good idea?'

'He believes your "joint brand" makes you stronger. I quote: "As a singleton she's cute but threatening; as part of a happy couple who have sorted their differences she's every woman's role model and every man's fantasy."'

'He called me a "brand"?' She had a look of revulsion on her face.

''Fraid so.'

'But what made him think you would do this "job" of his? After all, you hate Dan. Why on earth would Sheldon choose you as Dan's ambassador?'

'That's where it gets complicated. He's kind of blackmailing me.'

'Blackmail? What are you talking about?'

'Look Maya, this all stems from me loving you, caring about you, wanting the best for you, sometimes fearing the worst for you. And along the way, I've done things to help and protect you, and sometimes it's cost me money, and I've had to do things to get the money that are a bit tricky . . .' She looked alarmed all of a sudden.

'No, no, nothing bad, nothing really bad, just take out kind of loans against future earnings in the firm, and the thing is Sheldon knows, and he knows some of the things I did, and now he wants to use me to get you to do things you shouldn't, and I want to be open and honest with you, because that's the way we've always been.'

'I know, so come on, Steve, just tell me, what is it, what is the problem here? You're scaring me by not telling me.'

I hated that, the idea I was making her scared. I started to shape the events of recent weeks and months in my mind, and try to tell her the whole story, beginning with the moment I saw her black eye and became so frightened for her safety that I employed a private detective we used at Swift, then working through the complicated consequences, step by step, trying to make it as simple as I could. The trust she placed in me. The overwhelming instinct I had that Dan was lying about his club, which drove me to follow him to Sheila Hegarty's house. The coincidence of my meeting with Waller and the subsequent encounter with Stafford. The deal I struck to camouflage the nature of the commission until I got money myself. The panic and loneliness I felt on seeing what Stafford's soldiers had uncovered.

She listened intently to every word, her eyes saying little, occasionally shifting from my gaze to look at my lips. She didn't seem shocked though. I'd worried the mere mention of hiring a private eye would have provoked her, but she seemed fine.

She realised the story had some way to run, propped up a couple of pillows and leant back, clutching the sheets to her chest. It was when I reached the part about my early morning trip to Mr Lowe's greenhouse and his subsequent panicked visit to my office, that she spoke for the first time in several minutes.

'Hold on, Steve, I need to get this right. *You* put the package in Dad's greenhouse?'

'That's right, it was the only way of getting it to you without you knowing I had hired someone to keep an eye on Dan.'

'But that means you deceived me, Steve, you deceived my father.'

'Not deceived exactly . . . Or rather, yes deceived, I suppose, but only to protect you.'

'Protect me from what?'

'From a husband who was beating you, betraying you . . .'

'Listen, Steve,' said Maya, her eyes narrowing. 'Let's get this straight, once and for all. Dan did *not* hit me. He pushed me and I fell. Yes, he was being aggressive, but he was angry. *You* had made him angry. Second, I had strong suspicions about his affair and his cocaine myself. I'm a grown-up woman. I knew we had problems and I was sure I could work them through. As it was, the involvement of my dad, the idea that someone was watching me, keeping a file on me, perhaps intending to give the whole story to the press, that's what scared me, freaked me out. I panicked, same as Dad did. In those circumstances, there was no way Dan and I had a chance of mending things . . .'

'Mending things? But Maya, there were other women! That journalist who wrote your biography – he was sleeping with her too.'

Suddenly there was the same disgust on her face as when I said Sheldon called her and Dan a 'joint brand'. 'You know everything, don't you, Steve? I imagine you even know what kind of condoms they used.'

'Come on, Maya,' I said. 'It's not like that! I was doing this for you. I wanted you to know how you were being manip-ulated . . .'

'And so you manipulated me yourself,' she said.

'Because I had uncovered the truth, and I didn't know how to get it to you. OK, it wasn't perfect, maybe there were other ways I could have told you, but I couldn't tell you straight, not back then . . .'

'So you lied to me and you lied to my family.'

'Well, sort of, but look where it has led. He's out of your life, you're happy, you're free, you're a bigger star than ever, Maya.'

'And I've just found out that the one friend I thought I could trust was the most untrustworthy of them all. The one

I thought I could always rely on to tell me the truth was actually the biggest liar.'

'Don't say that Maya. I'm telling you the truth here, the whole truth . . .'

'And it hurts, Steve. It hurts a lot.'

She stood up, and her nakedness, last night so beautiful, now communicated a terrifying coldness. I'd never seen her so chilling, not even on screen, not even during our worst disagreements. It was as if she was withdrawing from me completely, as if I was some insalubrious stranger who had wandered into her room. I started trying to apologise but she wouldn't let me.

'I'm sorry, Steve, but you're going to have to leave, I can't handle this.' She put on a dressing gown and walked towards the door.

There was a fierce and horrible finality in her voice.

I got up from the bed.

'Don't react like this, Maya. I know it all seems sordid, believe me it *felt* sordid, but sometimes it's difficult to be honest when you're dealing with people who play dirty. They all play dirty, Maya. What will happen unless you change the people around you? Sheldon will carry on with his "branding" and Dan won't leave you alone. Nor will the press. I've saved you from that, Maya, I've saved you. You don't need them. You don't need that kind of empty celebrity. You've been saying it yourself.'

'Sheldon isn't the only agent on the planet, Steve. There are people who can help me other than you.'

'Maya, let me explain it all again, I've explained it badly, you don't understand what I was doing.'

'You explained it very well, Steve. I understand completely

now what you were doing.' Her voice was choking, and I moved closer to try to hear better what she was saying.

She picked up my jacket and threw it towards me.

'Get dressed,' she said. 'Then get out.'

'Maya, listen to me, you don't understand——'

'Steve, get out before I call security.'

'Maya!'

'Get out!' she screamed, picking up one of her green sling-backs and hurling it at me.

I realised I had no choice. She was already picking up the second shoe. I had no idea where my trousers were. Wrapping my jacket round my waist, I stumbled to the door and out into the corridor. As I closed the door behind me there was a thud as the second shoe hit it.

Once in the corridor, I stood still for a moment, adjusting my jacket to cover myself. I felt blinded by the harsh light. I didn't remember it being so bright. When we'd come back the night before, I'd noted the subtle lamps in the hallway. Then I realised I was not alone. With a sense of foreboding, I looked around for Dan, but instead saw a man wielding a camera, accompanied by two guys, one carrying a sound boom, the other holding a lamp, and a young man, dressed in a white buttoned-down shirt and deep red tie, who leapt up from an armchair by the door opposite Maya's as the light came closer to my face.

'Mr Watkins,' the young man said in a polite but adrenalin-fuelled American voice, 'can you explain why you spent the night in Maya Lowe's room last night instead of returning to your own?'

I tried to push past him but the combination of cameraman, soundman and lighting man was enough to block my way down the corridor. My jacket slipped as I raised my hand towards the camera. I hitched it back up then tried to barge aside the young man, but he was insistent.

'Mr Watkins, we have been here a while. We heard the shouting just now. So please confirm – you spent the night with Maya Lowe, you had sex with her, you had an argument this morning, she threw you out. Is that a fair summary, Mr Watkins?'

My own room was just yards away but I had to jostle my way through them to get to it.

'Fuck off out of my way.'

'Did you hire a private eye to dig dirt on Dan Chivers?'

'I said fuck off.'

'Did you use your company's money for that purpose? That is what we have been told. Are you aware that may be a criminal offence?'

I had had enough. The cameraman was now leaning against my door, his camera inches from my face. The soundman was standing against the lock in order to prevent me from swiping my card. The young guy in the red tie continued to fire questions at me. I tensed my neck and then uncoiled it to land a headbutt into the lens of the camera. It hurt. A lot. The cameraman fell under the weight of his own equipment. I butted the soundman too, to get him away from my door. It was the first time I had ever attacked someone, ever, in my whole life. I felt a cut opening above my eyes.

'Mr Watkins, Mr Watkins, don't make things worse for yourself. Just answer my questions.'

I pulled out the key card, managed to slide it through at the first attempt, and fell into my room.

The taste of my own blood warming my mouth, I stumbled into the bathroom, spat out a huge crimson blob. It was only when I looked up into the mirror that I realised I was crying. I sobbed, as quietly as I could, rocking from side to side, then backwards and forwards, banging my head gently against the glass.

I felt an overwhelming urge to speak to Vanessa. I had no idea what I would say. I just knew I had to speak to her, hear her voice, feel that familiarity, let her know, somehow, that in spite of everything I loved her. I dialled her mobile. It went to voicemail. I sat on the edge of the bed, blood from the cut above my eyebrow now dripping steadily, like a heartbeat, on to the brown carpet. Drip, drip, drip. I dialled Vanessa's mobile again. Voicemail. The next time I got an American engaged signal. There is no more aggressive engaged signal anywhere in the world. It's like a broken car alarm beeping into your head. It doesn't just say 'We're busy'. It says 'We do not want to hear from you. Ever again.' There was a tap on the door. 'Mr Watkins, can we sit down and talk like grown-ups?' said the young American. 'You won't look good fighting a cameraman. We can lose those pictures if you give us what we want . . .'

'Fuck off.'

'I'm only doing my job, sir.'

'Leave me alone. Just leave me alone.'

'I'll be here when you come out, Mr Watkins. Let's try to make it civilised.'

I went into the bathroom and tried to staunch the flow of blood. The cut clearly needed stitches. It was more than an inch wide, and deep. I must have hit the sharp rim that protects the lens. I couldn't go out there though. It was bad enough being filmed with your balls hanging out. I looked worse now, blood mixing with tears, a towel held to my head. I called Vanessa again. Voicemail.

Then my phone suddenly beeped with a message. Missed call. Vanessa. Fuck. It beeped again. Answerphone message. Fuck, fuck, fuck. She had been calling me as I was calling her. A marriage reduced to mutual phone engagement. I started to sob again as I dialled up the message.

Her voice on the recording sounded sharp, inhospitable.

'It's me. Call me immediately. I need to know what's going on.'

What on earth was she talking about? What else could be going on? I wasn't sure I could cope with much more being thrown at me.

Finally I got through to her.

'Vanessa, it's me.'

There was silence on the other end of the line.

'Vanessa, are you there?'

When she finally spoke, her voice sounded weak, like she had been crying.

'I want to know how you could do that to me, Steve? I want to know how . . .'

I felt fear strike through me, like a bullet into my guts. Somehow she knew. God knows how, but she knew. 'I don't know what you're talking about, Vanessa,' I said, in an attempt to stall.

'Yes you do, Steve. You know full well.'

'Please, Vanessa,' I pleaded. 'Explain to me. What is it you think I've done?'

'I'm with Dan, Steve.'

'Dan?'

'I'm with Dan, and Nick, and Dan's director. I'm sitting in

a van outside Maya's apartment, and it is full of TV equipment, and I have just watched a humiliating film of you with no clothes on. I came here because Dan told me where you were and what you were doing, and I didn't believe him, Steve, because I love you and I trusted you, but then Nick came along and he said "Vanessa, Dan's not lying, you need to see this", and so I saw it, Steve, and I heard it, and I have never felt so degraded in my life . . .'

'Vanessa, listen to me.'

'OK, Steve, I'm listening.'

But suddenly, I felt unable to say anything.

'I'm listening.'

I had no more lies left in me.

'Call me when you get to London, Steve. I'll be there myself by the morning. Goodbye.'

The phone went dead.

I dialled her number. Voicemail. I dialled it again. Voicemail again. Then a text came through from Sheldon: 'Sorry, Steve. Knew I couldn't trust you. Thought I ought to send an audience. Nick xxx'.

I wailed so loudly Sheldon's crew outside could hear.

'Mr Watkins, are you OK?' the young American called through the door. 'Is there anything I can do to help?'

But there was nothing anyone could do. I'd felt lonely before in my life, but this was different. This was like being far out in space, with only the cold stars for company.

Postscript

I made it to New England in the end, but not in the circumstances I'd intended. The autumn leaves here are wonderful: more colours than I could even name. I like the russet-red maples best. They remind me of Vanessa's hair – a deep red you could lose yourself in. I never thought I'd see the point of all that tree-hugging nonsense, but it's true. Nature can heal.

This afternoon I took a rowing boat out on to the lake. I was alone there except for an elderly couple thirty or forty yards away, who were letting their boat drift, having an intense conversation about the best college for their grandson, every word audible through the crisp, clean air. Then they suddenly leant towards each other and kissed passionately. I was taken aback. I hadn't expected it. I was filled with a longing for Vanessa and the holiday we never had.

As soon as she put the phone down on me that terrible morning, Vanessa went straight to the airport and flew home on the first available flight. Sheldon got her an upgrade.

By the time I got back to London, several hundred dollars lighter after needing four stitches in my head, she had seen a lawyer, and had a proposal ready. A straight fifty-fifty split on the house and contents, seventy-thirty to her on other assets and savings, inflation-linked monthly payments towards upkeep of the child, to the age of 16, unconditional access at least twice a week, with split holidays unless the child chose otherwise after the age of 7. I got the letter on my thirtieth birthday. She was nothing if not organised, and I was not in a position to fight. I agreed to it all.

I didn't even begin to try to persuade her to take me back. Pointless. I could see her mind was made up. She'd already put down a deposit on a flat in the Barbican. She wanted out of the area we had lived in all our married life. She wanted out of our life.

'How shall we handle the birth?' she asked. 'I don't want you there but obviously you'll want to see him.'

She knew by now that it was a boy. She was definitely going to call him Nathan, after her dad, and I had no say in the matter. It was her child. I might as well have been a test tube. That realisation as I left her lawyer's office in Shoreditch decided me: I would never see my son. Shame or selfishness, I don't know, maybe both, but I figured out that I had managed most of my life without a father, so he should be able to survive OK. If he wanted to know me when he was older, well, that was something we could think about then.

The one person I hoped might understand that I had at least started out with the best of intentions about Maya was Mr Lowe. I called him at his house in Taplow one Sunday morning. He was polite enough, if distant, in the opening exchanges, but I was doing most of the talking, and after one particularly rambling explanation of how I had hired Stafford, he said 'Steve, I don't think there is anything you can say. Sorry. Goodbye.'

As for Maya, she phoned me once, a few days after

Washington, to tell me she was changing her number, and to say she never wanted to hear from me again. I said I understood.

'I saw Bernard today,' she said.

'And?'

'And he knows who his journalist visitor was at his house in France. You didn't tell me that little detail.' There was a silence. It lasted several seconds.

'Your man made the mistake of saying he was visiting the British war graves. Bernard has a friend who used to be the head of the local police. His friend traced your friend and his wife to their hotel in Sainte-Preuve. He found out who your friend was and then found out what he did. Must be good money,' she said. 'He stayed at the Château de Barive no less, four stars, and he had the *menu gourmand*. Bernard's pretty furious about it. He was fuming about some comment the man made about the British saving the French from the Germans. He told me he was so angry he drove all the way to the war cemetery and left a message in the visitors' book: "To think these giants died so that pygmies could abuse the freedoms they fought for." I think he meant you, Steve, when he referred to pygmies. He wants your blood . . .'

She paused again.

'The Hunter Hunted, Steve.'

'I did it all for you, Maya.'

'You know what, Steve, I think you think you did. People can justify almost anything to themselves if they try hard enough. And if they try hard enough often enough, they end up believing their own bullshit. You did it for you, Steve, not for me. You were meant to be the rock. And all the time you were trying to turn my life to dust.'

'I'm sorry,' I said.

There was another long silence. I broke it.

'So this is it?'

'This is it, Steve. Yes. Twenty years, but this is it. You took things too far. You should have told me. No secrets, remember?'

'I do.'

'I'm sorry, Maya,' I said again.

'Yeah well.'

'At least I'll be able to know what you're up to.'

She gave a cold laugh.

'You will. Like the rest of the population. You'll know what I'm doing. But you won't know who I am, Steve, the spirit, the soul. Not any more.'

'I guess not.'

'Maybe you never did.'

And she hung up.

When she learned I had called her father, she sent me a lawyer's letter threatening me with a restraining order. I wrote her a postcard to say she had nothing to worry about.

I'd already lost my job by then.

When I finally got to the office at the end of the week, Brandon had been through all my files and emails to see exactly what I had been asking Swift International to do, and had discovered the invoices. I was escorted from the premises, having had to leave my company car keys behind. I walked for miles.

Brandon was good enough not to press charges immediately. He said I had six months to pay back the money or else he would take the matter to the police. I was penniless, with nowhere to go. Jerry offered to put me up, but I couldn't face it. All those children. His promotion. Brandon had decided not to replace me. He'd got Jerry to take over my role instead. Given him a pay rise. I went back to Acton, to stay with my mum and her boyfriend, but before long we were getting on each other's nerves. Mum had never shown the slightest interest in being a grandmother. Now that the possibility of playing a role in her grandson's life had been taken away from her, she seemed resentful. I had to get away.

I flew here at the beginning of October, two days after Vanessa gave birth. It was as I settled down into my seat on the flight to Boston, and the woman next to me took out a copy of *Hello!* magazine, that I caught a glimpse of the first major public step in Sheldon's 'Maya-Dan strategy'. I'd called his office to ask about whether I would be appearing in Dan's film. His secretary came on the line. 'Mr Sheldon has asked me to tell you that Mr Chivers no longer wishes the film to be shown,' she said. 'He said you'll understand why.' And there the two of them were on the front cover of *Hello!*, trailing a fifteen-page spread: 'Maya and Dan – on falling in love again'. She looked great. He looked like a dickhead, his teeth matching his white suit perfectly. Nothing had changed. In the interview Dan rambled on about how drugs made you do things you didn't want to do, the pressures of fame, and how he was 'the luckiest man alive' to be back with Maya. She talked about the importance of forgiveness, the need to understand the weaknesses of others, and how only she knew 'the real Dan'.

The woman, sensing I was reading over her arm as she picked at a bowl of mixed nuts, said, 'They got a million for that apparently.'

I nodded.

'Still, good luck to them. All adds to the gaiety of the nation, I say.'

There was a time I would have asked her if I could keep the magazine after she'd read it, or bought my own as soon as we landed, to store away in my files. Instead, I stared out of the window and tried not to think. I'd had a look through the inflight entertainment guide. *Fallen Angel* was among the movies on offer. Dan Chivers being booed on his own programme was part of a 'great telly moments special inflight package'. Other highlights included a former Labour MP wearing a leotard and drinking milk from a saucer on a reality TV show, chat-show host Michael Parkinson being attacked by a ventriloquist's emu, and Richard Nixon sweating in a US presidential TV debate. Somehow sleep seemed more enticing.

On landing, I took a bus to the Alamo car rental office, where a man with bad skin and a name badge – Andy – managed to get me a huge GM Saturn for the same price as a family saloon, with satnav thrown in for free. I have never known anyone who could click more quickly on the keyboard of a computer. I was in and out in under ten minutes. It was a lonely drive but the satnav guide kept me company. It had a high-pitched, rich American accent and spoke to me before, during and after every junction.

I suppose there is a part of me that thinks by coming here, making this journey, I am recreating some kind of link with Vanessa. Idiotic, I know. She won't even be aware I've been here, not for a while anyway, and even then she may not care. But I thought it would be a nice idea to go to the places we had planned to visit before events got in the way. Vanessa had wanted to take the coastal route up to a place called Camden in Maine, which she fancied because of the Camden connection back home. She had booked us into a harbour hotel called the Lord Camden Inn. I called ahead to make a reservation for a couple of nights to give myself time to find a lakeside place to rent.

Once I got used to the idea that I was going to be on my own for some months, I enjoyed the drive. When I was a child, Mum used to take me to the south coast for our holidays, sometimes Kent, sometimes Sussex. We stayed in caravan parks or, latterly, when she had a new man with a bit more money than us, guest houses. The countryside north of Boston reminded me of those journeys, except the trees and the cars seemed bigger. When I was bored, we would play a game in which I counted red cars and Mum counted blue ones. You got one point for each and the first to a hundred was the winner. Then we would play green vs yellow and the loser of round one could choose which colour to have. Green nearly always won so it would go to a third round, black vs white. The nearer you were to London, the likelier you were to win with black, because of all the black cabs.

As I reached New Hampshire, I invented a modern American version to play against myself – McDonalds vs Dunkin' Donuts. Dunkin' Donuts won easily. Parts of the turnpike reminded me of the Heathrow perimeter road, except that London's airline and logistics offices were replaced by food outlets. It doesn't take a genius to work out why so many Americans are obese. Just go for a drive.

I've loved this place though, from the moment I saw it, even if I would have loved it more had Vanessa been with me. Mrs Crowley has popped in a couple of times each week to clean and make sure I have everything I need. She's a good fifteen years older than me, but nice company, up to a point. Chatty without being too inquisitive. I like that.

I've eaten out a few times, mainly at the Waterfront restaurant in Camden, where the portions are so big I've been able to take a doggy bag home with enough for lunch the next day. There's also a great little ice-cream parlour behind the Lord Camden, and some days when I haven't been able to focus, I've been down there for a quick hit of pistachio mixed with blackcurrant and rum-raisin.

Having lived in London all my life, I've never been a scenery person. I am now. I'd been here four or five days when I realised I was spending up to an hour each morning, before settling down to work, just breathing in the air, learning to love the view and all it had to offer. The eagle has made four visits in all, each time delivering his warning croak to all lake-side inhabitants that he is on his way, then gliding by on an identical flight path every time. By the third visit I'd bought a camera. I've got some great pictures. He looks like he's smiling.

Some days I've found I just can't get down to it, so I sit and stare at the water, or the trees, or wait for the next cliff-edge daredevil to leap into the freezing water. There's no TV in the cabin. But I don't miss it. I could watch a patch of Lake Megunticook for hours. But in the main, I've stuck to the task in hand. Up early, get showered and dressed, enjoy the scenery for a while, then settle down to work. Half the days I've been here, I've written pretty much all day long, and some days a piece of the night-time too. Other days, I've disappeared for long walks in the woods until I've felt the desire and the capability returning. Anyway, the important thing is: the job is done.

It was my agent who recommended getting away from London, and doing this on my own, far from the people concerned. It seems odd to think I have an agent, I know.

She's from Newcastle, a hard-nosed woman in her thirties who thrives on selling books for outrageously high advances. Her name's Kate Osborne. I got in touch with her after reading a newspaper article about how she landed a book deal for the winner of a reality TV talent contest. I picked up a copy of his book in Borders. He dedicated it to her. When I got past her stonewalling secretary, I said I was Maya Lowe's lifelong best friend from childhood and I thought I had a book in me. She said she'd heard of me, 'vaguely', invited me to her office on Beak Street in Soho, and when I ran through the story, she agreed. We wrote a synopsis together and she got an OK deal, enough to pay off my debts at least, with a bit left over, but she said it depended on me being totally honest. I found it came easily to me. Writing. And being totally honest.

I had planned to be here for several months. In fact, it has only taken me a few weeks, which is lucky because the advance is running low. Last night, sitting alone outside the Waterfront restaurant, underneath a yellow street light, I read what I'd written from beginning to end, the whole story. It was gone midnight by the time I'd finished, and I felt drained. But I think it reads OK. It tells it like it was, warts and all, which is what Kate promised the publisher.

I called her this morning, to say I'm happy with it and I'll be home within the week. She sounded pleased.

'Do you have a title?' she asked.

I didn't.

She said she would have a think about it and throughout the day a series of text messages offered up a few ideas. *Maya: My Misery. Me, Maya and Maya's Men. My Life with Maya. My Life Without Maya. Maya: My Life.*

But when I went out in the boat this afternoon, it seemed

wrong for there to be any mention of me in the title. Who was going to buy a book because it was about me? It was Maya who counted, Maya who was the real subject. As the elderly couple headed for the shore, I looked out over the lake. A red cardinal was perched in a sycamore tree, filling the air with melodious song; two kids were diving screaming into the icy water from a pontoon across the way. I'd brought my manuscript with me. Putting down the oars, I pulled it out of my bag, took a pen from my pocket and wrote the word 'Maya' in large black letters on page one.

There could be no other title. It was my book, but her story.

I clutched the pages to my chest, and felt a wave of sadness come over me, that this was all I had left of the important people in my life. They were gone.

I wondered what kind of cover the publishers would use: some glossy, sexy shot of Maya that would make it look like all the other celebrity biographies on the shelf. But how many of them tell it like it is? They're written either by outsiders who don't know the truth, or insiders who won't tell it, because it might 'damage the brand'.

In the aftermath of that God-awful morning in Washington, Maya told me I would never again know who she really was. She was right. But I hope if she reads this, she will at least think I've captured a sense of her spirit. And the damage done when stardom enters the soul.

ALSO AVAILABLE IN ARROW

All in the Mind

Alastair Campbell

**Martin Sturrock desperately needs a psychiatrist.
The problem? He is one.**

Emily is a traumatised burns victim, Arta a Kosovan refugee recovering from a rape. David Temple is a long-term depressive, while the Rt Hon Ralph Hall MP lives in terror of his drink problem being exposed. Very different Londoners, but they share one thing: every week they spend an hour at the Prince Regent Hospital, revealing the secrets of their psyche to Professor Martin Sturrock. Little do they know that Sturrock's own mind is not the reassuring place they believe it to be.

Set over a life-changing weekend, Alastair Campbell's astonishing first novel delves deep into the human mind to create a gripping portrait of the strange co-dependency between patient and doctor. Both a comedy and tragedy of ordinary lives, it is rich in compassion for those whose days are spent on the edge of the abyss.

'Brilliant . . . A compelling and unforgettable experience'
Stephen Fry

'Eloquent and touching . . . A triumphant exploration of the imperfection of heroism' Tom Harris, *Mail on Sunday*

'Riveting . . . I'd rate this a landslide victory'
Derek Draper, *Observer*

arrow books

THE POWER OF READING

Visit the Random House website and get connected with information on all our books and authors

EXTRACTS from our recently published books and selected backlist titles

COMPETITIONS AND PRIZE DRAWS Win signed books, audiobooks and more

AUTHOR EVENTS Find out which of our authors are on tour and where you can meet them

LATEST NEWS on bestsellers, awards and new publications

MINISITES with exclusive special features dedicated to our authors and their titles

READING GROUPS Reading guides, special features and all the information you need for your reading group

LISTEN to extracts from the latest audiobook publications

WATCH video clips of interviews and readings with our authors

RANDOM HOUSE INFORMATION including advice for writers, job vacancies and all your general queries answered

Come home to Random House
www.rbooks.co.uk